Highest Praise for

"*A Sho...* ...m the first page to ...alive, and streng... ...kept me reading ...ay through to an ending I never expected."
—**Taylor Stevens**, *New York Times* bestselling author of *Liars' Paradox*

"By the end of the first chapter I was totally hooked on *A Short Time to Die*. I couldn't have closed the cover on Marly's story if my life depended on it."
—**Lisa Black**, *New York Times* bestselling author of *Suffer the Children*

"Gripping."
—*Publishers Weekly*

"Bickford's debut is an intriguing tale of murder and corruption that spans more than thirteen years. Riddled with twists and turns, *A Short Time to Die* features a family that is so evil readers will likely be looking over their own shoulders. The resolution is highly satisfying, more so because of Bickford's phenomenal writing talent. An A-plus for this great book!"
—*RT Book Reviews*, 4 Stars

"Bickford's tale of revenge, the dark reach and power of generational crime and violence, and of two brave and bright girls who become capable, fearless women, is gripping, chilling, and original. Add in a keen, exacting eye for character and place that transcends 'genre' and *A Short Time to Die* is sure to stay with you for a long, long time."
—**Eric Rickstad**, *New York Times* bestselling author of *What Remains of Her*

Books by

SUSAN ALICE BICKFORD

Dread of Winter

A Short Time to Die

A SHORT TIME TO DIE

SUSAN ALICE BICKFORD

PINNACLE BOOKS
www.kensingtonbooks.com

PINNACLE BOOKS are published by

Kensington Publishing Corp.
119 West 40th Street
New York, NY 10018

Copyright © 2017 Susan Alice Bickford

All rights reserved. No part of this book may be reproduced in any form or by any means without the prior written consent of the publisher, excepting brief quotes used in reviews.

This book is a work of fiction. Names, characters, businesses, organizations, places, events, and incidents either are the product of the author's imagination or are used fictitiously. Any resemblance to actual persons, living or dead, events, or locales is entirely coincidental.

If you purchased this book without a cover, you should be aware that this book is stolen property. It was reported as "unsold and destroyed" to the publisher, and neither the author nor the publisher has received any payment for this "stripped book."

All Kensington titles, imprints, and distributed lines are available at special quantity discounts for bulk purchases for sales promotions, premiums, fund-raising, educational, or institutional use.

Special book excerpts or customized printings can also be created to fit specific needs. For details, write or phone the office of the Kensington sales manager: Kensington Publishing Corp., 119 West 40th Street, New York, NY 10018, attn: Sales Department; phone 1-800-221-2647.

PINNACLE and the P logo are Reg. U.S. Pat. & TM Off.

ISBN-13: 978-0-7860-4597-6
ISBN-10: 0-7860-4597-3

First Kensington trade paperback printing: February 2017
First Pinnacle premium mass market paperback printing: September 2019

10 9 8 7 6 5 4 3 2 1

Printed in the United States of America

Electronic edition:

ISBN-13: 978-0-7860-4598-3(e-book)
ISBN-10: 0-7860-4598-1 (e-book)

Dedicated to

Kathy Bernhard, 1949–1966
George-Ann Formicola, 1951–1966
You deserved a future

and

George, Betty, Palma, Robert, and Erin
The wind at my back

This is a land where clouds come to die. Fresh young winds, born in Canada, migrate south, over Lake Ontario, where they pick up moisture, and transform into billowing clouds. Once the clouds reach the Empire State, they release their burden as rain or snow, lose elevation and bulk to land on these once-majestic mountains that the glaciers churned and scoured and ground into mere nubby hills. The clouds break apart and roll down the hills, down into the valleys, down into the deepest creases, down into farms and tiny villages that burrowed themselves into the hides of the steep hillsides and valley floors.

1

Marly: Quicksand

October 27, 2000

Marly Shaw peered into the night fog that crept in and settled around the Rock. She could see no sign of her stepfather's truck in the parking lot.

Charon Springs might be a tiny town, but as the only drinking establishment within ten or more miles in any direction, the Rock easily qualified as its most thriving business. Pickled from the inside out by beer, booze, and nicotine, the sagging two-story structure oozed a sour stench that permeated the car, even with the windows closed.

"What do you want to do?" Claire asked.

Marly studied the mist outside, tinged alternating shades of red and blue by the blinking neon lights.

"I should drop you home," Claire said with a sheepish glance at her passenger. "But we're already late. I'm supposed to be home by ten thirty and it's after eleven already. Straight to the dance, straight home."

And no detours into Harris territory. In this town, nice people like Claire's family avoided Marly's family as much as possible.

"Not to worry," Marly said. "Let me out down the

road. It's Friday night, so the bar is packed. He might have parked in the woods. If he's not there, I can walk home. It's not cold. Hard to believe it's the end of October. Maybe global warming is a good thing for Central New York."

"Yeah. A couple of times I had to trick-or-treat in a parka."

"Kids these days have it easy," Marly said. They both chuckled.

Marly rummaged in her large bag and pulled out a small flashlight and her tattered running shoes. She always came prepared to tramp across fields and down dirt roads, day or night.

"Great dance tonight," Claire said. "I can't believe we'll never go to another Halloween Gala. Next year we'll be in college."

"Some of us will be."

"You're a really good student and everyone says you'll do great. You might even get into one of the good New York State schools. That's what my mom says."

"Sure. Well, I hope so." There was no way Marly was going to reveal her deepest longings to a blabbermouth like Claire. Feigned indifference was the best spell for warding off jinxes. Her stepfather had taught her that lesson.

"Did you go to Laurie's funeral?" Claire asked.

"Yes." Marly drew out her response into a prolonged hiss.

"Do you think her mother and the bitches killed Laurie in a beatdown?"

"I wasn't there. But they are not nice people."

"It doesn't make much sense. She was their family."

Marly squirmed. She knew the rules—no talking to

outsiders about her family. *What is Claire fishing for? Titillation? Gossip? Just making conversation?*

"I don't know anything, Claire. Trust me." She studied the shrouded parking lot again. "Still no sign of Del. But I can't see anything very clearly. I should get out and look."

"Hard to miss a guy like him," said Claire. "You have to admit, he's easy on the eyes. And even my mom says he's smart."

Marly had one rule of her own. She never talked about her stepfather.

"I promised my mom I'd meet him here for a ride. She says it's not safe to walk home on these roads at night. And he'll be totally pissed off if he waited here for nothing. Thanks for the ride up to the dance, Claire. I'll see you on Monday on the school bus."

"If you walk, watch out. You're wearing all black. You're hard to see."

"I have a flashlight. And my sneakers are white. Don't worry."

Marly watched Claire's Civic fade into the fog before she walked to the back door of the Rock.

She slipped through the kitchen and gazed around the crowded bar, pool table area, and tables from the doorway. No Del.

"Hey, Red!" From behind the bar, Harry brushed his hand in her direction as if to push her away. "No underage kids allowed. Scram."

Marly forced herself not to wince. She hated that nickname, but she knew better than to let Harry know it. She vowed that once she left Charon Springs, she would never let anyone call her a name she didn't like. "I'm looking for Del," Marly said. "He's my ride home."

Harry crossed his arms, unmoved. "He left over an

hour ago. Good and drunk, too. I'm sorry, Red, but trust me—you're better off on your own. Now you need to go. I can't risk my license."

She should have known Harry wouldn't buy any hard-luck stories. Marly retreated to the parking lot and considered her options.

If she walked the long way along the twisting roads, she could cover the distance in about forty minutes. Or she could take a shortcut through the woods and over the hill. She would have to pick her way in the dark over rough terrain, but she would be home in less than twenty minutes. She opted for the woods.

She took one last look for Del's truck and sniffed. The earth was moist and fragrant from the spicy tang of freshly fallen leaves. She shouldered her bag and set out.

She left the Rock behind, plodded up a slight incline, and passed the Willey's General Store. *Nothing "general" about Willey's,* she thought, with the stock so limited and often dated, devoted to beer and snacks.

Down in the next misty dip, she passed the last streetlight. The pavement was rougher and rutted now. The shoulder disappeared. She straightened her back and switched to navigation by flashlight and familiarity.

Marly was making good time, her thoughts full of school and the dance, when she noticed a glow above the slight rise in the road ahead, the light amplified by the fog. A car. No, a truck. A truck with a distinctive ping from the engine. Del's truck.

Her ride.

Marly despised Del, and as much as she tried to hide this, they both knew it. For the sake of peace at home, she had to pretend to get along with her stepfather.

Harry had said Del was drunk, and that would make him unpredictable.

Perhaps the talk with Claire about Laurie had poisoned her mood. Or perhaps the sense of foreboding that had dogged her since summer had cracked through her firm emotional barricade. Deciding she didn't want a ride from Del, she stepped back off the road onto the narrow shoulder.

Del's truck spat up clouds of dust and pebbles and sped by, but Marly's relief evaporated when the truck screeched to a stop.

A slurred epithet floated out the driver's-side window. "Shit! Marly. I see you, girl. You get over here."

He made a U-turn, and Marly could see the outline of the distinctive broad-brimmed leather hat and bulk of the man in the passenger seat. Zeke—Del's father.

Marly cursed her white running shoes. She should go back to the truck. What was the worst thing? She would get a couple of dope slaps or maybe a punch to her ribs.

Or maybe something worse.

Propelled by the chill in her gut, Marly turned and sprinted the opposite way along the edge of the road.

This is crazy, she thought. *My mother lives with Del. He won't hurt me. He's just drunk. This will only make things worse. I need to stop.*

She heard an odd pop, and the ground in front of her exploded. She stopped to process what she had seen—Zeke or Del had fired a gun.

Marly hovered on the shoulder of the road, unable to move as she strained to push through a fog of panic.

She knew both Del and Zeke were dangerous people, relatives or not, and she had lived a life of meticulous caution around them. Had she somehow committed a mysterious capital offense, or were Del and Zeke in the grip of some alcohol-fueled phantom fury?

"Dad, what the fuck are you doing? Now she'll run for sure!"

Del's curse broke the paralytic spell. Marly's route back to the Rock was blocked. She turned her back on the truck and ran down the last stretch of semi-paved road.

With the truck close on her heels, Marly realized her old white running shoes with the peeling florescent stripes made her easy prey. She jumped to the right onto a narrow path, one of her favorite shortcuts, to a rutted road leading home. If he wanted to follow her, Del would have to drive farther on the main road before he could turn.

The path was slippery, with deep ruts where frequent washouts created an ever-shifting obstacle course of treacherous rocks and holes. The lopsided new moon had moved behind a dense layer of clouds. Marly flicked on her flashlight to scan for any changes in the familiar route before she continued to thread her way in the dark. She couldn't risk a fall.

The rocky path came to an end at a slight embankment. Marly dropped to all fours and clawed her way up onto the dirt track. She turned right and resumed running toward the deep woods hidden in the black night, several hundred yards away. This time the route was well lit—Del's truck had turned onto the dirt road and was headed her way, headlights blazing and closing fast.

The shots from Zeke's gun zipped by. She realized she made a clear target, leaping back and forth in the lights from the truck. Zeke was a terrible shot, but she needed to get off the road before her luck ran out. Rounding a slight bend, she jumped into the sumac bushes on her left, and forced her way through a narrow break of maple saplings.

The leafless branches reached out to snag her and yanked the bag off her shoulder. For a fraction of a second she struggled to pick up the bag, but the sound of Del and Zeke slamming shut the truck doors ran through her like a bolt of electricity and jolted her through the tree line into the open on a hillside potato field.

After the harvest and a week of rain, the potato field mud had turned the consistency of black snot that sucked at her feet. There were firm paths here and there, but those were invisible in the faint, hazy glow from the bashful moon. Marly hissed and sobbed. She traced a random zigzag up the hill in the deep mud and prayed she would stumble across solid footing to carry her to the safety of the woods.

The two men must have been as handicapped by the dark and the muck as Marly, but they were close behind and seemed to be gaining. At five foot nine, Marly was taller than most of the girls in her class, but Zeke and Del were both over six foot three. Each stride brought them closer to their prey.

She found the path she wanted, but not before she lost her right shoe in the mud. Thanks to the path, she could now move easier. She bent over to make herself a smaller target as she scrabbled her way up the slope.

Behind her, hidden in the dark, yelling had given way to wheezing from Zeke. She thought he might be a bit down the hill to her right. Marly could hear Del's breathing as he churned up the slope behind her, but she could not make her legs move any faster.

Shots coming from her right splatted into the mud. She prayed Zeke would run out of bullets and pause to reload, but those prayers were sucked up into the black night. The bullets kept coming. She wondered if Zeke had cat's eyes, because she could barely make out the ground in front of her. *What is he aiming at?*

The darkness was so opaque she hadn't realized she had reached the woods until she noticed the texture of the mud underfoot had changed from slippery and smooth to rough and spongy. The bright scent of rotting leaves washed over her.

She could hear Del just a few yards away and she had no more strength. She pulled up and stopped in surrender as two shots rang out from Zeke's direction. A burning sensation consumed her left thigh and she uttered an exhausted cry of defeat. The second shot drew a scream from Del, followed by a stream of invective. He was so close, she realized she could have reached out to touch him.

Del stopped in his tracks. Puzzled and winded, Marly backed up and scooted into the woods behind a dense section of sumac, burdock, and fallen tree trunks. Leaning against the trunk of an old maple to catch her breath, she tried to ignore the sharp pains in her right foot, the intense ache in her left thigh, and the buzzing in her head.

Del's curses continued, unabated. "Goddamn son of a fucking bitch, Dad. You winged me!"

Don't breathe. Don't breathe. Don't make a sound.

It was too dark to see her left thigh clearly. She told herself the wound had to be superficial or she wouldn't have been able to keep moving.

Zeke's wheeze grew louder along with the sound of the mud sucking at his feet as he slogged his way up to Del. "Why were you in the way? Why did you stop? I think I got her. Are you okay?"

"Yeah," Del said. "It just grazed my ribs. Hurts a bit."

"So keep going! Get her!"

Zeke's wheeze turned into a squeal.

"Dad! What is it?"

"Pain. My chest. Fucking little bitch. I chase her through this muck and now I feel like I'm having a heart attack."

"Shit. Are you okay?" Marly couldn't tell if Del was alarmed or angry. Their voices seemed close, amplified by the wet earth and the echo from the woods.

"All right. Not so bad, I guess."

"You head back to the truck. I'll settle this and come get you."

"Yeah. Make it quick."

Marly heard Del move closer to her hiding place. Surrender was now off the table and escape had new life. She prepared to run deeper into the woods, but paused at the sound of a strangled cry.

"Dad!"

Marly peered through the gloom. Del turned around to run to his father, who slipped and fell on the way back down the field. Del slipped and fell as well.

"Shit, that hurts," Del said, a whine of pain in his voice. "Are you okay?"

"It's worse," Zeke said. His groan floated across the field. "This is bad."

"Fucking bitch. This is all her fault. Come on. I'll help you. But I'll never get the truck up here in this mud. You need to get to the road."

"Need to get Marly," Zeke said between wheezes.

"Don't worry. She'll head home. I'll take care of you first and get her later."

"Call nine-one-one," Zeke said.

Marly grunted with satisfaction at the pain and panic she heard in his strangled cry.

"No coverage here. Besides, the phones are in the truck. Just keep going. It's not far."

Marly inched to the edge of the woods. The cloud cover over the moon thinned to reveal the black shapes of the two men, now in retreat in the mud. Zeke fell twice and groaned.

She risked a quick inspection of her left leg with her flashlight. Streaks of blood flowed down to her knee from a long crease, but far less than she had expected. She wrapped her scarf around her thigh and pulled it tight.

On quaking legs, she paralleled the progress of Del and Zeke but kept to the fringe of the woods as she edged back down the hill toward the dirt road. She narrowed her distance to the two men and hoped they wouldn't look back.

At the lower edge of the field, Del slipped and fell to his knees, taking Zeke with him.

"Shit," Del said.

"Help me up, Del."

"I can't breathe." Del spat. "Tastes bad. That's blood!"

Marly could hear an unfamiliar high-pitched quaver in his voice. Fear?

"I've been shot! It went in under my arm. You shot me!"

Zeke's mumbled response was too faint to hear.

Marly peered into the gloom as the two black shapes merged and gave birth to a new, four-legged, misshapen creature. Del must have helped his father to his feet. The unified mass lurched forward again. Their voices had dimmed to growls and grunts now. No more shouting.

She counted to one hundred and counted again. Her mind traced their slow trip back to the truck.

Now they'd be through the trees . . . Now they'd be on the road . . . Now they'd be at the truck.

Thanks to lack of coverage in these parts, their cell

phones would be useless, flashy toys here. They would have to drive to the Rock to call 911. At that point, the cops and EMS trucks would come, and Marly figured she would throw herself at their mercy. Witness protection seemed inevitable. She couldn't see any other way. Sooner or later, Zeke and Del would recover and relay instructions. She'd be dead.

She heard the faint sounds of the truck. Bright flashes filtered through the trees from the headlights signaled Del had turned the truck to start the return trip to the main road.

Marly eased herself through the sapling break, down onto the dirt road. Farther on, she crossed back into the field and retraced her steps up the hill with her flashlight. She was crying so hard she almost missed it, but she found her right running shoe, one yard off the path, halfway up the slope. Her foot still hurt, but at least walking was easier.

With no sign of the truck, she risked using the flashlight in the sumac, but could find no sign of her bag where she had cut through to the field. Her little purse was in there with her money, her driver's license, her school ID. She felt naked.

She sobbed in earnest and headed toward the paved road. Del must have reached the Rock by now. Help would be on the way.

And that would be the end of her life, one way or another. A mere half an hour ago, she was on track to be the first person in her family to graduate from high school and to have a shot at college and get the hell out of Charon Springs. Now she would have to leave her family and never see her sister Charlene's kids grow up.

Lost in mourning for her future, she rounded the next bend and saw the truck taillights. Startled, she jumped to one side into the bushes, her tears stifled.

She remained frozen for several moments before it dawned on her the truck was not moving and the tail-lights slanted to the left.

She inched up on the truck from behind. The massive vehicle had run off the dirt road and come to rest against a thick cluster of sumac. The fuzzy branches and brilliant red leaves caught the beams from the headlights and threw them up into the air.

She could see the heads of Zeke and Del, silhouetted against the windshield. Zeke still wore his distinctive hat—a silly affectation. This was Central New York and Zeke rode herd over petty criminals, not livestock or kangaroos in the outback.

Zeke was leaning left, against Del's shoulder. Del's head rested against the driver's-side window. Neither man moved.

Marly crept up along the passenger side. The light reflected by the sumac bathed the inside of the cab in a ghoulish red glow.

Zeke's pale gray eyes looked at her. *The look of a dead man,* she decided. She had never seen a real dead man, but in the movies dead people stared like that. She turned on her flashlight to take a closer look inside. His face was a pale blue. His eyes blinked and she dropped her flashlight. She picked it up and looked again.

Marly wiped her hands on her skirt to remove the mud and blood and eased open the door. The smell of alcohol and excrement wafted out. Stifling a gag, she reached in with a shaking hand to touch Zeke's neck. She couldn't find a pulse, but he blinked once more.

"You killed Beanie. My dad. You tried to kill me. Fucker," Marly said. She wanted to say much more, but her tongue froze and clicked with fear—Zeke's gun was still nestled in his limp right hand.

Even a bad shot like Zeke wouldn't miss at this distance. Marly's pulse pounded in her right temple and she stepped toward the back of the truck. She waited until she was certain Zeke wouldn't move. She reached in for the gun, but her movement jostled it out of his hand and it slipped between his legs to the floor and out of sight. He made no move to retrieve it.

All the while, Marly had been keeping a careful eye on Del. Sitting on the other side of Zeke, lit by the dome light of the cab, Del leaned against the driver's-side doorjamb, his face turned as if there was something interesting outside his window. His silence raised the hairs on her arms and the back of her neck.

Marly's bag sat at Zeke's feet. She tugged it toward her until it snapped free. She pressed the passenger door closed until she heard the soft click of the latch.

She eased around the back of the vehicle to the driver's side, where she could see the truck had come to rest in a precarious position. The left side of the dirt road gave way to a deep, narrow ravine. The truck was balanced along the edge, stopped by the sumac on the right and a pile of rocks on the left.

She pointed her flashlight inside the cab. Del's eyes were open a slit—enough to see them glitter with the bright blue she knew so well. Red foam covered his mouth, chin, and upper chest. She tapped on the window. He didn't blink.

She moved back to the right side and checked on Zeke. No more blinking.

Marly sat down on the running board with the two dead men sitting inches away.

She should run to the village and call 911 at the Rock.

What would be the point? Del and Zeke were dead.

Nothing would change. There would still be a big fuss. She would still have to go into protective custody.

Or she could just leave. There might be some evidence that could point to her—shoe prints, a little blood—but not much.

Marly moved back to the side of the ravine and used her flashlight to see what lay below.

The ravine was at least fifty feet deep at this point, but less than twenty yards across. A stream ran along the bottom. The usual sulfurous odors wafted up from the depths. In the spring, when the snow melted, the stream might rise about ten feet and would continue to carve down through the fetid layers of rock and soil.

The truck groaned and strained, still in gear, in search of its new destiny at the bottom of the ravine.

Marly eased open the passenger door again. This time Zeke's eyes stayed closed when she pressed down the lids. She started to close the door for the last time when a metallic flash caught her attention. Zeke's key ring dangled from his belt loop above his right front pants pocket.

The magic keys.

Zeke always carried those keys. Even Rosie, his wife, wasn't allowed to have copies of them. Marly knew those keys unlocked secret places. Places with money, hidden deep in the twisty hills and old limestone quarries. Beanie, her father, had shown her some of them long ago. She had also found some on her own.

The truck gave a lurch.

Marly reached in and pulled on the key ring clip. She slid back the sliding bolt on the clasp, but the opening would not come free of Zeke's belt loop. With one foot on the running board for leverage, she pulled on the keys with both hands. The belt loop gave way and Marly stumbled back, the trophy in her hands. Seconds later, the truck door slammed shut.

The truck shuddered from the blow, gave one final jerk, tilted left, and tumbled down into the abyss.

Lights from the truck now lit up the interior of the ravine. Marly inched forward and peered over the edge. Would the truck catch on fire? Would anyone notice the lights?

If so, she had better be far away.

The truck was almost invisible, even with the lights on. The bank of the ravine made it impossible for anyone to look straight down. A number of sumac bushes and a few maple saplings had been sucked over the edge to cover the truck on its way down to hell.

Marly released a sob. Del had been wearing his seat belt. Was it habit or fear that had prompted a dying man to buckle in?

Hobbled by the pain in her right foot, she gathered her bag and the keys. The pain in her left thigh had subsided and throbbed with a dull ache. Guided by her flashlight, she headed back up the potato field and ducked into the woods toward home. Her watch showed eleven forty-five. Barely thirty minutes had passed since Claire had dropped her in the parking lot at the Rock.

Such a short time to die.

She had walked through these woods thousands of times, but this was the longest passage. Every step aggravated the ache in her left thigh, and her right foot released a sharp jab. Potato-field mud clogged her shoes and caked her legs and arms.

Marly threaded her way past the pools of stagnant water and the hidden patches of quicksand. Stinky water smelling like bad farts percolated up through the rocks.

There were no lights from the house aside from the

blue throb of the TV in the living room. Her mother would be asleep or drunk or both, waiting for Del.

Inside their dilapidated barn, Marly hid the keys deep in a bag of grass seed where they would escape casual search. She stripped and put all of her filthy clothing into a plastic bag and hid it behind an old suitcase. Few items would be worth saving. As a last step, she used the hose to wash off the terrible mud and blood.

She eased her naked, dripping body through the back door to the kitchen. No one roused. Grabbing a towel and her gym sweats from the pile of dirty laundry, she slipped into the lavatory off the kitchen. Wrenching her gaze away from the wraith in the mirror, she dried her body, careful to avoid her left thigh. She pulled on her sweatshirt, wrapped her hair in the towel, and sat down on the toilet to clean the long, thin crease with copious wads of toilet paper. Most of the bleeding had stopped.

Marly recalled when Del asked her to help with a long cut sort of like this after he'd been in a fight.

Del. Shit. She leaned forward and rested her forehead against the cool surface of the sink until her nausea passed. With shaking hands, she poured peroxide on her wound and grimaced with a quiet scream. She applied butterfly bandages from an old package in the medicine cabinet and wrapped gauze around her leg several times. That would have to do.

The tremors had spread to her entire body, hitting her in waves punctuated by calm spells. She scrubbed the bathroom with more toilet paper and flushed the evidence away.

Marly's mother sat sacked out in her recliner at the front of the house. A sour smell of gin and sweat permeated the room. Marly threw a moldy blanket over the sleeping form and turned off the TV.

She tiptoed upstairs to the room she shared with her sister Charlene's two older children. Soft snores came from the bunk beds where Mark and Pammy slept, oblivious to her presence as she crawled into her twin bed, squeezed in under the window.

Marly tilted her chin toward the moon, which had peeked out from the clouds, framed in the white, naked branches of a birch tree outside. The window provided a fuzzy lens, covered by the plastic protection Del wrapped around the house each fall.

Her body shook violently, paused, and shook again. She counted her breathing, one to ten, then repeated the exercise until her shaking subsided.

One more time.

Before she reached five, she fell asleep.

2

Marly: Alone

October 28, 2000

"**W**hy are you still in bed? It's time to get up." Charlene, Marly's older sister, stood in the bedroom door. Her baby, Alison, screamed and thrashed in her arms.

"She needs changing," said Marly.

"You need to get up. All of you. It's nine o'clock. You are so lucky Del hasn't come home yet. He'll be furious if he finds you still in bed."

Charlene and Alison disappeared, leaving a trail of screaming baby and ammonia vapors behind.

Marly sat up. Her chest filled with a mixture of relief, confusion, and dread. *Del isn't home. Is it possible he really was lying in a ravine with Zeke?* She peered out the window to assess the weather, but the plastic winter covering masked all details and rendered the outside world as a collection of fuzzy gray shapes.

Marly rousted Charlene's two older children, Mark and Pammy, helped them dress, and made them brush their teeth. After shooing them downstairs, she stripped their beds for the weekend wash.

Dressing was a habit she had stepped in to enforce

for Charlene. No pajamas downstairs. Del zeroed in on vulnerability the way a lion noticed a limping gazelle. Kids in pajamas were vulnerable.

Ah. But Del isn't coming home.

She took her time in the shower. It was amazing how many small cuts she had accumulated. Each and every one of them stung. Thanks to the fall weather, clothing could cover most of the evidence. Her right foot seemed improved, but the gunshot crease on her thigh was swollen and sore, and it wouldn't tolerate the hot shower. Still, she didn't think it was infected.

She rewrapped her leg and put the old dressings under her mattress. She would dispose of those later. She pulled on her last clean clothes—jeans and an Avalon Central School sweatshirt—and stripped the rest of the beds.

Downstairs, Mark and Pammy fought over their favorite cereal bowl. Stranded on the kitchen floor, the baby continued to scream. Marly's mother watched TV in the living room, her usual spot in any crisis or upset. Charlene had retreated to the downstairs lavatory for a long sit.

Marly let Alison cry while she forced Mark and Pammy to sit down for cereal. That settled, she changed the baby. Calm descended.

Charlene ventured back into the quiet kitchen. "I didn't hear you last night. What time did you get in?"

Marly turned her back on her sister and stopped Pammy from ladling more sugar onto her cereal. Charlene might look like a carbon copy of their blond, blue-eyed mother, but one dysfunctional mother was enough.

"About midnight, I guess. I had to walk from the Rock."

"What? Del was supposed to give you a ride." Charlene sounded incredulous, as if Del were a pillar of reliability.

"Well, he wasn't there and Harry said he'd left, good and drunk, so I didn't wait."

Charlene gave a disapproving click with her tongue. Marly couldn't tell if Charlene's irritation was directed at her or Del.

Marly found the quiet disconcerting. All the ruckus had masked her jangled nerves, now exposed and raw. She busied herself at the sink as a distraction. Hell had been raging around them for years. This tiny moment of calm and safety would not last.

Denise, Marly's mother, entered from the living room, ready to assert her maternal authority. "We leave at ten thirty for the kids' checkups at the free clinic in Manlius. Then we go to visit Greg in Jamesville. Marly, you got cleaning and groceries."

Marly had just enough time to assemble snack packs for everyone, and also stuff the diaper bag with a few extra diapers and bottom wipes. Charlene and Denise would have taken off without those little bits if Marly hadn't placed them in a strategic location in her sister's car. No wonder the words "Mom" and "Mother" always seemed to stick in her throat. Now that Del had vacated the premises, perhaps she would be able to call her mother "Denise" again.

At least Marly would have her mother's car for a few hours to take care of several critical errands of her own while handling the family shopping.

"Say hi to Greg. Tell him that we're all hoping he'll be out by Christmas," Marly said. She helped strap the three kids into the backseat. She didn't much care for her sister's husband, Greg Harris, but Charlene would be calmer and less disorganized once he was out of the penitentiary.

Alone at last, Marly closed her eyes and tried to push her emotions into a thin layer surrounding her skin. She opened her eyes and scanned the dense woods. She half expected Del to lurch into the open.

They didn't have a driveway so much as a muddy parking spot teased out of the scrubby lawn. The two-story farmhouse sagged under its dull steel-blue asphalt shingles, a color that could have been plucked from the leaden sky that day. Half wrapped by plastic, the house stood waiting for Del to finish the job that would seal their home from the winter cold but locked them into a perpetual fog inside. Who would do that now?

In summer, dark woods pressed in on three sides from the hills around the house, but now, with most of their leaves on the ground, the maples and birches offered a permeable gray wall, anchored here and there by nests of dark green pine trees.

Thanks to inept planning, the town road sat higher than most of the yard. In the soggy climate of Central New York, that meant that water flowed off the road to flood their parking basin and stayed to drive rot and mold into the house and barn. It was always damp inside. Smells lingered, and bath towels often wouldn't dry from one day to the next.

If she ever wanted to leave this place for good, she would have to make careful choices. Once Del and Zeke were missed, the Harris family would look for culprits. Marly did not want to end up in their crosshairs.

No one would notice whether she cleaned the house or not. She emptied ashtrays and scrubbed the sinks and toilets while the first load of laundry ran, but decided to forgo a more thorough cleaning job until later.

Once the wash moved to the dryer, she gathered all her bandages and items to be thrown away or hidden. The next load of wash started, and Marly headed out in her mother's Honda Accord. The car's original blue color had almost disappeared under the assault from salt and sand over too many winters, but this dented and pockmarked vehicle provided Marly a tiny window of freedom. Marly gave an affectionate pat to the car's dashboard and wiped off the mist on the inside of the windshield with a rag.

Her first stop was the Charon Springs Public Library, located in one of the town's original houses and across the road from the Rock. Marly loved the elegant old building, originally built for a prosperous farmer and his family. The library had Internet access and even had a primitive website, created and maintained by Marly. Thanks to the library, Marly had a part-time job paying several dollars an hour over the minimum wage and a part-time job writing code for a small startup run by a couple of Syracuse University grad students.

The library didn't open until noon on Saturdays. Marly let herself in the back door and hid the special keys she'd pulled off Zeke's body in a secret hole behind the tampon dispenser in the women's bathroom. She had plans for those keys. Mission accomplished, she headed to Avalon, zigzagging up and out of their valley.

The hills in these parts weren't high, but their slopes were often steep. Hairpin turns had been added to this route long before cars and tarmac had come along. Each turn opened up a different view of the valley below and the surrounding hills.

She had to admit that Charon Springs was pretty— when seen from a safe distance. The village looked quaint, tucked into the nooks and crannies, softened by the persistent valley fog. A classic white church steeple poked through the trees. The hillsides still held spotty remnants of vivid fall foliage, with the red maples at the bottom, transitioning to yellow birches higher up, punctuated by clumps of intense purple-red sumac. The opposite hillside was so steep that the farms appeared to dangle, as if a painter had taken a flat landscape and tilted it on edge.

At the top of the rise, she drove out of the mist onto the flatter stretch, along the broad ridge. Marly's shoulders relaxed and she smiled. She looked forward to sliding into Avalon in another five miles.

On her left, her eye caught a mailbox at the base of Hubbard Road, "Fardig" neatly stenciled on the side. She had to pull over, her brief moment of calm evaporated, replaced by a deadly chill.

Elaine Fardig was a student in her class and so was Laurie Harris—or, more accurately—she had been. Laurie was also Marly's cousin and Del's niece.

Elaine had always rubbed Marly the wrong way. The two had competed for smartest in class during elementary school, and Elaine did not seem to like the threats to her status. She was always bossing the other kids around and giving advice when none was required. Denise had called the Fardigs "stuck-up." "They think they're too good for the likes of Charon Springs," she said with a sniff every time she saw Elaine's mother.

The rivalry had continued into high school, where Marly and Elaine had often been the only girls in computing club and science club, jockeying for the number-one slot in almost every subject.

Whenever Elaine had received an A+ on a paper or a perfect score on a test, she would lean over and ask, "Hey, Marly. What did you get?"

Marly had learned to cover up her paper so that the grade was hidden. True or not, she would grind her teeth, but smile sweetly at Elaine and say, "Can't complain, Elaine. Not one little bit." That often drew a scowl. Very satisfying.

On a mild early-September afternoon, Elaine Fardig had been jumped and beaten at the school bus stop by her mailbox. The police were tight-lipped about the status of that investigation, but everyone in Charon Springs seemed to know that Zeke's wife, Rosie, had organized the beatdown in retaliation for a spat between Elaine and Laurie, Rosie's granddaughter.

Not long after that incident, Laurie was dead, the victim of another brutal beating. Marly knew Rosie had been responsible for that as well. She had overheard Del yelling at his mother on the phone. He seemed more upset by the unwanted attention this would bring than his niece's "accidental" death.

Marly rested her head on the steering wheel. What had prompted Del and Zeke to attack her? Knowing them as she did, it was plausible that they had been drunk and in a bad mood that had crested when they found a vulnerable scapegoat. Perhaps she had just been in the wrong place at the wrong time.

Or they might have planned the attack, gotten drunk for courage, but screwed up because they were drunk. There was precedent for that, too.

All these years living with Del, Marly been stalked by the threat of running afoul of his family. Every day she needed to pay careful attention to each action and develop a practice of invisibility, both for herself and for her sister's children.

She had dreaded that sooner or later her luck would run out.

In September, it had.

On Labor Day, she had returned to their kitchen to

put away food and clean up after the family barbecue. The windows over the sink stood wide open, and she realized that she could hear Del and his brother, Larry, talking as they smoked dope on the side porch.

Max. They needed to take care of Max. Marly's heart pounded. Larry and Del had a very narrow definition of taking care of people they didn't like. She didn't know Max, but she couldn't help but feel anxiety on his behalf—and her own as well. She needed to get out of earshot right away.

She set down the pan, careful to avoid making any noise. There would be time to clean that later. She edged toward the back door, only to come face-to-face with Del's father, Zeke.

The two blinked at each other.

"Oh. Hi, Mr. Harris. I'm just bringing in things from outside." Her voice sounded high and shrill.

Zeke ignored her and cocked his head toward the windows. He listened before he spoke. "Hey, assholes! Shut the fuck up."

Del and Larry materialized in the kitchen. The three large men dwarfed Marly, who weighed less than a sixth of their combined weight. Before they could do or say anything, she sidestepped around Zeke.

"Well, lots more to bring in," she said, and rushed outside.

For a week, Marly had been on pins and needles, but Del didn't mention the conversation. She relaxed, but soon came the series of violent events that shook their community and Marly's peace of mind.

In late September, Marly noticed a news report that a federal Alcohol, Tobacco, Firearms and Explosives agent, Max Redman, had been found shot dead in his car in Liverpool on the other side of Syracuse. Marly's mother said that they were all torn up because Max had grown up in the Springs. She and Del and Marly's dad had all gone to school together.

Marly hadn't slept well all fall. Starting with the murder of Max, followed by Elaine's beating and Laurie's death in quick succession—the violence crept closer and closer, picking up pace and tightening like a noose. When Del and Zeke had tried to run her down the previous night, her nightmares had sprung to life.

Even if Del and Zeke were gone, that didn't mean that the rest of the Harris clan would be toothless or incapacitated. Quite the contrary.

What does Rosie know?

The Harris clan valued loyalty, but they didn't always share their plans. Even if he had a plan, Del might not have said anything to his family.

Marly knew she should keep driving straight to the police station in Avalon. Or to the state police in Chittenango.

She rubbed her forehead along the torn plastic on the steering wheel. She could not rely on the local police, the county sheriff's department, or even the state police. Over the years, all had repeatedly chosen to ignore Harris activities in Charon Springs. Marly was a Harris by blood on her mother's side and by association, thanks to Del, who was some sort of second or third or fourth cousin. Even if Marly were able to escape, she was certain the authorities would do nothing to assure the safety of her mother, her sister, Charlene, or Charlene's children. This was a risk she couldn't bear to take.

Marly straightened up and put the car in gear to continue her trip to Avalon. She would take her chances and manage without the police.

The ridge road was lined with old prosperous farms

intermingled with neglected ones. Many of the mail-boxes displayed the names of the families who had set-tled this area after the American Revolution: Lincklaen, VanLooven, Schwarzer, Lipe, Holmes, Jaquith, Kuntz, Schillinger . . .

"Everyone in our family was in this country before the Revolution," Marly's mother had said, repeating a familiar boast over dinner. The kitchen table was so small that their knees rubbed as they all squeezed in to eat. Marly squirmed and tried to turn to one side to avoid Del.

"It's true, Marly, and don't look at me like that. All us Harris people are descended from brothers Homer, Horace, and Wendell Harris. They got to New Hamp-shire in 1643."

"Weren't they kicked out of England for stealing sheep?" Marly asked.

"Those times were different. People got hanged for little things like stealing sheep. They were just mis-chievous boys. All our other ancestors were here be-fore the Revolution too. We were the first people in these parts."

"Mom, the first people around here were the Onondaga and the Oneida. Besides, I'm a Shaw, and the Shaws came from Ireland in the 1830s."

Marly's mother had paused. "Well, that was still a long time ago and they were Scotch Irish, not Catholic."

"Mom, there's nothing wrong with being Catholic. You do know that Del's mother was raised Catholic, right?"

Del jerked to attention, looking up from his spaghetti. "What? Marly, you talk with respect to your mother."

"Yeah, okay. I'm just really glad we got a head start here. That's made a big difference."

That remark had been worth the dope slap delivered by Del. *Totally.*

Closer to Avalon, old homes made of fieldstone, brick, and white clapboard became more frequent. At last she passed the familiar marker at the edge of town.

WELCOME TO HISTORIC AVALON
ESTABLISHED 1793
ELEVATION 1,200 FEET
POPULATION 7,039

Stopped at the first traffic light, she could see the glimmer of water through the trees. Grand houses, built when Avalon was a lake resort town over a hundred years ago, dotted the shores. Marly turned right onto Albany Street. The first stretch was lined with houses trimmed in gingerbread, followed by three- and four-story nineteenth-century brick structures that formed the center of town.

Even with her limited experience, Marly knew Avalon was considered charming. Today her admiration was muted by anxiety. She had important business.

Her bandages, muddy clothes, and shoes went into various public trash bins. Next she bought new running shoes at the cheap shoe store, followed by a replacement skirt and some odds and ends from the consignment store and new tights at the five-and-dime. So nice that Avalon was a wealthy town with many conveniences.

Last stop, she bought groceries at Wegmans, using their New York food stamp program cards and a bit of cash.

On the reverse trip home, the sun dropped below the

cloud cover to bathe the world in golden light before it headed for the horizon.

False promises, Marly thought.

"Still no word from Del," her mother said. She fixed Marly with a stare, her eyes narrow and watery from gin. "Didn't he pick you up last night?"

"No, Denise. And please don't smoke inside with the kids here. Claire dropped me at the Rock, but Del wasn't there. Harry said he'd left with Zeke about an hour before. I hung around outside for a bit and then I walked home, thank you very much."

"Don't sass me. You should call me 'Mom.' And just remember that we depend on Del."

Sure, sure, thought Marly. She dished out macaroni and cheese with hot dogs to Mark and Pammy. Del provided Denise with a pitiful stipend. Still, the thought of additional money problems made Marly's stomach ache.

Alison got a small, cooled lump on her tray, which she promptly smeared over her face. Calculating the amount ingested, Marly added incremental lumps until all three children were fed. Marly ate in between servings and keeping the peace. Charlene was dieting and confined her meal to the salad. Denise drank her calories at night these days.

Bath time for the kids. Charlene and Marly ushered Mark, Pammy, and Alison upstairs while Denise sat drinking in the living room, on the phone about Del and Zeke.

The Harris clan was coagulating into a mass of concern. By the time all three kids were bathed and in bed, Denise was in a knot of drunken worry.

Charlene showed no sign of concern. "Greg will be out on parole by Christmas," she said as the two sisters cleaned up in the kitchen. "We'll be able to move back to Syracuse and out of this mess."

"Mark and Pammy too?"

"Yes, of course."

"Mark's in first grade now, Char. I'm sure it's good to get out of the Springs, but you can't keep yanking them back and forth."

"Do you think I'd even be living here if Greg hadn't been picked up for cooking a little meth? We need to get back to living on our own as a family. He'll be out soon. I can't leave Mark down here."

"I'm just saying that—"

"Yeah? Saying what?"

"Are you sure Greg wants Mark and Pammy? They aren't his kids."

"So you think they'd be better off here with Mom?"

"While I'm still here, maybe. At least let Mark finish first grade."

Charlene glared and went to join their mother. Denise was drinking and sobbing in front of the TV, the telephone held to her ear.

Their mother hung up. "We've got to go to Rosie's tomorrow afternoon. Right after church."

"Has she heard anything? Did Zeke say anything before he left last night?" Charlene asked.

Denise sipped her gin and orange juice. "Just that he and Del had some business to clean up."

"What does that mean?"

Denise wiped her eyes. "Del's probably gone and got himself in trouble or dead, chasing someone his daddy didn't like. Or maybe he's just off and left me."

Marly leaned against the doorframe, trying to control her knees. There was no one she could go to. Confessing to her mother would do no good. Denise would betray Marly the same way Denise took up with Del right after Marly's dad, Beanie, had disappeared. Denise had also turned a blind eye and let Del crawl into Charlene's bed for years.

Somehow Marly had to avoid the trip to Rosie's. For the millionth time that day, she prayed that Rosie didn't know that the target of Del's mission last night was Marly herself.

Zeke wielded an efficient, if brutal, hand in managing their extended family business in a distant, dispassionate manner. On the other hand, Rosie was hot-tempered and impetuous. If her scope was narrower, it allowed her to focus her malice and controlling anger on the women and children in their extended familial team.

No wonder Del was so screwy. His brother, Larry, was worse and Larry's twin, Louise, was even scarier than Rosie.

Sunday will be a tricky day.

3

Vanessa: Bones

January 22, 2013

"**N**essa! Come in to my office, please."

Vanessa sighed. "*Espérate, espérate. Ya voy.*" *Hold on, hold on. I'm coming,* she said in Spanish. She loved her job, but she preferred to get settled in quietly first. Dumping her coat and bag at her desk, she carried her large Peet's coffee into Nick's office.

"Hey, Sergeant," she said. "Been doing some house-cleaning?"

Nick Bayhouth had the broad-shouldered build of a former athlete, now softened around the edges by encroaching middle age and too much office work. He always managed to look slightly rumpled, and this day was no exception, even in a clean button-down shirt and tie. Appearances aside, Nick ran a tight organization, which earned him high marks in Vanessa's book.

The state of Nick's office was a running joke in the Santa Clara County Sheriff's Department. He had a wonderful window office with California mountain views, but he kept the blinds pulled at all times, allowing books and papers to pile up against the walls and windows. On this day Nick had rearranged the mess and cleared off an extra chair to accommodate a visitor.

"Detective Vanessa Alba, meet Detective Jackson Wong. Detective Wong's from the Santa Cruz County Sheriff's Department. We're asking you to work with him on our mystery bodies."

"Yeah, sure." Vanessa nodded to the tall Asian man sitting in Nick's cleaned chair. "Nice to meet you, Detective Wong." She forced a smile and caught Nick's eye. She knew what he was telepathically trying to tell her: Play nice, share your toys.

Detective Wong gathered his long legs underneath him and rose to shake her hand. "Call me Jack," he said, offering a smile of his own. He turned to the oversized topographical map of the Santa Cruz Mountains on Nick's wall, sandwiched between stacks of old papers.

"The bones were found in Santa Clara County, but it looks like they washed down from the base of this cliff a mile or so west." His fingers traced the route on the map.

"It took us a while to figure it out, but the top of that cliff is in Santa Cruz County," Nick said. "Resources are too tight these days to get territorial, and the situation is not unique, is it, Vanessa?"

Vanessa flushed. She knew when Nick called her by her full name he was telling her that he wouldn't listen to any arguments.

"Absolutely not, sir," she answered. "It will be great to have some help." *There. That should make Nick happy.*

Nick slapped his palm down on a plain manila file folder sitting on his desk.

"Great news. We have a match on the DNA from the bones," he said.

Nick leaned back to read from the folder, which caused his chair to protest with a loud creak. "Two sets of DNA, of course. We already knew that these two were likely to be mother and son based on our own DNA testing. Now we've been able to do a match against the FBI CODIS DNA database. They belong to Louise Rasmussen, who would now be fifty-two, and Troy Rasmussen, who would now be thirty-four. They were a bit younger when they died, of course."

"The coroner said he figured they'd been dead four or five years, maybe as little as three," Vanessa said for Detective Wong's benefit. She turned her attention to the pieces of paper she'd snatched from Nick.

Bones are so impersonal. Hardly human. It was easy to forget they had once all been tied together into a package called a person. Now that she could see Louise and Troy glowering back at her from their old mug shots, they had become very personal indeed.

She checked the dates. These pictures dated back twelve and a half years.

Louise's profile listed her as white, female, five foot eleven and two hundred and fifteen pounds, hair red, eyes green. Louise favored the mullet look. Something that looked like a dead, frizzy animal framed her head. Her hooded pale eyes smoldered with smug aggression.

Troy was a carbon copy of his mother in most regards, right down to her chin stubble, except he was larger at six foot four inches and 297 pounds. At least he hadn't indulged in a perm for his mullet. A vague cast in his eyes caught Vanessa's attention. Despite his belligerent glare, Troy looked confused. *Drugs? Brain damage?*

Jack Wong crowded in to look over her shoulder. "Hmmm. Nice folks," he said, apparently not noticing that Vanessa's back had stiffened. "Louise—eight to ten for dual counts of aggravated assault and manslaughter, served four. Troy—four to six for more or less the same, served three. Last known residence, Charon Springs, New York."

"Presumably Mommy made him do it," Nick said. He waved them off. "Okay, go track down the details. Nessa, give Jackson that desk next to yours. I assume you brought your laptop, Jackson. I've already called IT for a monitor and all the access stuff you'll need."

After they'd situated themselves at Vanessa's desk, Jack tried to commandeer Vanessa's laptop, but she kept a firm grasp on the mouse and forced him to watch on the big monitor. Every good-looking cop she'd ever worked with had been lazy, crazy, or arrogant, and sometimes all three. Jack oozed enthusiasm, so perhaps she could cross off lazy in his case.

"Charon Springs, New York. Where the hell is that?" Jack asked. They leaned in and peered at the Google map. "Not very close to New York City."

"Not very close to anything, I'd say," Vanessa said. "It looks like Syracuse might be the nearest major city, but I wouldn't call that close. We're not talking about suburbia here."

Nick came to check on their progress just before lunch.

"We've located Charon Springs," Jack said. He pointed to the Google map. "Upstate New York."

Nick leaned in. "Nah. That's Central New York. You

should know the difference if you're going to talk to the natives."

"Do you know this area, Sergeant?" Vanessa asked.

"Sure. Didn't I tell you that I grew up in Utica?" Nick pointed to a location to the northeast of their little dot. "I've never heard of Charon Springs, but Avalon and DeRuyter I recognize."

"Louise and Troy dropped off the map about three and a half years ago," Vanessa said, consulting her notes. "Their New York driver's licenses expired and weren't renewed, and there were no new arrests, which was downright out of character. There are no missing persons reports."

Jack picked up the thread. "Lots of minor stuff on their records, but about twelve years ago they were both convicted of aggravated assault of a girl named Elaine Fardig, a local high school student at the time. It's not clear what the motivation was, aside from some sort of inter-family issues. Other relatives were convicted for shorter sentences. Bad stuff."

He continued. "A bit more disturbing are the assault and involuntary manslaughter charges. The victim in that case was Laura Rasmussen. She was Louise's daughter, and Troy's sister. From what I can tell so far, Laura was also in high school at the time. The two incidents seem to be connected, but I'll have to dig further to figure out how."

Nick scratched the back of his neck. "A place that tiny probably won't have their own police department. I'd check with the PD in Avalon and the Madison County Sheriff's Department. They'll tell you who covers this place. Even if Charon Springs isn't in their direct jurisdiction, they're likely to know charmers like Louise and Troy."

After Nick retreated back to his office, Jack and Vanessa walked to a Thai place along Saratoga Sunnyvale Road, dodging raindrops, passing anonymous office buildings and cookie-cutter restaurants. Vanessa ordered her favorite, Thai larb salad, and Jack ordered pad Thai.

When their food arrived and they started to eat, Vanessa realized with a start that Jack had sprouted a wedding ring. *Where the hell did that come from?* She had been working with the man all morning, sharing a keyboard, writing on the same tablet. She had seen his hands. Not a ring in sight! Now he had a wedding ring.

This confirmed her diagnosis: *Jack is crazy.* Did he really think she had been flirting with him when she snatched the mouse away? Was this a defensive move? Effective police work relied on trust, and at this point, she wasn't certain that Jack would be a reliable partner.

Back in the office, Vanessa placed a call to the Avalon, New York, police department. After a very brief explanation, she was connected to the police chief's office.

"Chief Chip Davis here," a man said, in a loud voice. "How can I help you?"

Vanessa wondered if Chip was capable of expressing himself in something like a normal tone of voice.

"Chief Davis, I'm Detective Vanessa Alba calling from the Santa Clara County Sheriff's Department in California. I'd like to have my colleague, Detective Jack Wong, join the call." She pushed the speaker button on the phone.

"Okay, okay. Hi there, Detective Wong. Call me Chip."

Introductions over, Vanessa continued. "Chip, about two months ago a local man found human bones up in the Santa Cruz Mountains here, just a bit southwest of San Francisco Bay. The bottom line is that we assembled the better part of two skeletons, one female and one male. We were able to match their DNA information to the FBI CODIS database, and we now believe that these bodies are Louise Rasmussen and Troy Rasmussen."

There was a slow hiss from the other end of the phone.

"Ah. Louise and Troy. Well, well. It sounds like they didn't meet with good ends."

"That's one of the things we're trying to work out," Vanessa said. "We can find no trace of clothes or jewelry at the base of the cliff or at the edge above or at any point along the way. Unfortunately, the bones were so dispersed and torn apart that we can't determine a cause of death. They might have been dead when they went over or died when they landed."

To their surprise, Chip Davis laughed. "Hoo hoo. Oops. Sorry. Louise and Troy Harris. Couldn't have happened to two nicer people." It was clear Chip was having a hard time controlling his glee.

"You don't seem very surprised or sad, Chief," Vanessa said.

"Did you refer to them as Louise and Troy Harris?" Jack asked.

"Ah. Yeah. Okay. Let's step back a bit," Chip answered. Vanessa noticed that his voice, although still warm and welcoming, no longer boomed.

"I was appointed chief about two years ago. Some years back, I had an early midlife crisis around giving back to my community and decided to make a career in law enforcement, mostly over in Vermont. I jumped at the opportunity to come back here and make a difference. I was born and raised here, and I can tell you that the Harrises have been a malicious disease in this area for as long as my grandparents can remember."

Vanessa and Jack swapped grins.

Chip continued. "Avalon is a gorgeous little town that is often called the gem of Central New York. Of course it's not perfect and we have crime like any place, but pretty much along the lines of what you'd expect. However, we also have a couple of smaller towns and villages that are part of the school system and also police coverage. To put it bluntly, Charon Springs is a carbuncle on our butt and that's where Louise and Troy come from."

"And Harris?" Vanessa asked.

Chip made a series of hums and clicking noises before he answered. "Well, I guess Rasmussen must have been the name of Louise's husband. It's a fairly common name around here. Lord knows where he went or came from, for that matter. Louise always used her maiden name, Harris, and Troy used that too. For them, being a Harris is—was—a badge of honor. For generations the Harris clan has been a sort of rural mafia around this whole area operating out of that pit."

"Were you aware they were missing? Did anyone file a report?"

Chip laughed. "No. Out of sight, out of mind, I guess. On our side, I have to admit that my predecessors practiced a containment policy. These Harris folks are so ingrained and inbred and insular, the primary goal was just to keep them penned up within their own boundaries. Not always a very successful policy, I might add. It is very unlikely that any of the Harris clan would have registered an official complaint or filed a missing persons report with us."

"Can you help us with next of kin? Who else should we talk to?" Jack asked.

"Wow. Next of kin. Well, of course Louise killed her own daughter, Troy's sister. I guess you might know that. Louise's mother, Rosie, died about four years ago and her father died about eight or nine years before that. Her parents, Rosie and Zeke Harris, ran the Harris clan for years. I guess Carl Harris, Zeke's brother, runs it now. But he's a different sort."

"Different?" Vanessa asked.

"Not as vicious. Sort of more like running a family business, tough but fair, although I'm sure there's stuff I'm not aware of. I know that sounds weird, but it's a big improvement over the brutal and personalized reign of Zeke and Rosie."

"Sounds like we should start with Carl."

"Yes, I'd start with Carl."

Vanessa exchanged looks with Jack. "If we came out your way to check on things, would you be able to help?"

"Ooh. Brave folks. Winter in Central New York. It *is* January, you know. There aren't many cheap places to stay around here, but it's the off-season. I suggest that you stay at Avalon House. They're located right across the street from the station, and the guy who runs it is a good friend. It's a bit more expensive normally, but we have a special discount. It's got a good restaurant and a nice beer cellar with pub food, plus they have a wing for extended stays. I'll get you the prices and you let us know. There's the Woodside Motel on the edge of town, but I wouldn't recommend that at this time of year."

* * *

True to his word, Chip emailed them the hotel rates an hour later. Vanessa printed the email and took it into their status meeting with Nick.

Nick must have been in a good mood. He listened to Vanessa's pitch for the trip to Avalon and the nicer hotel.

"Okay. It's January in Central New York after all. That motel would be close to unlivable. Just be sure you stay within the per diem for meals. If you want a drink, it's on you."

Shortly after, they each packed up to head home.

"Speaking about a drink, how about a beer down the road?" Jack asked.

Vanessa was in no mood to socialize. She would be seeing more than enough of him over the next few weeks. For now, she wanted to see more of how he handled himself at work. "Sorry, I have a commitment," she said.

Jack waved a farewell salute and headed toward his car. "Sure. Another time." He didn't seem to be put out. Vanessa watched him from behind. *Nice view.*

Vanessa had a nice view on the drive home as well, but as a cop she knew nice views could be deceiving.

Lovely mountains crowded around the San Francisco Bay at this far end. The Santa Cruz Mountains to the west were thick with the green of redwoods interspersed with Silicon Valley–fueled mansions. The mists rising from the hills in winter reminded her of slowly burning money. The Diablos on the eastern side of the bay had fewer trees and were now cloaked in the green fuzz of winter grasses with a thin dusting of white snow along the highest tops. The rains from earlier in the day had subsided, revealing a beautiful set of triple rainbows over Milpitas.

The drive to Mountain View was a smooth reverse commute, but she needed to keep focused on the road and not on the rainbows.

She hadn't explained that her commitment was to her parents.

4

Marly: Treasure Hunt

October 29, 2000

The anxiety in her stomach rose to Marly's chest and filled her dreams.

In the morning, she dragged herself to the bathroom and discovered that her discomforts had blossomed into a genuine malady. She had a cold. Her throat was sore and a quick check showed she had a low fever.

Thank you, thank you, she thought.

She went downstairs to announce to her mother and sister that she had to stay home—in bed.

"Rosie won't like that," her mother said in protest. "You've got to come along."

Marly forced up a cough, which turned into the authentic item. Her mother and sister took a step back.

Her mother reached forward and touched Marly's forehead. "Okay. Yes. You've got a fever."

Marly crawled back into bed and drowsed, soothed by the sounds of the others preparing for church. Under protest, she went on most Sundays but had no deep fervor for organized religion. Del had always refused to go, but Denise attended every Sunday.

Marly had pleasant memories of sitting on her father's lap in church when she was small, but that place had held no comforts for her since he had disappeared when she was seven. *Beanie*. She'd always called him Beanie and he had gotten such a kick out of that. She knew she looked like him.

There was only one church in the Springs, the United Church—a classic brick structure with a white steeple at the far end of the village—which offered a combination of Presbyterian and Baptist services. Catholics had to drive ten to twenty miles round-trip if they wanted to attend church. There were no practicing Jews in town, let alone Muslims. A few Pentecostal places had been set up closer to Avalon.

Marly jolted awake to find Rosie standing in her bedroom. Only in her mid-fifties, Rosie's skin was as wrinkled as an old apple, stretched over a lean, hard body. Denise stood nervously in the hall while Louise, Rosie's daughter, frowned from the doorway.

"Open," Rosie said.

Marly complied. Rosie studied the back of Marly's throat using a flashlight.

"Put this under your tongue." Rosie handed Marly a thermometer. Marly studied the ceiling and prayed that she really did have a fever.

"One hundred point two. And your throat's red. Denise, you'd better take her to Dr. Duckworth tomorrow. She might have strep throat."

"Sure, sure," Denise said.

Rosie turned back to Marly.

"Well, since you can't come and contaminate us all, you can tell me now. Did you see Del on Friday night?"

Marly sat up on the edge of the bed. "No," she said,

and coughed. In just a few hours her voice had roughened into laryngitis.

"No," she said, and started again. "I saw him at dinner. He went out and I went to the Halloween dance. Claire dropped me at the Rock at about eleven. Harry told me to leave and said Del and Zeke had gone and I couldn't stay inside. So I hung around for about fifteen or twenty minutes and I walked home."

"Which way'd you walk?" Louise asked, her eyes narrow. Louise tended to act like that with everyone, so Marly wasn't sure if Louise suspected something, but her fierce scowl made Marly's heart pound nevertheless.

Marly had given that inevitable question some thought. "Back toward Rippleton on Barrett and onto Dugway. I figured that Del would drive that way and he might see me," she said, tracing the route in the air with her fingers.

"You didn't cut through the woods?"

"Only for that last bit from Dugway. I was almost home."

Louise and Rosie stared at Marly. Denise shifted her weight back and forth, rocking herself. Marly held her breath.

"Okay," Rosie said. "Denise, you can bring the kids. Let's go."

Marly listened from the top of the stairs. Once she was sure everyone else had left the house, she dressed in jeans and her sweatshirt. She rushed to the bathroom and took the maximum dose of cold medicine and three aspirin. She ran downstairs, pulled on a Windbreaker, and grabbed a backpack plus a medium-sized duffel bag.

In the barn, she found a pair of rubber boots that

must have belonged to her father. She put them into the duffel, which she strapped onto the back of her bike.

Choosing her route with caution, she was able to take off-road paths through the woods to the closed and vacant library. She let herself in and retrieved Zeke's keys from the women's bathroom. Back outside, she crossed the main road and headed out on hunting trails to the spot she had in mind.

Keys, keys. Magical keys.

Word was that Zeke slept with them on. Marly knew that Rosie coveted those keys. They opened doors of hidden Harris treasure.

Marly had some ideas where to find those doors. Her father, Beanie, had been an avid hunter and loved the woods. He would take Marly on long walks, and he had shown her many of his favorite places and secret haunts.

Her memories of her father were both distant and clear, and this one was vivid.

She was headed to the place Beanie had called the Vault. It hadn't looked like much to Marly—just a more run-down version of a small, two-story farmhouse much like their own, tucked far off the road.

It was an easy place to miss—overgrown with vines and sumac in the summer and shrouded with snow in the winter. Only for brief spells in the spring and the fall did it emerge a bit to those who might be curious.

She had been curious a couple of years before, when she was fourteen. She had managed to sneak away keys that Del carried. She had checked out the little house but could not gain access to the fortified closet doors on that day.

Now, she was headed back.

The cold medicine and aspirin kicked in. The

weather turned chilly and bright. The crisp, sunny air soothed her throat, but she suspected she would regret it later. She rode without stopping for twenty minutes after leaving the library. She avoided the main roads and followed dirt tracks. She hated riding on dirt roads. The stones played havoc with the bicycle tires and she had to concentrate.

She felt almost normal and cold-free by the time she hid her bike, just off the deserted dirt track that led to this place.

She slipped on Beanie's old boots over her tennis shoes. The people who would come here soon would be hunters. She had already left enough of her own footprints around Beckwith's potato field.

Avoiding the overgrown driveway clogged with burdock, she climbed into the bushes and slid down the steep shale to the creek bed that ran along the edge of the property. She walked uphill in the shallow water, following the creek bed. As she climbed, the high walls of shale shrank until the water flowed at the same level as the woods. She climbed out and edged her way toward the clearing from the back.

Marly loved walking in the woods at this time of year, when all the brilliant leaves from the trees carpeted the surfaces of the rocks and fallen trunks. Soon the leaves would turn brown, but for the moment, the forest floor was a riot of color.

The boots were too large and they leaked. Once she reached the kitchen door, she slipped them off, put them beside the back porch, and unlocked the door.

She had gotten this far before. Getting this far was easy.

The house had deteriorated since her last visit. There were holes in the kitchen floor, and daylight shined in through the roof upstairs. The Harrises would have to find a new home for their treasures before long.

The door to the reinforced closet in the first upstairs bedroom was as sturdy as she remembered it, with two deadbolt locks. Last time, she had tried to punch through the walls. This time it took several tries to find the right keys.

She did a quick assessment. Cash in ziplock bags. Gold coins in plastic sheets. Some papers that looked official and might be interesting. She took about half of each without counting, shoving handfuls into her backpack, including some of the papers.

She locked up and moved on to the second bedroom, which had a similar closet, where she found more money and coins and followed the same routine. It was tempting to be greedy and take it all, but she knew that would be a clear sign of robbery.

Marly moved the dust around with an old broom to obliterate her footprints and returned to the kitchen on the first floor.

Time to go. Perhaps it was just the fever, but she was jumpy. If Rosie was holding a meeting with all the women and children, that meant the men and boys might be out hunting, checking the secret places.

Her hand was on the door to the back porch when she noticed that she could see the basement through cracks in the floor under her feet.

She opened the basement door and peered into the gloom. The basement stairs were treacherous. Every third or fourth step was missing.

The basement was empty, aside from a great deal of dust and crumbling wood on the concrete floor. Bright October light filtering in through the tiny windows.

Marly cautiously moved from the main basement

room to a second space under the front of the house. This room had a dirt floor and a ceiling so low that someone had dug a sunken path for those over four feet tall. At the end of that path, Marly found another fortified door.

The door opened without a sound when she unlocked it, revealing a set of stairs that led to nowhere. The top of the stairs must have been sealed off at some point, she realized. Each of the lower treads was loaded with bags, overall offering about four times what she had found upstairs.

She put handfuls of bags into her duffel bag, barely pausing to look, but still careful to take only a portion of each pile. She did note that the dollar amounts in some bags seemed larger. There was more gold. There were also individual bags of what looked like identity documents.

Finished, she picked her way up the stairs to the kitchen. A metallic sputtering sound caught her attention. All-terrain vehicles—ATVs. She dragged the broom and rushed to the front of the house.

A quick glance out a front window showed a group of five men gathering at the far end of the clearing, at the weedy patch that must have once been the front yard but was now claimed by milkweed, Queen Anne's lace, and burdock. Milkweed silk drifted through the air offering a hint of the snows that would arrive all too soon.

The men split up. Two started to approach the house. One was Larry, Del's brother, and the other was Troy, Louise's son. The other three fanned out. She knew they would start wide and move in.

Marly studied them. She pushed back her rising

panic. They were moving at a slow pace, slapping their way through the brush. She was sure they were there to check for Del and Zeke and to see if the treasures were intact. So far they weren't looking for her. *I hope.* She rushed back to the kitchen.

Inhaling in gasps, Marly locked the back door and pulled on Beanie's boots. She waited for the man circling to the right of the house to pass by in the woods, and she slipped under a tangled mat of vines, hoping that none was poison ivy. Without leaves, she couldn't be certain, but an itchy rash would be nothing compared to what would happen if Larry's team caught her. Her bags weren't particularly heavy, but they were bulky. At least they were dark green and dark blue, like her clothes.

Once Larry and Troy started following the logical path to the back door on the opposite side of the house, Marly crawled through to the front end of the vines, pushing the duffel bag and the backpack in front of her. At the far end, she crouched to survey the yard and woods. She took a deep breath and dashed to the right side of the clearing and into the woods. She hoped she would be out of sight once the searchers reached the dilapidated porch.

After a furtive glance over her shoulder, she scuttled down a short slope, praying the men would take her scuffling marks in the leaves for tracks left by deer or coyote dogs. She circled outward, turned, and headed back to the road once she was certain she had outflanked the searchers.

She was about to rejoin the old dirt driveway that led to the clearing, when she heard a cough. She caught the smell of a cigarette.

She froze. Elliot Harris, Zeke's nephew, stepped into view. If he looked to his left, he would see her, standing at the edge of the woods. Instead, in a simple stroke of luck, he turned right and went back to the ATVs.

Marly waited, fighting her nerves, before she crept away, certain that Elliot would hear her heart pounding.

Her bicycle was still tucked out of sight on the opposite side of the dirt road and had not been moved or uncovered. She pulled off Beanie's boots and shoved them into the duffel.

The trip back seemed both faster and longer. She felt more miserable as the brisk air now scoured her throat. She tried to breathe through her nose because it seemed less painful, but that was hard to maintain when going uphill. The wind chilled her. *My fever must have spiked.* She needed to stay calm. She needed to get home and crawl into bed.

Marly stopped first at the library. The keys went back into their place behind the tampons. The bags were stuffed upstairs in a storage space concealed behind a low wall where the ceiling sloped steeply toward the floor. She hoped the miniature tables and chairs of the children's reading area would provide additional camouflage.

The last push to her house was the hardest. It would have been easier on the road, but she couldn't be seen and that meant taking the off-road paths, with more rocks.

She pulled into their muddy parking area at five o'clock. The bike went to the barn. She crept into the house, grateful that Denise, Charlene, and the kids weren't back from Rosie's.

Marly dosed up again on aspirin. She didn't dare take her temperature. Two glasses of chocolate milk mercifully coated her throat. She shivered through a piping hot shower, brushed her teeth, crawled back into bed, and slept through the entire night without so much as rolling over.

5

Vanessa: The Empire State

As they waited for their travel approvals, Vanessa and Jack researched as much as they could about Louise and Troy. At Nick's suggestion, Vanessa took Jack on a tour of the crime scene in the Santa Cruz Mountains.

They started on the Santa Cruz County side, driving up rough, unmarked roads until they had to get out and walk the rest of the way. At each turn, Vanessa's irritation increased. The steep terrain did not invite intimacy, guarding many places where humans could not go. Or not go easily—like this one.

"Look at this," Jack said, spreading his arms as they clambered over a set of rocks and entered a ravine. "Gorgeous. I love working this beat."

"Yeah, well, you just grabbed a bunch of poison oak to haul yourself up over that rock. I don't know why it's not the state plant. There's so much of it around here. I swear I don't even have to touch it and I get a rash."

"No problem. I seem to be immune to the stuff."

"That figures," Vanessa said, muttering under her breath.

After about thirty minutes of scrambling, they stood at the base of a cliff, littered with boulders and the deposits from rockslides. The orange trunks of madrone poked through the debris, and the odor of bay trees perfumed the damp air. The concave cliff face was carved out of densely packed dirt and rock, arching to a ledge over two hundred feet above the base.

Guarding against poison oak, Vanessa kept her gloved hands tucked in her jacket pockets and gestured with her elbows.

"This is where the bodies landed. Their first stop. Pretty much on top of each other, as best we can tell. After they were eaten or fell apart, pieces washed down that way." She raised her chin downhill, toward Silicon Valley.

"Do you think they were alive or dead when they got here?" Jack asked.

"No way to tell, but I'm hoping dead. That would be a terrifying fall. I'm not sure anyone deserves that."

They hiked back to the car and wended their way through dark, dense stands of redwood trees pressing in over rutted dirt tracks. They lost GPS signals and used their detailed paper map until they found the road that they hoped would take them to the top of the cliff.

Abruptly the trees receded and the climb leveled out. They found themselves on a narrow plateau of mud and winter grasses. To their left, the land fell away toward the Pacific Ocean, hidden behind a sea of trees and lesser ridges. To their right, the cliff offered spectacular views of the South Bay and the Diablo Range in the far distance. There were no signs of human habitation nearby, only the glittering fungus of

Silicon Valley in the distance. *A spectacular place to die.*

Jack inched his way to the edge of the cliff and peeked over.

"Don't get too close," Vanessa said. "That ground is soft dirt and it's wet. Come over here, where the cliff curves. You can see better."

"Barely enough room to turn a car around," Jack said. "A couple of feet either way and they'd slide off the hill toward the ocean or fall hundreds of feet on the other side. This would be an odd place to meet."

"Maybe they weren't meeting anyone. Maybe they were brought here and thrown over," Vanessa said. "I wonder if they camped here. It would have been late spring or early summer and not rainy."

"No way to tell now," Jack said. "Stand there and guide me as I turn the car around. I don't want to become part of the scenery."

Several days later, Vanessa claimed the window seat and studied the suburbs and the multicolored bay as their plane climbed out of San Jose. She resigned herself to spending a long day in the air. There were no direct flights from the Bay Area to Syracuse. They had taken Nick's recommendation to fly through Pittsburgh as the least weather-risky connection at this time of year.

The plane banked and offered spectacular views of the San Francisco Bay and surrounding geography. She scratched the puffy rash on her right wrist as she tried to pinpoint the scene of their crime in the Santa Cruz Mountains.

Scratching her left wrist and cursing poison oak, she

looked over at Jack, already asleep with an inflatable cushion wrapped around his neck like a gray goiter. He wasn't as cute with his mouth hanging open.

Before long, the pilot announced that those sitting on the right side of the plane had a spectacular view of snow-shrouded Yosemite. Vanessa picked out Half Dome. There was no denying that the Sierras were more majestic than her Bay Area mountains. Vanessa wondered what secrets they held. She asked the attendant for a glass with ice, no water, and pressed the ice against the torturous rash.

Hours later over Ohio, the plane flew into a snowstorm and made its landing in Pittsburgh International Airport. By the time their connecting flight headed to the runway, the winter night had closed in around them.

The weather cleared for their connecting flight, and they flew sandwiched between brilliant stars overhead and the lights of towns and cities embedded in the white landscape below. She could tell that she would need all of her haphazardly assembled snow gear.

"Did the pilot really just say that it was minus twenty-five degrees?" Jack asked. He pulled down his carry-on backpack and ski jacket from the overhead compartment. "That must be a mistake."

"I wish I'd checked the weather site," Vanessa said. "Not that it would have made any difference, I guess. We would still have to make this trip." She hoped the padded jacket, gloves, hat, and simple hiking boots from Walmart would provide sufficient protection.

They picked up the keys for their car and crossed the snow-covered road to their vehicle in the covered parking garage. Even that short walk left them breathless, their lungs protesting the frigid air.

"My nose hairs are frozen," Jack said. He loaded their bags into the back of the car. "Okay if I drive? I drive to Tahoe all the time in the snow."

Vanessa hesitated, but agreed. "Sure. I'll thaw out and navigate."

The car had snow tires, a GPS, and heated seats. Chuckling at their own lack of winter weather experience, they found their way south to Syracuse.

"Chip said to take Highway Six Ninety to DeWitt and through Manlius. What are you doing? This is the exit," Vanessa said.

Jack pointed to the GPS screen. "No, it's more direct this way, V. Look. We go straight south and pick up Route Twenty East. Much simpler."

Vanessa slumped down and studied her paper map. "Call me crazy, but I'm thinking Chip had his reasons. Please remember that my name is Vanessa, particularly when we meet Chip and company. Our kind of work is not the place for cute nicknames. It's bad enough that I can't cure Nick of calling me Nessa."

Jack waved his hands over the steering wheel. "Okay, peace. Point taken."

The land had been quite flat near the airport, but now started to rise and fall, gaining elevation. Vanessa felt her shoulders tense with the unfamiliar terrain and icy road conditions. In the open areas, stiff winds carried wispy undulating waves of snow that hovered above the surface of the road.

"Can you see the road?" Vanessa asked. She noted how Jack leaned forward and his hands squeezed the steering wheel.

"Yes, Vanessa. Yes, I can see the road just fine."

Vanessa ground her teeth, noting that the car tended to slip now and again on white icy patches up and down the steep hills and especially along the high ridges. However, she had to admit that she was no better a winter driver than Jack.

After they turned east on Route 20, she pulled her gaze from the road to study the small towns along the route—islands of civilization illuminated by streetlights with houses of clapboard, brick, and stone, interspersed with more generic double-wides.

Beautiful and quaint, if a bit bleak, she thought. *It certainly doesn't look anything like home.*

Jack broke her train of thought. "Another hill. I wish we had chains. In the Sierras, we'd have chains."

Vanessa stared out the side window, her lips pressed together. *Shut up and deal with it. You picked this route.*

Tired and frazzled, they rounded the southern end of Lake Avalon and pulled onto the main street, where they found they had been transported to the nineteenth century.

"Founded 1793. Look at these houses!" Vanessa said. "It's gorgeous. And this main street is amazing."

"Amazingly cold." Jack pulled into the hotel parking behind the three-story brick structure facing the main street. They hauled their bags out of the back. "The car thermometer says minus thirty and it's only nine o'clock."

The hotel was as charming as the town itself. Vanessa noted that the ground-floor public rooms sported hardwood floors covered with Persian rugs and were furnished with what looked like genuine antiques. Chip's friend Rob greeted them by name at the desk and escorted them to their accommodations. Vanessa's eyes widened with pleasure at the sight of the four-poster bed, matching dresser, and desk in her room.

They dumped their bags and went down to the basement pub for beers and burgers.

"Adequate hamburger," Jack said.

"Oh, come on. It's very good and the fries are great. And it's cheap. And we don't have to go outside."

"You know, Vanessa, it's not like I asked for this assignment. I'm a good cop and I know what I'm doing. In a few weeks, with any luck, I'll be back in Santa Cruz for good, and I'll be happy to give you all the credit. In the meantime, I'd appreciate it if you wouldn't take issue with everything I say."

Vanessa stared at her plate. She hadn't intended to confront Jack, but now she didn't dare back away. She looked up at him. He seemed to be very engrossed in his burger, but she could see a flush moving up his neck, much like the one she could feel on her own.

She kept her voice flat and even. "Just keep in mind we're in unfamiliar territory. I need you to have your head in the game."

She leaned forward and tapped his left ring finger. "I don't know what's going on with your personal life. You don't need to share, but you need to focus on being right here."

Vanessa sat back and finished her own meal with feigned enthusiasm. She considered apologizing.

Jack spoke first. "Well, I'm done and I'm very tired. Let's say we start fresh tomorrow."

Was that an olive branch?

Vanessa nodded. "Sounds like a plan."

6

Vanessa: The Springs

January 28, 2013

The next morning the thermometer read minus fifteen degrees. Vanessa was wide-awake as soon as she stepped outside. *This kind of cold is better than coffee.* Vanessa and Jack trotted down the street to the police station at nine thirty.

"Whoa! Here you are. Welcome to Central New York," said the voice they had come to know rather well. "At least there's no slush—frozen solid."

Chip Davis was a short, stocky dynamo, just as Vanessa had pictured him. She guessed him to be in his early forties. His blond hair was half gray and thinning, but his blue eyes sparkled with impish pleasure.

"How about this great weather?" he asked. He shook their hands. "Not a cloud in sight. That's unusual around here. The nice thing about weather this cold is that it doesn't snow."

Vanessa shed multiple layers before she sat down in Chip's office. She noted that Chip seemed to be a clean-desk sort of person despite his oversize personality. Quite a contrast with her boss, Nick.

"My feet are freezing and I just walked down the road," Jack said.

"Ooh. Yeah. You should get some real boots for while you're here. You'll be tramping around in some snow and of course it's damn cold. There's a cheap shoe place just outside of town to the east, and there's a good used clothing store just a few doors down from here. I suggest you get some padded boots and some warmer stuff later today. Maybe your boss will cover that."

Jack scowled. "I hate spending money on stuff we'll only use for a few days."

Chip smiled. "Suit yourself. You could freeze to death in no time if your car were to break down."

Formalities over, Chip sat back and grinned. "So, where do we start?"

Jack leaned forward. "Let's start with Louise and Troy. We want to know about their family and friends, and Charon Springs."

"Fair enough," Chip said. "Let's start in the Way Back Machine. You may not know it, but this area was considered to be the frontier prior to the Revolution. White people weren't supposed to settle here thanks to treaties between the British and the Iroquois. Of course, that's neither here nor there now, but it did lead to a lot of chaos after the war. And within a few years the frontier had moved on to Ohio and beyond.

"The area was always fairly prosperous for farming compared to places like Vermont or Massachusetts. That's one reason people wanted to settle here. But as improvements in transportation like the Erie Canal came around, it became critical to be closer to those links to make money."

"The Erie Canal?" Jack asked. He gave Vanessa a wink.

"You've never heard of that? Clinton's Ditch? Clinton's Folly?" Chip's eyes widened in mock horror.

"Bill Clinton built a canal?" Vanessa asked.

Chip burst into song:

> *I've got a mule and her name is Sal*
> *Fifteen miles on the Erie Canal*
> *She's a good old worker and a good old gal*
> *Fifteen miles on the Erie Canal*

"Okay. Now don't tell me you didn't sing that in school," he said.

Jack grinned. "I seem to remember learning about the 1906 San Francisco earthquake. No singing required."

Chip threw up his hands. "Amazing. I must have sung that song at least once a week for thirteen or more years. Well, anyway, thanks to the canal, followed by the railroads, all those nice cities sprang up from Albany to Buffalo, like Utica and Syracuse and Rochester. All have gone through their rust belt phases recently, but these were great cities. Utica was the start of the transcontinental railroad, by the way."

Vanessa laughed. "My sergeant, Nick, is from Utica. He just told us."

Chip offered a crooked smile. "Good for him. For getting out. Anyway, my point is that gradually some communities got kind of left behind for one reason or another, and Charon Springs is one of those. This area is also referred to as the Finger Lakes, which are long, skinny lakes left by the glaciers. Here in Avalon we have this lovely small Finger Lake that attracted prosperous families from Syracuse in the summer. There's

Avalon College—a small two-year school—and Route Twenty was a major transit route before the days of big highways. So Avalon did very well. After the war, people moved here to commute into Syracuse. The gap between here and the Springs grew even wider."

Jack looked up from his notes. "So Charon Springs is a poor relation."

"Yeah. They're a good eight to ten miles away, but they're part of our school system. Responsibility for law enforcement has bounced back and forth over the years between our police department and the county sheriff. It's in our bailiwick now. Until very recently, going down there was like a trip back in time. Still is in a lot of ways."

"Sounds like more or less normal stuff," Vanessa said. "It is interesting but that's a scenario we've seen all over, even in California. What makes Charon Springs so different? Who are these Harris people?"

"Okay, right," said Chip. He cracked his knuckles. "Well, as best I can figure out, a guy named Elliot Harris more or less ran the Springs in the late 1800s. The water smells like shit down there. Literally. It happens around here in pockets. The rain hits the hills and runs down through a lot of ancient sediment and comes out smelling like sulfur. Hence Charon, as in the Greek guy who used to take dead folks to Hades across the river whatever."

"River Styx," Vanessa said.

"Yeah, that's right. Around here we say the Springs is the only place where you don't want to flush after a big one, you know? The smell dissipates right away, but it's still a nasty stink. Anyway, making lemonade out of lemons, Elliot figured that the water might be popular as a healing liquid and he tried to set up a sanitarium. That went belly-up, but it allowed him to take

control of most of the village. His son, Wendell, solid-
ified the Harris grip on that area starting around the
turn of the twentieth century. Their activities were
pretty low-level crap until Prohibition. That was when
Wendell came into his own and the Harris crowd grew
into a genuine, nasty, rural crime syndicate. We're not
real close to Canada, of course. Lake Ontario sits between Syracuse and Toronto, and it's a good haul to
Ottawa and Montreal, but it was close enough."

Jack and Vanessa wrote in their notepads, trying to
capture each detail.

"Let's take a break," said Chip. "I'm going to get
Paul Daniels, one of our officers. He was born and
brought up in the Springs and would have gone to
school with a number of our Harris friends." He rubbed
his face and leaned in to whisper. "Paul's not our
sharpest knife in the drawer. He barely passed the tests
years ago, and he's not very brave, quite frankly. Still,
he knows all the people down there and he'll know
how to talk to them. He might be cautious, but I want
you to pay attention. If he gets nervous, it could be for
a good reason."

Moments later, Chip returned, followed by a uni-
formed officer. Genetics had not been kind to Paul
Daniels, Vanessa decided. In his mid- to late forties, he
was on the short side, with bowed legs. His belly was
running to fat but his neck was thin and his shoulders
were narrow. He had an undershot chin and his hair
had thinned while his hairline stayed in place.

Chip erased his whiteboard. "I'll attempt to outline
the Harris family tree and explain where Louise and
Troy fit. Paul, you keep me honest here.

"First we have Wendell here at the top. Don't know
who his wife was. Anyway, he had a couple of daugh-
ters and one son, Homer. Homer was born in the early

1900s and Homer had three sons, named Zeke, Vernon, and Carl, in that order.

"Wendell had set up a nice little mini-empire in the twenties based on booze, but he died of appendicitis at the beginning of World War II. At that point, Homer ran things until he died, and his sons Zeke and Vernon began a friendly competition over who would run the family. That would have been in the seventies. Zeke won that argument and Vernon decided to play along. Carl wasn't a player at that point. He was sort of shoved aside and seemed content to take a 'consultative' role." Chip wiggled his fingers to indicate the air quotes.

"Not tough enough?" Jack asked.

"Plenty tough. My theory is that he was smart enough to realize he couldn't win at that point," Chip said. "He had a few run-ins with the law, but he went off and built up a good-sized legit construction business. Kept a low profile for many years. Still, he always kept a hand in and he now runs the whole deal, so I guess things worked out for him. Good things come to those who wait."

Chip turned back to the whiteboard. "But that's jumping ahead to recent events. Homer was considered brutal in his day. People who crossed him disappeared with regularity, but it was quiet stuff. When his favorite sons, Zeke and Vernon, took over, it all moved up a notch. Most of that was Zeke. Vernon had a health problem of some sort and didn't get engaged in the physical aspects of the business."

"Sugar," Paul said. "He had a sugar problem."

"Right. Diabetes. He'd led a hard life and he lost most of one leg and the other foot by his forties, so he did the planning. Zeke ran things. Zeke married Rosie Connor and she was his perfect match and then some.

From the seventies until just a couple of years ago when Rosie died, the Springs was under their thumbs. Zeke ran the hardcore monkey business, and Rosie kept order at home and with all the women and children."

"The women's auxiliary," Paul said. "Everyone called them the Coven. Even Zeke said he was scared of them."

Chip turned back to the whiteboard, writing some new names. "Zeke and Rosie had twins: Louise and Larry, and last but not least, Wendell—known as Del."

Paul gave a guffaw followed by a snort. "We used to call him Wendy in elementary school. That didn't last too long once he got bigger."

"Louise would be our Louise Rasmussen?"

"Yup. But she always called herself Harris. She had two kids herself, Troy and Laurie."

"Laurie as in the manslaughter and Troy as in our other body?" Vanessa asked.

"Absolutely. I guess you know that Troy and Louise were convicted of killing Laurie. They claimed that it was unintentional—just a family disagreement that got out of hand."

"Yikes," Jack said, wrinkling his nose.

"Okay. Finishing off this picture, we have Larry. He is Louise's twin. Larry didn't have any kids that we know of, thank goodness, and is doing a federal sentence for life. He and his brother, Del, were indicted on the murder of an ATF agent named Max Redman thirteen years ago. Unfortunately for him, Del and Zeke disappeared right about that time, and Larry took the full rap."

"Another disappearance?" Vanessa asked.

"All the time," Paul said. He coughed.

"There are lots of old quarries around here. Limestone mostly, plus other hidden places," Chip said.

"What did your investigations show?" asked Jack.

Chip gave them a long look. "Not much. We were rarely even called in. The Harris clan was too hard and too vicious to fight head-on. I'm trying to change that." He glanced at Paul and turned back to Jack and Vanessa.

"Anyway, Zeke and Del reappeared. They popped up a couple of months later at the bottom of a ravine in Del's truck."

"Zeke had shot Del," Paul said.

"Right. We—my predecessors—figured that they were chasing someone. Their clothes were covered in mud, and there's a big potato field along that track that was a match. Zeke had a gun and he'd fired a number of rounds, but no signs of bullets in return. They decided Zeke had a heart attack in that field but not before he managed to wing Del, under his right armpit. Of course it was possible that he was aiming for Del, but they both made it back to the truck, and started to drive out, so that wouldn't square with Zeke shooting Del on purpose. Unfortunately, Del died or collapsed at the wheel and they went over the edge of a ravine. Bled out. Zeke probably died at about the same time from the heart attack."

"Wow." Jack raised his eyebrows.

"No one was heartbroken," Chip said.

"Except Rosie," Paul said.

"Yeah. Rosie was obsessed with figuring out who got away."

"Don't tell me," Vanessa said. "She blamed the person they were chasing for the whole thing. He didn't roll over and get murdered as required."

Chip gave Vanessa a snappy two-fingered salute. "You got it. Before my time, of course. I was appointed two years ago, I'll remind you."

"Did she ever figure it out? Did you?" she asked.

"As best we can tell, she never did and we didn't either."

"Can we come back to the assault and manslaughter charges?" Jack asked. "What happened there?"

Chip leaned back in his chair and looked up at the ceiling. "About thirteen years ago, Zeke and Rosie made some big mistakes. First of all, Zeke tried to coerce a local guy into helping with some drug deals. Oliver Fardig was an old classmate of Del's, and he lived right on the edge of the Springs. He was an airplane mechanic up at Hancock Airport. Apparently, Zeke wanted Ollie to help with transporting drugs. Ollie said no, and Ollie disappeared."

"Surprise," Vanessa said.

"Yes, but this was a bit different because Ollie had never had anything to do with the Harris clan. Everyone else that I know of has been connected in some way. That was Zeke's bad call. About a year later, Ollie's daughter, Elaine, made some passing remarks to her classmate, Laurie Rasmussen-Harris, and some others that she might go to the police. Life was very hard for Elaine and her mother. They were in trouble financially. Zeke hadn't appreciated this middle-class thing. And that's where Rosie screwed up, and made things worse."

"Rosie beat up Elaine," Paul said.

"Their typical response to insubordination. Rosie took care of Elaine. Rosie pulled together her coven— Laurie, Louise, and one or two more. They beat the crap out of Elaine. She had a broken jaw, broken ribs, a broken arm, spinal injuries, and someone kicked her in the temple. She lost the sight in one eye." Chip tapped his left forehead.

"Elaine was only seventeen, so that got a lot of attention. And Elaine was also popular and a good student. Some kids up here in Avalon liked her a lot. Laurie was also seventeen. Elaine's friends started trailing Laurie around, whispering, taunting. Sure enough, Laurie showed up with a lot of bruises and some black eyes. She didn't say anything, but that raised even more questions. A couple of days later Laurie was found just outside of the Springs in a ditch. The state police figured that she somehow got away and crawled into the ditch to hide. She died three days later."

Chip cleared his throat. "Eventually, things narrowed down to Rosie and her crew."

"That's sick," Vanessa said. She reached for her cold coffee to wash away the sour taste in her mouth.

Chip studied her face. "No argument. Rosie and Louise said it was accidental. Fat chance. Anyway, that's the background. What's next?"

"We need to figure out why Louise and Troy went to California. Whom should we talk to? Next of kin? Business associates?" Jack asked.

"Oh yeah. Okay. Let's see." Chip leaned back in his chair to study the names on his whiteboard. "Well, Louise and Troy are both dead. Rosie's dead, thank God. Zeke is dead. Del is dead. Larry's in jail doing life. Other than that, I guess next of kin would be Carl, Louise's uncle. He runs things now and you'd want to check out what he has to say."

Vanessa took pictures of the whiteboard with her cell phone. Chip chuckled and asked to see the pictures, which she agreed to email to him. The team broke for lunch.

Vanessa and Jack strategized and did additional research with Paul throughout the afternoon. At the end of the day they packed up to go back to the hotel. Before the night shift arrived and Paul left, they met to discuss the plan to visit Carl Harris the next morning.

Chip offered his parting advice. "Stay alert and remember, Carl is more businesslike and not crazy, but he could still be trouble. I'm not saying that you shouldn't ask the tough questions. Just make sure you have a clear line of sight out the door."

Vanessa and Jack stepped out into the dwindling winter light.

"Do you notice that your feet squeak when you walk here?" Jack asked.

Vanessa laughed. "My poison oak doesn't itch as much in the cold and that's a blessing."

They reached the door of the consignment store and Vanessa stopped. "Okay. Sorry. Is it just me? All this talk of people disappearing and the casual attitude of the police here? You know they've been ignoring the victims."

"All this happened before Chip's time, Vanessa."

Inside, she picked out a heavy jacket, followed by a thick sweater, and insulated gloves. She even found a pair of stuffed moon boots, a half size too big. She added an insulated cap with earflaps. *Definitely not sexy.*

Jack also did well, except for boots. They had to traipse farther down the main street for some new ones, which put him in an even worse mood, as evidenced by his silent treatment.

"Listen, Jack, it's cold enough here as it is," Vanessa said. "Let's go back to the hotel, put all this on, and give it a test drive. I see there's an Italian place down the street. We could manage to get that far naked if we needed to."

By the time they regrouped in the lobby, Jack was looking less out of sorts, and he grinned once he realized that he could be comfortable outdoors in his new outer layers.

"Whooo. You know this is kind of fun when you're not in danger of dying of hypothermia. That hat is very flattering, by the way."

Vanessa was glad that they were on more pleasant footing.

The restaurant was about half full. A waitress showed them to a table in the classic Victorian front window.

"They're staring," Vanessa said under her breath. She studied the menu.

"Not a lot of people who aren't white in this town, I'm betting."

"Speak for yourself."

"Earth to Vanessa. You may look almost white in California, but here you have Mexican written all over you."

"My parents are from Colombia."

"Sure. That's the country just south of Mexico, right? The other one with all the drug and violence problems?"

Vanessa laughed.

The waitress approached. She looked too young to work, but was probably sixteen or seventeen, with wiry red hair and a plump, pink face, hidden by thick glasses. She had a cute figure, tucked into a white blouse, black pants, and a black cummerbund. A little badge with CLARA printed in bold type dangled at an angle from her right shirt pocket.

"Are you guys the cops from California?" Clara asked. Her eyes were bright.

Jack gave Clara a wink. "That's right. Word travels fast around here, I see. We're not used to weather like this. We need a recommendation for food that will keep us warm."

Clara's neck flushed bright red. The flush spread to her chin and cheeks.

"I hear that Louise and Troy are dead," she said. "Is that true?"

Jack and Vanessa exchanged looks.

"Did you know Louise and Troy?" Vanessa asked. "You look too young. They must have disappeared five or six years ago."

"Three and a half," Clara said. She flushed again, and stammered. "My dad was so scared. He'd had a fender bender with Troy and they got into a fistfight, right down there by the lake. Dad walked away, but we were about to leave town, he was so terrified. When we heard Troy and Louise hadn't shown up for Rosie's funeral and they hadn't been seen for a couple of weeks before that, Dad decided to wait and see."

"So you didn't leave," Vanessa said, hoping she looked reassuring. "Your father will be glad to hear that we have found their remains. We're trying to close the loop on how that happened."

"Dad will be relieved. Maybe he'll drink a little less." Clara wasn't blushing.

"It turns out he made the right decision to stick it out in this exquisite town," Jack said. "Even with this cold."

Clara's eyes glowed behind the thick lenses. "It's only like this for a little bit, right at this time of year. You should come back in warm weather. It's beautiful then."

"It's beautiful now. You tell your mother that Troy

won't be coming back. Now. Tell us what's best on the menu tonight."

Jack and Vanessa sat in silence until Clara returned with their baked ziti with sausage and pasta primavera, plus a large green salad and two Syracuse Pale Ales.

Vanessa spoke first. "I hope you get my point about the containment policy attitude of the police. I will grant you that Chip is new, but take a look at Paul. Chip has lucked out in taking on the Harrises when they are in decline or at least more tractable. There are victims all over this town and many more in Charon Springs, you can bet on that. They won't all be drug dealers and petty thieves. Some are going to be waitresses." She pointed her fork toward Clara, who seemed to glow each time Jack looked her way.

Jack studied his ziti. "I get your point."

"It does make this a bit more complicated. So many possible victims."

"Perhaps not as many in California." Jack finished his beer.

"How would we know? Every emigrant from this county could qualify. And that's just a start."

7

Marly: Called to Account

October 30–November 7, 2000

After his cursory examination, Dr. Duckworth informed Denise that Marly did not appear to have strep throat, but he would take a culture, just in case. Marly would feel worse or the same for another day or so and after that she would start to improve. By the next day, she wouldn't even be contagious. That was how it went with a virus, he explained in a slow monotone voice.

"He hates Medicaid patients," Denise said, once they were back in her car. "He talked to me like I was hard of hearing or something."

Marly didn't answer. She had no voice and she was too miserable. Her best friend Andrea's family had plenty of money and she had said that Dr. Duckworth hated patients with fancy insurance too. Marly vowed that once she was out of this place, she would never again see a doctor she didn't like. Another item on her checklist.

Dr. Duckworth was right. By Tuesday she felt much better and by Wednesday she was almost normal. She went back to school on Thursday, despite some laryngitis and a persistent cough.

After school Friday afternoon, Marly stepped into their empty house. She halted in her tracks and sniffed. What was that smell? The scent of cheap cologne mixed with nicotine and nasty body odor lingered in the kitchen. She listened for sounds in the house, ready to run, as she peered into each room and down into the basement.

In the kitchen, someone had pulled out the containers for flour and sugar and left them askew on the counter. Upstairs, someone had peeled back all the sheets and blankets from the beds.

Marly could pick up the same scent in their barn. Grass seed covered the floor, the bag emptied. Boxes had been rearranged.

The back of her neck prickled all evening. She said nothing to Denise or Charlene.

"Rosie's real worried. Larry too." Denise picked over the frozen lasagna Marly had heated up in the microwave.

"I'm sure they're upset about Del and Zeke," Marly said. She hoped she sounded sympathetic. "This situation must be very hard on them."

Denise took a long slurp from her gin and orange juice before answering. "It takes money to make money. That's what Rosie says. She's in a terrible state because Zeke has money hidden away. He had an accounting written down for her. Now some of that is coming up short. She is just wild to find out where that went."

Such a shame. The vision of Rosie in distress was

gratifying, but this was not good news and probably explained why their house and barn had been searched.

Marly's stomach churned every time she thought of Rosie. No longer able to eat, she cleared the table and started to clean up.

Lulled by the sloshing water in the sink, Marly thought through Rosie's motivations. Larry must have searched the house for his mother. It could be that he merely wanted to know if Del had squirreled money away at Denise's house without telling Rosie. The two brothers didn't always see eye to eye on money.

The search might also mean Rosie had decided that Denise, Charlene, and Marly were suspects in the disappearance of Del and Zeke.

Charlene and Marly carried multiple grudges against Del. Marly was quite certain that Rosie knew this. Over ten years before, Beanie, Marly's dad, had disappeared after a conflict with Zeke. Even at the age of seven, Marly recognized the whiff of scandal when Del moved in with Denise several months later. In addition, Marly knew that most people—including Rosie— thought that Del was the father of Mark and Pammy, conceived when Charlene was underage. As best as Marly could tell, at least no one thought Del was sleeping with her.

There have to be some advantages to being the homely daughter.

Marly tried to put herself into Rosie's frame of mind. She acknowledged that Rosie would have good reason to suspect all of them of taking the money.

Denise had a part-time job as a nurse's aide, but as a family, they subsisted primarily on a mix of Aid to Families with Dependent Children, food stamps, Medicaid, and welfare.

Marly knew that Zeke gave Denise a small cash stipend

every month or two—guilt money for Beanie. Del contributed money for food but little else. His rationale was that he still owned his own place—a double-wide over on Dugway Road. Charlene once mentioned that Del also gave her money every month for Mark and Pammy.

Charlene did not have a real job, aside from a bit of dabbling in the drug trade. Marly would often wake at night filled with dread over what might happen to the children if Charlene were arrested.

Marly's job at the library paid better than most in the area, as did the startup with the addition of worthless stock options. She tried to save for college, but gave half of her salary to Denise.

Finished cleaning up, Marly headed to the library on her bicycle for her Friday evening shift. She fretted that Rosie and her crew would search there as well.

It wasn't like Zeke and Rosie lived high on the hog. Their large main house in the woods had been improved a bit around the edges, but it remained just as tired and sad as Marly's house, only bigger. All the Harris family insiders drove new GMC trucks and carried fancy guns, but flashed few extras. Del, Zeke, Larry, and Louise flashed cell phones, but those were mostly for show since there was no coverage in the Springs.

Marly was the only one on staff at the library from six to nine. Visitors were rare after seven. On this night, the place was empty by seven thirty.

Marly retrieved her duffel and backpack from upstairs and took them to the librarian's office, located off the main reading room. She closed the door halfway and sorted through the contents she had taken from the cabin in the woods.

Keeping a watchful eye on the entrance, Marly pulled out the bags of cash she had taken from the first upstairs closet. Her fingers fumbled and she had to count twice: $18,000, about half in twenties and the rest in fifties. She packed those away. The second set of bills from the other closet came to $25,000.

She next examined the plastic sheets of gold coins. Each sheet held twenty coins tucked into individual slots. Most were gold dollars but there were also Krugerrands from South Africa. Marly counted two sheets from the first closet, one from the second.

Marly repacked the backpack and placed it in a file cabinet. She took a short break to check the front desk and empty library.

She didn't know much about gold or coins. She used the library computer on the front desk to search the Internet for the price of gold—$280 an ounce. She confirmed that each one-dollar coin and the Krugerrands were one ounce. Marly signed off and did the multiplication in her head. She had acquired approximately $16,000 worth of gold from the upstairs rooms of the cabin.

Marly knew exactly how she would use this money: college. True, her family also needed this money, but she knew that getting an education would be a better investment.

She had planned to attend one of the State University of New York colleges. The SUNY schools were all considered very good, but she ached to attend someplace like Yale or Princeton or Brown. Andrea's parents had included Marly on a college tour the year before that included Brown. She had decided that Brown would be the perfect fit.

Even a SUNY college would be expensive by her standards, and Brown or another private school would be much more for four years, even with scholarships.

Now she had a Harris scholarship, courtesy of Zeke. She looked inside the duffel bag filled with the loot from the basement storeroom. Library closing time was near. She needed to step up the pace.

She counted an additional $25,000 in cash, two pounds of gold, plus something potentially even more valuable—identities. Her quick glance at the additional bags had been correct—four bags, each with a social security card, birth certificate, and other documents that would allow the holder to change into a new person.

Marly repacked the duffel bag and replaced that along with the backpack in the eaves behind the low wall upstairs. She rubbed her hands together, both excited and scared. No wonder Rosie and Larry were so angry.

She rode home after she closed the library and noted with chagrin that living with Del had rubbed off in ways she hadn't appreciated or even recognized before. Take this little matter of money laundering. She knew she couldn't walk into a bank and deposit tens of thousands in cash without drawing unwanted attention. In some ways, having too much money was just as bad as having too little. Assuming she managed to keep the money, she'd need to figure out some way to get access to it for college.

Marly recognized that she had painted herself into a very tight corner. She had stolen a great deal of money and that was a crime, regardless of the source. She couldn't go to the police now.

She ran through scenarios of how she might return the money to the Vault or directly to Rosie.

Forget that.

Rosie would never overlook the insult, plus she would know that Marly was involved in the disappearance of Del and Zeke.

Marly spent another sleepless night. No amount of counting breaths helped. She needed to move her treasure. If Rosie and the Harris clan suspected her, they would search the library.

Because she was under eighteen, Marly could not open a safe-deposit box without her mother's involvement. Even if Marly used an alternate identity like the ones she had lifted, she would need to get farther afield from the Springs—which had no bank at all—or Avalon, where she would be identified.

She couldn't use her own bank account. Someone would notice a big influx of money. Plus, her mother had drained her account the previous spring. After that, Marly had kept most of her assets in cash, hidden in Andrea's garage in Avalon.

She dismissed sharing her fortune with Denise or Charlene. Some of this was greed, she did admit, but it was also much too risky. Denise could not be trusted to keep her mouth shut or to spend the money carefully. She would go out and splurge on something bold and stupid, and sooner or later she'd talk. Charlene was almost as hopeless.

The next morning, Saturday, shopping in Avalon helped solve the first part of the money problem. Marly picked up the bags and Zeke's keys at the library and drove to Andrea's house.

Marly's stomach unknotted and she could feel her neck relax as she pulled into the Melvilles' driveway. By Marly's estimation, Bob Melville made lots of money as a lawyer. He and his wife, Jean, had welcomed Marly into their home ever since Andrea had dragged Marly to meet her parents at the beginning of junior high school.

Andrea was one of the smart girls too, but did not see academics as a field of battle for supremacy. She enjoyed learning and figuring things out and developed a wide range of enthusiasms, pulling Marly along with her. Marly would never have taken up team sports or learned tennis or sailing without Andrea or her parents, who faithfully drove the girls to practices and games. Mr. Melville had taught Marly how to swim, moving her beyond her clumsy doggy paddle to become a confident and graceful swimmer. Every time Marly felt she might be submerged by her life in the Springs, Andrea's friendship provided a warm lifeline and a glimpse into the better side of human nature.

If Mrs. Melville was put out to find Marly at their back door on this day, she didn't show it. She made her famous, gooey grilled cheese sandwiches for the two girls and disappeared on her own errands.

Seated in the breakfast nook with Andrea's cat in her lap, Marly savored the taste of warm cheese and the contentment of sitting in a house that was old and graceful, rather than old and moldy, filled by people who seemed to get along.

"I need to put something in your garage," Marly said, after her final swallow.

"Sure. No problem." Andrea never meddled in Marly's family affairs unless Marly wanted to share.

As far as Marly knew, Andrea had never so much as looked into the other bags and boxes Marly had delivered for safekeeping. And so what if she did look and found the gold? Marly would have happily shared everything with Andrea.

The Melvilles' garage, a former stable, had ample storage space upstairs with an abundance of natural hiding spots. Marly deposited her backpack behind some boxes in the attic and put the duffel up on the rafters of the garage, along with Zeke's keys.

With a quick wave good-bye, she left Andrea's oasis and headed back into the real world of obligations and worry.

On Sunday before church, a small crowd gathered around the town librarian, Mrs. Haas. There had been a break-in at the library the previous night. All agreed that it must have been kids, out for fun.

Marly could think of nothing else throughout the service. She went through the motions of worship. Could this have been Larry or Louise? Would Rosie have told them to search the library because Marly worked there? She trembled at her narrow escape, glad she had moved her treasure the previous morning, and offered a genuine prayer of thanks.

"That's too bad about the break-in," Marly said to Mrs. Haas after the service. "Do you know who it was?"

Nancy Haas patted her immaculately coifed gray hair as she looked right and left, as if to make sure that no one was listening. Apparently satisfied, she gave Marly a long look.

"Yes. That was obvious. You be careful, Marly." She tugged the front of her Sunday-best tweed jacket as she straightened her back to reach her full five foot two inches and headed toward the parking lot.

Marly swallowed and drifted away to find her family. *Larry and Louise.* If they were looking in the library that meant Rosie suspected Marly. It also meant Mrs. Haas knew that too.

On Monday, she sat next to Claire on the school bus. Marly had been home with the cold most of the previous week and they had not spoken since the night of the Halloween dance.

"Rosie and Louise Harris came to see us on Saturday," Claire said.

"What did they want?"

"They wanted to know about the night of the dance."

Marly stared. "I don't think there was much to tell."

"Exactly. I told them I'd dropped you at the Rock to get a ride with Del, but that his truck wasn't there."

"Thanks. Of course that's the truth."

"Yeah, well, they weren't very nice about it and kept asking. My mother was scared shitless. Dad, too. My mother made them stand on the porch. She wouldn't let them inside. Jeez, Marly. Your relatives are not nice. Now my mom's furious. She says we can't be friends anymore."

Marly stared out the window. "I guess I can't blame her."

"I'm so sorry. Mom thinks we should be living in Avalon and not stuck down here. She hates the Springs. She wants my dad to get the principal's job up in Avalon."

"That's okay, Claire. I get her point. I'd get away from here and my family too if I could."

"I'm still your friend, Marly. But I can't help you anymore."

"Yeah. I know that."

Marly's mood darkened. Just as she had feared, Del's disappearance hadn't improved anything.

At the end of the day, she stepped off the school bus and trudged down the road to her house, deeply absorbed in her own thoughts. She jerked back to high-alert status when a car came to a squealing stop in front of her.

Two hulking figures, Louise Harris and her son, Troy, jumped out. Louise was taller than most men, with a solid, beefy build. Troy was her mirror image, but taller and run to fat. For as long as Marly had known her, Louise had only shown two emotions: pissed off and furious.

Now Louise was smiling. Marly realized that she was about to be hauled off and beaten to a pulp.

Troy grabbed her, but Marly managed to kick him in the groin. He bent over and slumped against the car. Marly ducked a punch from Louise but caught a backhand on her right eye. Louise grabbed Marly's school backpack and tossed it into the front seat of her car.

Before she could recover, Marly found herself in the backseat of an old Corolla, where she continued to kick and struggle with Troy. Out in the open, Troy had the advantage of his enormous bulk and strength, but in the backseat of a small car, Marly was able to maneuver better. She had only one thought—*don't go easy*.

Louise slammed on the brakes, throwing Marly hard into the backs of the front seats. Louise leaned over the seat and gave Marly a sharp rap on the top of her head.

"Troy, you keep that bitch quiet until we get to Rosie's."

Switching tactics, Marly went limp.

We're headed to Rosie's. Rosie wants me alive. For now.

Troy yanked Marly up beside him and wrapped his right arm around her neck.

Louise put the Corolla in gear, leaving a cloud of stones and dust in their wake. She paid no attention to the double yellow lines and didn't seem to worry about oncoming traffic. Several times Marly worried that she might die in a car wreck rather than from a beating.

Louise slowed down and turned into Rosie's yard. Louise and Troy pulled Marly out of the car. She forced her muscles to relax and sag heavily. When Troy turned to close the car door, she twisted, broke free, and dashed for the woods. For a few seconds, she saw freedom, but she slipped in the deep mud. That gave Louise a chance to catch up and tackle Marly. Louise and Troy dragged her by the hair and arms up to the house.

Marly found herself sitting on a hard chair in the first-floor side parlor. Louise and Troy stood against the wall in back of her, breathing hard. Louise's twin, Larry, leaned against the wall to her left. Rosie stood in the center of the room, staring.

Marly forced herself to appear quiet and defeated, but she looked around for an opportunity to bolt.

Vernon Harris rolled into the room in his wheelchair, pushed by his son, Elliot. Vernon was Zeke's younger brother and they were as physically different as oil and vinegar.

Zeke had been a bigger-than-life presence, tall and broad with a large paunch. Vernon was whip thin and considerably shorter, although it was a bit hard to tell since he always sat in his wheelchair.

Marly hadn't understood the connection, but the word was that childhood diabetes combined with a hard life had somehow caused Vernon to lose the lower part of his left leg when he was younger, followed by his right foot. He was now in his late fifties, and his face was wizened and his complexion an odd shade of yellow. If Zeke and Del were the operations part of the Harris business, most said that Vernon was the brains.

Elliot was vain and considered to be a pretty boy, like Del. Everyone said he was just waiting to step into a bigger role.

Rosie slapped Marly.

"Why'd you give Louise and Troy a hard time?" she asked.

Marly narrowed her eyes and tried to glare, but her voice came out in a sob. "Why did they jump me? I would have come if they'd just asked. I was so scared. Girls are getting killed around here."

Vernon cleared his throat. Rosie backed away.

"Did you kill Del and Zeke?" Elliot asked.

"What? Of course not. I would never do anything like that. Del is my stepfather. Zeke is family."

"Tell us again," Louise said. "What happened on that night?"

Between tearful gasps, Marly retold her story. "I went to the dance. The Halloween dance. Claire dropped me at the Rock, but Del wasn't there. The bartender will tell you. He saw me and told me to leave because I'm underage. I waited for a bit outside and then I walked home."

As Marly ducked her head to avoid another blow from Rosie, the door opened and Zeke Harris walked in. No, it was Carl, Zeke's youngest brother. Carl looked so much like Zeke that Marly thought Zeke had returned from the dead. She noticed the others jumped as well.

"What's this?" Carl asked.

"Just a few questions for Marly," Rosie said. "Why are you here?"

"Are you fucking crazy? Picking up a girl in broad daylight? How do you think I found out? The police might already be on their way."

Carl stepped to the middle of the room and everyone moved back. He studied Marly's face.

"Okay. You go upstairs to the back bedroom. Elliot, you take her and lock the door. Once that's done, you come back."

On her way upstairs, Marly turned to face Elliot. "I need the bathroom. Now."

"Fine, but I'm leaving the door open."

Marly used the toilet and washed her hands. She snuck a quick look in the mirror. Her right cheek was bruised and she'd have a black eye for sure, plus her upper lip was swollen in two places. Her ribs were sore too.

The back bedroom sat directly over the room where she had been held downstairs. Elliot made her sit on the bed and locked the door behind him.

Marly had never been upstairs in this house. The room was smaller than the one below, tucked in under the eaves. It was just big enough for an old iron bed and a battered pine bureau. Faded floral wallpaper had peeled back to reveal strips of lath and plaster. Outside, dusk had settled around the house and provided a dim, watery glow through the one small window.

A bare bulb dangled from the ceiling. Marly flicked the switch by the door several times and heard the ancient wiring crackle before the light turned on.

All she could think of was how to escape. She searched the dresser drawers, hoping to find something that might be used as a weapon. Nothing. The door was locked and the window was painted in place. Even if she had been able to open it and squeeze out, she would have a long drop to the ground.

Marly calmed down enough to realize that she could hear the argument in the room below through the heating vent. She left the bed to lie on the braided rug, her ear next to the opening.

Some parts of the discussion were clearer than others. Rosie's voice dominated. "That little bitch has been a thorn in our side since day one. Her father was a Shaw, not a Harris. She always hated Del and disrespected him."

Carl's laugh gave Marly a glimmer of hope. She didn't know Carl well. She knew he kept his distance from Harris family politics most of the time. She wasn't sure that his opinion would carry any weight with Rosie.

"By 'disrespected,' I assume you mean Marly refused to let Del sleep with her," Carl said.

"She accused Del of sleeping with Charlene."

"That was true, as far as I know. You're saying it wasn't? And she didn't complain to the police. She complained to Zeke."

Louise took up the argument. "Marly was the last one to see Del and Zeke."

"As far as I know, Harry at the Rock was the last one to see them and he backs up Marly. And that girl, the principal's daughter, she says the same thing."

The shouting subsided. The conversation was still heated, but not as loud. Marly couldn't make out much. She squeezed her knees to her chest to keep from shaking.

Carl spoke up again. "Just what did you have in mind? Do I need to remind you that two high school students have been found in ditches this fall? We're already in the crosshairs of the police."

"Laurie was a mistake," Louise said. She mumbled something else.

Carl's voice was sharp and loud now. "Shut up, Louise. Thanks to you, a very simple complaint from a stupid teenager turned into a disaster. You could have just ignored Elaine Fardig. No one else was paying any attention. But no. You had to beat her up and send her to the hospital. Then you went after Laurie for reasons I don't quite understand or want to. Your own daughter, Louise. And she died. I can assure you that the cops won't ignore one more."

Someone laughed.

"Careful, Elliot. The word is that Del and Larry are going to be indicted for killing that ATF agent. You could be going away too. Which brings up my next point. How do we know Del hasn't just skipped out ahead of that indictment?"

Doors slammed. What did that mean?

Marly scrambled back to sit on the bed.

The lock turned and Carl came in. He turned her left cheek to face the light, and then turned her face to the other side. His touch was not gentle or affectionate, but at least he did not seem inclined to hurt her.

"I suggest you have a good story in mind that doesn't involve Louise or Rosie. Come on. I'm taking you home." He handed her a plastic bag filled with ice wrapped in a dirty towel.

The downstairs seemed deserted although cooking smells oozed from the kitchen. Rosie, Louise, Troy, and Larry must have been in there, but they did not come out. Marly was not inclined to ask what was for dinner. It did not smell very good. She picked up her backpack where it had been dumped at the foot of the stairs. She and Carl left by the front door and got into Carl's Lexus.

The car's soft gold finish showed no signs of winter rust. Inside, Marly settled into a cushy leather seat and sniffed the new-car smell. Carl stared ahead at the rutted driveway and turned the ignition.

Carl had come to her rescue, but Marly wasn't sure

where she stood with him, or where he stood with Rosie, Larry, and Louise. She remembered that Del had always snorted whenever Carl's name came up. He had referred to Carl as The Loser. Still, he apparently had some pull. Whatever his agenda was, she needed to make certain Carl viewed her as his pawn, not Rosie's. Perhaps she knew something he might value.

"Mark and Pammy aren't Del's kids," Marly said.

"What?"

"Mark and Pammy. They aren't Del's kids. They're Johnny Martinson's kids."

"So?"

"Johnny is your stepson, right? Or he was before he disappeared. Your wife, Betty, is Johnny's mother. She'd be their grandmother."

Carl did not check for traffic, she noticed. He made a smooth turn at the end of the long driveway as if he owned the road into town.

"As far as we all know, Johnny's still alive on the West Coast," Carl said. "He wrote letters. He could show up anytime. But I'll bite. How do you know that?"

Marly knew Johnny was dead, just like her father was dead. However, this was not the time to argue that point. She needed to keep Carl as an ally.

"It's basic biology, Mr. Harris. Of course Charlene said they were Del's, but last year in biology I figured it out."

"High school biology?"

"Sure. You can learn a lot of good stuff in high school."

Carl shot her a look. "Watch the lip, Marly."

"Okay, okay. Mark and Pammy have cleft chins. That's a genetically inherited characteristic. Think Kirk

Douglas and Michael Douglas. The cleft chin gene is dominant, the smooth chin gene is recessive. It would be very unlikely that Mark and Pammy could have cleft chins since neither Charlene nor Del have one. But Johnny had a cleft chin, plus they do have his coloring with the same dark hair and blue eyes. Besides, they aren't the right blood type."

Carl let off on the gas and pulled to the shoulder.

"Fine, Miss Smarty-Pants. Tell me about the blood."

"It's not that complicated, Mr. Harris."

"Just explain and don't be a smart-ass."

Marly leaned across the burl wood console separating their seats. "You don't need fancy DNA testing for the basics. It is all forensics had for most of the twentieth century. It's really easy and cheap to test for blood types and you don't need much blood. We had a homework assignment and I tested everyone at home. Del wasn't exactly pleased, but I got blood from him, too."

"And?" Carl tapped his fingers on the steering wheel.

"Del couldn't have been Mark's or Pammy's father based on blood type. Del is Type B. Type B is recessive. That means that he can only pass along Type B. Charlene is Type AB, like me. We can only pass along Type A or Type B. If the kids were either AB or B, Del might be their father. But Mark and Pammy are Type O."

Marly wondered if Carl was following this. The Harris clan wasn't known for being very educated.

Carl nodded. "Type O."

Marly saw her opening. Carl was listening.

"Type O is a dominant blood type. If your Mom gives you an A gene and your Dad gives you an O gene—or vice versa—Type O always wins. I don't know for sure what type Johnny was. Maybe Betty would know. One thing for sure is that Del couldn't be the father of Mark or Pammy if Charlene is AB. They'd have to be B or AB." Marly leaned back and faced out the front window.

Carl put the car in gear. "Plus the chin."

"Plus the chin."

They drove in silence. Marly relaxed, wiggling her backside down into the heated leather. She decided Carl wasn't going to hurt her or turn her over to Rosie, and her face felt better thanks to the ice.

Carl took his foot off the accelerator and let the car drift to a stop.

"You need to get away from here, Marly."

Marly sat still and stared at the road.

"You're a good kid. But Rosie and Louise won't forget. You need to leave."

"I graduate in the spring."

"You might consider leaving early. I assume you want to go to college?"

Marly thought of the gold sitting in Andrea's garage.

"My mom wants me to stay here and get a job in Fayetteville or Syracuse. School is expensive."

"Where were you thinking of going?"

"I'm going to apply to SUNY Binghamton and New Paltz. And Syracuse."

"Those are nice and close to home. Too close to home," Carl said.

"Brown wants me to apply. I visited last summer with my friend Andrea and her parents."

"Where's that? Boston?"

"Providence, Rhode Island."

"Providence. That might be far enough."

"It's a lot of money, so it had better be," Marly said. "Even if I get in, student aid won't cover everything."

Carl leveled a flat stare straight into Marly's eyes. "I'm talking about your life, kiddo. What is your life worth? You think I don't know this is hard? I had to send my own boys away to keep them from harm."

Marly blinked and slid away until the passenger-door armrest pushed into her back. Perhaps Carl was more like his brother Zeke than she gave him credit for.

"I didn't realize you had sent them away. They were a lot older than me and I didn't see them much. I am really sorry."

Carl swiveled back to study the road, his face hard to read in the reflected glow from the dashboard and the headlights hitting the asphalt ahead. "I do not need your sympathy. I was making a point about what it takes to survive in this family."

Marly focused on her lap where her fingers twisted the ice pack rag. "I guess I know something about that too."

"It's your call. If you do stay, you had better lie low, graduate high school, take out some loans, and get the hell out of here and don't come back."

"Not ever?"

Carl pushed on the accelerator. "If you're asking my advice, then the answer is no."

Carl pulled into Marly's muddy driveway and turned the car around so its nose faced out toward the road.

"Get out, Marly."

Marly clambered out of the car and headed to the house.

Denise was sitting at the kitchen table with Charlene. Both women had been crying, their faces blotchy and red. Denise burst into tears when she saw Marly.

"Oh, my Marly. My baby. I thought they'd kill you. Look at your face. Oh dear. I'm so sorry."

The taste of loathing filled her throat like bile.

Marly raised her right fist and took a step toward her mother.

In that moment, Marly despised her mother even more than she hated Rosie. All of her terror and desperation were wrapped between her fingers, aching to be released against Denise.

Her mother closed her eyes and her face crumpled inward, waiting for Marly's blow.

Charlene's voice broke the spell. "Marly, don't."

Marly turned her back on her mother, clutching her hand against her gut.

"Shut the fuck up, Denise! You've never been any good to me. You knew they were going to grab me and you did nothing. You knew Del was crawling into bed with Charlene and you did nothing. They killed Beanie and you did nothing. They killed Johnny and you did nothing. You just drink and do nothing. You're no mother to me and I'm no baby to you."

Charlene got up to stand at the sink and looked out the window into the foggy black night. Denise sat back down and sobbed.

Marly wobbled on unsteady legs. She wasn't finished. "If the police ask me what happened, I'm going to tell them that you did this. When they come to talk to you, I dare you to say it was Rosie and company." She stopped, wishing she could withdraw her empty threat.

Denise rose and made herself another gin and orange juice and stumbled to the living room on wobbling legs. Marly gripped the kitchen counter.

Marly turned to her sister. "I know Mark and Pammy aren't Del's kids. It's basic biology. I'm going to leave after I graduate and you need to build a new life that isn't here. And by the way, I see you didn't leave me any dinner."

As Marly made a couple of ice packs wrapped in clean towels, Charlene shouldered her sister aside and pulled out a covered plate of food from the refrigerator.

"Marly, I'm glad that life for you is so black-and-white. For me it's always a gray fog," Charlene said. She wiped off the remains of the children's dinner from the table. When the microwave signaled the food was warm, she pulled out the plate and set it down in front of her sister. She handed Marly a knife and fork.

Marly ate, chewing with care to avoid sore spots, and started her homework at the kitchen table, swapping ice packs and wiping away tears.

Despite the food, Marly felt hollow inside. She had perpetuated the same evil Del had brought to this house when she threatened to hit her mother. Now that she knew how that felt, she knew she could never unlearn it. She would have to guard against it forever.

The rhythms of homework were soothing and distracting. She bent over her calculus book, absorbed in solving problems that were so simple compared to the rest of her life. She knew that her future could not be here. She would escape and that required discipline, even on a night like this one.

8

Marly: Alliance

November 8–12, 2000

Despite makeup, Marly's appearance on the bus the next day was greeted with quiet gasps and whispers.

Marly stiffened her back and marched to the rear of the bus, taking her usual seat. She ground her teeth and pretended to study for her upcoming Spanish test.

During the break between second and third period, she rushed up the staircase to the third floor and stopped short of bumping into Elaine Fardig. They both started. Marly hadn't realized that Elaine was out of the hospital and back at school. She stared at Elaine's black eye patch.

"Watch where you're going," Elaine said. Her voice was petulant. Frowning, she stepped back. "Nice black eye."

"I fell off my bike."

Elaine broke into a grin. "Yeah. Me too."

Marly grinned back, and they went their separate ways. Marly turned to watch Elaine inch down the stairs, leaning heavily on the banister for balance. She noticed Elaine still wore a light cast on her right wrist.

Perhaps her old rival had some redeeming qualities after all. She was certainly resilient and had stood up to Rosie.

By Saturday—shopping day—Marly's bruises had turned green and yellow. A year ago, she had been thrilled to take on this family chore. Saturdays with the car had provided a liberating alternative to riding the school bus in and out of the Springs every weekday. Now it felt like one more noose around her neck, tethering her to the bottom of this valley.

Marly contemplated her mother's pockmarked Honda. The damage from winter salt was not limited to appearances. The suspension was almost rusted through. Lifting up the carpet under her feet, she checked the size of a hole that gave her a clear view of the mud below. Yes, the hole was larger.

Deep in thought, she wove her way up and out of the Springs. At the top of the long hill, she turned at the Fardigs' mailbox. She followed the driveway up another winding incline and pulled into a broad gravel parking lot.

No wonder the Fardigs don't think they are part of Charon Springs. She stepped out of the car to survey the view. From this angle, the steep hillside down into the village had disappeared and all she could see were the soft, rolling hilltops formed by the moraines left from the ice age.

Marly had never been to Elaine's house before. The broad pastures and large, empty barn next to a watering pond indicated that this had been a dairy farm at one point. The lines of the two-story house were elongated vertically so that the windows appeared narrow and tall. She was more attuned to the short, squat lines of her mother's house.

She straightened her jacket and wondered what sort of reception she'd find here. Most folks in these parts didn't care for surprises, particularly from the Harris family.

"Hi, Mrs. Fardig," she said as Elaine's mother opened the door. "I was on my way into Avalon and wanted to stop by to see Elaine."

Helen Fardig, Elaine's mother, frowned, studying Marly's face, probably assessing just how dangerous this girl was to her daughter.

"Marly! Thanks for stopping by. Right on time." Elaine appeared from a back room. She offered Marly a wink over her mother's shoulder. "Let's go up-stairs."

Marly stepped around Mrs. Fardig into the spacious kitchen. Elaine could think on her feet. *A good sign.*

Mrs. Fardig was baking something sweet that smelled fabulous. Elaine handed Marly a hot oatmeal cookie, scooping up one for herself, and beckoned for Marly to follow.

Marly trailed after Elaine and took in every detail. Elaine's house wasn't plush or elegant like Andrea's place, but it was pleasant and clean. And it didn't stink of mold.

Elaine's room was at least three times as large as the room Marly shared with Mark and Pammy, with tall ceilings and long windows that looked out to the north and west. Marly gave a small sigh as she caught sight of the double bed made from some kind of light-colored wood plus a matching dresser and desk. Elaine even had her own computer, complete with monitor and printer.

"How's it going?" Marly leaned forward to study

Elaine's left eye, which was not covered by the eye patch that morning. "I heard you'd lost your sight and I thought you'd lost the whole eye. It looks normal."

Elaine offered a lopsided smile. "Right. Just can't see worth shit. It might improve a bit if they try some surgery, but it won't be normal again. I keep bumping into stuff. Going down stairs is torture. Reading is incredibly hard. And forget driving."

"Hmm. You've lost your depth of field perception. I hear that most people adjust with some time." Marly coughed. "Sorry. That sounds cold and analytical. I know it must be hard."

Elaine sighed. "You sound like my doctors."

Marly rocked back on her heels, studying Elaine, who sat on the bed.

"We have lots in common. Two smart girls from the Springs. And now we're pariahs, you and me. I'm a Shaw but tied to the Harrises. And you've crossed them, so you're toxic too."

"Hey. Not true. My friends helped me. They knew that Laurie was one of the bunch who attacked me. They tailed Laurie. She was scared when they touched her up." Elaine's eyes were narrow and angry. "I didn't tell the police anything, but I remember that it was Laurie who kicked the side of my head right here." She pointed to her left temple.

Marly stared at Elaine for a bit. "Still, Rosie and them punished Laurie again for being caught off her guard. She didn't deserve to get beaten to death. It's not your fault—it's not even your friends' fault—but I know the way the Harrises think. They thought Laurie had been sloppy and someone had talked. Rosie had her punished for real."

Elaine paled. "I didn't want her dead. I wish the police would arrest Rosie and her crew."

Marly sat down on the bed to wrap her arms around Elaine. "Rosie and Louise—they're evil. Sick. I don't think they even wanted Laurie dead, but they just didn't care enough to stop. In a way, it's a good thing that your friends were under observation for that little bit or they'd be the ones suspected when she was found in that ditch."

"Same ditch as me."

"Why'd you tell Laurie that you were thinking of talking to the police? Are you crazy? You should have known she'd tell Rosie. Look at me. I got this for doing nothing."

"My dad. He just disappeared last year. My mom cries all the time and I know she's worried about money. She can't even collect his life insurance."

"My dad disappeared too. Almost ten years ago. He didn't have insurance."

"Yes, but your dad was part of the Harris clan. My dad is—was—an aircraft mechanic. I wanted to know where he went and get the police to do something to help."

Marly stood and leaned in, looming over Elaine on the bed.

"Elaine, Beanie wasn't part of the Harris clan. He just made a living dealing a few drugs, and they didn't like the competition or thought he might blab. Your father had access to allow them to move drugs and stuff, but he said no and threatened to turn them in. I know where he went. He went where Beanie went and where Johnny Martinson went. He's not alive. They're all buried someplace in those hills down there. That's the way it works. As far as Rosie and Zeke are concerned, we are all part of the Harris clan because we live in Charon Springs. They think that makes us their property and they want to suck us all down into their mucky world."

Elaine started to sob. "I can't cry. I shouldn't cry."

Marly went to get a wet washcloth from the hall bathroom. No sulfur water, she noticed as she ran the tap.

She checked to make sure Elaine's mother wasn't hovering, then slipped back into the bedroom and pressed the washcloth to Elaine's face.

"I can't believe you had the nerve to say anything. Now we need to plan for the future, and we need to help each other."

"What?" Elaine hiccupped.

Marly sat in the desk chair and reached out for Elaine's good hand.

"Things are going to change and we need to get ready to bust out."

"Hunh?" Elaine pushed back farther onto the bed, yanking her hand free.

"Del and Zeke have disappeared. Did you hear that?"

"Yeah, I heard. But what about Rosie?"

"First of all, Rosie, Troy, and Louise are all under suspicion for killing Laurie and for beating you up too. They are very nervous. Plus, Rosie doesn't have much support without Zeke and his money to buy loyalty. The word is that Zeke's secret money stores came up short."

"I'm still scared of them."

"Good. That's okay. We need to be alert. Meanwhile, we—you and me—we have a small window of opportunity to get out while those Harrises are tied up."

Elaine flopped back on the bed and pressed her palms to her face. "I won't graduate in the spring at this rate. I've missed too much school and I'm so far behind. I was going to go to SUNY Albany. But I think even a state school is out. We don't have the resources for me to put in extra school time. I guess I'll get my GED, but I can't even get a basic job flipping burgers."

Marly stood up and paced with the rhythm of her thoughts. "I know we aren't great buddies. We didn't even like each other that much way back in elementary school. Still, we have a common cause and I owe you. If it weren't for you, I might be dead now myself. I'm going to help you. I'm going to tutor you to catch up. And I'm going to take you to basketball practice. We need a scorekeeper for the team. You can practice with us to improve your adjustment to one eye."

Elaine blotted her face. "I don't get why you want to do this. Why do you want to help me?"

"Because I need your help, too. I'm not going to escape the Springs without the help of someone I can trust. You're smart and brave. I know I can trust you. And I'm going to get you a job."

Elaine stopped crying. "What job? How do I help you?"

Marly smiled, happy to reveal her plan. "First of all, you can code. I'm better, but I know how good you are. Plus, you're better at the design side. I'm working part-time for this startup out of Syracuse University. It's just piddly stuff. They pay okay, and it's great experience. I work for them when I go to the library. The problem is they're doing more and more business and I'm overloaded. I need someone who can pick up the slack. I know you can do this. And you have an extra car. Your dad's old car."

Elaine sat up. "I can't drive," she said, and motioned to her eye.

"Hey! I can drive. And you'll be able to drive sooner or later. You work it out with your mother that I can take your car. Tell her we need to avoid the school bus and she can't be your chauffeur. She'll buy that because it's true. She needs to go to work, right? I'll pick you up in the morning and drop you off at the end of the day. We'll also need to work in the library for Internet access. I'll take you home after that. Plus, we'll need to go to some meetings with these grad students in Syracuse."

Elaine looked puzzled. "Internet access? We've got dial-up. Doesn't everybody?"

Marly laughed. "No. We don't even have cell phone coverage." She sat down at Elaine's desk and ran her hands over the keyboard. "We can work here, too. I have a laptop. It's just that I get to double-dip at the library. Mrs. Haas doesn't mind if I do other work as long as things are slow and I'm caught up."

"Could I work at the library too? Mom would like that."

Marly sat back and studied Elaine. "I doubt it. The library has almost no money. But if you help, I'll work out a split with you."

Elaine's mother refused to let Marly have access to the car on that day but relented several days later, worn down by Elaine's persistence.

On Tuesday, Marly's mother was alarmed to find the addition of a clean Nissan in her driveway. Denise was mollified by Marly's glib explanation that Helen

Fardig was trading use of the car in exchange for help and tutoring for Elaine.

After some encouragement from Marly, Mrs. Haas agreed to a few hours a week of employment for Elaine at the library.

The girls got their way and the plan moved ahead.

9

Vanessa: Family Matters

January 29, 2013

Vanessa and Jack met Chip in the police chief's office the next morning after breakfast, where they were joined by Paul Daniels, the officer they had met the day before.

Chip suggested that Vanessa call Carl Harris to break the news about Louise and Troy and ask for a meeting.

"He'll be more friendly if a woman calls," Chip said.

Vanessa had her doubts, but dialed the number Paul provided.

"Harris here," said a deep voice after four rings.

"Mr. Carl Harris? I'm Detective Vanessa Alba from the Santa Clara County Sheriff's Office in California, calling from Avalon."

Carl waited to speak. "What's this concerning?"

To Vanessa, his voice sounded neutral. Studied.

"Mr. Harris, our office recently identified two sets of bones that have been found in the Santa Cruz Mountains, just south of San Francisco in California. We have determined that they belong to Louise Rasmussen and Troy Rasmussen. I believe that they are relatives of yours, is that correct?"

She heard a faint cough. Carl answered. "Louise was the daughter of my brother Zeke. Troy was her son."

"Yes, sir, we've been checking on that. My colleague Detective Wong and I are assigned to work the case. We're here in Avalon to see if we can determine why they might have been in California."

"I don't know that I can help you much."

"I see, sir. Nevertheless, we need to make sure we've covered all the bases. We'll plan to stop by in about an hour."

Carl uttered a grunt and hung up.

"How did he sound?" Jack asked.

"I couldn't tell. He didn't express emotion one way or the other."

Vanessa was glad they'd picked up better boots and outside gear.

"Minus forty degrees last night," Paul said. "Do you know that's the only temperature that is the same in both Fahrenheit and Celsius?"

"Fascinating." Vanessa wondered if Paul tested on the autism spectrum, or if this was his idea of small talk. "Well, it's minus ten now. Fahrenheit. I wonder what that is in Celsius?"

Paul fell silent. "Minus twenty-three," he said at last.

Vanessa was surprised when Jack got into the backseat of Paul's squad car, leaving her the front passenger seat. Maybe Jack was a good guy after all.

Chip came down to see them off. "Warming up, folks." he said, and clapped his palms together. "That means we'll probably see snow tomorrow, so it's good to get the trip to the Springs over today. Meanwhile, remember not to set the parking brake or you'll wait a long time to get moving. Paul knows."

They left the village and picked up the road heading south toward the Springs. At last Vanessa had a chance to check out the landscape in daylight.

The road started on the flat, curled and rose with hills on their right and rolling country to their left.

"It's pretty in summer," Paul said. "This is all green then."

"So we've heard. It's pretty now," Vanessa said. "It's just a bit stark with the snow. Oh, look. There's a round barn."

"Octagonal," Paul said. "That means it has eight sides. Lots of barns like that around here."

Vanessa wondered if Paul was going to treat them to this detailed description of every tree and building. She looked over her shoulder at Jack, who smiled.

Such a monochromatic world. Even with the bright blue sky, the landscape around them was stark white, rimmed by lines of gray, leafless trees and punctuated by evergreens so dark they appeared black. Many of the older houses were white too, with black or dark green shutters. Others were made from gray stone or red brick. She had not seen a single stucco house yet.

After four miles, Paul nodded to a road leading up a hill to their right. "Up there is Fardig's place."

"Do you mean Elaine Fardig? The girl Louise and Troy beat up?" Jack asked, craning his neck.

"Yeah. Of course, she doesn't live there now. Her brother, David, took over the place after her mother left."

"I thought Elaine recovered."

"Oh sure. Except for that eye. But she left to go to school and just kept going, so she did okay. Her mom decided she'd rather leave too."

"Where did Elaine go?"

"I think she went to school in Albany."

Vanessa resolved to be patient. She tried again. "And that's where she still lives?"

"Oh no. She worked with Marly on that technical company. It turns out the two of them were working out of the library on that so that they could get onto the Net. And when that got bought Elaine moved someplace else."

"California?" Vanessa asked.

"Yeah. Don't know where exactly."

Jack cleared his throat.

"Who's Marly?" Vanessa asked.

"Oh. Marly. Marlene Shaw."

Jack leaned forward from the backseat. "I don't suppose she's a Harris, is she?"

Paul wagged his head back and forth. "Well, kinda. She is some sort of Harris but not real close, you know. Her father was Beanie Shaw. He wasn't a Harris. His real name was Bernard, but we called him Beanie. Me and him were in the same grade. Beanie took off at some point at least twenty years ago, maybe longer."

"Did anyone investigate?" Vanessa asked.

"I doubt it was ever reported, you know. Not too long after, Denise took up with Del Harris, Zeke's son. Chip talked about them yesterday. They didn't get married or anything. They were cousins. Denise said that Beanie had gone to Oregon."

"Oregon," Jack said. "Nice place."

"Yeah. So I hear. I'd like to go there sometime. Anyway, Del died. Chip told you about that. A little after, Denise hooked up with Elliot Harris, Vernon's son. Now *him* she married, cousins or not. So I guess you could say that Marly was a Harris cousin and a Harris by stepfathers."

"And does Marly still live here?" Vanessa asked.

"Nah. She went to college too. Someplace fancy in New England. They've all pretty much left. Her mother, Denise, still lives here. Marly paid to fix up her house real nice with the technical money. That place was a dump. Elliot died all of sudden four years ago. Cancer in his belly."

Vanessa wished she had recorded the conversation and made a note to revisit the diagram from Chip's whiteboard. All she could track was that everyone was related to everyone else.

The land dropped away in front of them, revealing the steep decline into a valley with a matching hillside several miles away. Both Vanessa and Jack gasped. Paul navigated the hairpin turns down the hill and they slipped and slid into the village of Charon Springs.

Perhaps it was just the clean white of the snow, but Charon Springs looked like a nice place to Vanessa. Paul hung a left and they drove by a church, a bar, a small country store, a liquor store, and two buildings under construction on the opposite side, with nice old houses in between.

"Looks kind of quaint," Vanessa said.

"Yup. We're undergoing some Marlyfication. They're doing a lot of work on the library there, adding a wing, and that's the new health clinic."

"Did you say modification?" asked Jack.

Paul chuckled, pleased with himself. "Marlyfication. As in Marly Shaw. When her company got bought, she did pretty good and I guess that paid some of the college. She and Elaine did another one and that did real good too. Marly gave some money and paid for some of this stuff. I guess she felt she owed something to the library. And of course everyone wanted some sort of medical clinic here. Now they'll have a doctor down here once or twice a week and a nurse most days. There's free wireless going in and they'll have real cell phone coverage soon. Chip wishes that she would help Avalon a little too."

Two miles out of the Springs, the hills flattened out to reveal a broad valley. Paul pulled off the road onto a well-plowed single-lane driveway that followed a break of trees and an old stone wall. The road ended in front of a large pale yellow farmhouse with an attached barn and a spectacular view over the valley. Two additional barns, one small, one large, sat on the opposite side of the yard.

Jack started to open his door, but Paul turned in his seat and spoke up, his voice sharp. "No, no. Don't do that. Just sit here. He'll let us know when to come in."

The side door swung open and a tall, barrel-chested man with a full head of white hair stepped out onto the deck and motioned to them.

Following Paul's lead, Vanessa and Jack shed their boots and coats in what looked like a big closet, which Paul referred to as the mudroom. From there, they passed through the door into an open-plan kitchen and sitting area. Carl was adding logs to a wood stove.

Carl looked like a shaved polar bear, Vanessa decided. Sort of like Santa Claus without a beard.

Carl turned and shook each of their hands. Vanessa noticed that Paul had developed a small bead of sweat on his upper lip.

"Have a seat. I suppose you Californians aren't used to this kind of cold."

He turned, sat down in a large club chair, and offered them two smaller chairs on the other side of the stove. Paul shuffled his feet and slipped onto a small couch facing the other three.

"What do you think of Central New York?" Carl asked. His tone was amiable. His eyes were hard to read. *Santa Claus with a secret life.*

"This is a beautiful house, Mr. Harris," Vanessa said. "It would be worth millions out where we live."

"Yes, of course. But this is not California. So you've found Louise and Troy."

"That's right," Jack said. "Some bones were found in a creek bed by a hiker in the Santa Cruz Mountains. They were traced back to the base of a cliff where we found some more. We identified the remains as Louise and Troy using DNA from CODIS. That's the centralized FBI database that tracks forensic data of convicted felons."

"Interesting to see that technology pay off. How did they die?"

"That's not clear," Vanessa said. She watched Carl's face closely for signs of emotion. "There had been too much trauma and disruption and the time frame isn't very accurate. We're assuming that they fell from the cliff, but we're not sure if they were dead when they went over or not. It would not appear that they died as the result of an accident. There were no traces of clothing or jewelry and no sign of a car or vehicle up on top."

She stopped and waited to see how Carl would respond, but he continued to regard her with a flat, expressionless stare. "Apologies for being so blunt. We were hoping you might shed some light, Mr. Harris. When did you last see Louise or Troy?"

Carl's gaze never left her face. "It seems a long time ago now."

"They didn't come to Rosie's funeral," Paul said, and flushed. They all turned in his direction.

"Right." Carl shifted his gaze back to the Californians without turning his head, giving the impression that he was watching the three of them at once.

Jack continued. "From what we've been told, Rosie died about three and a half years ago, so that timing fits. Louise and Troy were missed at Rosie Harris's funeral and seem to have gone someplace about two or three weeks before that. Does that sound right?"

"I was never close to them," Carl said. "We shared certain family assets, but I didn't track them or socialize with them very much. I do remember that they weren't at the funeral, now that you mention it, but when they went away, I can't say."

"We got a warrant to check Rosie Harris's phone records. From that we tracked down the cell phone numbers for Louise and Troy," Vanessa said. "They must have called her two or three times a day while they were away. Based on those calls we believe they left here about three weeks before she died. There's no coverage at the top of that cliff, but we do know that Louise called Rosie for the last time at five thirty on Sunday, June fourteenth, two thousand nine. Rosie died on the seventeenth. Is that correct?"

"That sounds right. She died in June that year. I'd have to look at a calendar."

"We're of the opinion that they died on or close to June fourteenth or fifteenth."

"That would make sense, I guess. We figured they might have died because they didn't return from wherever they had gone. Louise and Troy weren't the types to wander off, and they had no reason to disappear. I guess it's good to know for sure."

"Are there any family members you can think of in Northern California? Or maybe they wanted to do some sort of business?" Vanessa asked.

"Sure. Well, I suppose there are relatives, here and there. You're thinking they went out there to do some business?"

"Or take care of some," Jack said, his eyes hooded.

"Speaking of business, Mr. Harris, the word is that your family controls all the crime in this area and that Louise and Troy were key enforcers," Vanessa said. "Care to comment?"

Carl turned to face her. He sat motionless and stared.

"That's an interesting rumor, Detective. Did Paul tell you that?" Carl swiveled to look at Paul, whose face was pale and sweaty.

"Let's say that it seems to be common knowledge," Vanessa said, pulling his gaze back to her.

"I don't know anything about that stuff. I have a legitimate construction business."

"Louise thought she was going to inherit leadership of the Harris family business, didn't she, Mr. Harris?" Vanessa asked. "She felt that she had become the brains and the muscle, and that women had been pushed aside long enough, isn't that right?"

Carl's eyes were cold and hard, although his voice was still warm.

"The Harris 'business,'" he said, in an echo. "Who knows what that woman thought? She was an idiot. But let me make it clear that I had no motivation to have them killed. I was here when Rosie died."

"And you don't know why they went or whom they met with?"

"No."

"They must have left some belongings. Some property," Jack said. "Any chance we could look through those?"

Carl pursed his lips. "They lived at Rosie's house. They didn't work. Not in the normal way. Rosie gave them money for stuff—sort of an allowance. In her will, she left the house to her sister, Diane. Diane wasn't fond of Louise and Troy, you could say. Diane blamed Louise for implicating her in a sad incident. She waited about six months and threw out or gave away everything she could find that belonged to Troy or Louise."

"This incident—would that have been when Louise and Troy killed Laura? Or when they beat up Elaine Fardig?" Jack asked.

Carl blinked.

"I'll take that as a yes."

"Louise and Troy didn't leave wills, I suppose?" Vanessa asked.

Carl's smile conveyed no warmth. "I doubt that they understood the concept or the need, quite frankly."

A movement in her peripheral vision pulled her gaze to the windows. Vanessa saw that a Subaru station wagon had pulled into the parking area. A few moments later, they were joined by an attractive woman in her late fifties or early sixties.

"Hi there, I'm Betty," the woman said. "Please pardon my sniffles. That cold makes my nose run. I'm Carl's wife. You must be the detectives from California that Carl mentioned."

Betty's hair was white and cut short. Her eyes were a remarkable sapphire blue, almost violet. Vanessa leaned forward to study them and decided the color was not the effect of contacts.

Betty hustled around the kitchen, putting away groceries. "I'm going to make some tea. I assume all of you would like some," she said.

As she prepared the tea, Betty exchanged pleasantries about the weather and asked questions about California. Carl was quiet but kept his gaze fixed on Vanessa. She forced herself not to squirm.

At last the conversation returned to Louise and Troy.

"Well, I'm sorry to hear that they're dead, of course, but they were very difficult people. Very temperamental," Betty said, and gave her husband a quick smile.

"Did they say anything to you before they left?" Vanessa asked.

"Not a word. I didn't even realize they were gone until Rosie died. We did not socialize with them or Rosie."

"Can you think of anyone they might have visited there?" Jack asked.

Betty and Carl exchanged glances. "We didn't hear from anyone we know that they'd seen Louise or Troy," Betty said.

The tea was cold. Carl stood up. The interview was over.

Jack confirmed that the coroner could contact Carl about the remains.

"We can't bury them until spring, as you might understand," Carl said. He waved his hand toward the frozen landscape. "We'll put them in the family plot once things thaw."

Vanessa headed toward the mudroom, but stepped aside when she noticed a bookcase, filled with framed photographs.

On the top shelf there were pictures of a younger Carl and Betty. Carl looked as though he'd been stuffed into his suit. Betty wore a simple pale pink dress with big shoulder pads and held a matching pink bouquet.

"Are these your wedding pictures?" Vanessa asked.

"Carl and I married eighteen years ago," said Betty. "I was Betty Martinson before."

Betty pointed to the next row of photographs. "That's Carl's son Jason. He's a builder in Syracuse.

Those two are Jason's children. And that's Carl's other son, Judson, with his wife. He's a lawyer. They have three children."

Vanessa leaned in for a closer examination. "Where does Judson live?"

Betty bit her lip and glanced at Carl. "Stockton."

"Stockton, California?"

"Yes."

"And they didn't mention seeing Louise and Troy?"

"No. Absolutely not. Judson and Troy did not get along. Judson would have said something."

"Fine. Why don't you give us Judson's contact information, okay?"

Betty's face folded into a faint scowl.

Vanessa focused on the next row of pictures. Judson and Jason had reddish hair. The people in this row had dark hair and blue eyes.

"That's my daughter, Julie," Betty said. She pointed to a series of photographs with a young woman, laughing and holding small children. "Those are all the grandchildren from my side. We keep a very blended family these days."

Vanessa stared at the pictures.

"Julie has your eyes," she said. "So do most of your grandchildren. Julie has a lot of kids."

Betty smiled at the pictures. "Those three are Julie's. Those two are Mark and Pammy, my son's children. He's dead, sad to say. And that little girl is Alison, their half-sister. I include her in my family."

"How old is your grandson?" Jack asked. "He looks a little different in these two pictures."

Betty was staring at Carl. She seemed distracted. "What's that? I'm sorry. Oh. That's my grandson, Mark, on the right, and that was his father, John, when he graduated from high school."

"Both kids look like their father, but Mark could be his twin," Jack said.

Betty smiled but looked a bit sad.

After donning their winter gear, Paul, Jack, and Vanessa made their way back to the squad car. Vanessa had used the downstairs lavatory at Carl's house, but Paul and Jack insisted on stopping at the bottom of the hill to pee in the snow, standing at the back of the car.

Jack finished first. "That's an activity you only need to do once. I swear that pee was frozen before it hit the ground."

"Too much information, Jack," Vanessa said, eye-balling Paul, still outside the car. "I hope we don't have to get a description of every rock on the way back."

"Give the guy a break, Vanessa. Paul is infatuated with you. He asked if you were single. He's trying to impress you."

Vanessa made a gagging gesture. "Carl and Betty were hiding something, probably related to Jason. And Paul is nervous. This is not a winning combination."

10

Marly: Dreams Come True

November 18, 2000

By mid-November, the regular rains had turned to snow showers, and a bitter pre-winter chill settled down into the valley.

The Harris clan seemed to be keeping their distance. Ever vigilant, Marly was thrilled to hear from her mother that the Shaws—Denise, Charlene, Marly, and the kids—weren't invited to Rosie's for Thanksgiving. That suited Marly just fine, although Denise grew weepy for Del at the news.

On the Saturday before Thanksgiving, Marly was about to leave for her usual weekly shopping trip to Avalon when a black Lincoln with New Jersey plates pulled onto the shoulder of the road. It was followed by an Avalon police cruiser.

Two tall men in thick, black, wool coats climbed out of the Lincoln. Both wore suits and ties under their coats and their identical black shoes gleamed. Even their hair was the same color gray.

A matched set. Marly couldn't recall that she'd ever seen anyone dressed like that in the Springs, even at funerals.

Paul Daniels, a local Avalon police officer she knew well, flung open the door of his cruiser. Paul heaved himself up and out of the car, clapped his hands, straightened his uniform, and put on his hat, before he slammed the door shut and turned to gaze at Marly.

She kept still but mentally shook her head. Paul always made such a production of getting in and out of his car. *Loser*.

By the way the three men stared at her, it was clear that they expected her to come up to the road, but she waited until they slipped down into the muddy parking area.

One of the men from the Lincoln pulled out some papers and waved them at her as well as a badge.

"Agent Thomas and Agent Rockwell. FBI. We're looking for Wendell Harris. This is an arrest warrant. I assume you're his daughter."

"Could I see that?" she asked.

The agent handed it to her.

Marly opened the warrant and studied it, fascinated. She'd never seen one before. She also took a close look at Agent Rockwell's badge. "He's not here. He disappeared three weeks ago. I'm not his daughter. He's been living with my mother, but they aren't married."

She looked up at Paul. "This is a murder warrant. For killing Max Redman. You think Del did that?"

Paul nodded. "Yup. Him and Larry. This is a federal beef, Marly. Max was an ATF agent. ATF means Alcohol, Tobacco, and Firearms, you know."

Marly stared at Paul. His winter uniform suited him, she thought. He was thin where he should have been muscular and thick where he should have been thin. The puffy winter uniform jacket hid that, and his winter hat covered his thinning hair. He looked almost handsome.

Paul had been in the same high school class as Beanie—her father—and Del. Elaine's father too, for that matter. This Max guy—the victim—had been in the same class as Larry and Louise. She thought back to Larry and Del talking about him on her porch and her run-in with Zeke. It was all just a bit too cozy.

Marly squinted at Paul, trying to assess the officer's new accent—some sort of cross between Tennessee and Utica from what she could tell. She wasn't sure that Paul had ever been out of New York State. *Must be another attempt to be cool,* she decided.

"Are you arresting Larry, too?"

"Took care of that this mornin'," Paul said in his strange new drawl.

Things were looking up, Marly thought. She shifted her gaze to the other two men. "We haven't seen Del since October twenty-seventh. He went out drinking at the Rock, met up with his dad, and we haven't seen either of them since."

Agent Thomas's hair wafted in the breeze, pushing up his comb-over like a gray sail.

"So we've heard. We've also heard you were the last to see him." His voice had a genuine Southern twang to Marly's ears.

Marly repeated her familiar tale. "No. I saw him at dinner and after that I went to the Halloween dance at the high school. He was supposed to give me a ride home from the Rock, but he was gone when I got there, so I walked home."

"Well now, Marly," Paul said. "I don't suppose you'd be knowin' where he's gone? No? Well, maybe your sister? Everyone knows Del was pokin' her all these years. And she's had his kids."

"Paul, what is wrong with your voice? You sound sick."

Paul coughed.

"Is that true, Ms. Harris? Was your stepfather sleeping with your sister?" Agent Rockwell stared at her.

"My name is Marlene Shaw. Del wasn't my stepfather. Not legally. He stopped bothering Charlene."

The two agents shuffled their feet.

"Oh, come on, Marly." Paul's voice was back to the normal Central New York twang. "We all knew about that."

Marly stared at Paul until he blinked. Keeping her tone low and level, she said, "My sister was twelve years old when that started. You were a cop by that time. If you knew and you were a cop, wasn't it your duty to do something?"

Paul backed away, his eyes down. Marly stepped forward and leaned in, not letting him off the hook. "No wonder we have such a great relationship with the police."

Marly turned back to the other two. "Del stopped because we complained to his family. No thanks to the cops. And those kids are not Del's. Charlene's married now. We don't know where Del went."

"Do you mind if we look around?" Agent Thomas asked.

"Go ahead." Marly stood aside to let them pass.

The FBI agents minced their way across the parking area, followed by Paul. Marly trailed behind, pulled by curiosity and the obligation to protect her mother's house.

An icy prickle raced up her back to her scalp and down her arms. She had prayed for someone to come take Del away for a long time and now that day had arrived. Del should be cowering in the kitchen or sitting unaware on the john. In a few minutes, he should be leaving the house, his hands cuffed behind him with an agent on either side to keep him from falling into the muck. She should be feeling a flood of relief. But it was too late.

After the agents finished with the barn, they entered the house and wiped their shoes on the mat by the back door. Paul showed no such manners and stepped over the mat.

"Hey," Marly said, and mocked his fake drawl. "'Y'all' can wipe your feet too."

Paul squinted at her and his cheeks turned pink. He turned around and swiped each boot once on the mat. Marly felt her face go warm. Taunting Paul was a habit she'd picked up from Del. He had often referred to his former classmate as "Officer Runt of the Litter" or "Officer ROL," sometimes right to Paul's face. *Time to kick bad habits*.

The agents opened every door and closet. They searched the basement and found the access to the attic crawl space. Paul stayed close behind. After ten or fifteen minutes, the three regrouped in the mudroom and studied the dirty laundry.

"No men's clothing in here. And no fresh mud on those boots in the corner," one agent said. The other agent agreed with a low grunt.

Marly escorted the agents to their car. Paul had already removed his hat and climbed into his warm cruiser.

"Ms. Harris, did your stepfather ever talk to you about this investigation? Did he seem nervous or upset that we might be closing in?" Agent Rockwell asked.

Marly forced herself to look him in the eye. "This is all news to me."

"What about Max Redman? Did you ever hear Del or his brother or anyone else in his family talk about him?"

"Wow. No way." She widened her eyes and hoped she looked young and clueless.

Del should have known she wouldn't talk. Even after all the trouble he had brought into her life, she never would have betrayed him. That was the problem with Del. If he had known her, if he had only shown faith in her loyalty, he would be alive today. Zeke too. She wouldn't have had to save herself. She wouldn't have this crushing weight in the middle of her chest. Del would be sitting in the back of this Lincoln or on his way out of town, ahead of the FBI.

"Ms. Harris?"

Marly swiveled her head toward the woods. "Why did you wait so long? Where were you three weeks ago?"

"Excuse me? What was that?"

Marly turned back to face the agents, her hands on her hips. "I said my name is not Harris. It's Shaw."

11

Vanessa: Friends Matter

January 30, 2013

Vanessa could tell that the weather had changed as soon as she woke up. The room was warmer and noises from outside were muffled.

A quick look out the window confirmed that snow was falling in thick sheets. The local TV channel announced that it was a balmy five degrees Fahrenheit.

On their walk to the police station, Jack laughed. "My feet don't squeak."

With Chip's assistance, they scheduled a trip to Pennsylvania the next day to visit Larry Harris in federal prison and to a New York State prison the day after to visit Greg Harris. That accomplished, they ditched Paul for the day and drove their own car south to the Springs.

As promised, David Fardig waited for them in his house at the top of the hill. His wife and children had long gone by this hour, but he had agreed to forgo the long commute into Syracuse to meet with them.

The heavy snow cut visibility to less than a hundred feet. The nearby barn was a mere shadowy hulk, shrouded in a veil of falling flakes. Vanessa had always been a bit claustrophobic. Enclosed by the impenetrable storm, she felt her heart rate rise.

The tall, gracious lines of the house and its gingerbread details fascinated Vanessa. The structure was ancient by her California standards, but there were signs of recent renovation. The windows were insulated and looked expensive, and the driveway, from what could be seen, was composed of pavers. Triangle-shaped wooden teepees sheltered small trees, arranged around the yard. She thought she caught the signs of a pool and patio under the snow in back.

David answered the door. He led Vanessa and Jack into the mudroom, a feature Vanessa now recognized as standard as a bathroom around here.

Fortified by fresh coffee, they settled in a large family room that featured a walk-in hearth, complete with blazing fire.

Vanessa studied David over the rim of her cup. Average height, average build, mid-thirties, not homely, not cute. He leaned forward, forearms on his knees, his head cocked to one side as he looked from Vanessa to Jack and back to Vanessa.

"Too bad you weren't here yesterday," David said. "This view is the best, although the wind can howl. Now you can't see very much."

Jack spoke first. "Mr. Fardig, as we mentioned on the phone, we're here to conduct an investigation into the deaths of Louise and Troy Rasmussen. We'd like to ask you about them and your family's connections to the Harris family."

David sat up straight in his chair and rolled his shoulders. "We don't have any connections to the Harris crowd. In fact, only our mailbox sits in the Springs."

Vanessa studied David's face. "Mr. Fardig, I want to get straight to the point. Your sister, Elaine, suffered a

severe assault after she tried to figure out what happened to your father. People—Harris people—went to
jail over that incident and at least one girl died as well.
Now two of those people have been found dead in the
Santa Cruz Mountains. From what we can tell, Louise
and Troy had never left the Northeast before, and yet
we found them in California. I would think you would
want to make sure that your sister and your family will
continue to be safe."

David relaxed into his chair. "Please call me David.
We don't have anything to hide. Troy and I were classmates. Can you believe that? He was a jerk even as a
kid. And Laurie was in the same class as Elaine. There
was one class per grade in the Charon Springs Elementary School, so we knew everybody. For me, when I
got to Avalon for high school, the world opened up."

"What about Elaine? Did she feel the same way?"

"Yeah. We all did. My brother, Curtis, me, and Elaine."

"Curtis lives in Boston, is that right?" Vanessa referred to her notes. "He's a financial analyst? And you're
a lawyer."

"That's right. Curtis is in Boston. I live here and
work in Syracuse. Corporate law."

"And Elaine?"

"Elaine is a high tech entrepreneur."

"Where does she live, David?"

She cocked an eyebrow in Jack's direction.

"Is she in California?"

David took a long sip of coffee before he answered.
"Yeah, exactly. She lives in Mountain View. So does
my mother."

Well, well. Small world. Vanessa coughed a bit and
swallowed coffee.

"Mr. Fardig—David—did your sister or your mother
say anything to you in the spring or early summer of

2009 concerning Louise or Troy? Is there any chance Elaine or your mother saw them or ran into them?"

David stood to put another log on the fire and stirred the coals with a poker.

"David?"

"I was just trying to recall. That was a long time ago," he said. "I'm sure I would have remembered if they had said anything and they definitely would have been upset. They would have called the cops. There's been too much bad blood between our families to be polite."

"So that's a no?"

"That's a no. I would have remembered."

"Tell us about this bad blood," Jack said.

David drained his cup. "My dad would always tell us just to mind our own business and not let the Harrises get to us. He had lived here his whole life without any issues. But at some point, all the Harris madness caught up to Dad and I think that's what changed things for Elaine."

"Your father was killed, is that correct?"

"That's the assumption. His body was never found and he was eventually declared dead."

"Tell us about those events."

David pursed his lips and gazed at the ceiling, as if the story were written there. "I wasn't living here at the time, so most of what I know comes from my mother. What I remember growing up was that Dad always figured that he was immune. He had this benign, uninteresting job at the airport, until one day Del came to him and said that they wanted his help to pick up drugs that would come in on planes. That's what Dad told my mother. I know Del kept after him about it and Dad mentioned he might have to go to the police. He might have even said that to Del." David pressed his palms to his eyes briefly and wiped his nose with a napkin. His voice was soft and ragged. "He went off to work one day and just—poof—disappeared on the way home."

"Your mother reported that," Jack said.

"Oh yeah. That pissed off Del and Zeke to no end but led to nothing with the police. Fucking do-nothing idiots."

"They were scared to come down here?"

"Yes, and that's not in the past tense. They still are. When Zeke and Del died, the Harrises took a blow, and the cops became a teeny bit more responsive." David produced a grim smile. "Del had been the engine behind the Harris future. I hoped that once his successors, Vernon and Elliot, died, the whole lot would fade away for good. But it turns out Carl had ambitions." He raised his hands, palms up in apparent surrender.

"I gather that Del and Zeke died about the same time as Elaine ran into their buzz saw, isn't that correct? Was there a connection?" Vanessa asked.

David nibbled on a hangnail before he answered. "It was kind of an odd coincidence but no connection that I could see. Like I said, Curtis and I were already out of the house when that happened. I was working in New York and planned to go to law school. Curtis was in college at SUNY Buffalo. For Elaine and Mom, things were grim, Del or no Del. Mom was a registered nurse, but she had stopped working to study to become a nurse practitioner. She had to quit school to go back to work. She was terrified she wouldn't be able to pay the property taxes."

"So Elaine started to dig," Jack said.

"She started asking questions. My sister is a bit of a pushy person once she knows what she wants. She made comments that she wanted to talk to the police."

"Sounds brave."

"More like reckless. Just after school started in the fall—she was a senior—she didn't come home from school one day. Mom didn't think anything of it at first. Elaine did lots of after-school activities. When Mom headed off to her night shift at about five, she found Elaine in a ditch about a half mile away. It's a miracle she even saw Elaine.

"To this day Elaine still doesn't remember how she got there. The doctors said that isn't uncommon with a bad concussion. She might have been dumped there, or she might have run until they caught up with her."

"Tough times," Vanessa said. "You must really hate the Harris family."

David stood and walked to the hearth, came back, and sat down again, his hands clenched on his knees.

"Like I said—bad blood. Elaine was in the hospital for almost two weeks, followed by another three weeks in a physical rehab place. At that point, my mother had to bring her home because we couldn't afford any more care. Good thing that Mom was a nurse."

"Elaine must have missed a lot of school," Vanessa said.

"In some ways, that was the worst part. Elaine had been one of the top performers in her class. She might have even been valedictorian. The school sent homework, but at first she was too drugged to follow it, and after it was just too hard to catch up. Plus, trying to read with one eye was a strain."

"And the police?" Jack asked.

"The cops did respond, but just barely. It wasn't until Laurie died that they got serious and Rosie, Louise, and Troy plus several others were charged." David's voice was softer, edged with bitterness.

"And they felt it was all Elaine's fault, I assume," Jack said.

David gave a snort. "Oh, quite. That's the Harris mentality. It's always your fault that got you killed or beaten up or whatever."

"How did all that play out? Did Elaine have to testify?" Vanessa asked.

"She wasn't called because she couldn't remember enough, but her doctors gave compelling evidence about the damage. Mom was terrified and by that point Elaine was also very traumatized."

"But she got caught up at school, right?" Jack asked.

"That was amazing. She worked so hard and graduated with her class. But she couldn't have done it without Marly. That was how she began working on the startup."

Jack raised his eyebrows. "That would be Marly Shaw? Isn't she a Harris? What brought that about?"

"Her mother is some sort of Harris cousin. Her father had disappeared years before and Del was her stepfather."

"I'm surprised your mother approved," Jack said.

"I don't know her very well, but Marly can be just as pushy as my sister in her own way. Apparently, they figured that she and Elaine needed to team up—sort of like a smart girls club from Charon Springs. It was all planned out. Mrs. Haas, the town librarian, even gave Elaine a job. I don't think she was given many options either."

"And?"

"And Elaine caught up. She graduated with her class. She managed to finish in the top ten percent. Marly was in a tie for valedictorian, by the way. That spring was great. Zeke and Del were gone. Larry got locked up for good. Rosie, Louise, and Troy were in jail or headed there. The whole place took a deep breath and the peace lasted for a couple of years, until Rosie and crew were out again."

"Elaine went to college?"

"Sure. She went to SUNY Albany. Marly went to Brown on a big scholarship. Albany was a stretch for us. But that startup sold just before Christmas their freshman year. We were surprised as all get-out. Elaine ended up with a nice percentage of the company because there hadn't been much money for real paychecks. The deal was tiny by Silicon Valley standards, but Elaine got enough to fund college. In addition, she got a job at the new parent company at a very nice salary just to keep her off the market. What impresses me is that Elaine was the one who nailed those parts as a condition of the sale. I think that even surprised Marly."

Vanessa kept her voice neutral. "That was when she moved to California, right?"

"Yeah. Elaine transferred to Stanford. Eventually Mom rented a place in Palo Alto. That was a financial stretch, but she said Elaine needed help. I think she just wanted to get away from here.

"Things just continued. In their junior year, the non-compete period was over and Elaine and Marly began another startup. Marly moved out there to go to Stanford for grad school and Elaine signed up for an MBA. After three years, the company was acquired again and this time she did much better."

"Like how much?" Jack asked.

David demurred, waving his hands. "Hard to say exactly. Elaine says not to believe everything I read. Still, I could retire now thanks to her and so could my brother and I know Mom could. Elaine paid to have this place fixed up and after that was done, Mom sold it to me for a song. Elaine bought a cute home for Mom in Mountain View and a place for herself almost next door."

"What does she do now?"

"Ah. Do you know JaX?" David smiled. "That's the name of her newest venture. Something to do with augmented reality. I barely understand it. We're hoping Elaine and Marly will hit the big time."

"Another great Silicon Valley success story," Jack said.

"Not bad for two smarties from the Springs," David said. "I'm so proud of Elaine. Still, it's not all about the money for her. She's very competitive."

"So Marly also lives out there?" Vanessa asked.

"Yeah, kind of close by."

Vanessa leaned forward, her arms on her knees. "Would Marly have called the police in California if she saw Louise or Troy?"

David's eyes were round and he blinked several times. "I think so. I mean, I'm sure she would. Del was her stepfather but she isn't really a Harris. No way she'd let Louise or Troy get close."

Jack walked over to a wall covered with framed pictures.

"Tell me about these folks," he said, beckoning to David.

Vanessa followed and gave a grunt when she recognized three children she'd seen in Betty and Carl's pictures.

"I know who those kids are," she said, and pointed. "That's Mark and Pammy. And that's Alison. They're Betty's grandchildren."

David came to stand at her shoulder. "There's Betty with my mother in that picture. In elementary school, I was best friends with her son, Johnny Martinson, and

Judson Harris, Carl's son. Our moms were all real tight. When we went to high school, we drifted into new friendships. Betty married Carl after his wife died. Carl being a Harris meant she and Mom stopped socializing for a while after Elaine's problems. But now they're good friends again."

Vanessa looked over all the pictures. "Is that Elaine and your mother?" She studied the handsome middle-aged woman with short gray hair and wire-frame glasses. Mrs. Fardig was tall with a broad, muscular frame. Her daughter had a more delicate build with the same fair coloring as the man in the next picture. There was no visible indication of which eye had been damaged. Vanessa pointed. "That must be your father, right?"

"Yes, that's right," David said.

"Where's Marly?"

"Family joke. Marly's always the one who takes the pictures. I think there's one at the far end."

Two young women stood together with their arms around each other's shoulders in front of an ocean view. Both wore floppy hats and sunglasses. All Vanessa could determine was that Marly was white, slender, and taller than Elaine.

"Who is the mother of those kids? Where is she?" Vanessa asked.

"Marly has custody of them, but she is their aunt," David said. "Marly has an older sister, Charlene. Pretty, but not as bright by a long shot. She was in the same class with me too. After Del moved in with their mother, we heard that Del was sleeping with Charlene after Denise passed out."

"How old would she have been?" Vanessa tried to keep her voice level and unemotional.

"Thirteen or so. Maybe fourteen. I know she was in the eighth grade because we all took the bus up to junior high in Avalon. All the kids seemed to know. To be frank, I think we were a bit in awe. Charlene was cute and looked a lot older, plus Del was the local main guy and a lot of women had a crush on him. We didn't dare say anything or even tease her. Now I have kids and as I look back at it, I'm ashamed."

"Did she get pregnant?"

"No. At least not right away. She did get pregnant when she was a sophomore and she had the baby later that year. But that was with Johnny Martinson, Betty's son. I'm told Del had been minding his manners by that time."

"He stopped?" Vanessa asked. "That would be kind of unusual for a sexual predator."

"I don't know much about it, only the rumors. I gather that Zeke had told him to stop."

"So the baby wasn't his?" Vanessa asked.

"A lot of people assumed Del was the father, but no. Two years later, Charlene had a little girl and Johnny went missing right after that. Del said the kids were his and no one dared say otherwise until after he died."

"And Betty was able to reclaim her grandchildren."

David nodded. "Over time. But that's about right."

"You said Marly took custody of the kids. How did that come to pass?"

"Charlene had married Greg Harris and they had Alison. Greg was always in some kind of trouble, but things got very complicated and tense after Del and Zeke disappeared, with Rosie fighting for control. Greg got caught in the crossfire. He was busted for a huge drug deal that went bad. I was told Rosie set that up. No one died, but it was a close call. Charlene got pulled in as an accessory. She went to prison for a while. The kids went to California."

Vanessa wondered if her eyes were as round as

Jack's. She took a swig of cold coffee to wash away
the nasty taste in her mouth.

"Where do things stand with Marly and Charlene
now?"

"Let's see. I don't keep real close track. Charlene
got out about three years ago. I'm not a criminal attorney but from what I know, she was damn lucky to
serve only eighteen months. She lives out there with
Marly, I hear. I am not going to pretend that I'm the
least bit sorry to hear Louise and Troy dead."

"We're scheduled to meet with Greg Harris in At-
tica. Would he know why Louise and Troy went to
California?" Jack asked.

"He might. He's connected to Carl somehow."

"And Carl won." Jack scribbled on his pad, updat-
ing his notes. "He outlasted everyone else."

"Yeah, I suppose. I'm not sure that the Harris clan is
a worthy prize these days. New people are moving into
the Springs. Now that the Internet and cell phone coverage have arrived, these folks have enough money
and resources to ignore Carl. Not that Carl is toothless,
mind you. Watch out for him."

"Carl Harris doesn't seem like a good guy to cross,"
Vanessa said.

"That would be an understatement, although he's a
real gentleman compared to his predecessors." The
knuckles in David's hand turned white around the coffee mug.

Vanessa studied her notes. "Do you think Carl carried a grudge against Louise and Troy?"

"I'm sure Carl hated them."

Vanessa tapped her pen and frowned. "More to the
point, would he have thought they were a threat? Is it
possible he sent them out there to get rid of them?"

David raised his eyebrows. "You mean like a

setup?" He held his hands up in mock surrender. "No idea. You're asking the wrong person. I'll just say that Carl should not be underestimated. We all used to think he was the nice Harris."

Vanessa and Jack exchanged glances and a quick nod.

"I think we're done here, David," Jack said, offering his hand for a farewell shake. "Please get in touch if you think of anything else. We'd like the addresses and contact information for your mother and Elaine. And Marly."

The driveway down to the main road had accumulated several inches of new snow, but the road down to the Springs was well plowed and sanded.

"To think I didn't believe this interview would be interesting," Vanessa said once they were underway.

"Do you really think it's possible that Carl had Louise and Troy taken out?" Jack asked. He kept his eyes focused on the road and both hands wrapped around the wheel.

"He's definitely capable of it and he had a mountain of motivation. He might have connections with common values in California."

"Any thoughts about Elaine? Or Marly?"

"From what we've heard, they don't strike me as Carl's kind of peeps." The car went into a skid and Vanessa's voice failed as she stomped on the phantom brake under her feet.

"What if Louise and Troy went to pay them a visit?"

The car straightened out and Vanessa released her death grip on the door handle. "I don't see it. Louise and Troy had already come out losers trying to take on Elaine. Plus, Elaine seems like a real straight arrow.

Her mother, too, I gather. I think they would have contacted the police. And Marly's a Harris. She's family."

"With family like that, who needs enemies?" Jack chuckled at his own wit.

Vanessa peered out ahead, mesmerized by the stream of snow careening straight into the windshield. "True, but you do need friends. The right friends could make all the difference."

12

Marly: Orpheus

December 2–16, 2000

The phone rang and rang and rang.

Why doesn't Denise get an answering machine?
Marly could not leave Alison unattended on the changing table. The baby thrashed and screamed from the pain of a diaper rash but did not want her diaper changed.

"My mother should answer her own phone and your mother should be the one changing you," Marly said as she struggled to clean and lubricate the baby's red bottom.

Someone picked up the phone. Or perhaps the caller had given up.

It was Saturday. Marly wanted to leave for the standard errands. After that, she needed to pick up Elaine and go to the library for work.

Now dry and diapered, Alison cooed and reached for Marly's nose. "Mmmly." Marly melted and gave her niece a big smacking kiss, which drew giggles.

From downstairs, Charlene yelled, "Mom. Mom. They've found Del and Zeke. Their truck is in that ravine off Beckwith Road."

Marly bent over the changing table and buried her face in Alison's neck. She savored the sweet soapy scent of the baby's skin and waited for her gagging to subside.

Charlene was calling her. Marly hoisted the baby onto her hip.

"Let's go find your mother and see what's up with Del."

Charlene and Denise had already stuffed the older two kids into jackets and boots.

"Marly, you won't fit in the car. Sorry," Charlene said.

Denise grabbed Alison and wrapped the baby in her winter coat. The entire family, minus Marly, headed to the ravine in Charlene's car.

Marly called Elaine.

"It looks like Del and Zeke have been found in a ravine off Beckwith Road."

"You mean they wandered in there? Are they alive?"

"I don't see how they could be alive. They were found in Del's truck," Marly said. "Do you want to go see? I think half the village will be there."

"Including Rosie and Louise?"

"I'd count on that."

"My mother would have a fit and I'd rather not. I don't want to be included in any Harris gatherings."

"Got it. Okay. I'll take Mom's car. She won't like that, but I'll work it out." Marly had made a promise to Mrs. Fardig that she would only use Elaine's car for activities that involved Elaine's benefit.

"Couldn't you walk through the woods? That area must be close once you're over the hill."

"It's cold. I'd rather drive." Marly smiled. How like

Elaine that she would pick up on that simple piece of rural geography.

Marly pulled on her new walking boots. Winter weather had arrived but a slight warming trend left many frozen places a bit defrosted, including—she hoped—Beckwith's potato field.

She parked her mother's car near Beckwith Road, not far from the Rock. There was no shoulder to speak of. She joined a long line of parked cars crowding out the right lane.

Since that night in October, Marly had made a point of avoiding this route, either by car or on foot. Now she noticed little dips and bumps where she had stumbled and faltered. She wondered whether some of those deeper divots were bullet holes.

The beat of her heart in her ears propelled her through the crowd along the road at the base of the hill above the ravine. She noted with some satisfaction that little kids and a few teenagers were running around in the half-frozen muck of the potato field. If any of her footprints remained, they would soon be camouflaged.

Once in the lane, she passed two ambulances that idled in the ruts. A small crowd of police officers peered over the edge of the ravine and the heads of a few more could be glimpsed down below. Tad Morrison's tow truck sat at an angle across the dirt road. The cable attached to his winch ran down to Del's truck.

Rosie and Louise glared at all around them. Marly decided to back away a bit and bumped into Paul Daniels, who was making some pretense of crowd control.

"This is terrible. You are all disturbing the crime scene," he said. "How will we figure out any footprints or evidence?"

"Wow. That's too bad." Marly tried to sound sympathetic. "Who found them?"

"Deer hunters. After bow season's done there are more around. Beckwiths post this land but of course people come through here."

Tad's winch began to turn.

"How did they die?" Marly asked.

"Can't tell yet. The coroner will take a good while, I'd say. Lots of decay."

The truck emerged like a muddy fish from the ravine, dripping water, and dragging branches like moldy fins. The common sulfurous smell from the hard water mixed with a different stench and spread across the crowd.

Many gasped and moved away. Marly imagined what the corpses inside might look like.

Now that it was time to remove the bodies, the crowd was pushed back and screens were put up to prevent casual glimpses.

Paul stood close behind her and spoke in a low voice.

"You know it could be dangerous for you around here. I could pick you up at school and drive you home."

Marly turned and stared.

"Okay then, at the bus stop," he said. "You could use a friend in the police department."

"No thanks, Paul." *Loser.*

"Marly, I'm just trying to keep you safe. And we could get cocoa or coffee or something."

Marly bit her lip and ignored him.

Paul moved forward to supervise the crowd as the body bags emerged from behind the curtains and were loaded onto gurneys and from there into the ambulances.

After Del's truck was hauled away, the spectators lost interest and dispersed. Marly mingled with her neighbors and made her second escape from Beckwith Road.

Home life that night was weepy. Mark and Pammy sat quiet and wide-eyed as Denise sobbed her way through a very nice roasted chicken dinner. Even Alison ate in silence until she dumped her bowl of rice onto the kitchen floor, signaling she was full.

"At least we know where he's gone," Denise said.

Marly considered herself an atheist but wondered if her mother thought Del would go to heaven.

"Yes, Denise. It was just awful not knowing," she said.

Denise patted Marly's hand. "Now at least we can settle his estate and get some money coming in again. Lord knows we need it."

Marly looked at her sister, who was trying to stuff more chicken into Alison. The baby banged on her tray. *Leave her alone, Charlene. She'll start crying in a moment.*

"Did he leave a will, do you think?" Marly asked.

"What do you mean, did he leave a will?" Denise's eyes narrowed.

Marly knew she should shut up. Saying more would hurt her mother, but someone had to explain the facts to dim Denise.

"You weren't married. You can't inherit if you're not the wife or if there's no will."

"I couldn't marry him!" Denise said. Her face flushed bright red. "Your father had disappeared, so it wasn't like I was a widow. And besides . . ." She stopped.

And besides, Del was your cousin, completed Marly in her head. At least she didn't say that out loud.

"But children can inherit without a will," Charlene said. Her voice was quiet and soft.

Denise, Charlene, and Marly all turned to look at Mark and Pammy, who jumped up and ran off to get ready for their baths upstairs.

Denise tottered into the living room to finish drinking while Marly and Charlene cleaned up.

"I'm glad he's dead," Marly said.

Her sister stared at the suds.

"Charlene, he raped you for years. He's gone at last. You can talk."

Charlene dunked the children's glasses under the soapy water and wiped around the rims. "You know, he treated me so nice. He was so sweet in bed. I felt special. And the girls at school were so jealous."

Marly's eyes widened.

"He always said Mark and Pammy were his." Charlene's voice had a new assertive edge.

"You know that's not so." Marly wanted to scream.

Charlene held up a glass and looked at Marly through the bottom, still smiling.

"The point is, he said it. He wrote it. I have letters. Zeke sent money every month since Mark was born and a bit more since Pammy."

"That will piss Rosie off. Everyone knows that they aren't Del's kids. If you go after his money or his property, you could alienate both sides of the family. Now that Zeke's dead, Vernon and Elliot may make a play to run things. But if Rosie wins, you know she'll always think that you cheated your way into some money and she'll use Mark and Pammy to get back at you."

"They have lots and lots of money. They don't spend it right, but they have it stored away." Charlene's voice turned low and bitter. "That's our money. That pays for Daddy. That pays for Johnny."

"Yeah, but I bet that all Del's worth on paper is that quarter acre with his old crappy double-wide, plus a little bit in the bank. The property isn't worth shit and the kids might have to pay taxes on anything they'd get. You could end up owing money. Just sit back and wait. Let Rosie make an offer and let her take on the liability. I want you safe."

Charlene finished the last saucepan. "And what about Mom? She needs the money Del used to give her."

Marly thought of the money she'd stolen and how she mentally counted it every night to lull herself to sleep. She pushed away the guilty twinge. *No turning back.*

"I don't know. They'll come talk to you. Don't ask for much but ask them to treat Denise like Del's widow and make sure they keep up the payments for Beanie. I think these things take a long time to settle without a will. Tell them you will not make any claims if they just do the right things and that includes Denise."

Charlene gave Marly a black look and went upstairs. Marly had a sinking feeling that her sister had not changed her plans.

After a few nervous days, Marly was pleased with the initial assumptions published by the police. Pending the official autopsy, it appeared that Zeke had succumbed to a heart attack and that Del had died from an arterial bleed caused by a bullet wound. They also verified that the bullet had been shot from a gun in the truck with Zeke's fingerprints on it. There was evidence that the men had been climbing around in the potato field based on the mud on their boots and clothing, and to a limited extent based on footprints they could find near the field.

No explanation was offered as to why Del and Zeke were near the field or if there had been another party involved.

There was no avoiding the funeral service for Del and Zeke a week later.

Denise was allowed to sit in the front pew with Rosie. Marly's diminutive mother was barely visible, squashed between the gigantic Harris family members.

Marly, Charlene, and the kids were relegated to the back. Attendance was spotty, Marly noted. Aside from family members, most in town avoided the service. She was surprised to see Mrs. Haas, the librarian. As usual, she was impeccably attired, this time in a charcoal-gray wool suit, pearls, and pristine cranberry-red pumps that matched the reading glasses she used to study the flimsy service agenda.

Marly stared at the hymnal and tried to avoid looking at the huge photos of Zeke and Del over their closed caskets.

She wondered who had chosen the pictures. Zeke was smiling and looked twenty years younger and downright avuncular—the kind of guy you could have asked for a cookie or talked to about how much you missed your daddy. Not the kind of guy who could turn on a dime and knock you off the porch because you spilled lemonade.

And Del. There was no question he had been "a specimen," to quote Claire. Her classmates had always glanced at her when his name came up, even in Avalon. Del was gorgeous. Marly could see that. Most Harris men tended to be tall and barrel-chested, with reddish hair and hazel eyes. Del liked to wear pale blue to highlight his eyes, and tight-fitting shirts, even in winter, to show off his broad shoulders and flat belly. He was meticulous about his haircuts—not too long, not too short—so that his blond waves would bounce just so.

He had been smart, too. Marly had underestimated him more than once. He was unpredictable when drunk, but he was careful not to show when he'd been drinking. He ran Zeke's snotty empire like a little Swiss watch, according to Paul Daniels. Now that watch showed signs of poor timing. Events had spiraled out of control.

Marly kept a careful eye on Rosie during the service. Denise bowed her head and bobbed in time to the music, but Rosie stayed stiff and upright the entire time. Reverend Rick spoke in glowing tones about the virtues of both men. There were no other testimonials.

Once the singing and praying were done, they rode to the cemetery behind the outdoor hockey rink. The weather was still too warm for ice, and the rink sat empty. In a few weeks it would be filled with children and the sounds of skates on ice, and slap shots.

Marly bobbed Alison on her hip and watched the two caskets lowered into the ground.

"Good thing they turned up when they did," Charlene muttered under her breath. "Otherwise the ground would have been too frozen and we'd have had to wait until spring for this."

Marly suppressed a grin. "Too bad there are only two holes," she said into Alison's neck.

Charlene buried her face into her scarf, pulling it up to her nose to hide a snicker.

Carl was right, Marly thought. *I am the lucky one.*

13

Vanessa: The Snow Man

January 30, 2013

The snowstorm tapered off by the time Jack and Vanessa pulled into Denise Harris's driveway, allowing Vanessa to appreciate the transformed landscape. Dark evergreens were white, a stack of snow perched atop every twig on every tree and along the power lines. The half-plowed driveway surface appeared to be covered with thick, lumpy oatmeal, a mix of snow on top of sand and salt.

"We can't stay long, Jack. We could have a hard time getting out if the snow starts up again."

"Got that," Jack said. "Stuck in Hades."

Beneath the gloss of the Marlyfication Paul had mentioned, Vanessa thought she could see the bones of the old, run-down farmhouse this must have once been. Snow slid smoothly off a metal roof, and the clapboard siding looked freshly painted. The windows boasted they were new, showing manufacturer stickers here and there. Off to one side, a small barn had been painted the same antique yellow with white trim as the house.

A figure exited the rear of the house onto an ample deck and waved them up.

Denise's mudroom sat off the back deck, next to a spacious laundry. Vanessa felt she was becoming a connoisseur of mudrooms.

Denise Harris hovered as Jack and Vanessa removed their boots and jackets.

"Hello. Hello. I'm Denise. I'm Denise. How about tea? I'll get you tea."

It was evident that Denise had once been quite pretty, and she still could have been if she had relaxed into a more natural look, Vanessa decided. Once a natural blond, the older woman's hair was now bleached and the texture of dry straw. Her face showed blackheads and rough areas that indicated neglect the heavy makeup could not hide. In spite of those signs of a hard life, Denise's figure was lithe and attractive, and she dressed to show that off in tight jeans and a form-fitting, fuzzy pink sweater. Her blue eyes brightened at the sight of Jack, as if he were a new kind of candy she'd like to taste.

Jack blushed and stood behind Vanessa as they moved into another part of the house—a large family room with a gas stove.

"I hear Marly fixed this place up for you, Mrs. Harris," Vanessa said.

"Oh, yeah." Denise turned around and waved her hands toward the new appliances and the open-kitchen format attached to the family room. "The house used to end right there." Denise drew an imaginary line across the floor. "Can you believe that we all used to eat around a tiny table in that kitchen? Now I've got a breakfast bar and a nice big dining table and this sitting area with a gas fire. No wood required. And there's a master bedroom and huge bath through that door there, plus the original living room in front."

"She's been very good to you," said Jack.

"She's been a pain. I'm worth a lot of money now on paper. Can you believe it? But it's in a trust and she has me on an allowance. A drip. I need to ask for extra money when I need it."

Jack picked up the ball and turned to Denise with a big smile.

"This is a gorgeous place, Mrs. Harris. As we mentioned on the phone, we're here to try to figure out how Louise and Troy Rasmussen died. We'd like to ask for your help."

Denise directed a coquettish grin at Jack. "Oh, but they died in California, *n'est-ce pas?*"

Jack raised his eyebrows and laughed. "*Mais oui*. But they started out from here. We hear you are something of an expert on the Harris family. We're hoping you can provide some background."

Denise waggled her shoulders and pouted. "I never cared for Louise or Troy. I didn't socialize with them any more than I had to. Once my Elliot passed, I hardly ever saw them."

"Do you remember the last time you saw them?" Jack's voice was smooth and soothing.

Denise put a finger to her lips. "Let's see. I'd say that was about a month before Rosie died. Rosie was Louise's mother, you know."

"I don't suppose you'd remember the occasion?"

"Rosie had a birthday party for Del. He would have turned forty-five if he had lived. It just broke her heart when he died." Denise's lips quivered and she dabbed at her eyes.

"You must miss him a great deal," Jack said.

Vanessa tried to keep her expression neutral. *What a pair of ham actors.*

Denise sniffed. "I've had bad luck with my husbands. First Beanie ran off, then Del ended up in that ravine, and Elliot died from cancer. They were all so sudden. Even Elliot. He started throwing up and just couldn't stop. So he went to the doctor and two months later he was dead."

Vanessa resisted the temptation to look at Jack. *Tough luck indeed.*

"But Del had his flaws," Vanessa said. "He did molest your daughter Charlene for several years, isn't that right?"

Denise squirmed. "Charlene led him on."

Vanessa felt a surge of heat ripple through the muscles of her back. "She was twelve or thirteen when that started, I hear. He was a grown man. In your heart, do you believe that Charlene seduced him?"

Denise sat up straight and gave a snort. "Well, he stopped. And I don't like to speak ill of the dead."

"Why did he stop?"

Denise simpered and sniffed. "She should have talked to me first. I'm her mother. She went straight to Zeke. Rosie was furious."

"Charlene did that?"

"No, no. Charlene's a good girl. That was Marly. She'd gotten it in her head from school that she should say something. She told Zeke that someone would bring this to the attention of the authorities sooner or later and Del would be in big trouble."

"That was brave."

"That was stupid is what that was. Del swore that it was all Marly's imagination and Marly got a proper touch-up over that."

"But he stopped."

Denise turned her face away from Vanessa.

Vanessa studied her notebook to calm down. She rather doubted that Marly hadn't raised the issue with her mother.

"The word is that Charlene's children were Del's," Jack said. "They came along several years later."

"Rosie liked to believe that Mark and Pammy were Del's," Denise said in a stage whisper. "We humored her when she was alive. But Charlene said they were Johnny's and as they got older it was clear they looked just like Johnny."

"Rosie didn't like Charlene very much, did she?" Jack asked in his own stage whisper.

Denise gazed out the windows and spoke in a normal tone. "She blamed Charlene for leading Del astray, of course. But Charlene kept her mouth shut and moved on with Greg. And Charlene did her time in prison for Greg and didn't say anything about the family. But Marly. She sure did dislike Marly. I could never quite figure that out. Of course Marly had complained to Zeke that once, but she was punished for that. And Marly never blabbed to outsiders. She attended family events and meetings, and she was even more polite than Charlene."

"She got along with Del?"

"Oh, so-so. Del told me that he felt that Marly was always sneaky and he said she'd been listening in on his conversations. Business conversations."

"What about Carl's sons, Judson and Jason? What did Rosie think about them?" Vanessa asked.

Denise scowled. "Judson and Jason? They haven't been around for years. Jason is a bit older than Charlene. Judson was not an easy boy. Carl had to send him away."

"He lives in California, correct?"

Denise's eyes shifted away. "I guess so."

"You don't see him when you visit Charlene and Marly in California?"

"Sometimes. When Betty comes out, she wants to see all the California grandchildren," Denise answered.

Vanessa continued to stare at Denise, but she mentally clapped her hands.

"Of course they're a little farther away. Sacramento," Denise said.

"Who did Rosie think Del and Zeke were chasing when they died?"

Denise wet her lips, as the question appeared to rattle around in her vacant brain.

"Oh. Well, it's hard to say. When Del and Zeke disappeared, Rosie was like a crazy woman. Every day she had another person to blame."

"Was Rosie mad that Marly had made friends with Elaine?" Vanessa asked.

"Sure. That was another slap as far as Rosie was concerned. But Marly had reached that age where you can't tell them anything. Lucky for her, Rosie and Louise and Troy all got scooped up and sent to prison for a while. When they got out, Marly was long gone."

"In your opinion, why would Rosie have sent Louise and Troy to California? A drug deal?"

Denise made a tsking sound. "I certainly do not know. I could never figure out what ran around in their heads and I never meddled in their business."

"Did Carl get along with Rosie?"

"Carl tried to keep things cordial, I guess you'd say. There was some bad blood because he wouldn't give work to Louise or Troy. But they all got along good enough."

"What if Rosie wanted to punish someone? Like Charlene? Or Judson? Or Elaine?" Jack asked.

Vanessa held her breath.

Denise squinted at her hands. "No. Charlene was

still in prison and Marly was long gone when Rosie died. She had lost interest in all of them as best I could tell. She was real sick from that chemo. Lung cancer."

Vanessa had one more line of questioning. "Mrs. Harris, on the night Del and Zeke died, where were you?"

Denise flushed. "I was right here, of course. I had Charlene and her three kids living here, plus Marly, and Del, and the house was much smaller, mind you."

"Was Charlene here all night?"

"Yes. Marly was the only one who went out. She went to the high school Halloween dance. It was the last Friday in October, I remember that so well." Denise dabbed her eyes again.

"Did you see Marly when she returned?"

"Of course. She always came in and told me if she got home after I was asleep. She would have told me if anything was wrong."

Vanessa forced what she hoped was her most charming smile. "You know, Mrs. Harris, I've seen mug shots of Louise and Troy but no personal photographs. Do you have any family pictures we could see?"

Denise stood up and laughed. "Oh, yes. I've got lots of photo albums in the living room." She waved them through the kitchen to the original front of the house.

This was where all the old furniture went to die, Vanessa decided. Musty loungers and a tired old couch crowded the room. A wood-burning fireplace with a scorched mantel sat at the far end, surrounded by bookshelves. Denise was not a big reader—the shelves were filled with the plastic binders of photo albums.

Denise pulled down selected binders. "Marly says she'll have these moved to the computer but she still hasn't done it."

She studied the labels on the spines and grabbed one album from thirty years before.

"This was Beanie, my first husband. He was a sweet man, but he couldn't read very well. Learning disabilities. That made it hard to make money. Thank God my girls got their smarts from me."

Vanessa stared at the photos of the young man in his teens and early twenties. He was just shy of handsome, with regular features, a wiry build, wavy red hair in a classic mullet, and a warm smile. Even in the somber pictures, she could detect a certain humor behind his eyes. Two little girls, Marly and Charlene, held their dad's hands, sat on his lap, opened presents.

Denise paged through a different album. "Here. This is one you'll like. This is me and Del."

A youthful Denise smiled into the camera with a handsome man at her side.

"Wow," Vanessa said, caught by surprise.

"Yes. We were young and beautiful. Del was just wonderful. Here are some family pictures. These were from about six to eighteen months before he died."

Vanessa and Jack studied several pages and paused on a large family group, posed in front of a pond or lake.

"That's Carl, and Zeke next to him, and that's Larry." Denise pointed. "That's Louise and Troy, just to their left."

"Yikes," Vanessa said. "Talk about land of giants."

The Harris clan seemed to have two body types—big and bigger. Carl, Zeke, Larry, and Troy were all tall—six foot four or more—with beefy shoulders and potbellies. Zeke was downright obese. Louise had a similar build but appeared small by comparison. Del was almost as tall as his father, but more muscular and lean. A tall, skinny woman with lank black hair glared at the camera from the center of the scene.

"That's Rosie, I assume." Vanessa pointed.

"Oh yes. She never took a good picture. And there's Elliot. He became my third husband. That's his father, Vernon, next to Del and Greg. Greg's my son-in-law. Married to Charlene. That's me, of course," Denise said. "That's Charlene and her kids, and there's Marly."

Vanessa and Jack leaned in.

Denise flipped the page. "Here's another picture, a bit closer up."

"Charlene looks just like you," Vanessa said, focused on Marly.

"My spitting image. Marly takes after her dad—red hair, greenish eyes. But you know, I always told Marly she could be just as pretty as Charlene if she just smiled."

Vanessa flipped through the binder. There was handsome, confident Del, radiating crafty intelligence. Here was sweet, oblivious Denise. Charlene always smiled and appeared happy, if a bit blank. Rosie glowered. Zeke seemed half asleep. Larry's eyes were full of implied menace. Troy postured and showed off his tattoos. Odd. She hadn't thought about Troy's skin until that moment.

Denise was right. Marly almost never smiled. She didn't scowl, but she had a fixed stare. Was that Beanie's humor behind those hazel eyes or grim determination? It must have been hard to smile at the people she knew had murdered her father.

"Marly looks different here." Jack pointed to a picture. "She doesn't seem very happy."

Denise leaned in to look. "Oh, that's not Marly. That's Laurie Harris. Laurie Rasmussen, I guess, to be accurate. Louise's daughter. Laurie and Marly were the same age. When they were little we couldn't tell them apart. So sad when she died."

"She was killed," Vanessa said. She looked through several more binders searching for Laurie and Marly. Denise was right. As younger children they could have been twins, but as teenagers, Laurie was taller and plumper. And angrier.

"We'd better go, Vanessa. The snow has started up again," Jack said, pointing with his chin toward the window.

The sloping driveway was a slippery toboggan run with new snow. Jack backed up the car and raced for the road several times before they broke free of the driveway.

"So much for snow tires," he said when they gained the road at last, the car fishtailing back and forth.

As they rolled into the village, a building caught Vanessa's attention. "Stop at the library. The lights are on. It must be open."

Jack stomped on the brake and turned the wheel. The car performed a delicate pirouette on the empty road, turned around in place, and stopped. Vanessa swore in Spanish until she had to stop and gasp.

"Jesus, Jack. You are so lucky there's no traffic."

"Okay, okay. We're both lucky." He inched the car into a half-plowed parking spot.

The snow topped Vanessa's boots as she climbed out of the car and she winced. The two detectives slogged their way through a slushy mix up to the door of the library.

The wood-paneled foyer offered a classy spot to shed coats and boots. Vanessa considered it the nicest mudroom so far.

To the left of the foyer, they found a comfortable reading room with the librarian's desk at the far end. A large fireplace dominated the interior wall, trimmed in carved wood that matched the wood trim around all the doors.

A middle-aged woman with short gray hair glanced up, peering over the nameplate on the counter that read MRS. NANCY HAAS.

"Are you visiting?" she asked. She stood, revealing a gray boiled-wool jacket, trimmed in green and red over a black turtleneck. She slid her red reading glasses from her face to dangle against her thin chest from a beaded chain. "We don't often get visitors here in Charon Springs."

"We're sheriff's detectives from California," Vanessa said. "The remains of Louise and Troy Rasmussen were found there in November. We're here to investigate why they went to California so that we can determine what happened to them."

Mrs. Haas pressed her lips together before she answered. "They didn't come in here very often, I can tell you that much. Not big readers. I can't say I'm sad to hear they won't be back."

"Did you know them?" Jack asked. He gazed around the reading room and took in the walnut paneling that covered the open walls. Long library tables stretched end to end.

"My family were Judsons," Mrs. Haas said. "Judsons settled this place. This house was my family's house before it became the library. I know everyone."

"And that's why you still live here?" Vanessa waved her hands toward the frigid exterior.

"It's a beautiful place once you appreciate winter and can see with a clear mind. Do you know "The

Snow Man," by Wallace Stevens? No?" She led them to a framed poem on the wall.

Vanessa leaned in and recited:

One must have a mind of winter
To regard the frost and the boughs
Of the pine-trees crusted with snow;

And have been cold a long time
To behold the junipers shagged with ice,
The spruces rough in the distant glitter

Of the January sun; and not to think
Of any misery in the sound of the wind,
In the sound of a few leaves,

Which is the sound of the land
Full of the same wind
That is blowing in the same bare place

For the listener, who listens in the snow,
And, nothing himself, beholds
Nothing that is not there and the nothing that is.

Jack cleared his throat and backed away. Vanessa said, "I thought it meant to have a frigid heart of winter, but it's just the opposite. Sort of like Zen. Be in the moment and see the beauty."

Mrs. Haas rewarded her with a slight bow. "Even in summer, I try to feel like the snow man."

Jack went to a side window to study the large, half-built extension in back. "I hear that's called Marlyfication."

"Marly and Elaine both gave, but Marly was key,"

Mrs. Haas said. "This place was a refuge for her and I was happy to give it to her, and to many other children, by the way."

"You didn't feel that way about Elaine?" Vanessa asked. She had found the section with all the old elementary and high school yearbooks and pulled one out, from forty-five years back.

"I have those all digitized now, by the way, thanks to Marly. In any case, Elaine didn't need help in the same way. She had a good family and they made a respectable living. Don't get me wrong. She was a very nice girl and smart. When she hit trouble, she did need help. But her parents wanted to be from Avalon. She didn't need this place the way that Marly did."

"You gave Marly a lifeline. Elaine as well after her beating," Vanessa said.

"In a job like this and in a little town like this, you hope you make a difference, but more often than not you don't know what to do. Some kids come through okay, but a lot don't. All those sweet little faces. Marly was sweet and bright. She needed a place to get away from her family."

"What about Laurie Harris?" Vanessa pointed to a third-grade picture. Marly and Laurie stood like twin bookends at either end of the middle row.

Nancy Haas's face darkened in a soft scowl. "She had a chance, briefly. By the time she got to eighth grade, I could no longer reach her. That was very sad."

"Too bad that nobody tried to get her help."

" 'Somebody' did try to help once," Mrs. Haas said, her eyes angry.

"Oh?"

Mrs. Haas plopped her hands down on the table. "It came to nothing. Laurie was at the bottom of a deep well. 'Somebody's' arms were just too short and we were out of rope." Mrs. Haas continued to fix her dark stare on Vanessa.

Vanessa blinked first. "That would be hard for a listener in the snow. I'm sorry to hear it."

"You said that Marly wanted to get away from family. Did you mean Louise and Troy?" Jack asked.

"I was talking about Del. He was a conniving little boy and later he was mean underneath. I was about six years older, and I remember him from school. My younger sisters had crushes on him. Larry was nasty but so dumb you could see him coming. Louise always wanted to be as tough as the boys, but she couldn't run things like Del did. Besides, Rosie and Zeke believed that Del was their anointed prince."

"I gather that Del did not have a mind of winter," Vanessa said.

"More like a heart of winter."

Jack thumbed through the yearbooks. "We were told that Del and Larry ran things for Zeke."

"Larry and Louise did what Del told them to, even though Del was a couple years younger. Del was smarter and almost as vicious as his father, Zeke, just in a smoother way. He got other people to do most of his dirty work. In many ways, he was amazing. When he died, that was when things began to change here."

"Rather convenient that they died together," Vanessa said. "Do you think that was planned?"

"Doubtful. More like a happy accident. They went after someone who didn't roll over and die. The coroner said that Zeke had a heart attack right after he fired a wild shot from his gun that hit Del." She burnished the tabletop, erasing the smudges and fingerprints. "I call that just desserts."

"Do you know who their intended victim might have been?" Vanessa asked.

Mrs. Haas gave a dignified snort. "Definitely not and I am not going to indulge in idle speculation."

"Anyone from the Springs you could eliminate?" asked Jack.

"Only the ones who were already dead." Mrs. Haas walked stiffly back to her desk.

Vanessa wandered around the library. She used the bathroom, now half torn-up for the upgrade. She studied the exposed hole in the wall where the tampon dispenser had once provided feminine products.

"What about Carl Harris?" she asked when she returned to the main reading room. "It seems like he was out of the picture for a long time. Would he have had problems with Louise or Troy?"

"Carl was a wolf in sheep's clothing, but I saw through his clever waiting game. I know he didn't get along with Louise and Troy, but they didn't get along with anyone, so that's a low bar."

"Did either of them ever come in here?"

Mrs. Haas licked her lips. "Right after Del died, Larry and Louise tore this place apart for Rosie. I don't know what they were looking for, but they didn't seem to find it."

Jack scowled. "They broke in?"

"Hell no! They walked right in on a Saturday late afternoon and made me close the library while they searched. I was terrified. They kept saying that if they found anything, it would be my fault."

Vanessa put her hand on the woman's arm. "That must have been terrible. Did you call the police?"

Mrs. Haas stared at the two detectives. "You must be kidding."

Winter twilight was closing in outside. Mrs. Haas helped Jack and Vanessa make copies of selected pages from the yearbooks and agreed to email them a link to the digital versions, which they could order for a small fee.

"I see that Del was a football star in high school," Vanessa said.

"Del had quite a run as a football player. But in his senior year, he missed some practices and got into an argument with Coach Pasco. Zeke beat up Coach. End of high school for Del."

The car didn't want to leave the library parking spot and spun its wheels. Vanessa agreed to drive while Jack pushed from the front until they were free.

Once on the road back to Avalon in the dark, the snow flew straight into their windshield. Vanessa thought that perhaps the car had shown good sense in its desire to stay put someplace safe.

"Don't drive with your high beams on," Jack said.

"Shut up." Vanessa rested her forearms on the steering wheel and peered into the flying snow. She did as he suggested. Several seconds later, they agreed to go back to high beams.

"How could they rent us a car without all-wheel drive at this time of year?" Jack asked.

"We didn't pay much money for this heap and it does have snow tires. We'll be fine. Just remember, you must have a mind of winter."

They climbed up the steep slope out of the Springs and inched ahead less than a mile, when Vanessa caught movement along the right shoulder.

"What the hell is that?"

"It's a man!" Jack said. "He's flagging us down. He must be in trouble."

"Jack, something's not right. He's wearing some sort of mask."

"It's just a scarf. Look at your dashboard. It's not even five degrees out there. He could die. Stop the car."

Vanessa pulled over, about one hundred feet beyond the man, and put on the flashers. "Do you have your gun?"

"What? No. I left it in the hotel safe."

"Shit. Did you leave your brains there too?"

Jack opened his door and got out as the figure trotted up to the back of the car.

"Jack. Be careful. If you're worried, raise up your arms and wave them around. I'll be watching. If we do give him a ride, he sits in front and you sit right behind him with my gun."

Vanessa watched in the rearview mirror. She unzipped her jacket and hoisted her sweater to pull out her warm gun from its shoulder harness. She made sure it was ready to fire. She eased out her LED flashlight from her right pocket. A quick glance at her cell phone showed no bars. Calling for Chip's cavalry was not an option.

The man appeared to be gesticulating off to the right. What was taking so long? What were they talking about? Vanessa could feel her pulse build and throb in her temples.

She thought Jack was raising his arms. His hands were about shoulder height.

Vanessa opened her door and slipped out. She left her door open and stopped just short of the trunk. She flipped on the flashlight, flinging the two men into bright light.

Jack didn't turn. He kept his eyes fixed on the other man, who now blinked into the light. A ski mask covered the man's face. Traces of a goatee and bushy eyebrows pushed out through the openings, collecting snow.

"This is Terry," Jack said. His voice was a flat monotone.

"My car is stuck, just down that road there. I think I need a jump," Terry said.

"I've been explaining to Terry that this car isn't very sturdy. But we can give him a ride into Avalon."

"It would just be a moment," Terry said.

"I like that idea of Avalon," Vanessa said. "Tell you what. I'll show you my ID and you show us yours."

She pushed the gun in front of the halo from the flashlight so that Terry would be certain to see it. Jack started to reach into his left armpit. Vanessa knew there was no gun there, but both gestures appeared to catch Terry's attention and he froze.

In the corner of her peripheral vision, Vanessa noticed a bright flicker in the field to her left, but she kept the light and her focus on Terry. There was a roar of an engine from the field, followed by a cocoon of headlights glowing in the dense snowfall.

"Well, hey. Looks like my car is okay after all," Terry said. He backed up, turned, and charged over the snowbank into the field.

"Get in the car, Jack." Vanessa's voice crackled with relief. Jack needed no additional encouragement.

Vanessa drove the rest of the way to Avalon with her eyes fixed on the road ahead as Jack stared out the back. No lights behind them, he reported.

Chip and Paul were still in the office.

Chip flushed and slapped his desk at the news. "Shit. Of course it's hard to tell for sure, but it doesn't sound like this Terry was up to any good. Paul, do we know anyone named Terry in the Springs?"

Paul turned so pale that Vanessa was glad he was already sitting down.

The four of them studied a paper map to pinpoint the location.

"Not much there. Here's a track that used to service some limestone quarries. No houses," Chip said.

"Schwarzer's quarry. Down that road about a mile," Paul said.

"Who owns that?" Jack asked.

"I'm thinking Carl must own that part now. But that doesn't tell us much substantively," Chip said. He rubbed his jaw, his brow furrowed. "Lots of people know about that road, and it's not like it's patrolled or anything."

"Maybe you could go down there and look for tire tracks," Vanessa said.

Paul twitched his shoulders. "Eighteen to twenty-four inches tonight. No one's going down there."

"Shut up, Paul," Chip said. He turned back to Vanessa and Jack. "We'll go check tomorrow. We have a snow emergency for tonight. There will be critical situations here and on Route Twenty."

Back at the hotel, Vanessa noticed that items in her room had been moved around. The contents of her drawers had been shuffled. Some of the furniture had been shifted, although everything was still neat and organized. A prickle lifted the hairs on the back of her neck.

Jack waited for her in the hallway. "Funny thing about my room," he said. "Things have been moved."

In the lobby the manager, Rob, squinted at them over his desk.

"I'm so sorry. I'm sure we did not give out any keys. It must have been the cleaning staff. I'll check with them. It's odd that happened to both of you. You're sure you're not missing anything?"

Vanessa pinched the bridge of her nose to keep from snapping at Rob. The residual tension after the confrontation on the road had settled into her gut and threatened to bubble over into a full-scale tantrum.

"Not that I can tell," she said between clenched teeth.

She cut the discussion short and dragged Jack to the beer cellar to soothe her anger with food and a good brew.

"This is spooky, Jack," Vanessa said. "Do you buy that it was the cleaning staff?"

"Only if their last name is Harris," Jack answered.

"Maybe it was Terry and his pal in the car," Vanessa said. "Very reassuring that Chip was so concerned about that incident. His support is wonderful."

"They're still scared of the Springs."

"So am I, Jack."

"These hamburgers are growing on me," Jack said after a long pause. "How's your salad?"

"Between you and me, not very good. But I don't want to go outside."

Vanessa leaned forward and snatched a couple of French fries off Jack's plate.

Jack stared into his soda as if it were fine wine. "I'm thinking Carl knows more than he's saying."

"Duh."

"Maybe Larry will be more forthcoming. Still up for the trip to see him tomorrow?"

"If the snow lets up a bit, yes. Chip said Paul would

drive us and I assume that cop cars have good snow tires. Man, I hate visiting prisons."

"I don't know which is worse, the cold or this snow. Or Paul. He sets my teeth on edge."

"I thought you were the one who loved skiing in the Sierras."

"In the Sierras it snows like crazy but the sun— warm sun—comes out, the roads clear, and you need sunscreen." Jack added a dramatic groan. "I won't forget this place, that's for sure."

"I won't forget the Springs," Vanessa said. "Look at this."

She pulled a sheaf of papers, copies of yearbook pictures, from her bag. "Second grade, forty-four years ago. Seven boys, eight girls. Here is Beanie, Marly's father. He disappeared and is presumed dead. Here's Max Redman. He's the one who became an ATF agent and was killed by Larry and Del. And there's Ollie Fardig. Presumed dead. There's Larry. In prison doing life for killing Max. And there's Louise—dead. And that's Elliot Harris, Denise's second or third husband, depending on how you count. He died of cancer, miraculously. Five people met violent deaths, one is in federal prison doing life, and one died from cancer. That defies the odds. And you know that pattern is repeated in a lot of these class pictures."

"This is you, pissed off at the Avalon police again, isn't it?"

"It's me, pissed off at them all. Even Mrs. Nancy Haas. She helps but she still hides them."

"Are you crying for anyone in particular?" Jack asked. He fidgeted with his napkin.

"Johnny, Beanie, Ollie, Max. All those people who must have been so terrified and all those left behind."

Vanessa mopped her eyes as her second beer arrived. "And no help in sight. No wonder Denise was such a slut."

"I suppose whoever led Del and Zeke on that final chase was terrified. I wonder if Louise and Troy were terrified in the Santa Cruz Mountains."

Vanessa leaned forward and reached for more of Jack's fries as Jack pulled his plate out of her range.

"So, Jack. I see you're not wearing your wedding ring today. Aren't you afraid that might terrify the locals?"

Jack studied his burger and rubbed his left ring finger. "I'm getting divorced. I mean I got divorced. I tried like hell to save this marriage for five years, but we've been separated for over a year and now the deed is done. I've just started experimenting without the ring."

"No girlfriend?"

Jack gave her a wistful smile. "I've dated a little. Maybe now that things are final I'll feel that I can move on."

Vanessa gave an appreciative grunt. "That doesn't sound like a pleasant parting."

"It wasn't easy, speaking for myself. It didn't seem to bother her very much. My wife—my ex-wife—has a booming career in high tech corporate marketing. She decided I was an underachiever."

"That is so Silicon Valley," Vanessa said. "What about your parents? Do they care that you're a cop?"

"My parents own a couple of dry-cleaning stores. They believe my job is a sign that we're real Americans. Lucky for me, my brother has come through in the income department. He's a corporate lawyer in high tech. They wish I could speak better Chinese. I did the whole Chinese school thing every Saturday, but I wanted to play soccer and baseball. Chinese went in one ear and out the other. I did master the abacus."

Vanessa chuckled. "I live with my parents, believe it or not. I had a relationship with this guy for almost eight years, but he did not want to get married or have kids and I had to call it quits. The house was his, so I moved home for a while. You know how expensive things are and I wanted some time to plan my next move before I decided where to land. Once I'd been there a couple of months I realized my parents had major health struggles that I knew nothing about. They hadn't wanted to worry me because they wanted me to feel free to forge my own way. But if I lose them, I lose everything. We don't have any other family in this country. So I stayed."

Jack shoved his plate back to the middle of the table and offered her two French fries. "Good for you."

14

Marly: The Mind of Winter

December 2000

When Rosie, Louise, and Troy were arrested for Laurie's death on December fifteenth, Marly figured her best Christmas present ever had landed in her lap.

A cold front moved in overnight, and by the time Marly left to pick up Elaine for their regular Sunday study time blended with startup work at the library, a thin layer of ice and snow had blanketed the Springs.

Given the weather, Marly was tempted to stay home, but they had a software delivery deadline by the end of the day. She found the coding challenges of their email security application to be like solving one delightful puzzle after another, but the user-facing parts were tedious and boring. Happily, it turned out that Elaine enjoyed working on those components.

At the top of the hill, a horizontal wind tried to push the car into the right-hand ditch, but Marly made a smooth turn into the Fardigs' driveway, where Elaine waited outside, dancing a bouncy jig.

"Did you hear?" Elaine asked, adding a high-pitched squeal as she climbed into the car. "I can't believe it."

"It was on the news last night," Marly said. She turned the car around and they inched back down the hill. "Plus, our phone has been ringing nonstop."

There wasn't a car in sight, but Elaine leaned toward Marly and whispered as if revealing a major conspiracy. "The police chief called us yesterday. Paul Daniels stopped by too. Louise and Troy are in deeper shit than Rosie. They're accused of my assault in addition to Laurie's death. According to Paul, they told the police that was a misunderstanding and unintentional."

"Fuck that," Marly said. "The only thing unintentional was that they were too stupid to realize they'd be caught."

"Yeah. Rosie's been arrested as an accomplice after or before the fact of whatever in both cases."

"I'm not sure that amounts to much. Plus, I'd bet my laptop that she was there in person."

"Paul says Troy and Louise will get high bail, so they might stay in jail until they go to trial. He thinks they'll get up to ten years, but that may come to about three to five in prison."

"It's a sad day when you have to trust Paul for legal advice. Sounds optimistic to me. What about Rosie?"

"She'll probably get lower bail. Maybe no one will post for her. I can't imagine she has many friends these days. Even worse, she might not get much jail time. Maybe none."

"That sucks. The wheels of justice have a flat tire."

"Mom says that at least this is better than what happened in my dad's case."

Marly pumped the brakes of the old Honda Accord as they approached the base of the hill and hoped she wouldn't smack into a car that had emerged from their right and turned onto the hill road in front of them after ignoring the stop sign.

Some people drive like they own the road.

"Shit," Elaine said. Carl Harris cruised by their bumper in his gold Lexus. Rosie sat in the passenger seat.

Marly's car swerved to a full stop, and both girls swiveled to watch Carl's car disappear up and around the next bend.

"Jeez. That didn't take long," Marly said. She swallowed hard to push down the icy pain that filled her chest. "We're going to get out of this place before long, but meanwhile, we keep up our guard."

"By the way, Mom said to watch out for black ice," Elaine said as Marly put the car in gear.

The next day, Marly and Elaine drove to Andrea's house in Avalon to work on their college applications together. The three compared their choices, proofread one another's essays, and provided moral support, fortified with a steady stream of snacks from Mrs. Melville. Submission dates were closing fast.

"I am not going to wait until the last minute," Andrea said. "I hate being rushed. I want to be able to polish these. Mom wants me to go to Williams, but Middlebury is still my first choice."

"State schools for me," Elaine said. "Probably Albany. I'm just glad I'll be able to graduate and go."

Marly stayed focused on her application for Brown. If it fell through, she had her fingers crossed for Boston University. Her third choice was SUNY Stony Brook, which she figured was the State University of New York school farthest away from Charon Springs.

If she did get in to BU, Brown, or Stony Brook, she would have to figure out how to pay. Applying for financial aid had introduced Marly to a new form of torture, but Helen Fardig had stepped Marly through the daunting process. One more hurdle completed.

Now she was almost done. Marly offered a silent blessing for Mrs. Haas, who had sorted through the forms and reviewed every answer and essay, and offered Marly the use her own credit card to pay for submitting the applications.

One more pass. Marly adjusted another sentence. She held salvation in her hands. She couldn't afford to relax yet.

Marly's brother-in-law, Greg Harris, was released from the county jail two days before Christmas. As holiday presents go, Greg was a mixed blessing.

First and foremost, he was a Harris. Until Marly had started junior high school in Avalon, she hadn't realized that cousins marrying cousins would be considered unusual. She endured many tedious jokes about birth defects and low IQ due to intermarriage, and vowed at thirteen that she would never ever marry anyone from Charon Springs.

Greg was not smart enough, tough enough, or illtempered enough to make a good living as a criminal. He had been picked up numerous times on minor offenses for stupid reasons. Hence his recent sentence spent in the county clink. Marly worried that Charlene allowed herself to be pulled into his schemes.

Marly could feel her shoulders tense every time Greg entered the room. He laughed too much, tickled the children too often, and ate like a convict, hunched over his plate surrounded by his forearms.

In spite of that, Marly couldn't help but like the guy. He seemed devoted to Charlene, adored Alison, and treated Mark and Pammy with cautious affection. He hated Rosie and considered himself to be part of Carl's branch of the family, the lesser of multiple evils in Marly's book. Greg was also a moderate drinker by Harris family standards. He only got drunk a couple of times a month.

He didn't stay long, as it turned out. Greg's mother lived in a double-wide on the road to Avalon, and she was about to head to Florida for the winter. Greg, Charlene, and the kids moved there before New Year's and planned to stay through spring so Mark would be able to finish first grade without changing schools.

Left alone with her mother, Marly wished that they would all move back right away. Without the noise and distractions, Marly's anxiety expanded, unfettered, to fill the drafty old house, lined with the accumulating residue of cigarette smoke, black mold, the stench of half-digested booze, and the ghost of Del in every corner.

After a prolonged flirtation, winter moved in for an extended stay. Marly tried to complete wrapping her mother's house in plastic—a job left unfinished by Del. The plastic kept the house warmer, but looking for any weakness, the bitter winds would often slip in behind her clumsy workmanship and make the plastic snap and rattle, while mysterious drafts of cold air swirled along the floors.

Snow began its steady accumulation. Plows and trucks spread the corrosive mixture of sand and salt, and rumbled up and down the roads, day and night.

Marly decided to live at the library until school restarted, paid or not, and go home only for required meals and sleep. She read books to preschoolers, reorganized the nonfiction section, and worked on her startup, adding more rules and features to protect email users against prying outsiders.

During quiet times, Mrs. Haas would let Marly start a fire in one of the four fireplaces on the first floor of the library. Marly preferred the fireplace in the office, which Mrs. Haas explained had been a parlor for entertaining guests or family when this building had been a private home. Like the main room, the cozy corner space also had matching walnut trim around the doors, windows, and the mantel.

"Did you really live here growing up?" Marly asked, as they sipped tea one afternoon before New Year's.

"From time to time. This house belonged to my great-uncle Henry Judson when I was small. We would stay over at Christmas and Easter."

The comforting growl of a snowplow rattled the windows in their frames. Marly mounted her Christmas gift to Mrs. Haas—a framed print of "The Snow Man," a poem by Wallace Stevens.

"I don't know why you like this poem. 'A heart of winter.' That's what was wrong with Del and all the Harris family. Maybe they caught it from living in this place."

Mrs. Haas held the framed poem while Marly placed the mounting fixture. "That may be so, but that's not what Wallace Stevens meant in 'The Snow Man.' He wrote about the mind of winter, meaning that when you slow down and pay attention, the world is vibrant and beautiful. That's what happens when your chattering self-talk and imposed emotions drop away."

"If you say so." Marly hung the frame on the wall, stepped back to check the alignment, and adjusted the poem so that it hung straight and true.

* * *

Paul Daniels was right. Louise and Troy had to stay in jail after the district attorney asked for a very high bail for each of them. Larry was never going to see the light of day for the murder of Max Redman, the ATF agent, if the reports were true. Rosie showed unexpected self-restraint and stayed out of sight.

Not everyone was thrilled with the turn of events. On the night of December twenty-seventh, Rosie was leaving the pharmacy in Fayetteville's upper village when someone tapped her on the shoulder. She turned and received a full blast of hot coffee in the face followed by several fast body punches. Her assailants remained unidentified.

"Couldn't have happened to a nicer person," Elaine said on their ride to the library. She and Marly snickered into their mittens.

15

Vanessa: Larry

January 31, 2013

Vanessa insisted on taking the backseat of Paul's car for the drive to Pennsylvania to visit Larry Harris in prison. Craving some alone time, she closed her eyes in fake sleep. The snow stopped falling from the sky. Now it flew horizontally, carried by the wind and splashed up from the road as brown slush that coated the windows. She could hear Paul's wipers beat a steady rhythm in between applications of windshield washer fluid, sliding the mushy mixture back and forth across the windshield. Outside, it was a wonderful twelve degrees—above zero.

She opened her eyes in narrow slits from time to time to study the back of Jack's head as he talked to Paul. She had suffered from worse partners over the years. Jack didn't reek from halitosis, cologne, or the lingering stench of cigarettes on his clothes. Visits to his hotel room showed no sign of dirty laundry on the floor. Practical jokes were not part of his repertoire, and he didn't laugh too long or too loud. Best of all, he was competent, smart, and respected her desire to call the shots—most of the time. Refreshing.

"Hey, Vanessa. We're in Binghamton. Not much longer." Paul swiveled around in his seat and turned back to give the windshield another squirt.

Vanessa sat up, studied the leaden sky, and glanced at her watch. She must have fallen asleep.

"It's odd that all these cars are kind of the same color," she said, and yawned.

Paul gave a laugh of appreciation that made his shoulders shake. Jack turned around and grinned.

"That's the salt and sand," Paul said. "You won't see many cars over ten years old either. The salt eats them apart. Anyone with a good car puts it away for the winter because this never lets up."

Thirty minutes later, they rolled through the gates of the federal prison and went inside to sign in. They were shown to an interview room where they met first with the warden, a tall, broad-shouldered man with gray hair and a world-weary squint.

"I'm skeptical that you'll get much help, so don't be disappointed," he said. "Larry's a big guy who only likes white people, and not many of those, either."

"His sentence was twenty-five to life," Jack said. "Does that mean he'll be up for parole soon?"

"He might have gotten out within a year or two, but he killed another inmate about ten years ago. It was a bit unclear as to whether that was self-defense, and that added another five to ten, concurrent. There is the issue of his less-than-stellar attitude. No sign of remorse or change in behavior. I'd like to say he'll go the full twenty-five and die here. But it won't be up to me."

"We can always hope he continues to call this home for a long time," Vanessa said. Some people might be unhappy to see Larry Harris a free man. She wondered what Carl thought of that.

The warden left and the trio waited another twenty minutes for Larry to arrive.

Vanessa wished that Paul would calm down or at least stop pacing the room and popping his finger joints. She caught Jack's attention and tilted her head toward Paul. *Please help,* she signaled.

"Do you remember Larry?" Jack asked Paul.

"Larry. Oh yeah. I remember Larry real well. I was in Del's class. Larry and Louise, they were a couple of years ahead. Everyone said Larry looked just like Zeke, but Del was more like him. Del always told Larry what to do. Del and Larry, they always said Carl was a wimp."

Vanessa looked at Jack and raised her eyebrows to let him know his approach wasn't working.

"Okay, Paul," Jack said. "Sit down over there. You don't need to say anything to Larry. You just drove us here."

"Right. Chip told me to drive you," Paul said. He stayed on his feet and bobbed his head up and down.

They were spared more of Paul's reminiscences when the door opened and a manacled Larry Harris was escorted into the room. Paul sat down with a plop and clamped his mouth shut.

Vanessa had to admit that Larry cut an intimidating figure. He looked like someone had taken Carl Harris and pumped him full of air to add another thirty percent. Larry stood half a head taller than Jack, with a massive barrel chest and broad shoulders. He wore his white hair long and slicked back, with a matching Vandyke beard. The sleeves of a white T-shirt had been rolled up to reveal beefy arms covered in prison tattoos of the racist kind. His eyes may have been listed as blue on his rap sheet, but they were dark and hooded now. Those eyes were fixed on Vanessa as he eased himself into a chair on the far side of the interview table.

"You do have a certain family look, Mr. Harris," Vanessa said. "I would have picked you for a Harris anywhere."

Larry's face remained neutral as he continued to stare at Vanessa. "Hello, Paul."

Paul shuffled his feet and gave a little wave. "'Lo, Larry. Chip asked me to drive these California detectives down to see you because they found the bodies of Louise and Troy."

Larry leaned forward across the table and inhaled deeply. "Ahhh. Nice to smell a woman, even if you aren't white. I don't get that often."

Vanessa kept her game face planted, her eyes on Larry. She gathered that Jack did as well since Larry leaned back in his chair.

"I am Santa Clara County Sheriff's Detective Vanessa Alba and this is Santa Cruz County Sheriff's Detective Jackson Wong," she said, in case Larry wasn't up to speed. "As you've been told by the warden, the bones of your sister and her son were found at the base of a cliff in the Santa Cruz Mountains."

If Larry was upset about his twin sister or nephew, he hid it well as he stared back in stony silence.

Jack picked up the thread. "They may have been killed first or tossed over alive. Either way, it appears that Louise and Troy went over that cliff naked. There was no clothing found and nothing like jewelry or watches. We believe that they went out to do some kind of business and got ambushed. We'd like to figure out what they were doing there and who killed them."

Larry turned his head in a slow, steady rotation, keeping his eyes on Vanessa. "I haven't kept up with events. I don't know why they went out there."

"According to Carl, your mother, Rosie, was about to die when they left town. Are you saying that no one told you that Louise and Troy were headed to California?" Vanessa asked.

"Nope. I'm sort of out of the loop these days. Nobody tells me nothing."

"Somehow I don't quite buy that. Were they going to take care of old foes one last time for Rosie, or did they go on other business?"

Larry cleared his throat in a low growl. "I told you. I don't know why they went. Maybe they went on a vacation."

"That's the story of your life, isn't it, Larry? You're the big muscle but not the one who knows."

Larry scowled. Vanessa was happy she was on the far side of the table next to Jack, with Paul and the prison guard for backup.

Jack spoke up. "You were always happy to be the punisher. You liked that. But you needed help figuring out what to do. You didn't mind taking a few blows. You are tough. Not like Del. Del was soft. A pretty boy. In fact, you wouldn't be here today if it weren't for Del. You're lucky you didn't get the death penalty for killing Max. That was Del's idea, wasn't it?"

Larry blinked and Vanessa caught a glimmer in the hooded eyes.

"You searched the town library after Del disappeared," she said. "Looking for the odd rare volume?"

Larry shifted his eyes her direction.

"Rosie figured Marly was hiding stuff she'd stolen from Del and Zeke," he said.

"What *stuff* would that be?"

Larry shifted his weight to one side and released a noisy fart. "For the record, Del wasn't all that bright. I knew lots of things he didn't. I knew Del was pissed as hell with Marly. He was certain she was going to talk about family business. Like Max. She'd heard talking. Del and Zeke thought Marly needed a lesson and hinted it might be soon. And there's that field and the ravine. If you look on the map, you'll see those are over the hill from Denise's house. Marly and them would have used that route all the time as a shortcut into the village. Marly knew the way across that field and those woods. Tricky places. Odd bogs and quicksand and unmarked paths. She was running for home. I'd lay money on it."

Vanessa stared past Larry at a crack that zigged and zagged down the far wall, like lightning striking Larry's head. She thought of the girl with the determined eyes, trapped and scared.

Larry yawned. His breath would have peeled paint, Vanessa thought.

"And you think she was responsible for their deaths, is that right?"

Larry glared at her. "Rosie figured Marly didn't stand and take it like she deserved. It would have all been over with no fuss. She must've ran."

"Your father fired his gun and shot Del by mistake. Do you think they were just going to beat up the person they were after?"

Larry leaned back in his chair. His grin gave Vanessa goose bumps.

"What exactly were you looking for when you searched the library?" Vanessa asked.

Larry took his time to answer. "Marly was always sneaking around. Her father had shown her lots of places he shouldn't have. Things were missing. We looked in her mother's barn and house. We looked in the library. Nothing. Didn't matter. Rosie was sure."

Vanessa made several mental notes on things to check, while Jack kept the patter going.

"Louise wanted to run things, didn't she, Larry? Rosie had managed to hold on and run the business after your father and your uncle Vernon died. Del was dead. You were gone. Now it should have been Louise's turn, not Carl's. She took Troy to California to prove something—a deal, revenge . . . What was it?"

"I. Don't. Know. But Louise had others who backed her. Not everyone sided with Carl."

"Like who?" Vanessa asked.

Larry grunted and smiled. He leaned toward Vanessa.

"You should figure out who killed my mother. Sure, she was sick, but I'd heard she had months or a year or even more. That chemo was working. Sort of funny that Louise and Troy go missing and she ups and dies a day later, don't you think? Her sister, Diane, was living with her. She's a nurse. She'd know how to kill some-one, quiet-like. She hated the family business. Plus, she and Carl's wife, Betty, are best buddies. That's what you should be looking into."

"Not exactly our jurisdiction, Larry. We're from California, remember?"

"Yeah, but Marly lives in your jurisdiction, remember? The word is that Marly and Carl did a deal. Right after Rosie died."

"What kind of deal?" Jack asked.

"A truce, of course," Larry said with a snarl. "He'd get some of that high tech money. Marly'd get protec-tion, sitting under Carl's wings along with those kids and her sister. No more looking over her shoulder all the time. I hear that as a bonus, her sister Charlene's husband, Greg, will be getting out on parole a few years early. Carl knows how to pull those strings."

Vanessa studied Larry with new appreciation. He

wasn't a dim bulb, as others had described him, and he seemed to have his fingers on some sort of Harris pulse. On the other hand, he showed signs of a significant personality disorder and paranoia that had twisted him into a freakish, amoral monster. How many of his thoughts on Rosie, Carl, and Marly were delusions?

"Do you think Diane killed her sister? Is that what you'd like me to tell Chip Davis?" Vanessa asked.

"Hey. I'd like you to tell Chip that he's a bitch. He should watch his ass. You too, Paul. I'm done," Larry said, and crossed his arms.

By the time they reached the car, Paul's color had returned to his face. He protested, less than thrilled, when Vanessa and Jack insisted on stopping to see Rosie's sister, Diane, on their way back to Avalon. Vanessa called Diane from the car. Diane didn't sound thrilled either.

"She lives at Zeke and Rosie's old place," Paul said. "Carl lets her stay there. Not a nice spot."

The lanes on Route 81 were hard to discern as the snow fell, mixing with the brown slush. Vanessa was glad that Paul was driving as the winter night closed in around them.

Closer to Avalon, they pulled off the highway onto local roads. Vanessa felt claustrophobic, hemmed in by the dense night and flying snow. She tried to follow their progress using GPS, but coverage on her cell phone was spotty.

Paul guided the cruiser through the twists and turns up into the steep hills above Charon Springs. The roads were narrow and rutted, filled with slush. Trees bowed over the roads like ghosts, laden with wet snow on each branch and twig.

This place is a lot creepier than Carl's house, Vanessa thought. They had left their weapons in the trunk while visiting Larry. Now she was glad to have her gun again, tucked under her arm.

On the bright side, Paul wasn't nervous. He was normally a weather vane of caution.

Vanessa leaned forward and tapped Paul on the shoulder. "Tell us about Diane," she said.

Paul obliged, as if she'd pressed a button. Vanessa wondered how much else Paul might tell them if she managed to tap him on the right spot.

"Diane Connor is Rosie's younger sister. Never married. She's a nurse. Much nicer than Rosie. By a long shot. She'd be in her sixties now, I guess. Rosie sucked her into that business with Elaine Fardig. Diane had only driven the car, but that almost got her sent to prison and she lost her nursing license. She moved into Rosie's house while Rosie and them were in prison, and she stayed when Rosie got out. I guess she figured Rosie owed her something. Louise didn't like that much."

"So Rosie left her that place?" Jack asked.

Paul made a humming noise. *Like waiting for the gears to mesh.* "Well, that was a bit muddy. Most people thought it would go to Louise, but it might have also gone to Carl, depending on who ended up running the family."

"Didn't Rosie have a will?" Vanessa asked.

Paul skirted a large pile of drifted snow. "Not all that common with them. Or maybe there was a will and it just got lost."

"But Rosie died, Louise and Troy disappeared, and Carl let Diane stay in the house. Is that how it worked?"

Paul caught Vanessa's eyes in the rearview mirror. "Pretty much, I guess."

"What about all that stuff Larry said about Marly Shaw and Carl? Did they make a truce? Was he saying Diane had killed Rosie?"

"Marly left here years ago and has never come back that I know of," Paul said, his voice soft. "If she had a truce with Carl, she'd come back to visit her mother and her friends. Larry's crazy and it makes him mean—or maybe it's the other way round. Marly is the nicest person in that entire family. She's missed around here."

Paul's eyes met Vanessa's again.

Oh. An ache shot through her heart. Mrs. Haas wasn't Marly's only friend in Charon Springs. *Poor Paul.*

Paul turned his eyes back to the road, maneuvered around one last corner with the easy grace of a man who had grown up driving in this weather, and pulled into a large yard with a faint trace of an unplowed parking area. *Castle Harris.*

This was the compound where Zeke had reigned, like his father before him. This was where crimes were plotted and fates were sealed.

Closer inspection revealed why Carl might have left the place alone. Even in the dark, Vanessa could see that the outbuildings sagged, and tar paper covered large sections of the main house. *No Marlyfication here.*

Rosie's—now Diane's—mudroom was part of the kitchen. A single dim lightbulb overhead revealed a wood subfloor that peeked through the clean but worn linoleum tiles. The cheap kitchen countertops were chipped and stained.

Diane was a surprise. The pictures of Rosie had shown a tall, dark, scrawny woman, with a perpetual glare. Diane was average height and plump with clear blue eyes, a blond-gray pixie cut, and an engaging smile. She had brewed coffee and steered them to the front living room, where she had laid out cookies beside a blazing fire.

The firelight cast a cheery façade over the sad couch and chairs. The seat of Vanessa's chair sagged so low that her knees were higher than her bottom. The best she could say was that the house was clean and orderly.

Jack smiled, presumably to show off his disarming personality, and repeated the story about finding Louise and Troy.

"I'd heard you were here," Diane said.

"You don't sound upset," Jack said.

Diane smiled, but not with her eyes. "I think most of us assumed they were dead. It does give us closure."

"Including ownership of this house?" Vanessa asked.

If Diane was offended, it didn't show. "Carl offered to let me have this place free and clear with about twenty acres. He won't contest it. That's very generous considering the gentrification going on these days. And now there's the fracking. Maybe we'll share in that if it comes to anything."

Jack glanced at the snow hitting the windows and pressed ahead.

"Do you know why Louise and Troy went to California?"

Diane pressed her lips together and frowned. "No. I knew they were on some sort of business, but I stayed out of all that shit, if you'll pardon my language. After I got caught up in the mess with Elaine, I made it clear where my boundaries lay."

"You lost your license to practice as a registered nurse and received twelve months of probation, is that right?"

Diane spoke to her hands, folded on her lap. "I'd spent a lifetime keeping out of Rosie's messes. One night. One goddamn night she asked me to drive her someplace and I lost everything. I lost my house and my savings staying out of jail."

She clenched her hands into fists and then relaxed them. "But I learned to draw my lines. Now I've got my license back. I'm working in DeRuyter and I have this house."

"You looked after Rosie in those last days," Jack said. "Are you certain she didn't say anything about where Louise and Troy had gone?"

Diane looked up. "Betty, Carl's wife, helped with Rosie. She was a nurse too, and she was here the night that Rosie died, so I could go to work. I never asked Rosie about Louise and Troy and she never offered. I know that they would call her at least once a day and sometimes I had to answer the phone. But I never wanted to know. I detested them."

"Rosie was trying to set up Louise to be her successor. Could Louise have been on a mission of revenge?"

"It's hard to believe that revenge alone would be enough to retain control." Diane studied her mug. "Rosie had so many enemies and people she hated. I'm not the expert on that."

"Let's go through a few possibilities," Vanessa said.

Diane set down her mug and turned her palms up, as if in surrender. "I can't even begin."

Jack ticked off the list. "Carl? Judson Harris, Carl's son? Elaine Fardig? Marly Shaw?" He continued with several more names.

Diane raised her shoulders. "Who knows? She complained about all those folks and many more. It's not as if there was one demon."

"You're very different from your sister, aren't you?"

Vanessa said. She struggled to pull herself forward out of the chair, for more coffee.

"I hope so. I also hope I'll have a little bit of money to update a couple of things here. The Harrises were never rich. They were like all of us. This place was a bit better when Zeke was alive. He had a couple of big cars and trucks. He and his sons called all the shots. Everyone was beholden to them. Rosie loved the power and she had a huge chip on her shoulder. She got to act out, but that didn't scratch the itch. It just seemed to make her better at acting out. I saw that. I was eight years younger. I decided to get out. I became a nurse. I lived in Manlius."

"Still . . ." Jack said.

"Ah. This place is like quicksand," Diane said. "It doesn't kill you outright, but it holds on to you until you die of starvation or hypothermia."

"You survived," Vanessa said.

"Oh? I'm still here. Stuck."

Vanessa stopped fighting the chair and leaned back. "Larry thinks Carl and Marly made a deal after you killed Rosie. His belief is that Rosie wouldn't have died for at least another year because the chemo was working. When Louise and Troy didn't call or show up, you saw your opportunity. You're a nurse. You'd know how to take care of things."

Diane laughed. The laugh faded and she put her face in her hands. "Oh shit. If that idiot ever gets out of prison, I'll be dead meat. But he's full of crap. He wants to chase this trail of Del and Zeke and Rosie. She was gravely ill. You can go get her records. I won't stand in your way. She had Stage Four lung cancer. The chemo was working on keeping her alive, but not cured. She was still a drinker and a smoker. She'd started doing heavy pain medications and the chemo was wearing her down. She was very weak. She was just one minor infection or health incident away from death. Her doctors will tell you that and that's what happened. The stress of the illness and the medications caused a heart attack. No one killed her."

"You were here when she died?"

"I had left for my night shift. Betty was here. When I got back, Rosie was asleep and in the morning she was dead."

"Was there an autopsy?"

"The coroner did a basic examination since she died unattended. He agreed."

"Was she cremated?" Jack asked.

"Oh yes."

"What about Marly?" Vanessa asked.

"Marly? I hardly knew her. I've never heard about any deal with Carl. I don't know where Larry gets that notion. She's long gone from this place, lucky stiff."

Vanessa made a final note on her pad and heaved herself up and out of the collapsing chair.

"We need to leave now, Ms. Connor. Thank you for your time and the coffee on this cold night," she said.

Back in the car, Vanessa slumped in the seat, exhausted.

She longed for a glass of wine and a long hot bath and room service.

Vanessa said good-bye to Jack as they passed his door and he slid his card key into the lock. As she opened the door to her room, she saw a sock lying on the floor by the door. She paused, frozen by the sight of something that wasn't right. *What the . . . ?*

She heard a noise over her shoulder and turned. Jack was running toward her, his face pale and gun drawn.

"Vanessa. Wait. Wait. Something's wrong. Don't go in. Someone broke into my room."

Vanessa pulled out her gun as Jack took up position on the opposite side of the doorway, his back to the wall, gun pointed down, ready for action. The two exchanged signals. On the silent count of three, Vanessa kicked the door open and covered Jack as he moved into the room.

Clothes had been pulled from the drawers and the closets. The dresser lay facedown on the rug and the antique desk had lost a leg. The mattress and bedsprings sat upended on the far side of the room. Their search of the bathroom showed that Vanessa's cosmetics and toiletries had been smashed in the sink and bathtub. A faint scent of cigarettes lingered in the room, but the perpetrator was long gone.

16

Vanessa: Farewell to the Empire State

February 1, 2013

Rob, the hotel owner and manager, rushed back from home as soon as he received the call from his night manager, arriving moments after Chip's officers started their examination of the hotel rooms. He quickly took charge of moving Vanessa and Jack to the two nicest rooms in the main building. Free meals and accommodations were theirs for the rest of their stay.

By the time she crawled into her new bed, it was close to two in the morning, and Vanessa was grateful but too tired to care about the gesture. His remorse and concern appeared to be genuine and heartfelt from what Vanessa could tell. Still, who knew how far Carl's tentacles reached, even in lovely Avalon? As best she could tell, most of her belongings were still intact, which was also a blessing since she didn't plan to spend precious time shopping before returning to California.

Still shaken, they were back on the road with Paul after breakfast the next morning, headed to a medium security facility near Lake Ontario, current home to Greg Harris, husband of Charlene Shaw Harris. He would be their last interview.

Paul gave them the background as they rolled down the flat Dewey Thru-y, as Paul called New York State's Thomas E. Dewey Thruway.

"Greg's just a minor player in the Harris family," he said. "His dad was a cousin to Carl and them. He died of a heart attack and Greg moved in with Carl. He started running errands and stuff for Zeke before he graduated from high school. Carl didn't like that, but Zeke always got his way. Greg married Charlene Shaw and they had a baby girl named Alison."

"How did Del take that?" Jack asked. "Denise Harris told us he thought the other kids were his, right? Didn't Charlene's boyfriend Johnny disappear? I'd have been very nervous if I were Greg."

"Oh, Rosie approved of the whole thing, according to my mom," Paul said. He checked his rearview mirrors and gave the windshield another squirt. "It wasn't like Del was ever going to marry Charlene, what with her being his stepdaughter and all. But Rosie liked to keep things tight. In the family."

Vanessa's head gave an involuntary quiver. "Yuck."

"I think Charlene loved Greg," Paul said. "At least until she divorced him. I guess she'd finally had enough. He'd led her astray, doing drugs, selling drugs, making meth. He'd done some small time for minor drug stuff, but then he went to Florida for Vernon, Zeke's brother, a couple of years after Zeke died."

"A drug deal, I assume," Vanessa said.

"Oh yeah. A big one and it went wrong in a big way once he got back. He said that Vernon's son, Elliot, had set him up and then dropped the dime. Elliot was married to Charlene's mother by that time. There was no love lost there."

"Was that true? Did Elliot set up his cousin?" Jack asked.

Paul strummed his fingers on the steering wheel. "It could be, it could be. I'd never trust a Harris as far as I could throw him." He seemed proud of his own wit. "Anyway, Charlene got pulled in trying to help Greg. That was supposed to be after the fact, but I think that was a deal Greg cut with the district attorney so that she'd get less time and he'd get more."

"That was when the kids went to California?" Vanessa asked.

"Yup. All three. Gone."

Greg had the Harris look in a scaled-down way. Just over six feet tall, he had red hair, peppered with white that matched the bushy eyebrows over his green eyes. He was hefty, but more muscular than Larry. Vanessa was pleased to note that his face was relaxed, with an open gaze, thinly disguised under tough posturing.

Jack went through his now-familiar patter about the bones and the DNA as Greg listened.

"Louise and Troy," Greg said. "Tough. Nasty. I was already here when Rosie died and they disappeared. I can't offer much."

"Rosie was trying to set Louise up to take over when she died," Vanessa said. "Were you on board with that? Louise had the chops for it. She was smart and she was willing to make the hard decisions. Not like Carl."

"Del was the brains of the family. When he died there were slim pickings on who could lead. Elliot and Vernon tried for a while and they failed, big time. Louise was an idiot, but it's not like I got a vote. Besides, Carl was the one who took me in after my dad died. No way I'd be a supporter of Louise."

"So you say now," Jack said. "Why do you think Louise and Troy went to California?"

"Keep in mind I'd been in here for close to two years by the time Rosie died. Charlene was in Bedford and she was divorcing me, and the kids were all in California with Marly. No one was telling me anything. I didn't know what was going on. I don't get many visits. Marly makes sure the kids write me every week and send email, and we talk on the phone, but that's not inside information. I did hear that Rosie was sick and that it might be terminal. My complaint was that she didn't die fast enough. I figured Uncle Carl would take over and things would be sane and my kids would be safe."

"How about these days?" Vanessa asked.

"I hear from Betty, Carl's wife, pretty regular, but I don't ask about what Carl's up to. I'm up for parole soon and I'm keeping my nose out of that business. My daughter's fourteen. I might have a chance to know her a little bit."

Vanessa gave a mental squint. *Is this guy for real or is he faking this good attitude stuff?*

"Why did Charlene divorce you?"

"I guess that's kind of obvious. I dragged her into this mess and she did time. Plus, I wasn't a great husband. I didn't protect Mark and Pammy. I liked meth and I could never hold a real job. Who could blame her? Now I'm clean and I'm going to stay that way. I screwed up, but if I'm lucky I'll get out in time to build a different life."

"Marly gave you money, didn't she?" Vanessa asked. "You're under Marlyfication."

Greg let out a guffaw. "Marlyfication. That's good. No money. Yet. Marly is all about positive motivation. If I mind my manners and keep working on my education, I'll have a stake to start again and access for visits."

"It sounds like Marly could be cut from the same cloth as Rosie," Jack said.

"Nah. Marly can be like a dog with a bone, but she has a soft heart. She knows what it's like to miss an imperfect father. She wants me to have a relationship with Alison. Mark and Pammy, too. She's a healer. She builds. Rosie was about control and punishing. 'Forgive and forget' was lost on Rosie. She could never forget an insult, so she could never forgive. No vision, just punishment."

"Who were Louise and Troy sent to punish in California?" Jack asked.

Greg's face hardened and he stared at the table.

"Your cousin Judson? Marly? Elaine Fardig? Your children?"

Vanessa watched Greg's face as Jack recited the list. At first Greg frowned, but his eyes widened at the mention of the children and his mouth drooped.

"I can't see that Rosie would go after Judson," he said. "That would be suicide. Carl wouldn't stand for it. He'd pull out all the stops to get revenge. Still, Rosie wasn't known for being the most rational person on the planet."

"What about Marly or Elaine?"

Greg's frown had the effect of squeezing his eyebrows together to form a long, hairy line. "Rosie did not like Marly, but she'd left town. Rosie was one of those people who have to see their demons to stay focused. And she'd been burned once before when she messed with Elaine. I think she'd learned to leave the Fardigs well enough alone."

"And your kids?"

"Doesn't make much sense either. Mark and Pammy

are Carl's step-grandchildren. She'd be courting major hurt if she touched them. Besides, going after children would be weak. I can't see how that would help her set up Louise to take over."

As they got ready to leave, Greg offered one parting remark. "You know what surprised me is that nothing happened to Carl. I was worried for him."

"You mean that Rosie planned to have Carl killed?" Jack asked.

"It might seem far-fetched, even for them, but if Rosie wanted to leave Louise in control, Carl would be the biggest obstacle."

Back on the Thruway, Jack and Vanessa went over their notes. "I'm glad we touched all the bases, but I don't see that we learned much," Jack said.

Dusk settled in as a heavy snowfall picked up just short of Syracuse. For all his shortcomings, Paul was a steady driver. Vanessa dozed as they rolled along the flat darkness and didn't rouse until they passed through the lights of the tollbooth and headed for the twisting road up to the Avalon ridge.

"That truck has been following us for a long time," Jack said, looking over his shoulder.

Vanessa sat up straight, wide-awake. Paul was studying the rearview mirror more than the road ahead. Jack fumbled under his coat for his gun.

Vanessa looked out the back, but all she could see were the lights of a large vehicle, close behind. Very close. As she turned back to face front, the truck's high beams flipped on, along with a row of bright lights on the roof of the cab, flooding the inside of their car with light.

"How long has he been there?"

"Since the other side of Syracuse, as best I could tell," Paul said. He shot another look in the rearview mirror and kept both hands visible on the wheel. "Maybe before that, but since the last Syracuse exit there's been no traffic. I couldn't get him to pass me and I couldn't pull away."

Vanessa reached under her armpit for her service revolver, grateful that she had removed it from the trunk when they left the prison.

"Should we call it in on the radio?" Jack asked.

Paul's head turned back and forth in a very slow, minimal move. "No. Don't reach for that. If those folks are up to no good, they may have a radio with police band. We'll be in Avalon in about fifteen minutes."

"I'm going to duck down a bit and call Chip on my cell phone," Vanessa said.

"Keep that hidden. Tell him we're on the river road."

Vanessa placed the phone in her lap and hit the speaker function after she dialed the Avalon Police Department number.

An officer she'd met once picked up. She wasted no time and explained their situation and relayed Paul's information.

"Tell Paul to keep driving. We're on our way. I'll tell Chip," he said.

The truck edged forward, riding their bumper, mere inches away, from what Vanessa could determine.

"Should you pull over?" Jack asked.

"Not a chance," Paul said. "There's no shoulder and those snowdrifts on either side are very high. I'm going to hog the road and go slow. This cruiser is big. He won't be able to pass or force us off the road. If he pushed us hard enough to turn us sideways, we'd block the road and he'd be trapped behind us."

"What if they have someone waiting up ahead to cut us off? They could force us to stop," Vanessa said, hoping her voice sounded firm.

"All the more reason to go slow and steady," Paul said. "Keep your weapons handy."

Vanessa had to hand it to Paul. He was jumpy about silly things, but when the situation looked serious, he was focused.

Time seemed to crawl slower than the pace of Paul's car, but after ten long minutes the two vehicles reached a high, straight section of road. A flash of blue lights bobbed in the distance. Moments later, the truck made a sharp right and veered away down a side road.

Chip jumped out of one of the two parked cruisers as Paul skidded to a stop. Vanessa felt a flash of concern for Chip, planted in the way of Paul's slipstream, but Paul deftly landed his car facing across the road.

Paul rolled down his window.

"Well, well," Chip said. "Glad to see you're all here and intact."

"As usual, not much concrete to go on," Chip said. His face was flushed and his eyes had lost their characteristic twinkle. "I'm glad you're leaving tomorrow. It seems that someone has decided you're a threat. I can't promise we can always be able to help."

Vanessa's body tingled as she tried to push away her anger. "Don't you think you should send out a couple of cars to track down that truck?"

Chip snapped back. "Welcome to my little corner of hell, Detective Alba. I'll call the county sheriff, but I don't have the resources to look under every snowflake."

"You know that Carl had to be behind this, right?

And at the hotel? And on the road from Charon Springs? Are there other Harris factions we don't know about?"

"You're a cop, Detective. I can't just go and arrest Carl. He doesn't even own a truck. If I could bring Carl to heel, I'd be man of the year around here." Chip's mouth was pressed into a grim line.

"He's protecting someone."

"Brilliant deduction."

"Isn't that kind of an odd way to show his affection? Doesn't he realize that we now know we're getting close to someone?"

Chip's eyes brightened and his voice regained its cheerful volume. "Detective Alba, I have learned to never overestimate the intelligence of the Harris crowd. Which doesn't make them any less dangerous."

"What about Marly Shaw?" Jack asked. "She's smart. Would Carl protect her?"

Chip rocked back on his heels and considered Jack.

"Marly's not a Harris. And she's been gone a long time. Long before my time in office. In my opinion, the connection is very tenuous and doesn't seem likely. You two should go get dinner and a good night's sleep. We'll keep looking, but don't expect much. Paul and I will come by to see you off tomorrow morning."

Vanessa and Jack retreated to the hotel, where they raided the minibar in Jack's room several times before they calmed down enough for dinner.

"Ready to go home tomorrow?" Jack asked. They had turned down Rob's offer of a more elegant meal and planned to go back to their preferred Italian place.

"There is a lot more buried. That's clear. It's like unraveling a sweater by pulling on one string. Still, I don't know that we can get more for our case here. I have to say that I am also looking forward to leaving this kind of winter behind."

"Yeah, it's official. We're weather wimps," Jack said. "But when it comes to Louise and Troy, it feels like a lot of heat but not much light."

"That bugs the hell out of me. Let's face it. The crap here is neck deep when it comes to the Harrises, but we aren't going to solve any of that or get any closer on our case by staying in New York. The only one who might know is Carl, and he'd never talk. My boss is also having the team run down the cell phone calls for the time Louise and Troy were in California and checking on Judson Harris. We may get some more information from that."

"Gut feel?"

Vanessa tossed back the last of her minibar vodka. "Nothing good. But there are several people in California whom I'm looking forward to meeting."

17

Marly: Breakout

January–August 2001

The aftermath of the 2000 presidential election provided a welcome distraction from Marly's self-absorbed obsession with staying alive. Charon Springs was a bright red Republican dimple in a very conservative district, even though most of the state voted for Al Gore. Marly dabbled in basic statistics, calculating odds, sampling the election data, and became a news junkie. She didn't have much of an opinion on the aftermath of Bush versus Gore, but she was grateful for the distraction.

At last, all was settled. From her perch on the second floor of the library, Marly monitored the impromptu inaugural party for George W. Bush at the Rock despite wretched January weather. A fight spilled out into the parking lot.

By the next election she'd be able to vote. She crossed her fingers and prayed she would be registered somewhere far from Charon Springs.

January exerted an eerie pall that frayed her nerves and kept her looking over her shoulder for Del. The intense cold combined with wood smoke and exhaust emissions to create a hazy fog that sank to the bottom of the valley and kept everyone huddled indoors. Key Harris family members had been arrested, but their presence still haunted each stretch of vacant road and silent woodlot.

Marly followed Machiavelli's advice: Keep your friends close and your enemies closer. She raised no objections when her mother smoked inside the house. She made her mother gin and orange juice cocktails. Through gritted teeth, she called her mother "Mom" and—once or twice—"Mommy."

Won over by the charm offensive, Denise reported on Harris family activities to her newfound confidant. Rosie might have been confined to her home, but she was still very much a player, plotting to take control.

"She'd like to be the one in charge, one hundred percent," Denise said over dinner. "There's no way that will happen. She's only a Harris by marriage, you know. Besides, if she goes to prison for a bit, she won't be here to defend her territory."

Marly noted she should plan to be long gone before the next battle broke out. No matter who won, peasants like her always got the short end of the stick.

The new regime change also meant that Vernon's son, Elliot, was elevated to do most of the actual work since Vernon was confined to his wheelchair. That wouldn't have been so bad except that by the end of January, Elliot showed up at their house to court Denise.

After their third date, Marly cornered her mother over breakfast. The best time to talk to Denise was when she was sober but hungover.

"Mom, he's another Harris. And he's still your cousin."

"Well, so what? What do you expect me to do? I'm

thirty-seven. I need someone to look after me," her mother said. "And don't go saying, 'you need to look after yourself.' How could I do that? Your father got me pregnant when I was fifteen with Charlene and then you came along. I didn't finish high school. I couldn't go to college. Rosie isn't giving me any more money and my job pays shit."

"You built that cage yourself."

"Don't you lecture me, kiddo. Wait until you're my age and then we'll see what kind of cages you've made for yourself." Denise pushed back from the table and stalked to her usual perch in the living room.

By April, Elliot had moved in. His diabetes medications, syringes, and equipment filled the bathroom cabinets, including the downstairs lavatory. Marly moved her personal items and makeup to her bedroom.

Despite his reputation as a brutal enforcer for the Harris clan, Elliot was a significant improvement over Del in most regards. Due to his diabetes, he confined his drinking to outings with buddies at the Rock. He didn't seem inclined to try to get Marly into bed.

Elliot treated Denise to flowers and took her out to dinner on Valentine's Day. He bought Denise a better secondhand car.

What is the attraction? Yes, her mother was still pretty in a simpering kind of way, but she brought no assets to the relationship. Perhaps Elliot felt that he had to prove he was capable of filling Del's shoes in every possible way.

Despite her nerves and perhaps due to Elliot's presence, winter and spring passed with no new threats or run-ins with the Harris crowd. Marly's life wasn't exactly without its ups and downs, but at least it seemed like what a normal life might be like.

* * *

Even with Elaine out of the running for valedictorian, Marly's competition was stiff. She usually relied on her grades in math and sciences to stay ahead, compensating for slightly lower grades in English and writing-intensive courses. To her astonishment, Elaine's mother, Helen, stepped in to look over Marly's written homework, which helped close the gap. Marly could never remember Denise ever asking about school beyond the basic disciplinary and attendance issues. It never occurred to her to look to an adult for help with homework.

After a respectable basketball season—second place in the regional finals—Marly looked forward to a break from intensive extracurricular activities, but was quickly swept up into the spring play, *Our Town*. Charon Springs bore no resemblance to Thornton Wilder's idyllic setting, but her ability to memorize lines quickly earned her a leading role and an invitation to the senior prom from Sam, the leading man.

Sam was an Avalon boy. Marly knew his upper middle class family didn't approve, but he was attentive and sweet until another girl from Avalon caught his eye.

All the while, the startup continued to grow. Even though she was theoretically just a part-time employee, the demands on her time kept expanding. She considered quitting on a daily basis. The best decision she had ever made was pulling in Elaine, who had a cool head and more than pulled her weight when it came to staying on top of conflicting demands.

A tense, unrelenting, underground current continued to flow. Marly remained watchful and vigilant, counting down the days to the end of July when she would turn eighteen and blast off, college or not.

Over the course of one week in April, three thick envelopes arrived addressed to Marly, each one offering her freedom, escape, and education. The last envelope came from Brown University.

She blinked and rubbed her eyes to clear away her tears. Despite the pouring rain, she rushed outside and performed an ecstatic dance in their muddy parking area.

Back inside, Marly studied the financial aid package from Brown. It was generous but wouldn't pick up the entire tab. Even a part-time job wouldn't take her far. She would need additional resources.

Over her mother's objections, she accepted Brown. Her new challenge was to figure out how she would move money from her stolen treasure, hidden in the Melvilles' barn, to new accounts she could access. Perhaps one or two of the identities she had swiped could help, but she was in unchartered territory.

Sometimes when the Melvilles weren't home, she would sneak into their barn to count and recount her small fortune. An imaginary spreadsheet filled with opportunities that spelled escape. The routine exerted a hypnotic spell, releasing her anxieties so her mind could relax and regain a footing in logic and reason. *All will be well. Stay focused. Be careful. All will be well.*

In early May, winter finally loosened its grip on Charon Springs and warm breezes filtered down into the valley. Buoyed by the sunshine, Marly hopped on her bicycle and outraced the clouds of black flies to the library for her Saturday afternoon shift.

Mrs. Haas looked up and broke into a grin as Marly burst through the front door.

"I haven't seen you smile like that for months, Marly."

"It's like the spring has unfrozen my brain. Mrs. Haas, I need help. I need a student loan and I don't even know how to get to square one. Please."

"You sit and get settled. I'm going to get some iced tea first. This is going to take a while."

As Marly pedaled home for dinner, she ran through the calculations in her head. If she played her cards carefully, she would soon have the flexibility to make use of what she thought of as Del's Dough.

One final obstacle remained—Denise. Once Denise found out about the loan, she would want a piece of that action. Marly would have to swallow her pride and ask for help. Legal help.

Bob Melville had a beautiful law office in Syracuse, but he also had a small office in his house, which is where Andrea cornered him the following weekend, pulling a reluctant Marly with her.

"Tell him," Andrea said.

"I won't be eighteen until the end of July, but I've got money coming in from my student loan, plus our startup is doing better," Marly said as she swayed from foot to foot. "I need to put that someplace where my mother can't get to it so I can send checks to Brown. She already drained my account once last year. I can't kick her off my current account or set up a new one."

Mr. Melville studied her. "We need to have you declared an emancipated minor. It's straightforward. Let's start the paperwork."

Marly said nothing to Denise or Elliot. Despite assurances and advice from Mr. Melville, she hoped that she might be able to fly under the radar on this one.

Her luck ran out several weeks later.

* * *

Marly knew something was brewing by the way her mother was slamming pots around in the kitchen. Her mother never cooked.

"Is something wrong?" Marly asked.

"You want to be emancipated? You can just emancipate yourself right out of this house, young lady."

"I need to have a separate bank account for school. There will be a lot of money there for a very short period of time that needs to go straight to Brown."

"You don't need to have a separate account for that. If it's in a separate account, I can't help you manage your money."

"You managed me right out of two thousand dollars last fall. I can't afford that kind of help anymore."

"You owed me that. Raising kids takes money. And you should trust me. This looks terrible. I'm your mother!" Denise's voice had risen to a shrill shriek.

Marly rubbed her face with both hands. Fights with her mother were so illogical. Every time she backed Denise into a corner, her mother ran off with the argument in another direction and Marly ran right with her, down into the next rabbit hole.

"You seem to forget that I did trust you and you took all my college money." Marly tried to keep her voice level and not succumb to her mother's tantrum, but it was a losing battle. "If I go to college, I'll be able to give you much more over time. I need that money now. Besides, no one will know, if you keep your voice down and don't kick me out of the house."

"You should be sharing with me."

"That money is all spoken for."

"I need some for my wedding."

"Your what?" Marly felt as though someone had thrown cold water on her face.

"Me and Elliot are getting married."

"You can't marry him. You shouldn't marry him. It's too soon after Del."

"Since when did you ever give a fuck about Del?"

"You and Elliot are cousins. That's illegal."

"Elliot looked it up. We're second cousins once removed and that's not illegal in New York. So there, missy. We're getting married on August twelfth, and right after, we're going on a honeymoon to New York City."

"For how long?"

"For how long what?"

"How long will you be gone? You know I have to leave for college just a few days after that."

"Oh. Well, if you're so smart that you can go to a fancy college, you can figure that out for yourself, Miss Emancipation Proclamation!" Denise turned her back on her daughter. The conversation was over.

Marly stomped from the room, half hoping she would be kicked out. The argument had ended in a draw. Marly retained control of her money, and Denise retained the right to marry Elliot.

Denise stayed away for Marly's graduation, despite the fact that her younger daughter would be the first in their immediate family to finish high school. The term "valedictorian" didn't register with Denise, and it didn't seem to matter that Marly would be giving a speech.

Alone again, as usual, grumbled Marly to herself on graduation day as she stood to present her upbeat and forgettable thoughts about high school and the future. That was when she saw Charlene and the kids

plus Mrs. Haas, standing at the back. Helen Fardig
gave an encouraging wave and the Melvilles signaled
with a thumbs-up. Her favorite faculty members preened,
congratulating themselves. Marly cleared her throat
to speak.

Elliot and Denise were married in the United Church
on August twelfth, followed by a sedate party at Carl's
house, sans Rosie, who had decamped in July for a
two-to-three-year stint in prison following her plea bargain for the attacks on Elaine and Laurie.

Marly gave her mother and Elliot $200 cash as a
wedding present for their honeymoon. It was Harris
money, after all.

On the hot and steamy day before departure, Marly
looked up from her packing to see Carl Harris enter the
living room from the front door, off the covered porch.
No one used that door except Carl and he never knocked.

Carl scanned the grimy living room. "Your mother
and Elliot are still on their honeymoon I guess."

"Yes. That's right."

"I do like you, Marly, but having you here is not
good for the family. I want you to stay away. Rosie,
Louise, and Troy are in prison now, but they'll be back.
We can't afford any more stupid viciousness."

"So solve that with them." Marly edged her way toward the kitchen.

"Stand still and pay attention, Marly. That's not the
way it's going to work. You can stop by for a few days
now and again, but don't plant roots here. Stay up in
Syracuse with Charlene if you need to."

"But you mean I can't even visit?"

"No buts." Carl's voice was flat as he fixed her with an emotionless stare. "Get out and stay away until you hear that they're all dead. I wouldn't count on that being anytime soon."

Marly stared back. Carl pointed a finger at her. "Just do it," he said, and he turned to leave.

18

Vanessa: Loose Ends

February 2–4, 2013

A driving rain in forty-five-degree weather welcomed Jack and Vanessa to San Jose Airport. Their argument on transportation continued down to the luggage area.

"Vanessa, it's pouring. My car is in long-term parking. Let me give you a ride home."

Vanessa relented. She could have caught a cab and been home in twenty minutes. Instead they waited fifteen minutes for the long-term parking bus, bounced on their seats for another fifteen minutes as the vehicle snaked its way up and down the aisles in the parking lot, got soaked walking to Jack's car, waited ten minutes to pay and leave the parking lot, and at last headed to the highway for the short ride to Mountain View.

What's wrong with this picture? Vanessa studied Jack's profile outlined against the rain-streaked driver's-side window.

Vanessa had alerted her parents via cell phone, and they were waiting at the door as Jack pulled into the driveway.

"*Ay, hijita,*" her mother said, wrapping her arms around Vanessa. "*Cuanto te echaba de menos.*"

"I missed you too, Mom." Vanessa answered in English for Jack's benefit. "New York was beautiful but I don't think you would have liked the weather. This is my colleague, Detective Jack Wong."

"Do you speak Spanish, Detective Wong?" asked her father as they shook hands.

"*Un poquito,*" Jack said, holding the tips of his thumb and index fingers almost touching. "Please call me Jack." He turned to leave. "I'll see you on Monday, Vanessa."

Before Vanessa could wave her farewells, her mother jumped in. "Oh, you come here on Tuesday night. Always family night with good Colombian food on Tuesday night."

Jack shot a nervous glance at Vanessa. "Thank you so much. I'll—uh—see if that could work out."

"You should let him know that it's okay to come on Tuesday," Vanessa's father said as Jack pulled away.

"Dad, he is not my boyfriend. He lives way over in Santa Cruz somewhere. We aren't dating. He is a colleague."

"*Un colega muy simpático,*" her father said.

Vanessa agreed. *A very nice colleague indeed.*

Monday morning Nick greeted Jack and Vanessa with a knowing grin. "Frostbite anyone? I've loved your reports, Nessa. They made me glad I live in the free state of California."

"Do you get back home often, sir?" Jack asked.

"Only during the summer month."

"Yes, sir." Jack's face was expressionless.

"Month. As in July. It's a local joke, Jack. Clearly

you didn't spend enough time there." Nick bent over his desk to dig through the stacks of papers. Jack snuck Vanessa a sideways glance and a wink.

Nick handed a stack of paper to Vanessa. "We have some interesting news on the cell phone records. We've been able to pinpoint where Louise and Troy made most of their calls while they were here."

Vanessa reached for the reports and handed over the pages to Jack after she had glanced through them. She stopped at a printout of a map with a helpful X in the middle.

"What you'll see is that they made a lot of their calls to the phone number for a Rosalind Harris in New York from that location in the Santa Cruz Mountains. The property belonged to a woman named Angela Rodriguez at the time. It looks like there's a cabin at that spot."

Vanessa rotated the map to get a better fix on the location, to no avail.

"Even better," Nick said. "The cliff where Louise and Troy went over? That's owned by Miguel Rodriguez. Not our lovely heroine, Angela, but there is a Miguel Rodriguez who now owns the place with the cabin. But the best thing? Angela had some bad times twenty-odd years ago. She went East and tried her fortunes there. Things didn't go so good, and about fourteen years ago, she found herself in prison, for criminal assault and selling meth. After her release, she came home. Lucky us."

Vanessa pawed through the pages. "She was Louise's cellmate!"

"Bingo!" Nick said, lifting his palms up with a flourish, as if to ask for applause. "I'm sure you'll have some fun digging into that."

*   *   *

Vanessa stared out the car window at the steep red clay banks that lined their twisted route up into the dripping redwood forest.

"This is rather refreshing compared to slush and ice," she said. "Do you know where we're going?"

Jack squinted at a faded road sign that had somehow folded itself in half. "More or less. The GPS keeps cutting in and out, so keep an eye on that good old-fashioned map."

After several more false turns down one-lane roads, they located the steep driveway that led to their destination—a double-wide tucked under the redwoods overlooking a rushing creek. Vanessa felt as though she had driven to the bottom of a deep well.

The double-wide had seen better days, but sported a coat of fresh paint. A grayed redwood deck wrapped around the outside and provided below-ground accommodation for several large dogs of varying mixtures, who rushed toward the car, barking.

"Their tails are wagging," Jack said.

"Their ears are back." Vanessa made eye contact with the largest mutt, whose nose bobbed outside her window. She kept her seat belt buckled.

She caught a movement from the direction of the creek bed. First a blond head and then the body of a man appeared as he climbed up to the level parking area. He clapped his hands twice and the dogs stopped barking and sat down.

"Maybe we're lunch," Vanessa said, but she followed Jack's lead and climbed out of the car.

Jack flashed his badge. "Miguel Rodriguez?"

"Mike," said the giant.

He looks tame enough. Mike had cultivated the mountain man look from the sixties and seventies. He had to be close to six foot three in his stocking feet. Under his hoodie and jeans he had a physique that looked suited for a TV wrestling career.

Closer inspection showed that he was a bit too old for those possibilities. Vanessa took him to be about forty-five, maybe a bit older. But he was good-looking, no doubt about it. His skin looked clear, his eyes were bright blue, and his blond hair, laced with a few white strands, was thick and long, pulled back into a pony-tail.

Mike returned her appreciative look. "How can I help?"

He waved them up onto the porch and into the house, which to Vanessa's surprise was clean, odor-free, and bright, despite the looming trees.

No mudroom, of course. This was California. They stepped directly into the living room.

Vanessa let Jack take the lead after basic introductions.

The syncopated rhythm of raindrops splatting on the roof followed the story she had come to know so well, which allowed her to study Mike. If Mike was growing pot, he didn't seem worried, keeping in mind that he could have crushed them both with one hand and tossed them to the dogs.

"You mean those bones I heard about a couple of months ago? That was on my property?" Mike jerked his thumb to point up and west, looking more intrigued than alarmed. "I'll be damned."

"It took us a while to track down the ownership of that property, Mr. Rodriguez."

"Hey. No problem," Mike said. "I tend to forget I own it except at tax season. Once upon a time, that was a real road and a busy track to the main ridge road for the farms and ranches up that way. But most of those properties were acquired by Open Space or some other park, or turned into smaller lots or big vineyards, and the ridge roads got broken up. We own that narrow piece along the old road. Not good for much. I'm hoping I'll sell it someday for the view to some Silicon Valley billionaire and retire in style." He frowned. "So who were those people?"

Jack consulted his pad. "That's where we were hoping you could help. Or rather, your sister, Angela. We used DNA to trace the remains to Louise and Troy Rasmussen, mother and son. Louise Rasmussen was a cellmate of your sister's."

Mike's face darkened. "Yeah. I remember those two. Mother and son, my foot. More like demon and spawn. They came here about four years ago and stayed for a while."

"You didn't like them?"

"Nasty. Always looking to pick a fight—both of them. Troy was a bit taller and a lot heavier than me, but not very fast or smart. He did what Louise said. She was pretty big too, for a woman. Most nights, they stayed in a van they'd rented. Sometimes they'd visit Angela and they'd eat together. Angela lived in a little place just over that bridge there." He cocked his head toward the creek.

"How long did they stay?" Jack asked.

Mike puffed his lips, thinking. "Hard to recall. I'd say a week. Maybe ten days. I know it was mid-June when I finally ran them off. Troy killed one of my dogs. Knife. Just for the fun of it, as best I could tell. Goddamn asshole used a stun gun on me. That was how they managed to get away."

Vanessa leaned forward. "Could they have camped out along that cliff after that?" she asked.

"Yeah. That's possible. I hardly ever go out that way, and there aren't any neighbors up there."

"What about Angela? Would she have taken stuff to them? Could we talk to her?" Jack pointed his chin toward the little bridge over the creek.

Mike smiled. "Sorry. You just missed her."

"Will she be back soon?"

"No," Mike said. He pointed to an urn on a chipped and dented end table. "She died just before Christmas. She'd had hepatitis C for a long time and a couple of years ago she got liver cancer. Of course she'd already gone through a lifetime of hard living, so in some ways I was amazed she lasted almost two years."

"What did she tell you about Troy and Louise? Did they say why they were here?"

Mike stared out the window, as if visualizing the past. "They said they were here to see California. But they didn't do much sightseeing as far as I could tell, at least while they were here. They'd leave and go someplace and come back and not talk about where they'd been or what they'd seen."

"You said they had a van?" Vanessa asked.

"They had some sort of panel truck—the kind with no windows. I think it was green. Sorry. It didn't look new, but they said they'd rented it. They'd bought all sorts of stuff, like at a Home Depot. A chain saw, a little battery-operated cross saw. Lots of other things. Plus camping stuff like air mattresses and sleeping bags. Kind of creepy, now that I think about it. Well, I thought it was creepy at the time, but now it seems creepier."

Jack studied his pad. "Why do you think they were here? A drug deal? Some other business?"

Mike lifted his hands. "Louise glared most of the

time. Not a big talker except when she wanted something. At first she thought I was like Troy, but when she found she couldn't push me around, she avoided me. One night, Troy told me that Louise's mother was dying and they were going to take care of loose ends for his grandmother."

"Loose ends?" Vanessa asked.

"Yeah," Mike said. "That did make me curious, but the next day he started teasing Red, my best dog, and while I was out on an errand, he killed her, so we didn't have any more conversations." Mike turned his attention to outside the window where his dogs snoozed on the deck.

"Can you account for your whereabouts on June fourteenth through the seventeenth?" Jack asked.

Mike checked his phone. "Sure. I went on a fishing trip up in the Sierras, right after I kicked those two idiots out. I was gone for two weeks. You want the names of my buddies?"

"That would be a good idea."

Jack and Vanessa stood. They handed Mike cards with their information. Mike gave them a list of his fishing friends, the fishing camp location, and the dates of his trip.

Outside, the dogs rose to say good-bye. Vanessa held out the back of her hand to the largest one, who sniffed and gave it a lick, just as another put his nose to her butt and wagged his tail. She jumped.

Mike opened her car door and smiled. "Come back anytime," he said with a wink.

"Quite a conquest," Jack said as they pulled away. "How much pot do you think he grows?"

"He is quite nice-looking," Vanessa said. *Do I detect a whiff of jealousy?* "And he's a citizen—not a single arrest."

Jack ignored her. "Hmm. Who do we know that would rent vans? For cash?"

"I'll ask around. Nick will know. It's worth a check, but we're not likely to get much love and assistance from that corner. I think it's time to interview the loose ends."

19

Marly: California-Bound

October 2007–June 2008

In the autumn of 2007, the curse of Charon Springs reached out to suck Marly back into its vile orbit. Her worst fears bore fruit. Charlene and Greg were arrested as part of a drug deal that had gone upside down. The only good news was that no one had been shot or killed in the process.

Greg quickly cut a deal in hopes of sparing Charlene and he was serving a hefty prison sentence. Out on bail pending final resolution of her case, Charlene hovered for months as the judicial process ground through her life.

Andrea Melville, in the middle of law school, worked long hours with her father on Charlene's behalf. Half of Marly's life seem consumed with daily tearful phone calls from Charlene and Denise, and very matter-of-fact advice from Andrea and her father.

"We're doing our best, Marly, but Charlene is going to have to do some time," Andrea said in a call just after the New Year. "I think we can cut a deal for three years in medium or minimum security. Keep in mind, that could be much less if she stays out of trouble inside. You need to convince Charlene that this is going to be her best deal. Going to trial will not end well."

"I'll try again," Marly said. "Charlene is a very emotional thinker. She's just not rational about her options unless she has no choice."

"She has no choice, Marly. She just doesn't realize that."

"Are the kids doing okay? I call but they don't say much."

"They need a plan too. Charlene seems to think your mother will take care of them."

"She might as well leave them in the woods to live off of nuts and berries."

"Are you ready to step in as a mother?" Andrea asked.

"I sort of thought I already had."

Charlene continued to work through her denial phase until March. Hammered by Marly and Andrea, she called a truce and agreed to the plea deal.

"Will you take the kids, Marly?" she asked on a tearful phone call. Ever the optimist, she added, "There's a good chance I'll be out in a year or even less. It won't be for very long."

"Of course I'll take them. But it won't be for just a year. They need stability and security. We need to come to a permanent solution for them going forward."

"I guess I could ask Mom. But you know she would be a disaster. Since Elliot up and died so suddenly, she's been drinking and wandering around at night, sometimes stark naked. She might have died from hypothermia a couple of weeks ago if Paul hadn't found her when he was on patrol."

"I've tried to talk to her, Charlene, but she hangs up on me."

"You need to reason with her face-to-face. And you need to take charge of my kids before Rosie does."

"Rosie! Why would she want to take on raising three children?"

"Not for any good reason I can think of. But she's so insistent and I'm so frantic that she's wearing me down. Ever since she got out of prison, she has been hovering like a vulture. She keeps saying that Aunt Louise and Cousin Troy will be on hand to help her out with discipline and child-rearing. You've got to help."

"Shit." Marly hung up and booked her flight.

The Springs hadn't changed a bit and was still over-populated with the Harris family and their ilk. Marly kept a sharp eye out for Rosie and Louise at every turn.

"Things have changed. Charlene shouldn't worry about Rosie. She's got bigger fish to fry now," Denise said, keeping a firm grip on her breakfast orange juice and gin that Marly tried to pry away. "She's got cancer. Lung cancer. Not the right time to take on a bunch of teenagers."

"No kidding. You think?" Marly tried to spoon-feed some scrambled eggs into her mother's mouth.

"She's up in Syracuse at St. Joseph's and Louise is staying in Liverpool with a friend to be closer until they can bring Rosie home. She might die, you know."

"Yeah, I know." *The sooner the better*.

"I can take care of the kids now."

"Mom, I think it's time for you to have a break from looking after family. Let me take care of this."

With Rosie and Louise occupied elsewhere with their own problems, Marly focused on the tasks at hand.

Within the week, Bob and Andrea Melville started the process for Marly to become legal guardian of Mark, Pammy, and Alison. Marly recruited Mrs. Haas to help find a nurse's aide with a strong stomach and tenacious temperament to provide live-in care for Denise.

Marly wrenched herself away several weeks later, praying that nothing more would erupt while she took on her next challenge. There was no way she could live with three children in her studio apartment.

Fortunately, she was somewhat optimistic that she could afford an upgrade. She and Elaine had forged their second startup in the furnace of Silicon Valley as Stanford grad students. Joining the long list of entrepreneurs nurtured—or tortured—into successful businesses, their security company had been much more successful than their first. Although not extraordinary compared to many of their fellow strivers, Marly and Elaine had done well enough with their second acquisition.

Perhaps well enough to afford a house that could hold three children and one struggling adult.

Helen Fardig convinced Marly that she had to give up plans to live in Palo Alto or Los Altos. She needed to look for less pricy properties in places like Mountain View, which is where Helen and Elaine had houses.

As usual, Helen came through with a place that was big enough and needed minimal work, not far from her own house.

By the time Charlene started her prison sentence in June, Denise's behavior had stabilized. Marly flew back to shepherd her new charges to California.

She tried not to be resentful. She loved Charlene's kids, but she wanted her own life. Getting them settled in meant she couldn't go to England for the summer, as originally planned.

She feared this would mean the end of her long-distance romance with Tony Rochford. Their relationship had blossomed when she spent a semester during her junior year at Cambridge, where he was a medical student.

They each dated other people but kept drifting back together, sustained by semi-regular visits.

Marly marveled that Tony was willing to sustain his feelings with so little nurturing from her side. What did he see in her anyway? Even the best seeds need watering.

And now she needed to call him and explain that her summer trip was simply not going to happen. She was positive this would mean the end. Even if she could sneak away from time to time, she was going to be saddled with three children for the foreseeable future. Who would want to sign up for that?

20

Vanessa: Sacramento

February 6, 2013

"**M**an, your mother can cook up a storm," Jack said. They were heading out to Sacramento to meet Carl Harris's son Judson. "What did you call that rice dish?"

"Um—*arroz con lentejas y coco,*" Vanessa said, trying to stay focused on the highway, slick with rain and clogged with traffic. "Rice with lentils and coconut. I'll tell her you liked it. They were very impressed with your Spanish."

"Ugh."

"Jack, you did great. Your accent was very solid and you handled basic stuff well. Now, please let me handle the traffic."

Jack obliged and stayed silent until the onslaught of cars had diminished.

"You know, it's kind of ironic that Judson Harris works for the California attorney general's office," Jack said. "Didn't anyone ask him if he had any ties to organized crime?"

"'Organized' is not the word that comes to mind

with his family," Vanessa said. "But perhaps that's why he wants to meet us at his home rather than his office."

Judson's neighborhood had been upscale, but was now dotted with FOR SALE signs. Judson's own little piece of paradise was a two-story pseudo–Spanish mission stucco on a cul-de-sac. The surrounding houses looked to be in good shape with no FOR SALE signs in sight.

A blue plastic toddler-sized tricycle was parked on the front lawn next to two larger purple bikes, a row of shoes piled up on the front porch. Papa Bear, Mama Bear, and the Baby Bears—two sets of pink with sparkles and one set with a superhero on the sides.

As Jack reached for the doorbell, the door opened, revealing a tall Asian woman in crisp chinos and a black crewneck sweater that looked soft and expensive.

"I am Beverly Harris," she said. "If you would please remove your shoes here in the foyer."

Ah. A foyer, not a mudroom. So nice to be home. Vanessa and Jack removed their wet shoes. Beverly's accent was as crisp as her chinos. She did seem a bit tightly wound, but perhaps she was nervous. It couldn't be easy being married to a son of Carl Harris.

By the time Vanessa and Jack had removed their shoes, Judson and the children—two girls around seven and nine, and a boy of about three—had padded into the foyer. Judson was tall, like his father, but slim, with brown eyes and thinning reddish hair.

The children said hello and stared back with frank curiosity until Beverly shooed them back into the recesses of the home.

Judson ushered Vanessa and Jack into an office off the foyer and shut the door. The office was spotless. Judson took his scat in a high-end desk chair, leaving a futon couch for his visitors. He wasted no time getting down to business.

"My dad called me after your visit. I gather you found Louise and Troy up in the Santa Cruz Mountains. Or what was left of them. I used our department systems to check on the details."

Jack pulled out his pad. "It doesn't seem likely that they died a natural death. We need to figure out what happened."

"You're thinking a drug deal or something like that gone bad, I assume. That would certainly fit."

Jack glanced at Vanessa. "Could be. We're also thinking that they might have been here to settle some scores before Rosie died."

Judson studied his hands. "Yeah. Could be, I suppose. I've stayed away from all that stuff for close to twenty years, but Rosie did tend to think that way."

"Particularly if she wanted Louise to control the family assets, not your father," Vanessa said.

Judson cleared his throat and shuffled his feet. "Maybe. As I said, I keep myself away from the family business. One hundred percent."

Vanessa looked at the framed diplomas on the wall over Judson's computer monitor. He was a lawyer. Her radar said he was sincere, a good guy who wouldn't manipulate an interview. *Still . . .*

"You must have known Troy growing up, right?" She passed him copies of pictures of his first-grade class.

A fleeting smile crossed Judson's face. "Yes. All too well. Troy, Greg, and I were all in the same classroom in elementary school. My brother was a couple of years ahead. Troy was always trying to pick fights with me. A real asshole."

"Like Greg was a model citizen?"

Vanessa watched Judson's response closely. To her surprise, he grinned.

"Greggy was a good kid. He didn't escape like I did. I could have been just like him. He sends me email. He's got his GED now, plus an associate's degree in computer studies."

"How did you get out? And your brother?" Jack asked.

Judson gave a dry cough. "Until we got to high school, all the fights were over silly stuff. Jason was a couple of years older, and when he finished high school, my Dad sent him over to Rochester right away to work for a buddy to learn commercial building. For me, things got worse because our mom had died of cancer and I didn't have Jason. Dad was courting Betty, so he wasn't around much. One day during my junior year, Troy and I got into a fight waiting for the bus home. I don't even remember the point or what set it off. The trick with Troy was to not let him get ahold of you. He wasn't very smart or quick, but he was strong. I was a skinny kid and he was full-grown already, plus he had some sort of natural ability for 'wrassling.' I screwed up and he got me in a headlock. He was trying to break my neck. No doubt about it." Judson swallowed. "Man, I was scared. I don't even know how, but I wiggled loose. I kicked him hard in the balls and I pounded his head on the pavement."

"That must have gone over well," Vanessa said.

Judson offered her a twisted grin. "Yeah. Don't forget that Del and Zeke were the ones in charge in those days, with Larry as the enforcer and Louise and Rosie riding shotgun. Dad was terrified for me. He's a tough guy, but I have never seen him scared like that." He studied a hangnail. "In some ways it proved that he loved me."

"You left?" she asked.

"He sent me to a prep school in Rochester. I lived with Jason. Troy dropped out of school a couple of months later, but it wouldn't have been safe for me to stay. After high school, I got into the University of Rochester. I was the first one in my family to go to college. I think Dad was proud, not that he'd say so. When I got into law school at UCSF, I headed out here and never looked back."

"It sounds a bit lonely," Jack said.

"That has been the hard part. But I'm lucky. Beverly has lots of family here. Normal family. Happy family. I've even learned passable Chinese. Since Rosie died, Betty comes out two or three times a year. She's great. Her son, Johnny, and I were good friends in elementary school and I think she sees me as a link to him. My dad has come once or twice. He's better with grandchildren than with sons."

Vanessa's heart ached a bit for Judson. Freedom came at a price for the Harris clan.

"I don't suppose you saw Louise or Troy when they were out here."

"Hell no. Besides, I looked back on my calendar." He gestured to his computer screen. "I see that we were all in Southern California around the times you're talking about. Our first Disney vacation, after Harriet and Chelsea, but before we had Aaron."

"Any chance of other family coming out uninvited?" Jack asked.

Judson licked his lips and swallowed. He looked at the door, leading to the heart of his family life. "I hope not. And I rather think not. The good news is, they're a diminished group now."

Jack shot Vanessa a skeptical glance. "We can always hope, Mr. Harris."

*   *   *

By the time Jack and Vanessa started back to Cupertino, the rain had given way to brilliant late-day sun.

"He was scared of them. Even now," Jack said.

"But not scared of his father," Vanessa said. "A bit resentful, and not close, but not scared."

The next day, Nick greeted them with more news.

"Your good friend Chip called. Larry Harris was stabbed to death yesterday. They found him at the end of the day, stuffed into a shower stall."

"Convenient," Jack said. He stared at the report, clicking his ballpoint pen, meditating on the implications.

"Oh?" Nick's eyebrows reached up to his receding hairline.

"Convenient for Carl Harris. Convenient for anyone not aligned with the old Zeke-Rosie power axis," Vanessa said.

"Of course, Larry was the kind of guy to have lots of enemies," Jack said, continuing to click the pen.

Vanessa reached over and snatched the pen.

"We have two more sets of interviews: Elaine Fardig and her mother, and last but not least, Marly Shaw and her sister, Charlene Shaw Harris."

"I thought Charlene was still in prison at the time we're thinking of," Nick said.

Vanessa tapped on the report on Nick's desk. "Yes, but she may have inside information."

"And you think she's likely to be in the sharing mood given her history?"

"Attention to detail, sir," Jack said.

"Thank you, Jack. You stay, Vanessa." Nick dismissed Jack with a wave.

Jack offered Vanessa a finger wiggle as he backed out the door.

Nick planted both hands on his desk and leaned forward. "Vanessa, here's the deal. We need to move on, one way or the other. I know you have a reputation of running every case to ground. I like that about you. So does the brass. But we've spent a lot of time and money on this and we've got cases piling up. Righteous cases. Cases with real victims. Finish these interviews. But unless you come up with something concrete, I don't see that we'll be able to pinpoint anyone for these deaths."

"Hindering prosecution?" Vanessa asked.

"Good luck with that." Nick frowned. "Go."

21

Marly: Old Friends

June 14, 2009

Marly stretched her arms above her head and tensed every muscle, tip to toe. She had slept in—a luxury, even on Sunday. The large house was silent.

The thermometer outside her window read fifty-five degrees, under a gray, overcast sky. It was the start of another perfect summer day in Silicon Valley. The high fog overhead would burn off and give way to sun by midmorning. The temperature would rise to eighty degrees, give or take, and around five in the afternoon, the fog would peep over the top of the Santa Cruz Mountains and pull cool air back over the valley for the night. And no rain until October.

Marly padded down the hallway and opened the door to Mark's bedroom. Last year, her nephew had removed all of the cherry mission-style furniture she had provided when he had come to live with her. His mattress now sat flat on the floor, flush against the far wall, next to his meditation corner, defined by a rectangular Zen *zabuton* mat with a plump, lozenge-like *zafu* in the middle. An old coffee table served as his desk these days. He explained that it was the perfect height where he could study or read, squatted on his haunches or sitting in full lotus. Just watching him made Marly's knees and ankles ache.

Before she eased the door shut, she paused to study the one wall that was not stark white. On this wall, closest to the door, Mark had plastered soccer and baseball posters, and school pictures over every available inch of space.

The deep saffron yellow of Pammy's room seeped out the door and pulled Marly in to bask in the glow of her niece's spirit. The orange and green curtains and bright red rug competed for attention with the stacks of books and papers scattered in loose piles around the room.

Alison compartmentalized her room into neat pink and purple activity centers. Her shiny white bedframe with matching side tables took up the near wall. The clean surface of her art and project table sat under the window with toys stacked by size in the cabinet to the left, sports equipment in the cabinet to the right.

As she waited for coffee to brew, Marly picked up the phone and started to dial Mark's cell number. She put down the phone. The Zen Center did not allow cell phone use during the *sesshin*—a weeklong meditation session that would end on Friday. She had been concerned that Mark was too young for such a Spartan spiritual adventure. She agreed to let him go only after persistent badgering on his part. Pammy would return from her camp in the Sierras a few days after Mark. Alison was down in Santa Barbara with the family of her best friend, Tami, for the next week.

Her children would be home soon enough.

Over breakfast, Marly went over her checklist for their trip to England in two weeks. She had accepted an offer to teach a course on high tech entrepreneurship at Oxford, but the real reason for her visit was Tony.

Who would have thought a sane, rational, highly intelligent person would settle for a long-distance relationship with someone as screwed up as Marly? And if that wasn't enough, there were several needy children tossed into the mix as well.

Tony's willingness to actively embrace her dysfunctional situation and strange family continued to astound her. Marly thought she might be truly in love with this odd person. She hoped this summer would cement that for her, one way or the other.

After a lazy morning and late brunch, she rode her bike into work at the office of her newest startup, near the 101, on the other side of Mountain View.

As she locked her bike, she noticed that there was one car in the back parking lot—Elaine's—and a green van parked in the shade at the far end. She used her access card to enter the office.

Elaine stood in the reception area. She greeted Marly with crossed arms and a scowl. "You took your time getting here. I thought we were going to begin early. I've been here for over two hours already."

"You are not going to make me feel guilty about taking a few child-free personal hours. You know perfectly well that I put in plenty of time, plus I don't waste it trying to micromanage people."

Elaine's nostrils flared. She turned on her heel and strode into the adjoining conference room. She sat down, her back stiff and straight, facing the whiteboard, which was covered with handwritten notes and multicolored Post-its.

Marly strolled to the break room and filled a coffee mug. She started for the conference room, but turned around after a few steps to add half-and-half to her cup.

She knew that sauntering at a slow pace would drive Elaine crazy, but she needed a few moments to cool off.

At times like this, Marly missed Andrea, a friend with no rough edges, who knew how to bring out the best in the people around her by using positive motivations. Elaine had been a pushy kid in first grade and now she was a pushy colleague. Marly did appreciate the value of Elaine's brilliance and ambition, but on a personal level, she could be high-maintenance.

Although she often got the credit for saving Elaine, Marly knew she had been more than repaid. At seventeen, Marly's idea of escape from Charon Springs had been limited to getting through college and finding a job with a company like IBM, someplace far from Central New York. She discovered that Elaine was not going to settle for anything as prosaic as that and, since Elaine and Marly were now a team, Marly wasn't going to either.

It was at Elaine's insistence that Marly came to Stanford for graduate school where she was happy to ride Elaine's aggressive coattails on their second company.

Now the landscape had changed. Cell phone and mobile device apps were all the rage. The risks were higher than ever, but augmented reality presented thrilling new challenges that Marly loved.

According to Elaine, technical talent was overrated. Knowing how to blend business know-how and technology was the critical component. Marly loved building things, figuring out how to solve problems, and pulling people together to make those happen. On most days, she enjoyed making Elaine's visions successful.

Marly settled into a chair at the conference table, careful not to sit across from her prickly co-founder. Making direct eye contact with Elaine when she was in one of these moods would be like teasing a rabid dog. Most people had no idea Elaine was virtually blind in her left eye. By positioning herself slightly to Elaine's left, Marly was able to diffuse most of Elaine's fury.

Besides, Marly knew that Elaine was stressed over the materials they needed to send to a venture capital team that was interested in funding them. VCs could be notoriously picky, and Elaine had every reason to be concerned.

As Marly predicted, once she and Elaine started working, the temperature in the room cooled. The pieces of the puzzle began to fall into place. These golden moments, when their complementary skills synchronized and everything clicked, were magical.

At four p.m., Elaine stood and stretched. "Not bad. We have a long way to go but I think we've laid the foundations for what we need. See you at seven tomorrow morning."

Marly had no intention of getting to the office by seven a.m., but decided she would make that argument at nine the next morning. She waited behind to take care of a few emails, savoring a few minutes in the office alone.

Something flashed in the corner of her peripheral vision and pulled her attention to the conference room window.

In the middle of the parking lot, Elaine was struggling to free herself from the arms of a tall and beefy man with a scraggly mullet. He had wrapped his arms around her from the back and lifted her feet off the ground. As Elaine twisted, another figure, a rotund woman with a similar haircut, moved in and slugged Elaine in the face.

Marly pounded on the glass. "Hey. Hey. I'm going to call the police."

Elaine slumped to the tarmac, and the two figures turned toward the window. Marly stopped yelling and stepped back into the middle of the room. The two attackers were Louise Harris and her son, Troy.

Louise and Troy turned back to deliver more kicks and punches to Elaine, while Marly ran back to her desk for her cell phone.

As she started to dial 911, Marly noticed that Louise and Troy were loading a limp Elaine into a panel van. Marly realized that if Louise and Troy drove away, she would not be able to tell the police much about the van except the color. If she tried to follow them on her bicycle, they would soon pull away. She knew Louise and Troy well enough. They were not taking Elaine for another beating.

Marly dropped her phone and picked up a putter that their team had used for a game of office miniature golf.

This is stupid. Go back to the phone and call the police. Do not go out that door. Don't.

Marly raced across the parking lot. Troy was bent over, stuffing Elaine through the side door onto the floor of the van. If he heard her coming, he didn't stop or turn around. Marly closed in, set her feet, and swung the putter at Troy's back.

The putter shuddered in Marly's hands and bounced off Troy's well-padded flesh, as if she had hit a large rubber tire. Troy grunted and straightened up. As he turned toward her, Marly cocked her arms for another blow.

Before she could swing at Troy's head, she felt something hit her like a punch. And another. Every muscle contracted, her legs collapsed, and her head hit the pavement with a bounce.

"Nice of you to come greet us, Marly," Louise said. "I was wondering how we'd get you into this van."

22

Marly: Comeuppance

June 14, 2009

Marly was lying on her right side in the back of a moving vehicle. Her hands were tied with a plastic band in front of her and her bare feet were in some sort of similar restraint that kept them no more than a few inches apart. She lay very still, as she tried to process what had happened. She had not lost consciousness, but the impact of her head on the ground had dazed her. She was too confused to be terrified.

"Keep your eyes on the road, you idiot," Louise said. "And don't speed. We can't risk getting pulled over."

"Shut the fuck up," Troy said.

"Just do as I say. I'm going to call Mom."

"Tell her what a good job I did."

"Just drive."

Marly shifted her head and swallowed several times to make certain she didn't vomit. She struggled to pull in enough air through her nose.

She was lying on the bare, long metal bed of the windowless van she had seen in the parking lot. Rolling to her left, she could see Elaine lying on the other side of the van floor.

Elaine stirred at Marly's tentative touch but remained slumped on her stomach. She rolled her head and Marly's throat constricted. Elaine's right eye—the good one—was swollen almost shut and blood caked under her nose and around her mouth. A sour, ammonia smell leaked from her body.

Louise's voice floated over them from the front seat. "Yeah, we've got her. Don't worry, Mom. Yeah, Elaine too. We have a place in mind. No one will find them. Ever."

Pause.

"Yeah, the kids seem to be off someplace. But they'll be heading East once Marly disappears. Yeah."

Another pause.

"Yup, I've got the cameras. We'll have good movies. Once we've tidied up, we'll be headed home. We plan to be back on Tuesday night."

After Louise hung up, she turned to Troy. "She's doing better. The doctors are saying she may hang in there for a while. Amazing."

Marly paid attention to the driving. They seemed to be on a winding road, heading uphill. Route 9?

Louise swiveled in her seat. Marly pretended to be unconscious, but Louise gave her shoulder a rap with a hard stick, and Marly released an involuntary grunt.

"Hey there, smarty. You should get ready to die. Rosie's waiting to get the report. Including video. Now your family will know what it's like to suffer and wonder where their loved one has gone."

Marly tilted her head and realized that Louise was shooting video.

"You think I don't know what that's like? We don't know where my father went," Marly said. "And what about Johnny? And what about Elaine's father?" She was rewarded with a sharp rap on the side of her left arm.

"We'll get you to confess," Louise said, her features distorted by a sneer. She picked up a small chain saw that had been sitting at her feet. "Piece by piece. We'll get the truth from you about Del and all the rest."

Troy giggled.

Marly coughed as the air rushed from her lungs. Elaine whimpered.

"Don't you hurt my kids." Marly wracked her brain to come up with some argument that might convince Louise to change her mind.

"They'll be orphans," Troy said, his voice filled with glee. "They'll be so upset. They'll have to go to your mom."

"The Shaws have been thorns in our sides for a long, long time," Louise said. "Your mother's house is old—all wood. It could burn real easy."

"This is crazy," Marly said. "You have Elaine, too. The police will figure out that there was a connection to your family. They'll find out that you came here. They'll track this van. You have stun guns. Someone will know where you were planning to dump us."

Louise laughed. "Cash is still good. Cash and a new driver's license. You can even get a cash card to make reservations. You can rent vans for cash. You can buy what you need for cash."

"Carl will know." Even to her own ears, her voice was tinny and weak.

"Carl doesn't know shit and he can't do anything about it anyway. We'll take care of him. We have friends all set to move," Troy said. "We're doing this for Rosie. She needs this to perk her up. And she'll make sure my mother leads from here on out."

"She's been sick for over a year. I've heard she's dying," Marly said.

Louise smirked. "She's still got lots of life in her as it turns out."

Marly lay back and let Louise's raving, punctuated with Troy's chortles, wash over her. She kept gasping for air, her ability to reason swept away. She would never get to talk to Tony again. Or the kids. What would happen to them? She rubbed her face and tried to funnel her desperation into figuring some way out, but her thoughts kept circling in a deadly spiral.

The ride was both short and interminable. Given her position on the floor of the van, Marly couldn't see out, but she could tell that at some point, they turned off the main road onto something rougher and more twisting, followed by another turn and another until she lost track.

The sunlight hitting the front windshield was bright, but little filtered into the back of the van. Marly cast her eyes into every corner for some sort of tool or device that could give her hope. The floor toward the front of the van where she and Elaine lay was clear and barren. The floor at the back was covered with two deflated mattresses, two sleeping bags, two duffels, several piles of clothes, and a couple of boxes. There had to be valuable tools buried in those boxes, but she wouldn't be able to search without being noticed.

"Okay, I'll tell you about Del," she said. Her voice sounded small and scared. "They came after me in Del's truck. I ran down the road and up into that field. Zeke shot twice. One bullet nicked me and the other hit Del. I didn't kill them. They died in the truck and it went over the side of the ravine."

Louise put the camera aside long enough to climb into the back and slug Marly a couple of times. She gave Elaine a good knock as well. Marly tried to scoot out of the way. She saw Elaine try to turn her left side toward Louise to protect her right eye.

After a few more blows, Louise returned to the front and plopped down into her seat. "Idiot. We knew that. We know about your ways. Del. Precious Del. Such a wimp. He never wanted to do any of the hard stuff, little baby boy. He didn't mind a little touch-up, and he wanted to call the shots, but he had no stomach for the real thing. Larry and me had to take care of all the hard work. Why do you think Dad was with Del that night? Dad was so mad we'd got Laurie by mistake—it was supposed to be you, Marly. Del couldn't bear to take care of his little stepdaughter. He had to get all drunk. Dad went with him to make sure he manned up."

Marly swallowed, transported back years.

Louise continued. "I've always been the backbone and even more so with Larry away. And now I'm going to prove to everyone that I've got the balls and the intelligence to pull this off. Rosie will run things a bit longer and, when she's gone, I'll have it all."

Marly no longer wanted to argue. She had used the distraction of trying to evade Louise to twist around so that her head was at the back of the van where she could use her new position to roll and search for something, anything, in the boxes or under the piles of clothes.

Fumbling under a sleeping bag, her hands came back with a Phillips-head screwdriver. She had no time to dig for something better. This would have to do.

While Louise busied herself in the front seat, Marly sandwiched the screwdriver between her palms. With some difficulty she tucked the screwdriver, blade first, under the left sleeve of her sweatshirt.

"I want to know where my father's body is," Marly

said. "You owe me that much. I'll tell you about the money."

"We know about the money, bitch. We'll get that back one way or another," Troy said, followed by his signature giggle.

"Beanie is with Johnny at the bottom of Schwarzer's quarry under a ton of rock and fifty feet of water," Louise said. "Your precious Ollie, too."

"I can't believe Carl let you kill Johnny," Marly said, her voice a whisper.

"Carl. Jeez. Carl has been on the outside all these years. No one asked Carl. Carl was told after the fact."

Louise turned and leaned into the back section to strike Marly's shins with an ax handle before turning back to supervise Troy's driving.

With her feet now facing the front of the van, Marly used her squeal of pain to pull out the screwdriver. Rolling with the steep curves in the road to hide her movements, she started working on the plastic ties around Elaine's ankles. Marly feared that Elaine had fallen unconscious—she was so limp.

Using the head of the screwdriver to cut through all the plastic loops proved harder than she had hoped. At last Marly believed that Elaine could break the leg ties with one good jolt. Marly tried to get into position to work on her own, but the bouncing was now too severe and Louise had also turned around to face the back. Marly tucked the screwdriver out of sight.

The track was so rough that Marly was almost grateful when they stopped, even though she knew this would mean the end for both Elaine and herself.

"Okay," Louise said with a broad smile. "This is the place where you go over in pieces. I think we should start with your feet."

Troy got out and headed toward the back. Louise

stayed inside watching the two young women until he had the back doors open.

Marly swallowed her scream of helpless fear. She couldn't get the screwdriver free while Louise and Troy were on the alert for any suspicious movements.

Louise climbed out and joined Troy at the back of the van. "Wait, wait. Hold on. I've got to get the cameras going. I want to put one on the edge, looking down, and the other facing the flat area. Get out the chain saw and the rest. Once that's done, you can drag them close to the edge. We'll do Fardig first. Make her go to her knees. Parts go over and we'll toss what's left."

Louise picked up two tripods from the truck bed.

"Get undressed," she said to Troy. "Blood will go everywhere once you start cutting. Watch and rings, too."

Marly could hear Louise swearing as she set up the cameras. Troy stripped off his clothes, keeping his eyes fixed on Marly and Elaine from the frame of the back doors. Marly noticed with disgust that he had a hard-on.

Glancing out the open front passenger door, Marly could see Louise take her clothes off too. Things were about to get serious. Marly was breathing too fast. She couldn't think clearly. She tried to bury her face in her sweatshirt to minimize hyperventilating.

Plan B. Maybe she could throw herself over the cliff. She would die—no doubt about it—but at least her death would be sudden and quick.

Troy disappeared from sight. Marly could hear him arguing with Louise about whether to put down plastic and how to stabilize the tripods.

"Elaine," Marly said, careful to mask her voice from the two outside. "I've cut most of the way through the ties at your ankles. A couple of good kicks and they'll snap. You've got to fight—you've got nothing to lose. Wait for a distraction and then kick free and run."

Elaine wagged her head. *Was that a yes or a no?*

"I know you can't see very much. Try to follow the road. I can't tell you which way, but just run."

Louise's voice was now close to the van and the side door slid open. "Okay. Now we'll show these smarties that we're smarter than they are." Troy reached in and grabbed Elaine under her left arm, hoisted her out, and let her fall onto the dirt.

Marly had a brief chance to study their surroundings through the open door. The van had come to rest in a saddle in the road following some sort of ridge. The ground had been cleared to offer a view over the mountains and treetops, although from her vantage point she couldn't determine more than that. The smell of mountain bay trees wafted over her. She assumed that the cliff edge started where the dirt area met open sky.

Elaine squirmed and thrashed. *Were those ties weakened enough?* Her struggles provided a distraction and a sliver of extra time that allowed Marly to work the screwdriver out from under the ties around her wrists. She turned it in her fingers so that the tip faced out with the handle between her palms.

Marly lost sight of Elaine, but she could hear her friend's screams.

Troy climbed inside the back of the van. After a brief and futile spell of cat and mouse, he grabbed Marly's arms and yanked her out onto the dirt, headfirst. The blow knocked away all emotion and the world around her slowed down to a crawl.

Marly brought up her arms and bound hands to protect her head, clamping her fingers together so that she wouldn't lose the screwdriver. She rolled, got to her knees, and resisted with all her might as Troy started to pull her up, leveraging his three hundred–plus pounds.

He giggled. "Silly girl."

She resisted a bit more, paused, and reversed course, pushing herself forward. Troy stumbled back, but he had a good hold on Marly. He adjusted his stance and compensated by leaning forward.

Marly's initial, so-called plan had been to drive the screwdriver, point first, down behind Troy's collarbone or into his neck. Now she realized that he was too tall for her to stab him at an angle that would give her leverage, plus—remembering how the putter had bounced off his back—he was so larded over that she doubted she would have the strength to stab him anywhere on his torso.

This time as he came forward, Marly leaned back. She pointed the tip of the screwdriver toward his left eye, but his grip on her arms was too powerful and her planned blow was far off course. Her tethered feet tripped over each other and she fell forward into the bulk of his body.

If Troy noticed the screwdriver, he didn't give any indication. Locked in their strange waltz, Troy staggered. His head snapped back and then forward. As they fell toward each other, Marly's bound hands shifted the screwdriver to her left and, redirecting her aim, thrust the blade up into Troy's right nostril.

All movement stopped. Troy blinked and gave a grunt. He stiffened and pulled back, a puzzled look on his face. Marly loosened her hands and launched from her toes, slamming the crown of her head up into the base of the screwdriver. There was an unfamiliar crunching sound as she felt the screwdriver slide upward. She heard Troy grunt one more time before he flopped to the ground, still holding on to Marly.

Marly thrashed her way out of his grip and rolled. She looked up from the dust. Absorbed in her dark tasks, Louise had not turned around.

Marly pushed to her knees and made a dive for the nearest pile of tools. Her gaze fell on a box cutter. Troy had not gotten up, but his legs and arms were moving. She was sure he would be on her in a second.

The world moved faster. Elaine kicked her legs free and rose to her feet, unnoticed by Louise, who turned and froze at the sight of Marly crouched by Troy, box cutter in her hands.

The stench of excrement filled the air. Louise's eyes were drawn to her son and she yelled obscenities.

"Elaine! Run, Elaine!" Marly screamed as she sawed at the plastic ties around her ankles. Even barefoot, they had a good chance of running faster than Louise, who was bulky with fat and muscle but not in shape for a race.

Out of the corner of her eye to the right, Marly could see that Elaine had staggered to the front of the van.

Marly was almost done cutting her leg ties when she saw Louise stoop to pick something up and move toward Troy.

Marly yelled again, so loud that her throat hurt. "Elaine. She has a gun. Elaine. Run."

The plastic ties around her legs gave way. Freed, she scrambled toward the far side of the van, hoping that the vehicle would provide a better cover from bullets than the open ground. She tried to cut through the ties around her wrists as she ran, but the angle was awkward and she dropped the box cutter.

As she passed the back bumper, she heard a yell from Elaine, followed by a howl of pain.

Marly turned around. Rounding the back of the van, she saw that Elaine had located a shovel. Even with limited sight and with her hands bound in front of her, Elaine was swinging at Louise, landing blows on the older woman's head, shoulders, and neck.

Louise stumbled and fell. The next blow sent the gun spinning into a clump of poison oak close to the edge of the cliff. Marly dove for the gun, poison oak or not.

Concerned that Elaine might not be able to see with clarity, Marly shouted instructions as she hunted for the gun while keeping track of Louise. "To your right and straight."

Louise was circling around to her right, trying to outflank Elaine and Marly.

Marly located the gun. She struggled to her feet as the gun wobbled in her nervous fingers, her wrists still tied together. *Shit. Don't shoot your own head off. Does it have a safety? How this this work?* She had shot .22 rifles and shotguns before, but didn't know much about handguns.

"Okay, Louise," Marly said. "I've got the gun. Down on your knees, hands on head." She hoped Louise wouldn't notice her tenuous hold on the weapon.

Instead, Louise cursed and lunged at Elaine, who fended off the huge woman with another blow as Marly moved closer.

"Fucking, stupid bitch." It was Elaine's turn to scream. "Stupid, fucking idiot. Fuck you." With that she lunged in Louise's direction, using the blade of the shovel like a spear.

Louise swayed, stepped to her right, grabbed the shovel above the blade, and gave it a hard yank. Elaine stumbled but pulled the shovel free. Caught off balance, Louise lost her footing on the sloping ground and fell. As she wobbled to her feet, she met Marly's eyes and looked at the gun.

Distracted, Louise missed an incoming blow from Elaine, which landed on her right shoulder. Louise fell back and rolled, coming to rest with her feet at the edge of the cliff.

The soft dirt crumbled. Louise froze, her eyes round. In a crouch, she lunged forward to grasp the soft fabric of Elaine's jeans and yanked Elaine off her feet, pulling her toward the edge of the cliff.

The shovel went flying as Elaine's bound hands flew over her head. She thrashed side to side, desperate to find purchase in the barren dirt as the two women continued to slide.

Elaine and Louise were too entwined for Marly to risk firing the gun. The shovel was lying precious seconds away. To use it as a weapon would require going dangerously close to the fragile edge of the cliff.

Marly dropped the gun and bent to grab Elaine's hands in her own. The intervention stopped Elaine's downward slide, but Louise weighed at least as much as Elaine and Marly together. The three women came to a halt, frozen in their tug of war.

Marly felt her damp grasp slip on Elaine's smooth skin. In one swift movement, she let go of Elaine's hands, sat down, and slid her own hands down over Elaine's outstretched arms and head to her torso. Marly squeezed her knees into Elaine's sides, her arms wrapped around Elaine under the armpits.

Marly's rational brain recoiled in horror. *What the fuck did you just do? You're committed now, sweetie. You're going over that cliff with Elaine and Louise.*

"Shut the fuck up," Marly said out loud.

Hugging Elaine to her, Marly dug her heels into the dirt and started to butt-walk the three of them backward. Except that Louise wasn't moving. Elaine's jeans had slid down over her hips. Louise was losing ground.

"I've got you, Elaine, now kick. Kick!"

Anchored by Marly, Elaine kicked and the pants slipped down to her knees. Moments later, her left leg popped free. Louise let go of Elaine's right pant leg and grabbed Elaine's bare left foot and ankle with both hands.

"Kick your left ankle. Knock her hands free."

Elaine thrashed and smashed her feet together. Louise let go with a yelp. Another chunk of the cliff edge dropped away, leaving Louise's legs dangling in the open air. She pawed at the bare dirt for a handhold as Marly continued to pull Elaine away.

Marly had seen Louise angry many times, but never fearful. Even now, Louise looked more furious than afraid. It occurred to Marly that, perhaps for Louise, those two emotions had always been the same.

Balanced on the soft, crumbling ledge, Louise was beyond help—her upper body among the living and her feet already tasting death. Marly watched, transfixed, as Louise swore, scratched, and scrabbled, grasping at twigs and rocks, and slipped from view.

Still tethered to Elaine, Marly tilted her head back and yelled into the uncaring blue sky.

"Smarties win, Louise. See you in hell."

23

Marly: Cleanup

June 14–16, 2009

Elaine and Marly lay entwined on the dirt and rocks. Elaine's body quivered and twitched, but Marly remained frozen as she savored every breath, the hard earth, and the thin, brittle shell of delicious heat from the brilliant sun. A brief breeze signaled the impending arrival of the gray fog bank from the west. Her terror broke like a fever and tears flowed.

"Is she gone?" Elaine asked.

"She's gone. She went over the edge."

"Where's Troy?" Elaine's voice was sharp with fear.

"Dead too, I think. I hope." Marly sat up and looked to where Troy lay near the back of the van. He was not moving. "He's not getting up. Let's move back. We're still too close to the edge."

Marly pulled her arms free, eased herself upright, and helped Elaine to her feet. Marly felt light-headed and jittery. She didn't trust her own limbs, and she had to resist the temptation to giggle. *You're fine. You're okay,* she kept telling herself as she guided Elaine to the open sliding side door of the van. They both sat down on the edge.

"I couldn't even see her go over," Elaine said. She was crying. "I can't see much of anything."

"You're dehydrated and in shock. Let me cut through these wrist ties and I'll take a proper look at you." Elaine's distress had a soothing effect on Marly, allowing her to focus on something external. Elaine needed her. "And I'd better check on Troy."

Troy had fallen on top of the bright blue tarp he had unfolded at the rear of the van. Marly's knees shook as she drew close, and she gagged when she touched him. She could find no sign of a pulse. His eyes were open and fixed on the sky, his limbs spread-eagle. The screwdriver still protruded from his nose. Marly was surprised there wasn't more blood. A small trickle ran from his right nostril, down his cheek, followed the creases of his neck, and disappeared under his body. Troy's hips and upper thighs lay in a puddle of piss and excrement that escaped when he died. Marly gagged again.

She found the dropped box cutter and returned to Elaine and cut their hands free, starting with her own. Now calmer, she surveyed the site and noticed two large coolers in the shade of an oak tree. Inside the first cooler she found ice, water bottles, a Costco-sized half-empty bottle of vodka, a bottle of cheap sparkling wine, and a container of orange juice. The second cooler held more ice, a six-pack of Coke, four bottles of beer, chocolate bars, and two containers of onion dip. A grocery bag behind the coolers contained several bags of potato chips and a pile of granola bars.

"It looks as though Louise and Troy were going to toast our deaths with mimosas, beer, and potato chips. A real classy celebration. Now let me clean you up a bit." Marly handed Elaine a Coke and a granola bar. She planted a soft kiss on Elaine's forehead and swabbed her friend's face with paper towels and bottled water. "Your right eyelid is swollen with blood. You should still be able to see once that goes down."

Elaine moaned. "But I'm blind now."

Marly studied Elaine's right eye. "I don't think a doctor would approve, but I could make a cut along this bone, just below your eyebrow." She traced the line with her finger on Elaine's face. "I learned this from Del, believe it or not. I had to do it for him after a fight at the Rock. It's a trick boxers used to do when their eyes swelled up so much that they couldn't see to fight. The blood will release and the swelling will go down a bit."

"Do it."

"Are you sure? I'll put some butterfly bandages on it, but you'll need proper stitches and you may need to see a plastic surgeon."

"Jeez. Don't second-guess yourself, Marly. If Del didn't complain, I won't. Just do it."

"Okay, wait a sec." Marly gave Elaine ice wrapped in paper towels. "This will help make you numb. Hold it on your eye."

In the back of the van, she found a small first-aid kit and a package of new box cutter blades.

"Are your hands steady?" Elaine asked.

"Steady as a rock." Marly decided that this was no time for candor. She cleaned the area and her hands with vodka and made a short, clean slice with a new blade, following the line of the eyebrow. Blood gushed out into a clean paper towel but subsided with pressure. By the time she had applied her handcrafted butterfly bandages, Marly could see that Elaine's eyelid and surrounding area still looked terrible, but the swelling had gone down enough to reveal Elaine's blue iris.

Elaine sniffed and gave a short sob. The two hugged

and slumped back onto the van floor, holding each other in a tight embrace.

"I can see," Elaine said. "I was so scared. I felt so helpless not being able to see."

"You were amazing with that shovel. I can't believe you were so deadly even blind as a bat."

"I was so terrified that I peed myself."

"I was so scared that my body forgot how to pee."

Elaine cleaned up with some of the bottled water and changed into a pair of Louise's stretch pants, held up by a bungee cord belt.

Marly rummaged in the back of the van and found Elaine's bag with her computer and cell phone. In the front, she found two more cell phones belonging to Louise and Troy. She had left her own phone along with her laptop back at the office.

She tried to call 911 on each of the cell phones. She uttered a low growl of frustration and tossed the phones into the footwell of the van. "No coverage. I guess we'll have to walk or drive. I have no idea how far we'll have to go."

Elaine scowled. "I'm in no condition to walk a long way. If we drive, I guess we just leave all this?"

The two looked around. Marly jumped up. "Shit. Those cameras are still shooting video."

Before she turned off the second camera, Marly inched toward the edge of the cliff and held the camera on its tripod to check over the sheer face.

"Damn. It must be at least two hundred feet down to that first level," Marly said as they squinted at the playback. "I think that white spot there might be Louise in the trees."

Elaine gazed around the clearing and out over the horizon. "You have to admit, it's a beautiful place to die."

"Yeah, well. I like it better as a place to be alive."

Elaine watched as Marly dug through Louise's clothing for the keys to the van. "You know, it's not that much to clean up. Just that body over there."

The two stared at each other. Elaine spoke first. "You've walked away from bodies before."

"That's been my secret for a long time. It eats into me every day. If we clean this up and say nothing to the cops, we can never talk about it. Not to lovers or best friends or families. It's forever."

"Marly, I've known about Del and Zeke for years. Mrs. Haas came to our house to talk to my mother right after I started working with you at the library. You know how parents talk when it's a secret—all whispery, nod, nod, wink, wink. I hid at the top of the stairs and heard every word."

"Mrs. Haas? How did she know? I never told her."

"She told my mother it was obvious to anyone who paid attention and didn't look away from what was under their noses."

"Shit." Marly brushed away new tears.

Elaine laughed. "I was kind of envious. I was so tired of being a victim. The pity didn't help or change a damn thing. Going to the police wasn't a fix. Sure, Rosie and the rest went to prison for a little while, but it just made her angrier and more crazy."

Seeing Marly hesitate, Elaine persisted. "We aren't murderers, Marly. All we'll get is a world of hurt and no help from the police."

"What if they track us down?"

"Marly, think of how many people Louise and Troy killed. And then there's Zeke and Del and Rosie and Larry. Think of the ones they eliminated. We know how terrified and scared all those people were. The cops here will be the same as in New York. If push comes to shove, we've got those videos Louise shot. Besides, we have money. Money buys good lawyers and good PR."

Marly offered Elaine a slug on the vodka bottle and took two herself. "Not exactly what the doctor would order," she said to Elaine. They repeated the procedure.

"I think we'll have to tell my mother," Elaine said. "She's waiting at home."

"And don't forget that Rosie is waiting for final word back in Gateway to Hades, New York. I'd love to see the police scoop her up again."

"Think big picture, Marly. That didn't help before. If we call attention to this, we'll be on the lookout for Harris henchmen from now to eternity. You heard Louise. They were sent out here in secret. Keeping it secret hurts Rosie more."

Marly did not need much persuading. Hearing Elaine's arguments convinced Marly to pay attention to her own instincts and agree.

They set to work. Louise and Troy had provided helpful items, including several boxes of disposable latex gloves and an enormous roll of plastic bags. Tools were packed away first, followed by clothing, bloodied items, cell phones, wallets—all went into separate bags.

At last only Troy remained—a very large item of final business.

"Convenient that he undressed for us," Elaine said.

Marly removed an earring from his left earlobe and put it on the bed of the van, next to his watch and ring. Despite Louise's instructions, he hadn't removed those.

"Don't pull out the screwdriver until the last moment," Elaine said. "More blood might leak out."

They pulled on new gloves and rolled Troy's body into the middle of his tarp, and wrapped the edges over him like a blue shroud. That was the easy part. Lugging Troy to the edge of the cliff was trickier than they had anticipated, given his weight and bulk. Marly remembered how the soft soil had crumbled under Louise and wanted to stay a safe distance from the edge.

Marly laid down a new tarp, sliding it forward so that the far end drooped over the edge of the cliff. She popped open the sparkling wine and—after a few swigs—emptied the contents onto the tarp.

"Lubricant," she said by way of explanation.

They strained to position Troy, headfirst, at the top of the blue sluice. Marly removed the screwdriver, keeping her eyes averted. Elaine lifted Troy's feet and pushed forward as Marly tried to move his upper body. Troy seemed reluctant to go, but with additional encouragement from the shovel, he slid onto the wine-slickened tarp, twisted to his left, picked up speed, and tumbled over the edge of the cliff.

"Bon voyage," Marly said with a wave.

Elaine offered Marly a high five. "I hope he landed on Louise."

Fortified by granola bars and bottled water, Marly found new energy to finalize the cleanup. Elaine tried to help but struggled to stay on her feet. Her face was the color of sour milk, sending a pang of worry through Marly's gut.

"Go sit in the van, Elaine. Drink another Coke and put any papers you find into this bag."

Marly pushed a large pile of brush and wood over the edge of the cliff. She suspected that Louise and Troy had assembled the pile to bury her and Elaine down below. Now she would return the favor.

As her final step, Marly shoveled any shit, pee, or blood she could find over the edge of the cliff and smoothed out the open dirt area with the shovel.

That was when Marly found Louise's pendant—a small Iroquois mask, matching the design of Troy's earring and ring. There were no Native Americans living in Charon Springs that Marly knew of, and she had never heard Louise speak a kind word about folks from the nearby Onondaga Reservation. She had also heard that the Onondaga didn't approve of making copies of sacred masks. She had never had the nerve to ask Louise about this affectation, and now she never would know. She put the pendant into the same baggie with Troy's bling.

By the time Marly slid into the driver's seat and started the van, the sun had dropped down behind the ridge and the shadows were long and deep, although the sky was still light. The fog hovered at the tree line to the west like a crouching animal and would soon shroud this section of road in a gray blanket. The clock on the dashboard read 7:37.

"I couldn't find a map," Elaine said. "And GPS isn't working."

Marly executed a cautious K-turn, mindful not to send the van over the cliff to the east or down the steep mountainside to the west. "It's a good thing it's June and the days are long. Getting out of these mountains will be slow going, but at least I know how to start. The tire tracks end a few yards the other direction."

Tightening her grip on the steering wheel to keep her hands from shaking, Marly focused on the rutted road. The shadows were gaining on them. Minutes after leaving the site, she saw a mountain lion cross the road in front of her. Elaine gasped.

"Dinner down below," Marly said, realizing that bodies might not last long up here.

Navigating by trial and error, Marly headed northeast and downhill when the roads allowed. She made several wrong turns that led to dead ends or slide areas. Three times she had to back up before she had room to turn around. According to the dashboard clock, after twenty-two minutes, they merged with a tame dirt track, which led to a one-lane tarmac road. She went the wrong way again, but self-corrected and paused to check Elaine's phone. *At last. GPS.*

Elaine kept nodding off despite the cool air flowing through the open windows and Marly's efforts to keep up a conversation. She recalled that for a person with a head injury, falling asleep could be dangerous. *Is that true?* From time to time she would shake Elaine awake. Once awakened, Elaine would try to dial her mother on her cell phone, but she couldn't make out the display and would start to cry.

Marly patted her friend's leg. "I'm driving. Hold on, Elaine. We're almost there."

At eight fifteen she found the highway leading down out of the mountains. Shortly after nine, they reached Mountain View as the last bit of indigo daylight faded.

The closer they grew to home, the harder Marly cried. She made a brief stop as she pulled off of El Camino, the main commercial strip, to dump a bag with Louise's and Troy's smashed cell phones into a public garbage bin in a tiny park. Even with the batteries removed, she feared the phones' locations could be tracked, and she didn't want them in her house.

Marly pulled into her driveway, hopped out, and found a hidden set of keys in a combination box under the front porch. She pressed the numbers on the numeric keypad to open the driveway gate and pulled the van into the empty slot in her garage.

Elaine snapped awake. "We're here? Where is my mother?"

Helen Fardig picked up her phone on the first ring. "Marly. I'm frantic. I haven't heard from Elaine and we were supposed to have dinner."

"Elaine is here. Come to my house right away."

"Is she okay? What's going on?" Helen's voice quavered.

"Helen, please shut up and get over here. Bring your emergency medical kit."

Marly had already guided Elaine to the guest room and helped her into a pair of Pammy's pajamas. After she hung up, Marly put all of Elaine's clothes and her own into a new plastic bag and went to pull on clean sweatpants and a T-shirt.

"Mom?" Elaine asked as Marly tried to force her to drink more water.

The doorbell rang and Marly rushed to open the door.

Helen pushed by Marly, scanning the front room for Elaine. "What's going on? I—Oh my God! Marly. What happened to you?"

Marly grimaced and cleared her throat to hold back tears. "A run-in with Louise and Troy. They got to Elaine first. Take a big breath."

Helen stared. "They came here? From New York?"

"They're dead, Helen," Marly said. Her lips fluttered and she sobbed. "Now we need you. Elaine needs you. She's in the guest room. We got away. Come on."

Helen let out a howl when she saw Elaine, and Elaine wailed in return.

Elaine choked and gagged, her voice muffled in Helen's shoulder. Marly picked up the tale as Helen examined her daughter.

"Where are they?" Helen asked when Marly finished. "You drove the van down here and left them up there?"

Marly wiped her eyes. "I managed to shove a screwdriver up Troy's nose and Elaine used a shovel to get Louise to back up until she went over the edge of the cliff. We dropped Troy over the edge too. I suppose . . ." She paused to regain a shred of composure. "I suppose we should call the police now. Elaine needs to get to the hospital. We've destroyed the evidence, but we have the videos. It will be messy, but we'll hire lawyers—"

"Shut up, Marly," Helen said. "Go clean up and get some food ready for us. I'll come check you out in just a bit, but I think you're fine. I don't think Elaine will need to go to the hospital, but I need to make a closer examination."

Relieved that Helen's experience as a nurse had kicked in, Marly stumbled to her bathroom and climbed into the shower. She was amazed that she wasn't more banged up. She had a small bruise over her left eye, another on her right cheekbone, and a big one forming on her left shoulder. She could feel a few more bruises on the back of her head, hidden by hair, as well as a number of welts rising on her shins and legs. Her left wrist was rubbed raw from the plastic ties, as were both ankles, but her right wrist was clear. She would be wearing long-sleeved shirts and socks for a while. And forget shorts or a bathing suit.

Helen met her in the hallway. "Back to your room and strip. Let's take a look at you."

"How's Elaine? Why is she so sleepy? She was very alert for a while."

"My diagnosis is shock, dehydration, and possibly a mild concussion," Helen said. She sniffed. "But no sign of brain hemorrhage. I'll stay here to watch her tonight. Broken nose, cracked ribs. Her right eye is fine. I stitched up your cut. Good work on that."

Helen wrapped Marly in a long hug. "Thank God for you."

Half an hour later, the three women grouped in the kitchen for dinner. Marly kept track of the frozen lasagna heating in the microwave while Helen set the dining room table. Elaine wobbled in on unsteady feet and she spoke in coherent sentences.

Lasagna had never tasted so good. *This is a meal I almost missed.* Marly blinked back tears and forced herself to eat.

"We must have a story in case Elaine needs to go to the hospital," Helen said. Her lips were compressed into a straight line, her eyebrows pulled together in a scowl. Elaine must have filled in her mother on the decisions made at the top of the cliff.

Marly set down her fork. "If Elaine has to go to the hospital, we'll come clean and hire good lawyers. We have the videos. We'll plead shock and my terrible family history."

Helen clenched her knife in her right fist and her fork in the left, pointing them straight up, ready to attack. "If we go to the police, Louise and Troy will get a proper burial. That just sticks in my craw when I consider how many decent people like my Ollie will never get that privilege." Helen glared at her placemat. "I've decided it's best if we leave you out of this part, Marly.

If it comes to that, Elaine and I will make sure our stories work for the police."

Helen put down her utensils with a clang. "Time to go clean that van. Elaine, I know you're tired, but you should come help. You can sit if you need to."

Inside the garage, they all pulled on latex gloves and Marly covered the floor space with tarps. Elaine's assigned task was to attach the video cameras to a small LCD TV and screen Louise's cinematic efforts.

Marly and Helen unrolled the sleeping bags and turned them inside out, just in case they held any secrets. Once that was done, Marly rolled them up, put them back into their sleeves and into white plastic bags as Helen checked the air mattresses and rolled them up and into a bag along with the two pillows. They looked almost new.

Next, Marly brought out the duffels. She sorted through all the clothes and all the pockets. Underwear and torn clothing went into a discard pile. The rest of the clothes were repacked into the duffels and the duffels went into garbage bags.

The clothes and shoes Troy and Louise had been wearing received special attention and were stuffed into a separate bag. Marly also set aside some of Louise's clothes.

Helen turned and raised an eyebrow.

"I'm not sure what we'll do about the van. I might need to look like Louise if we return it," Marly said.

Helen sorted the boxes and tools, separating which items could be tossed without a problem and those—like the chain saw—that would require some creative thinking.

From time to time, Marly and Helen paused to watch video that Elaine wanted them to see. Marly was horrified to realize that Louise and Troy had been so close, watching and waiting. Helen had to sit down for a long break after watching the scenes in the van and the final fight at the top of the cliff. Marly went outside to throw up.

"I'm glad I couldn't see any of this at the time," Elaine said.

Helen put her arms around Marly. "Over the years, I've grown very fond of you, Marlene Shaw, but from this day forward, you are as dear to me as any daughter could be."

Until her tears subsided, Marly kept her head buried in Helen's chest. She couldn't remember the last time her mother had comforted her like this, patting her back, rocking side to side. Marly could have stayed that way forever, but Helen sniffed and gave Marly a quick squeeze and her bottom a brisk pat—time to get back to work.

When the back of the van was almost empty, Helen scrubbed the outside and Marly went over the empty rear of the interior. She found a few receipts, which she put into the pile to scrutinize later.

Moving to the front, Marly emptied the glove compartment, picked up everything on the floor, looked under the seats, and pulled down the sun visors. Harmless trash went in one pile, potentially interesting receipts went into another. She found a rental agreement for the van, scrawled by hand on a piece of stationery from a place named Johnson Garage in South San Jose. Louise had rented the van for cash, twelve days before, leaving a hefty deposit. Her fake name was on the papers, as well as Troy's fake name as an additional driver.

Helen had plopped the watch and jewelry in a bowl of bleach and water. Marly now took those pieces out, rinsed them off, and put them into a small sealable bag. Along with SIM cards from the phones and the cameras, these were among the few items they would save.

"I'll make a copy for you from the cards," Marly said. "I intend to keep mine in a secret bank box."

"What a nice idea. I'd like one of those too," Helen said with a wink.

"These things can be arranged." Marly winked back, thinking of the identities she had stolen long ago.

Marly spent a restless night. At six, she crawled out of bed and dialed Tony's number in England. As the distinctive double ringtone began, tears threatened to overwhelm her and she hung up. Much as she needed to seek comfort and reassurance, she knew she would spill all her secrets if he asked her what was wrong.

After a trip to the kitchen for coffee, she tried again. This time, she kept her voice casual and let Tony do most of the talking about all the things he had planned for her upcoming visit. She let the sound of his voice fill her head, driving out memories of Louise and Troy, if only for a few minutes.

Refreshed and calm, at seven, she drove to her office, where she loaded her abandoned bike onto her car rack and retrieved her phone, laptop, and keys.

By the time she returned home, Elaine and Helen were up, puttering around the kitchen. Helen and Marly assembled scrambled eggs and muffins, pretending not to watch Elaine as she fumbled with the coffeemaker.

Once she had wrestled the machine into production, Elaine turned to the other two. "Give it a rest, you guys. My depth of field vision is crap and I hurt like hell all over, but I'm fine."

Helen studied a printout of Louise and Troy's travel itinerary and the small stack of two false driver's licenses and credit cards. "They were going to fly out tomorrow, at eleven from San Jose. Their names were Henry Leonard and Alice Haynes." She chuckled, pointing to the picture of Louise as Alice Haynes. "You know, I may have found my long-lost twin. Look at this. With green contacts and red hair, this could be me."

"I can help you with that," Marly said. She went to her closet and came back with a box of wigs and cosmetic contacts in a variety of shades. "Just part of my stash."

"I'll use these this afternoon when we return that van," Helen said. "After that I'll dispose of the IDs and credit cards. Leave that to me."

Marly pulled out the pieces of Louise's clothing that she had set aside and added dark glasses and a cap for Helen's disguise. Helen gathered up the rest of the clothing and headed to a coin laundry over on Calderon to wash everything so that no traces would be left at Marly's house. Elaine was sent to re-mop Marly's garage.

While the clothes roasted in the hot dryers, Helen went to a nearby self-service car wash to scrub the van again, paying special attention to go over all the places the would-be assassins might have touched without gloves.

Loaded up with excuses for Elaine, Marly went to work at their startup. Long sleeves, a bit of makeup, and some colorful braided bracelets covered her injuries quite well.

Their company was still small. Elaine was their CEO and head of marketing. Marly ran engineering and operations. Their old friend Steve handled sales, and they employed four engineers, plus Katy, who took care of the office and organized events, part-time.

Marly announced that she needed a few days off and Elaine would be out as well with a bad cold. She called their venture capital contact and pushed their meeting out one week. As soon as she was certain that Steve knew what to do, Marly headed home.

At two that afternoon, Helen donned Louise's cap, sunglasses, and jacket, supplemented by the green contacts and reddish blond wig. Louise had been much heftier, but Helen had broad shoulders and was almost as tall. Success hinged on Helen passing for Louise at the rental garage where the crew had seen Louise only once.

Helen drove the van with Marly and Elaine following in Marly's car. Their caravan made a stop at Goodwill to dispose of all the remaining clothes, mattresses, pillows, and sleeping bags before proceeding to the address on the van rental agreement.

Marly and Elaine slowed to watch Helen turn into the garage lot, continued another block, and parked around the corner off the busy four-lane road. Marly wanted to walk back to check on Helen, but Elaine insisted that Marly stay put.

Twenty minutes later, Helen hustled around the corner and jumped into the car. Marly wasted no time on small talk until they were well away and headed back to Mountain View.

"Well now, that was quite a place," Helen said, her face beaming from relief and the adrenaline rush. "It's just a garage, not a genuine rental place. No surprise. The boss was out, but a very nice man accepted the van and worked out the figures. He gave me all this money in cash from what was left of the deposit. Twelve hundred dollars."

"I was tied in knots waiting for you. Are you sure they didn't realize that you weren't Louise? Did they ask about Troy?" Elaine asked.

"Nah. They didn't speak much English and I don't speak much Spanish, so we kept things simple. I just scowled and glowered a lot," Helen said, overcome with nervous laughter.

Marly dropped Helen and Elaine at Elaine's house and headed home. Mother and daughter Fardig lived a block apart, a short distance from Marly's house. They agreed that Marly would return to Helen's house for dinner.

Marly stopped at home long enough to find a special key in a hidden envelope before she walked to the local Wells Fargo bank to visit her secret life. She did her personal banking at Bank of America, several blocks away on Castro Street, but Wells Fargo was where she stored the identity documents she had stolen. Over the years, she had created false accounts and driver's licenses—a silent, secret army, waiting to be summoned.

Marly took her bank box to a private stall. Evidence bags went in, a driver's license for Edith Martinson and credit card were pulled out, along with a wad of cash. *Time to make your move.*

* * *

As Helen fixed dinner, they reviewed the remaining items that needed attention. Marly laid claim to the watch and jewelry.

"I need to take them with me tomorrow."

"Where are you going?" Helen turned from the stove.

"I'm flying into New York. To the Springs. I need to attend to some family business."

Helen turned off her stir-fry and sat down. "Marly, we've got as much of a reason to want Rosie dead as anyone. But she will die soon enough, even if she's had some improvement."

"I'm not going to kill Rosie," Marly said. "Not that I wouldn't love to. But I need to check on my mother. And warn Carl. If others are about to pounce, he needs to know about all this. It's not something I'm going to talk about on the phone."

"I'll go with you," Helen said. "We'll talk to Carl together."

"No, Helen. That's not how it works. Even if he believes me about Louise and Troy, I cannot bring in an outsider. For that, I'll get no thanks. In fact, quite the opposite."

"Marly. Don't do this. You haven't murdered anyone. Louise and Troy were killed in self-defense. Del and Zeke made their own destinies. This would be very different."

Marly smiled. "Relax, Helen. I'm not going to kill anyone."

After dinner, Marly went home to pack. She wouldn't need much—a small backpack with one change of clothes and her toothbrush, the bag with the watch and jewelry, and a prepaid cell phone.

* * *

Helen insisted on taking Marly to San Jose Airport at six the next morning. Waving good-bye, Marly headed for check-in. She had used a blond wig for her original Edith Martinson ID. For this trip, she pulled her hair back into a tight bun and prayed. Her heart was pounding.

The TSA screener squinted. "Your hair is different."

"It's a chemical thing," she said. He laughed.

As a rule, Marly hated flying to Central New York. It took so long, since she had to change planes in Pittsburgh or Chicago. This time the long flight suited her.

To push away images of Troy and Louise, she daydreamed of a savior. Much as she cared for Tony, he didn't fit that mold. She wanted to believe in a redeemer. She ached for someone who would take over managing teenage children, sweep away adversaries, come home and take her in his arms and . . . *Ah, but that was what my mother wanted and look how that turned out.*

Marly landed in Rochester in the midafternoon and—as Edith—picked up a rental car. She had selected Rochester over Syracuse to reduce the likelihood that she might be recognized. The drive from Rochester would add at least ninety minutes to her commute to the Springs, but that also suited her plan.

She drove with the windows down and the air-conditioning off, even though the day was hot and humid. She soaked in the sight of soft, rolling hills, lush with tall trees and green pastures, so different from the rugged California landscape, now turned brown—golden to the natives—until the winter rains started again.

A few minutes after seven, the sky still bright, Marly worked her way on back roads toward her mother's house and slid down a wooded logging road parallel to her property. She eased out of the car and stretched.

Unlike California weather, the evening was warm and close. A short walk in the dense woods confirmed that the summer foliage would hide her presence.

Marly returned to the car and lowered the back of the passenger seat until it was flat. She needed some sleep before she visited Rosie.

24

Vanessa:
Mountain View Connections

February 8, 2013

Although she lived in Mountain View, Vanessa could not claim to know the so-called Old Mountain View section well. Many of the oldest houses in town were inside that area, and it reserved a certain status with charming streets and close proximity to Castro Street, the central part of town, crowded with shops and restaurants.

Vanessa eyed their destination—a one-story bungalow—as Jack pulled his car to a halt along the opposite curb. *Nineteen twenties,* she thought. She had always loved the Craftsman style. This house with its low lines, big windows, fine details, and deep porch made her sigh. The light sage green color with white trim and the cherry red door spoke to her, and the garden oozed professional attention. She suspected that the inside had gone through a tasteful renovation as well. This was the house she wanted for herself.

The house belonged to Helen Fardig, Elaine's mother. On the phone, Helen had made it clear that her job as a nurse practitioner meant that she would not be available until after three, at the earliest. Elaine was more flexible. A meeting time with Helen and Elaine had been set for three thirty.

Jack and Vanessa arrived early and planned to sit in the car, but a woman with gray hair came out onto the porch and waved for them to come inside.

They walked straight into a modest-sized living room with an adjoining dining room. Through a glass door, Vanessa could see a generous kitchen with French doors leading to the backyard. She craned her neck to catch a glimpse of a bathroom and the hint of bedrooms on the other side of the house.

Helen was a tall, big-boned woman, with broad shoulders and hips. Her wiry gray hair was cut to accentuate natural waves, and her brown eyes snapped with intelligence. Through her brisk handshake, she exuded a clear-eyed vitality and energy that made Vanessa envious on behalf of her own parents.

"My daughter will be here in a minute," Helen said, showing a toothy half smile. "Please sit. I've already made tea."

Vanessa thought to object but realized that this was not an option. She and Jack sank into comfortable wing chairs framing the brick fireplace.

Helen came back with a tray, which she placed on the mahogany coffee table, and gave Vanessa and Jack each a saucer holding a delicate china cup of tea—no milk, no sugar—before she took her own seat on the couch, facing them.

"Helen," Jack said, about to start his speech. "May I call you Helen?"

Helen consulted the business cards they'd handed her. "Only if I can call you Jackson. If you want to be Detective Wong, then I'm Ms. Fardig or Mrs. Fardig to you. I prefer Ms."

Jack blinked rapidly. Vanessa hid a smile as she

scrutinized her blank notepad. *Way to go, Jack. Lose control of the interview right up front.*

Helen took the initiative to move things along. "Detective Wong, I assume you want to talk about Louise and Troy." Helen spoke with rapid-fire speed and a nasal twang that Vanessa recognized from Central New York. "At times like this I relish freedom from the Springs. What a couple of losers. But crazy like a fox, both of them. I have to say that I'm quite relieved they're dead."

Vanessa admired the rug. It looked expensive and better than anything she'd seen in Helen's former residence back in New York. "Do you know why Louise and Troy would have been out here? Did you ever see them?"

"I avoided them like the plague back in New York. I barely ever saw them there and I would have run like hell if I'd ever seen them out here. They never struck me as the tourist types," Helen said. She scowled. "I suppose I would have gone to the police, but I don't know what you would have done. I don't suppose it is a crime to visit California."

"No, that's not a crime, but I'm sure, given your history with the Harris clan, that the Mountain View Police would have paid attention."

Helen raised her eyebrows. "There's always a first time. Regardless, I didn't see them."

Jack cleared his throat to ask a question, but his eyes were pulled toward movement on the front porch. A young woman came in and joined them.

Vanessa recognized Elaine from the pictures in David Fardig's house and the library yearbooks. Elaine gave her mother a quick kiss and shook hands with the detectives. She was as tall as her mother but with a fine-boned build, delicate features, and crystal blue eyes. Her natural hair color must have been a light, mousy brown, but a cute haircut and a deft highlighting job had given Elaine a natural-looking, trendy sheen.

"You look like your father," Vanessa said, nodding toward a picture on the mantel.

Helen jumped in to answer. "Oh yes. No doubting that. You met David. He looks more like me."

Elaine shooed her mother toward the kitchen. "Mom, why don't you get me some tea too? And please bring in some milk and sugar. And cookies." Turning back, she said, "I'm sure she didn't give you any choices."

"No problem," Jack said. Both detectives glanced at their untouched cups.

"Ms. Fardig, we want to get straight to the point," said Jack, taking advantage of Helen's absence. "We know from phone records that Louise and Troy Rasmussen-Harris were in this general area in 2009, starting on May thirtieth. They dropped out of sight after June fourteenth. We need to know if you—or your mother—had any contact with them, however remote, during that time."

Elaine pulled out her smartphone. "Right. I've got the dates. It looks like I was here during that time. I might have visited friends or been at parties, but I was around."

"No chance that you saw Louise and Troy, I suppose?"

Elaine raised her hands, palms facing out. "No way."

Helen bustled in from the kitchen with the tray, updated to include a cup of tea for Elaine, a pitcher of milk, a sugar bowl, and a plate of plain crackers.

"I already answered that question," Helen said.

Vanessa settled back in her chair and studied Elaine. *Which is the blind eye?* There was no evidence of scarring.

As if to answer, Elaine rotated in her seat and turned her head very slightly to the left so that she was facing Vanessa.

Vanessa caught the subtle compensation move. *Aha. It's the left eye.*

"Do you think Rosie Harris held a grudge against Marly?" she asked.

"Rosie was a head case, but we weren't on speaking terms," Elaine answered. "I know Marly didn't get along well with Rosie."

"Oh yes," Helen said. "I remember that day Marly first came to our house. She had a big black eye and her cheekbone was scraped. I knew right away that she must have hit trouble at home. I almost didn't let her in. We had already had so much to worry about."

Elaine rotated to her right to face her mother. Helen turned to study something out the window; her neck was covered in a red, blotchy flush that quickly rose to her cheeks. Vanessa studied the unspoken exchange between mother and daughter. *Interesting. Had Helen talked out of school?*

"It wasn't unheard of for Marly to turn up with bruises now and again, but she never complained or asked for help," Elaine said.

"David told us about your ordeal," Vanessa said. "It must have been very hard."

"To this day I don't remember a lot about the actual incident, but I sure as hell do remember what came after. It was an awful, painful, confusing time. Out of the blue Marly came by and said we should team up."

"Marlyfication. That's what Paul Daniels calls it," Jack said.

Elaine chuckled. "Absolutely. I was her first project."

"Too bad that Laurie Harris wasn't part of that escape plan," Vanessa said, watching for Elaine's response. "She was a lot like Marly."

"It took a village to kill Laurie Harris. In fact, it took a couple of villages. It took a couple of villages' worth of people looking the other way and trying to keep the Harris family penned up in Charon Springs. They ignored children like Laurie and Marly. Now it just eats at me to think how miserable Laurie's life must have been. Much worse than Marly's. I think it might be too much to ask a couple of teenagers to have saved her."

Vanessa and Elaine locked eyes. *She knows something,* Vanessa decided. *She's helping now in ways she couldn't years ago.*

Elaine's voice was soft and somber. "At the time I was too angry to be sorry for Laurie. It seemed to me that we were all entitled to some kind of bright future up until that point. Even Laurie had been a sweet little girl once upon a time. However, as I look back now, over half of our class from the Springs elementary school floundered within a few years after high school, all victims of bad decisions—theirs and others'. Laurie wasn't the last one to die before her time, I might add, just the first."

"Speaking of decisions, joining that startup was a stroke of luck for you," Jack said.

"Yeah," Elaine said, a faint, wistful smile on her lips. "That was part of the library thing. We wrote code like crazy."

"And the rest was history," Helen said. "Those girls just kept going. They left the Springs behind and didn't see Louise or Troy ever again."

Elaine blushed. "We've had an amazing run."

"Elaine bought me this house," Helen said. She sat up straighter and beamed at her daughter.

"I bought a place around the corner," Elaine said,

adding a laugh. "I love my mother, but we are not going to live together."

Vanessa felt her throat tighten with Silicon Valley envy. She wished she could afford to do the same for her parents.

Jack consulted his pad. "Marly became the guardian of her sister's children a year and a half prior to the dates in question, is that right?"

"Oh, that was quite a time," Helen said. "Marly was so upset those children were in danger. No small thanks to the actions of their parents, of course."

"Mother—"

"Well, it's true, Elaine. The way Charlene put it, you'd think those children had wandered off into some deep dark woods all on their own or invited vampires into the house."

"Our friend, Andrea Melville, was in law school by then," Elaine said. "She and her father took care of custody issues in New York, and Mom helped Marly get ready back here."

"Of course it was sad in some ways, but it was also very exciting," Helen said. She tilted her head and she gazed at a point that seemed to sit halfway between Vanessa and Jack, as if a vision of that happy past were mounted in the fireplace. "Those kids arrived with nothing but the clothes on their backs, I swear. We bought a house, furniture, curtains, clothes, bikes, computers, cell phones, a bigger car—two cars." Helen stopped for breath. "Wow. That was so much fun. And the kids have done very well."

"Now Charlene is out here too, is that right?" Jack asked.

Elaine spoke for the two of them. "Marly was adamant that Charlene was still their mother and she needed to have a relationship with the children. A supervised relationship, I might add. She told Charlene to study programming and computer classes while she was in prison. I have to say that she's worked out well for us as an employee. I had my doubts, but I guess there were some neurons firing in there after all."

"Did Marly ever confide in you that she'd been involved with the deaths of Zeke and Del?" asked Vanessa.

Elaine's body jerked as if she'd touched a live wire, but to Vanessa, Elaine's face appeared composed.

"What? No way. She definitely never said anything to me. I don't believe she knew anything about it. Like I said, she didn't talk about her family much when we were growing up."

"Doesn't it seem odd that she wouldn't have talked about them? She must have hated Del. Wouldn't she have been thrilled when he died?" Jack asked.

Elaine stared at the rug. "She was relieved that he was gone in some ways but she was sad that he was dead. I think her feelings about Del were complicated. *He* was complicated. He was an asshole but he did keep a lot of the Harris clan crap away from Denise's family. Compared to most of that bunch, he was a step up. When he disappeared, Marly was more exposed. That was when she came to find me."

"Ms. Fardig, is it possible that Rosie Harris sent Louise and Troy Rasmussen to take revenge on Marly Shaw?" Jack asked.

Helen shot to her feet. "What a lot of hogwash."

"That seems bogus," Elaine said at the same time, her voice sharp and emphatic.

"And you would be willing to swear that Marly Shaw showed no signs of injuries or seemed unusually upset or nervous in June of 2009?"

"Yes!" the two answered in unison. Glaring, Helen

resumed her seat and wiggled her backside into the cushion.

"I saw Marly every day of the week in that time. We were getting our company off the ground. I would have noticed," Elaine said.

"Would you be willing to take a lie detector test to answer these questions?" Jack asked.

Before Elaine could respond, Helen answered. "What is this? A movie? Lie detector tests are a bunch of pseudoscientific bullshit and you know it. Not even admissible in court."

Elaine set down her cup of tea on the coffee table. Her lips curved into a smile, but her eyes were unblinking and cold. "Detectives. I am happy to help your investigation, but I am not interested in participating in a fishing exercise that uses an approach that I consider to be specious. You know perfectly well that I had my own run-in with Louise and Troy years ago. The mere mention of their names makes me break out in a cold sweat."

Vanessa stared in reluctant admiration. Before her eyes, Elaine had transformed from an agreeable daughter to a focused, incisive leader—a young woman with hidden talents. *And perhaps a few secrets about her friend as well.*

Elaine handed a business card to Vanessa. "However, if you are serious about pursuing this, please contact my lawyer."

Vanessa studied the card. "Andrea Melville. Your old high school friend? This card is from your company."

Elaine handed another card to Jack. "Andrea moved out here and is working for us with our corporate counsel team, but she has experience in criminal law. I will rely on her judgment."

Vanessa tucked the card into the back of her note-book. Elaine had threatened to lawyer up and that signaled the end of this conversation.

Jack and Vanessa said their good-byes, slipped on their coats, and headed for the door. Helen Fardig moved in behind, herding them onto the porch.

She wasn't going to let them go without having the final word. "I'll have you know that Marly Shaw is a very special young woman without a dishonest or vicious bone in her body. I am as fond of her as I am of my own daughter. If you tangle with her, you're going to tangle with me." Helen turned on her heel and disappeared into the house. The door shut with a thud.

"That went well," Vanessa said once they were seated in Jack's car.

"I feel like I came to question Goldilocks and got my hand bitten off by Mama Bear," Jack said.

"Overreaction? Maybe Marly did see Louise and Troy, and Helen knows that. Elaine's no Goldilocks. I think she's quite capable of fighting her own battles."

"You know what I think? I think they all did it. Helen, Elaine, Marly, their lawyer friend, those kids . . . They all ganged up on Louise and Troy, drove them to that cliff, and kicked them off. As if we'll ever prove it."

"Be serious, Jack. What about Angela Rodriguez? We like her for this too, right? Angela was a big, tough broad, like Louise, and her brother Mike could handle himself. Besides, I rather think this could be standard operating mode for Helen."

"Yeah. You could be right about Helen. You could sell tickets to watch her take on Louise. The problem with Angela is that she's dead and I hate dead suspects. Plus, her brother has an ironclad alibi."

Vanessa picked up Jack's right hand and turned it around in her own.

"Your hand looks okay to me. You'll live. I think Helen's reaction is kind of sweet."

"Excuse me?"

Vanessa squeezed Jack's hand and released her grip. "Helen loves Marly like a mother bear. Poor kid never had anyone in her corner, let alone a proper mother. Now she has Helen."

25

Marly: Operation Rosie

June 16, 2009

The sound of crickets and tree frogs woke Marly at nine. *What a racket.* She had forgotten how noisy night could be in these woods. She climbed out of her car and the tree frogs fell silent. She smothered a laugh, remembering how hard it was to catch those cagey little buggers. She knew they'd start up again as soon as she walked away.

Slapping at mosquitos, she hiked over the ridge in the fading twilight to gaze at her mother's house. With Louise and Troy dead, would her mother be safe now? The house looked so vulnerable.

All the lights were out and her mother's car—the one Marly had bought—was gone.

Marly let herself into the small barn. In recent decades it had held tools and general storage rather than animals, but these days it also served as a halfway house for furniture that Denise still held dear.

Upstairs, Marly located the locked cupboard where her father stored his hunting guns. As usual, the keys hung in plain sight next to the cupboard. Marly kept the guns clean until she went away to college, but she doubted they had been cleaned since. Pulling on disposable gloves, she retrieved the shotgun and several handfuls of shells. The shells looked clean and intact, but she felt a nagging concern that the gun might blow up in her hands. She hoped she wouldn't have to fire at anything or anyone.

Marly eased open the back door to the house and stepped into the rebuilt lavatory off the kitchen. She would have to remind her mother to lock her doors.

As Marly had hoped, Denise hadn't thrown out any of her third husband's diabetes paraphernalia. Elliot's blood testing kits, syringes, and insulin continued to crowd the shelves of the medicine cabinet. *Would the insulin still be good after almost two years?* She took two syringes and four insulin ampules and put them into a fresh plastic bag.

Rosie's place was thirty minutes away on foot, which gave Marly time to think—not that she hadn't been thinking constantly since Sunday evening—strategizing, fuming, grinding her teeth, finalizing her plan. She wanted to punish Rosie over and over, but the woman could only die once.

Marly hoped Rosie would be alone. Based on information that Denise had relayed from time to time, she assumed that Rosie was still more or less bedridden or at least weakened by cancer treatments.

If Rosie was up and ambulatory, Marly planned to use the shotgun to get her old nemesis into some sort of chair and secure her to it with the plastic ties. She would show Rosie the trophies: Troy's watch, ring, and earring; Louise's pendant. She might even show Rosie some video of the action on the cliff. *No. Too complicated.*

Once the gloating was over, she would inject Rosie with a large dose of insulin. Or a painkiller if that was handy. Or both. Presumably, Rosie had a shunt in her chest for easy administration of drugs and chemo. That location would be ideal.

Picking her way through the woods, Marly felt as though she had stepped back in time. Only she had changed. Twilight gave way to night, and stars emerged, fireflies darting in imitation. At her home in California, the nightly fog, compounded by ground lights, obscured stars much of the time. As her feet hit rocks and roots, they stirred the leaves and rich earth. She inhaled the damp smells she so missed in the Bay Area. For better or worse, this was the land that had raised her.

She heard a sharp snap behind her and stopped. Animal? Human? The tree frogs were silent. *What or who is back there?*

Her teeth chattered and she shivered despite the warm night. After a few deep breaths she flipped on her flashlight and probed the woods behind her. The light caught the red eyes of a skunk who stomped his feet and raised his tail. She turned off her flashlight and backed away, picking up her pace with new caution.

Marly headed for a faint glow in the distance like a moth drawn to a flame. She looked over her shoulder every few paces. The light grew brighter until it became individual lights from Rosie's windows. Flood lights on the kitchen porch and barn lit up the yard and parking area. She counted three cars.

From her mother's reports, she knew that Betty, Carl's wife, and Diane Connor, Rosie's sister—both nurses—had taken on the task of providing care for Rosie. Diane worked nights at a nursing home closer to Syracuse and should be leaving very soon. Betty would stay a bit longer and go home to Carl in an hour or so. Marly could wait.

She drew closer and spied Betty and Diane talking in hushed tones on the side porch. Marly stood out of sight around the corner, straining to hear.

Diane was a bit of an unknown. Marly knew that Diane had played a minor part in the beatdown of Elaine but little else. Betty—Mark and Pammy's true grandmother—was a bit of a wallflower in the tough and raucous Harris crowd. She never raised her voice or made a fuss. A wimp, in Marly's opinion.

"I'd say it was a panic attack," Betty said in a soft voice. "Of course, it is so hard to tell. She is still a sick woman, plus all that chemo. She's surprised us before."

"She's waiting," Diane said. "For Louise and Troy. She keeps saying they're supposed to be home tonight."

"Sometimes things like that make a difference. You can leave for your shift. I'll make sure she's comfortable."

Diane headed to her car, and Betty returned to the house.

Marly circled the building, looking in windows. She hoped Rosie wasn't in an upstairs bedroom.

The sound of a television pulled Marly along the back of the house to an open sliding-glass door into the downstairs parlor. The room was dimly lit from a single lamp that sat on a bedside table next to the sliding door. She couldn't see the head of the hospital bed on the other side of the table, but she could make out a pair of spindly legs stretched out on the white sheet.

How fitting. This was the same room where Marly had taken a beating from Rosie, Louise, and Troy, years before. The addition of assorted modern medical equipment—monitors, tubing, an oxygen tank, and the hospital bed—made the rest of the room look even shabbier by contrast. Along the ceiling, faded wall-paper hung in loose flaps, breaking away from the wall. An ancient TV rested on top of a battered bureau. A chair with a caved-in seat sat by the bed.

Marly waited until she heard Diane's car pull away from the house before she inched forward to stand outside the screen door.

Betty stepped into Rosie's room. "Hi, Rosie. Diane has gone to work. I need to swing home for a bit. I'll be back in about an hour."

Marly heard a low murmur from Rosie, and could see Rosie's left hand rise and fall back to the bed.

Marly backed away to the edge of the woods, where she leaned her shotgun against a tree and set down her backpack. Leaving the shotgun behind, she pulled out the sealed plastic bags and her supplies, and tiptoed back to the house. She teased open the screen door and slipped into Rosie's sickroom.

Absorbed in her television show, Rosie didn't shift her gaze until Marly sat down on the rickety chair beside the bed. As the older woman moved her focus, Marly's throat tightened. Always skinny, Rosie was a skeleton now, every bone visible under the thin summer nightgown, her lank black hair plastered against her head.

"You," said the gaunt figure through cracked lips. Her black eyes glittered.

"Hi, Rosie," Marly said. "This is your night to die and I've come to make sure you do."

Rosie hissed and sat up straight.

Marly held up Louise's Iroquois pendant, dangling the chain between her fingertips. "Louise and Troy aren't coming back. See this? Just for the record, those two were as dumb as sticks."

She had so much more to say. *What's happened to my fine speech?*

Rosie choked and struggled over her words. "You fucking bitch. You will pay for this."

"Maybe so, but not tonight." Marly stood and pulled out a syringe from the second bag.

Rosie froze, her face covered in a sheen of sweat. Marly leaned closer. She removed the cap that protected the needle tip and put her left hand on Rosie's chest, searching for the shunt.

Marly felt a violent tremor run through her body. Her hands shook and her feet wobbled.

It was one thing to push a screwdriver up into Troy's brain when he was about to chop her into little pieces, or to fight off Louise at the edge of the crumbling cliff. It was one thing to run away from Del and accidentally pull him into the line of fire. It was one thing to walk away from two dead men in a truck. But this was another thing. This was murder. She couldn't do it. She straightened up.

After all that. Fuck me. Fuck me, fuck me, fuck me.

She replaced the protective tip on the syringe and put it back in the plastic bag.

Behind her, Marly heard the door from the kitchen open and Diane's soft voice. "Rosie, I just came back to— Marly! It's late. What are you doing here? Why aren't you in California?"

Marly moved to the bottom of the bed to face Diane. "I'm here to say good-bye."

Diane's forehead wrinkled as she attempted a smile. "You didn't have to come all this way for that. It looks like Rosie will be around for a while."

Rosie moaned, and Marly stretched her mouth into what she hoped was a grin.

"No, I've come to say good-bye from Louise and Troy."

"Louise and Troy?"

Good Lord, Diane is such a dim bulb. But Rosie understood and uttered a mournful, wordless cry.

Marly held Troy's earring between her thumb and forefinger, and turned toward Rosie.

"They're in hell, Rosie," Marly said. "They went over that cliff screaming."

Rosie started to climb out of bed, but Diane crossed the room and pressed her back into the pillows.

"What are you talking about?" Diane said, still behind the curve.

"Jeez, Diane. Shut up and listen. Louise and Troy came to California to take Elaine and me up to a high cliff, chop us to pieces, and throw us over. But we showed them." She gasped, overcome by a surge of hate-fueled bile in her chest. "We showed them and they're dead."

Rosie yelled something incoherent. She squirmed and thrashed her legs, struggling to free herself from Diane's hold.

Draping herself across the bed, Diane held Rosie down. "Marly, stop. You're crazy. Please."

"I'll tell you what's crazy. What's crazy is all sorts of people going missing and no one cares. Louise and Troy told me. My father, Beanie. He's up in Schwarzer's quarry. Ollie Fardig, too. And Johnny. Carl couldn't protect Johnny and he can't protect Mark or Pammy or Alison or my mother. And neither can you. Louise and Troy were planning to burn down my mother's house once the kids were back here."

Marly's voice failed her. She bent over and rested her fists on the foot of the mattress. Rosie's chest heaved and she arched her back like a bow against the hospital bed, her head thrown back against the pillows. Diane went limp and sank onto the chair, her face buried in her hands.

Rosie rolled back and forth, cursing. "Bitch, bitch, bitch. You should be dead. Elaine should be dead. We'll take care of you."

Moving faster than Marly would have thought possible for someone so ill and distraught, Rosie opened the drawer in the table next to her bed. Marly's eyes widened as she saw that Rosie was reaching for a gun nestled in tissues.

Marly's body was trying to move two directions at the same time. One part told her to run from the room while the other wanted to rush forward, shove past Diane, and pull the gun away from Rosie.

As Rosie's hand dipped into the drawer, Marly's attention was drawn by a movement in her peripheral vision. A figure stepped through the open screen door and pointed a shotgun—Marly's shotgun—at Rosie's head.

Marly stopped breathing. Diane jumped to her feet. Rosie shut up and froze in place. She dropped the gun back into the drawer.

"That's it, Rosie," Betty said in a hoarse whisper. "Helen wants you to know that you have fucked with her family for the last time. That goes double from me."

Betty smiled a humorless grin, keeping a careful bead on Rosie. "Diane, why don't you take that gun? Marly, what's in that bag?"

"Syringes," Marly said. "Insulin. But I couldn't do it. Fuck." She wiped her nose with the back of her hand.

Betty made a soft tsking sound. "Marly, you are overwrought. Helen called me this afternoon and told me you might be paying a visit tonight. I didn't move quite fast enough to stop you, but you made the right choice. Now you need to take a break. Give Diane your bag with the syringe. And that one with the jewelry, too."

Diane stood and staggered to the bedside table. She removed Rosie's gun from the drawer, holding it as though it were a dead rat. She clenched her jaw several times and turned.

"Yes, Marly. Give me all that. There's some food in the refrigerator. Go use the bathroom. You look terrible. Clean up and get something to eat."

Too drained to protest, Marly relinquished the bags and stumbled out of the parlor to the bathroom off the kitchen.

By the time she'd finished in the bathroom, the door into Rosie's room was shut. Marly rattled the doorknob. *Locked.* Only a few soft murmurs escaped. Marly wondered if she should warn Betty not to pull the trigger of that shotgun.

The refrigerator revealed a crusty pot roast, boiled potatoes, and some limp broccoli. She wrinkled her nose and grabbed a can of sweetened iced tea and a brownie from a pile on the counter instead.

The sugar definitely made her feel better. She paced the kitchen and checked out the other rooms.

Betty came out and shut the door behind her.

"Time to go, Marly," she said. She held out the two bags and let them drop with a soft plop onto the table. "I think you might want to dispose of all this."

Marly studied the contents. The syringes and ampules looked the same as when she'd handed them to Betty. "What about Rosie?"

"Don't worry about her."

"Where's Diane? Did she talk to Helen too?"

Betty shook her head. "Don't worry about Diane."

"Betty—"

"I had an understanding with Rosie. I never discussed it with Carl, but he knew the bargain I'd struck. I wouldn't say anything about Johnny. I wouldn't say that Mark and Pammy were Johnny's children—my grandchildren. If I kept my mouth shut and made nice, she'd leave them alone, even in California. That meant leaving you alone, too, because they needed you."

Betty went to the sink for a glass of water. "Maybe they would have killed those children in your mother's house. Maybe not. Louise might have made up that part to scare you more. But no question, Mark and Pammy would have been so hurt and damaged if anything had happened to you. And that was not our agreement. My precious grandchildren."

Marly's voice came out in a ragged whisper. "According to Louise, they have arranged for 'friends'— that's a quote—to jump Carl. They are just waiting for the word, which Louise was going to deliver tonight."

Betty sank into a chair. Her face twisted into a mask of pain, then softened back into her placid, calm façade.

"I'll tell Carl. He'll most likely know who she meant," she said, and waved her hands. "His business."

Marly rested her forehead on the table, too tired for tears. "How do I make peace here? I can't take this anymore. I can't go to the police. They can't keep us safe."

"I assume you are the one who stole all that money. That gives you leverage. Carl will be taking over soon. Once things are clear, you call him. Maybe in a week or two. You tell him you want to make amends. You say that dealing with Rosie was not an option but that he's different. You'll make him whole. You'll return that money you stole, and in return I can come see Mark and Pammy and be their grandmother, for real. And he can come too."

Marly groaned.

"Just from time to time." Betty patted Marly's head and smoothed her hair. "That's not such a bad thing. Now you go."

"I want to see her."

Betty stood. "Leave now, Marly." She returned to Rosie's room, closing the door. The lock clicked.

Marly finished her brownie and let herself out the kitchen door. She circled the house, but Betty and Diane had shut the windows and pulled the shades to Rosie's room. Exhausted, Marly worked her way back into the trees where she found her backpack and the shotgun where she'd left them.

She called Betty's name and heard it echo back to her from the woods. Only the tree frogs answered. Alone in the dark, she walked back to her mother's house by starlight.

26

Marly: Sic Transit Gloria

June 17–25, 2009

The dirt road to Schwarzer's quarry was rough going. Marly parked at the top of the rise, not certain that her low-slung rental would be able to clear the roadbed for the rest of the journey. She wanted her presence in Charon Springs to remain a secret, but that would be impossible if she had to hike out to find someone to tow her car. She walked downhill using her flashlight to find her way along the vestiges of the old road, most of it washed away by runoff from heavy rains.

Growing up she had avoided this place, although like all kids, she had sneaked in to look several times. Hidden in the woods, about twenty feet off the old deserted road, lay the quarry, a mere fifty feet across and seventy feet long. Starlight winked innocently from the surface of the water.

Everyone knew this was an evil spot. There was no way out once you had jumped or fallen into the deep waters that filled the hole left after Old Man Schwarzer had tired of extracting limestone. The sheer sides dropped straight down all the way around, ten to fifteen feet. Her friends Chuck and Harry had once come with a rope, vowing to swim, but they both chickened out. No one jumped in. Voluntarily.

Marly wondered if her father had been alive on his last trip here. She hoped not. Had he thought of her, Charlene, or her mother? Had he been as terrified as she had been at the top of that cliff in the Santa Cruz Mountains?

Marly pulled out the bag with the syringe and insulin ampules. They appeared unused, but she would take no chances. Using her gloves and a cloth, she wiped off each item and replaced them. She filled up the bag with sand and small pebbles, squeezed out the air, and tossed the sealed unit into the center of the quarry. She repeated the same procedure with her second package: the pendant, ring, earring, and watch she had taken from Louise and Troy.

Someday, someone would drain this cesspool. Bodies and evidence would pop up. She wondered if that would be her in lifetime.

Marly sat in meditation, caught up in the memories of her father and the other people she knew who were resting just below her feet. But she couldn't stay here forever. She wanted to go home—to her mother's house. When Marly had returned the shotgun to the barn, Denise had still been out, but she would be home by now. Last call at the Rock was two a.m. She ached to hug her mother, but knew that would be a sentimental mistake.

Instead, Marly hiked back to her car and drove to a secluded spot on the far side of Charon Springs. She dozed until dawn. At first light, she headed for Rochester.

Stopping at the top of the western ridge out of town, she parked in the middle of the road and walked back for one last look down into the village. She watched the new sun bathe the hillsides, the trees, the church steeple, the rooftops, and even the Rock, in gentle, healing light, as mists released from the valley and drifted up to embrace the sky.

She cried for her father, who had never had a chance, and for her mother, who had no inner compass to guide them out of harm's way. Vicious human nature had robbed Marly of her place in this world and made her hate this lovely valley that had both molded her and driven her away. She cried from relief that she hadn't killed Rosie.

Back in the car, Marly drove at a slow pace to Rochester and checked in for her flight to California. This time Homeland Security waved "Edith" through without comment. Marly considered an upgrade to first class, but decided that would be tempting fate.

Once she boarded the connecting flight from Pittsburgh to San Jose, she planned to sleep, but she spent her time pretending to read, lost in her reveries.

She was no murderer. The abuse and sense of helplessness accumulated over the years had crested into a fury so consuming that she had walked right up to the edge with Rosie. But she had backed away.

Marly didn't think she was a sociopath, either. She had empathy. She didn't think that she was above the laws that governed others. She believed in consequences. She didn't own a gun. She respected cops and believed in law and order and did her best to make sure that Mark, Pammy, and Alison thought the same way.

She'd been squeezed into some tight corners and thought that she had no one to help her. But over the years, Andrea, Mrs. Haas, Elaine, and Helen had come through. And Betty.

Law enforcement was not up to the challenge of determined Harris mayhem. That fact required continued self-reliance on her part. Witness protection was a non-starter. Even if she qualified for the program, her mother would never have been able to adhere to the rules of a new identity. Leaving Denise behind was not an option.

Over the Rockies, Marly settled back for a nap. As her anger receded, she could recognize how much Tony meant to her. She would build a healthy, normal family with him. If he would still have her. She would tell him about Del and Zeke, but she would never tell him about Louise and Troy, and she would not lose any sleep over that. If she made her peace with Carl, the Harris threat might be neutralized. *For the time being.*

Once upon a time, she had been a listener in the snow, savoring life in a frozen landscape. Now she had grown up.

Marly tossed her disposable phone in a trash can in the San Jose Airport lobby and caught a cab home. There was one message waiting on her answering machine. It was from her mother.

"Oh, Marly. I have the worst news! Rosie died in her sleep last night. This is just awful. Please call me."

Perhaps it had not been a dream after all. Diane. Betty. It was after eleven at night in New York, but her mother picked up on the second ring.

"Hi, Denise. Mom. It's Marly. I just got your message. What's up with Rosie?"

"I can't believe it. Rosie's doctors had told her that she was doing better. Betty helped put her to bed and Diane checked on her when she came home at three in the morning and she said Rosie was fine. But this morning she was dead."

"What did the doctors say?"

"Oh. Dr. Duckworth said that she must have been worn out from all the chemo and the lung cancer. These things happen, I guess. It's just not fair."

"He came down to examine her? In person?"

"No. You know he never comes to the Springs. He talked to Diane and Betty. They're both nurses, so he trusts them."

"He's going to sign the death certificate?"

"Oh yeah. He's the coroner, you know. No question about it. Heart attack."

Marly vowed never to say another bad word about the good doctor.

"Will you come for the service next week?" Denise asked.

"I can't do that, Mom. Mark and Pammy come home on Saturday and Alison comes back on Sunday. We head to England for the summer next week, so there's a lot to prepare for. It's too crazy."

Denise sniffed. "Rosie thought so highly of you, don't you know? She was always asking about how you were doing. A couple of weeks ago, she was saying such nice things about you, how she admired you, and how glad she was to hear the kids were doing great."

Marly squeezed her eyes shut and spoke from between clenched teeth. "That's real sweet."

"She's going to be cremated. That worries me. She was raised Catholic, you know. She went to our church sometimes but she wouldn't let Del or Zeke be cremated. She was adamant. Now Diane insists that Rosie told her she wanted cremation. It's in writing."

"It sounds like she had a change of heart, Mom."

"And she wanted her ashes dumped into Schwarzer's quarry. Of all places."

"Kind of out of the way," Marly said. "But I'm sure she had her reasons."

"I wish you were here."

"You'll see us in England, right? We have a house lined up in Oxford and you'll be there in about a month."

"Yeah, that will be real nice, I guess. I don't know that I'll feel comfortable there. And don't ask me to drive. I hear that's really hard."

"Fine, Mom. Don't worry, I wouldn't dream of asking you to drive."

The next day, Marly's morning run ended at Helen's house.

"Hey, Marly," Elaine said as she opened the door. "Mom's making pancakes."

Helen waved a spatula. "Sit, sit. Elaine, get Marly some coffee."

Marly studied Elaine's face. "You look better."

"Ugh. My ribs still ache and this black eye will take forever to fade. I'm going to have to come up with a story. But otherwise I'm feeling fine."

"Betty told me about your phone call, Helen."

Helen raised her eyebrows. "What? I haven't spoken to Betty in years."

Marly looked from mother to daughter. It was clear that neither was going to admit to anything.

"Okay. Have it your way. I do have news, fresh from Charon Springs. My mother called last night, quite upset. Rosie died in her sleep late Tuesday night or early Wednesday morning."

Elaine crowed and raised her coffee mug in a mock toast.

Helen cocked her head and saluted with her spatula. "That's a shame."

"My mother's a bit worried because Rosie's going to be cremated. She was raised Catholic. Practicing Catholics don't usually choose cremation."

Helen's smile faded. "Is that true? I had forgotten that."

"According to my mother, Diane says that's what Rosie wanted. She also wanted to have her ashes deposited in Schwarzer's quarry."

Helen turned her attention back to the pancakes. "That's as good a place as any. *Sic transit gloria Rosie*."

After breakfast, Marly walked home, puzzling over the circumstances of Rosie's death. Had Rosie died of a heart attack, perhaps brought on by the distress over the news about Louise and Troy? Or had she been given some assistance from some combination of Betty and Diane, in consultation with Helen? Marly wasn't certain that she wanted to know.

She wondered what else she didn't know about Helen. Or Betty.

One week later, Marly called Carl.

"Congratulations on your new position. I'd like to settle some accounts with you," Marly said after they'd exchanged pleasantries. "Now that Rosie's dead, this is an option for me."

"I make that to be about a million dollars," Carl said.

"You have several choices for payment." Marly kept her voice light. The amount Carl mentioned was extreme, but she wanted to stay focused on the bigger picture.

Carl remained silent. She took his lack of response as an opening and continued. "You can have that, principal plus interest. No problem. After, we are done forever—with both you and Betty. Or you can choose to invest a more modest amount for shares in our latest company."

She let that sink in. "My startups tend to do very well."

"So I hear," Carl said, breaking his silence.

"You could end up with a lot more money. Of course there's no guarantee. Startups aren't for the faint of heart."

Carl grunted. "Don't be a smart-ass, Marly."

"Keep in mind that option two does have some other advantages. Visiting privileges for Betty, for example."

"And me?"

"I was under the impression you didn't care about Johnny's kids."

"You'd be smart to—" Carl cleared his throat. "You might be surprised to know that I think of Johnny's kids as my own grandchildren."

"And Alison?"

"Of course. She's Greg's so she's family too."

"I want advance notice for visits. No surprises," Marly said.

"Done."

"Option two? Three hundred thousand?"

"Make that five hundred and it's a deal."

"I don't suppose you'll be coming to England this summer?" Marly slumped in her chair, weak with relief.

"Nice try, Marly. You know I've got new responsibilities here. This would not be a good time to go wandering off. But I'm sure Betty would like to go."

Marly hung up and pondered how she could bounce money back to Carl without arousing suspicion. He had turned out to be much more ambitious than she had ever suspected. Now Carl would control the Harris clan, and he would own a portion of her company. She wondered if she had just been sucked back into Charon Springs.

27

Vanessa: Marly

February 11, 2013

Vanessa's gasp was audible as they pulled up in front of Marly's house.

Jack grinned. "I thought you wanted Helen's house. You do realize that in places like Avalon, this would not be impressive."

"Context is everything," she said. "Teardowns here can cost over a million bucks. You know that."

Although the house lay in Old Mountain View, this section of town was mixed. Some houses had been renovated, but many had not. A number of the properties here were large compared to the typical lots nearby, and this was one of them. Vanessa estimated that this property was almost twice the average width. The original bones of the house appeared to date from 1900 to 1920—ancient by California standards.

The house sat high off the ground and the porch was deep, complete with inviting outdoor furniture. It stretched across the front, wrapped around the side, and ended where the house jogged out along the ample driveway. She recognized the same soft yellow from Marly's mother's house in Charon Springs, with white trim, dark blue sashes, and dark red doors. A fence across the driveway cut off views into the backyard, hinting that the best features might lie out of sight.

Jack looked at his watch. "Four thirty-seven. Let's go meet Marlene Shaw."

The rooms at the front of the house were dark, but several seconds after Vanessa rang the doorbell, one side of the lace curtain that covered the glass of the front door moved. Vanessa recognized Alison's heart-shaped face from the pictures she'd seen on Betty's shelves.

Offering what she hoped was her least threatening smile, Vanessa pulled out her badge. "Hi there. I'm Detective Alba and this is Detective Wong. We're here to see Marlene Shaw and Charlene Harris."

The face disappeared. Vanessa resisted the urge to check her watch as the seconds ticked by. At last, the door opened and Vanessa recognized Mark. Betty's pictures must have been several years old, but this was the same boy. The tall girl standing behind him had to be Pammy.

"Hello, Mark," Jack said. "Could we come in?"

Mark held his ground. "Strict orders. No strangers inside when Mom or Marly aren't here. You can sit on the porch if you like. Mom should be back from work any second. Marly and Tony went to the doctor. I'll call them and make sure they're headed back."

Vanessa took in Mark's and Pammy's coal black hair and violet eyes. Whatever had possessed Rosie to think these were Del's children?

"I don't suppose you'd talk to us while we're waiting, Mark?" Jack asked. "You're over eighteen now, right?"

Mark stepped out onto the porch. His two sisters crowded in behind him, standing in the doorway.

Taking that as a yes, Jack lobbed a softball question. "I guess you've heard about Louise and Troy, right?"

All three nodded.

"Did you happen to see them in June, about three and a half years ago, here in California?"

"Nope," Mark said.

Pammy put a protective arm around Alison.

"But you did know them, right? You would have recognized them if they were around here in June of 2009?"

"We knew them," Mark said. "Not nice people."

"I saw Troy kill a kitten once," Alison said. "And Louise spanked me for no reason at all."

"Shitheads," Mark said. "Good riddance. Besides, I think we were away."

"That was right before we went to England for the summer," Pammy said. "That's why I remember. We came back from camping and had to get all kinds of things for the trip a week later. It was beyond hectic. We heard that Rosie had died and there was some discussion of stopping in New York for the funeral. Which we skipped."

Alison wrinkled her nose at Rosie's name. Her eyes lit up, and she pushed by Vanessa and Jack and ran down the steps toward two cars that had pulled into the driveway.

The woman driving the second car, a Subaru Outback, climbed out first. That had to be Charlene Harris—a younger image of her mother, with ash blond hair and blue eyes. A tall man with wavy brown hair, dressed in khakis and a leather jacket, got out of the passenger side of the other car, a BMW SUV, as another woman emerged from the driver's side. *Marly.*

Vanessa walked around the corner of the porch to get a better first assessment of Marly.

She could tell right away that Marly was taller than her sister. Her coppery hair was pulled back into a ponytail, and her face was fuller and softer than the pictures Vanessa had seen. She was not a classic beauty like her sister, or a cute sophisticate like Elaine, but her firm chin, full lips, and straight, no-nonsense gaze conveyed a calm and focused intelligence.

Marly stepped around to the front of the car and Vanessa gave an involuntary start. In all their interviews, even with Denise, no one had mentioned that Marly was pregnant.

"Ms. Shaw?" Jack asked.

Marly's smile was pleasant but formal. "Hello, Detectives. Please call me Marly. Sorry we're running a bit behind. We had a visit to the baby doctor." Turning, she called to the kids. "Okay, folks. Please come and help bring in groceries."

The cars were emptied as Marly escorted Jack and Vanessa past a long outdoor table, through the side porch door, and into what Vanessa would now have called a mudroom, connected to the large kitchen.

Marly waved them to a small sitting room area at the front of the house on the opposite side of the island and breakfast bar. "We'll be just a few minutes. Let me get things organized."

The man in khakis introduced himself. "I'm Tony Rochford, Marly's husband."

"That's Dr. Rochford," Alison said. "He's a surgeon at Stanford."

Vanessa studied him. His accent was British. He was tall and slim with a nut-brown complexion and dark brown eyes. She put him in his mid to late thirties.

Tony gave Marly a kiss. "Let me go get changed. After that I'll come back to keep the wheels turning."

Jack and Vanessa sat and watched the family dynamics unroll.

"Alison, what's the homework situation?" Marly asked.

"It's okay."

"Mark, please go check on what she needs to get done. Are you going to be here for dinner?"

Mark indicated that he would stay. He disappeared with Alison down a long hallway.

"Pammy, how's your homework?"

"Almost done, just a little bit of Spanish and a short essay."

"Are you cooking dinner?"

"Yup. Orange meal. Salmon steaks, butternut squash, Moroccan carrot salad, and couscous. Mango ice cream for dessert." She turned and scampered off after the others.

Vanessa heard Jack's stomach growl. Like her, he seemed to appreciate the orange meal.

Marly was no Helen Fardig, but it was clear that she ruled the roost while Tony and Charlene played the supporting roles. Mark, Pammy, and Alison knew who was boss, but nothing in their behavior indicated fear.

Marly turned to her guests. "We'll go to the back apartment where Tony and I stay."

"Interesting house," Jack said.

Marly acknowledged him with a slight bow. "The renovations were done before I bought it. The front here was the old part, built around 1915. That room used to be the living room, fireplace and all. Now I use it as our dining room. This room was supposed to be the new dining room, but I've always liked having a separate place for eating, so I made this part into a family area off the kitchen."

Vanessa recalled how cramped Denise had said her

kitchen had been. Those were the days when Charlene and Marly crowded around a tiny table for meals, sitting knee to knee with Del Harris—thief, crime boss, pervert, murderer.

With Charlene in tow, Marly led the detectives down the corridor past a hall bathroom and four bedrooms. Vanessa caught a glimpse of private baths through two of the open doorways. "This was the end of the original house," Marly said.

Past the bedrooms, the corridor ended in a large living room.

"This new part is what sold me on the house," Marly said, waving her hands to encompass the open beam ceiling, the big fireplace, and a loft area overlooking the main floor. "I hate living rooms that never get used. The kids have nooks and crannies where they can study and we can still be here together."

They passed an indented office area where Mark was helping Alison. Pammy poked her head over the edge of the loft and watched them parade by.

"Mark's at Berkeley now. He's a sophomore," Marly said, the pride rich in her voice. "He's an excellent student. They all are."

They passed another hall bath and two more bedrooms, one set up as an office.

"That's our guest bedroom and office for now. Tony and the baby and I will move into these two rooms this summer when the baby is a little bigger and sleeping better—we hope. Meanwhile, Tony and I stay in an apartment in back of the garage."

They stepped out onto the back deck and Vanessa heard Jack give a low whistle. Pavers from the driveway merged with a back entertainment space and outdoor kitchen, complete with a small pool and Jacuzzi.

Marly gestured toward the pool. "We'll need to lock

those down or just get rid of them. I'm so nervous about having an inquisitive toddler. Plus, we would have more space for a play area. After all, there's a city pool just a few blocks away."

Marly led the way up onto a smaller deck and into the apartment built into the back of the two-story garage.

The downstairs living room and small dining area sported a tiny kitchen on one side plus a lavatory under the stairs. Glancing up, Vanessa could see that a loft ran the length of the second story. Evidence of impending changes were stacked around the living area—a big box with a picture of a crib on the side sat near the kitchen, and another showing a changing table was propped against the stairs. The back wall was occupied by a chest of drawers in a similar style, and storage shelves were already stuffed with diapers, wipes, and onesies.

Tony came down the stairs in jeans and a white button-down shirt.

"You may stay if you want to," Marly said.

"I know all I need to know about your family, thank you very much, and I have nothing to contribute." He offered an amiable nod to Vanessa and Jack and left.

Charlene flipped the switch for the gas Franklin stove, and Marly busied herself making custom coffees and teas from the single-cup machine on the kitchen counter.

"The main house was pretty much as you see when I bought it," Marly said. "But this apartment was a raw space. It's one of the few improvements I did on my own."

Marly served the hot drinks, and the conversation died away.

Vanessa kicked off the interview. "Now that I've

spent some time in Charon Springs, I'm curious. Do you think that Laurie Harris was jumped by mistake instead of you?"

Marly raised her eyebrows, her eyes round. "That's a new one. No, I don't believe that. When we were little, we looked very similar, but by our senior year, we weren't much alike. Laurie was taller and much heavier than me—like her mother. Even in the dark, anyone would have noticed the difference right away. Quite frankly, I don't see what this has to do with Louise and Troy out here."

Vanessa considered Marly's response. "I'm sure you can understand that we are interested in a pattern of clashes between you and Rosie and her crew."

Charlene spoke up. "I'd have to agree with Marly, Detective. It seems very unlikely to me. That being said, I don't think I'll have much to offer you. Of course I knew Louise and Troy, but I was still in prison that June. I didn't get out until the end of November."

"That is when you moved out here, is that correct?" Jack asked.

"Marly had a job waiting, so we were able to negotiate my move. I never would have found a job like this without her."

"You still work for Marly?"

Charlene gave a genuine grin. "Yeah. Well, the same company, not directly for Marly. It's great. I'm a senior engineer now."

"And you have some stock," Marly said. The two sisters exchanged smiles.

More Marlyfication. Still, there were limits. Charlene may have become a model citizen with a good job, but her blue eyes had a vague, placid cast, as if she were watching the meeting from a great distance.

"You knew that Rosie held a grudge against Marly?" Vanessa asked Charlene.

"Yes and no. Rosie had a grudge against everyone. She even hated Louise."

Vanessa turned back to Marly. "Rosie believed that you were the one Del and Zeke were chasing the night they died, isn't that right?"

"Oh please. She knew that wasn't the case. I went to the school dance the night they disappeared and I walked home from the Rock. For all we know, they didn't even die that night. There were plenty of nights when Del didn't come home."

"Come on, Marly. Rosie sent Louise and Troy out here to take her final revenge on you for the deaths of her husband and son."

Marly sat very still, her arms crossed, as if Vanessa had not said anything.

"You were here when Louise and Troy arrived, correct?" Vanessa asked, trying a new approach.

Marly uncrossed her arms. "Sure, I guess that's right from what I heard about the dates. I was the only parental unit in those days. The kids would have been away most or all of that time. After they got back, we left for England."

"That's where you met Tony?" Jack asked.

"I'd met him at Cambridge when I spent my junior year there. He was this sexy guy in medical school. I was too young and unsophisticated at that point, but he waited around and it worked out."

"And now a baby. When are you due?" Vanessa asked.

Marly shifted in her chair. Was her patience wearing thin or was she simply uncomfortable?

"One more week, in theory."

"One more time, for the record, you didn't see Louise or Troy during that June?" Vanessa asked.

"Give that a rest already. Are you done?"

Jack set his mug on the coffee table and leaned toward Marly.

"Do you know how Rosie died?" he asked.

"Sure!" Charlene said, startled. "She died of lung cancer."

Marly shot a glance at Charlene and turned back to Jack. "My mother told me that she'd died in her sleep. Not a bad way to go, considering. We didn't go back for the funeral."

"I don't suppose you paid her a farewell visit? Around June sixteenth of that year?"

Marly blinked. "Excuse me? Back into the belly of the beast? No way. I haven't been to the Springs since I went to pick up the kids and bring them here. I'm sure you can check flight records if that's a serious question on your part."

Vanessa assessed Marly's response. For the first time, Marly's jaw had tightened and her eyes had flashed before she composed herself. Vanessa wondered what this young woman might be capable of if she needed to defend her family.

"What is your opinion of polygraphs—lie detector tests?" Jack asked.

"I assume that's not merely an idle question, Detective Wong. I think they rank one step higher than drowning trials for witches. Using them exploits the underprivileged and less educated."

"Which you are not."

"Which I am not," Marly said, her voice flat and expressionless. "Should I contact my lawyer?"

Jack looked at Vanessa, and they both rose to their feet.

"We'll let you know if we plan to go that route," Jack said.

Vanessa thought she and Jack might be forced to leave through the side yard gate, but Marly made no objection as Charlene led the group back through the house. The kitchen was filled with laughter and the smells of cooking. Alison was setting the dining room table while Pammy prepared dinner. Seated at the kitchen island, Mark and Tony were playing some sort of card game.

Tip of the hat, Marly. I'm sure your mother's kitchen never felt like this.

"What was all that about Rosie?" Vanessa asked, as Jack started the car.

"An itch I needed to scratch. Something Larry said."

"You certainly got her attention. Should we check airline flights?"

"I think that would be wise, just in case."

"We can do that. Do you really think she slipped back to Charon Springs and took care of Rosie somehow? Even if it were true, it's not our jurisdiction. I'm still not convinced Marly killed Louise and Troy."

"I don't know, Vanessa. I'm just making sure we've ticked all the boxes. If it turns out she did travel and lied to us about it, we can use that to justify pulling her in for a real interrogation."

"But if Marly did kill Louise and Troy, we know that was self-defense, right?"

"Could be, but that would be a call for the DA," Jack said.

"Here's the thing. I keep wondering what I would have done if I were Marly and found out that Rosie had sent her hounds of hell after me."

"You would have done the right thing and gone to the police."

"I suppose. But I was brought up by great parents. Marly had to bring herself up."

"Vanessa, you know we could say that about almost every person we arrest. It's sad but no excuse."

Vanessa pulled her gaze away from the bright windows of Marly's house. "We could say that about a lot of victims, too."

Jack put the car in gear. "How about dinner? There are great places on Castro Street. I miss having dinner with you, and we don't need extra padded clothing now."

Vanessa laughed to cover the spark of excitement that blossomed deep inside. She wondered if Jack could see her glow in the dark.

28

Vanessa: Promises

March 11–12, 2013

Jack and Vanessa spent a full day tracking down the garage where Louise and Troy had rented the van. The owner was unapologetic about his unlicensed side business. He wasn't stealing business from Hertz, after all. His clients were people with bad credit who needed help.

The owner remembered renting to Louise and Troy. He even ID'd their pictures. Louise had left a $3,000 cash deposit, but he hadn't been around when she'd brought the van back and collected the balance. Yes, a middle-aged woman had returned the van, according to his guys. Sorry, the van was long gone. Lost in a wreck.

It took longer to check airline records for any sign that Marly might have traveled to New York in June of 2009. When that investigation came up empty, Nick pulled the plug.

"Vanessa, I've read your reports. Quite fascinating. Talk about sick people. Maybe this young woman, Marly, was involved, but you don't have any evidence to justify further investigation on that front."

"We've still got Angela Rodriguez, sir," Vanessa said. "We know Louise and Troy stayed with her and had a falling out. Someone returned that van. Angela was about the same size and age as Louise. She could be a fit."

"Too bad she's dead. And you say her brother has an alibi. That's inconvenient."

"He seems like a regular citizen, sir. Spotless record. Quite the opposite of his sister."

"That's it then. We are done. Are you comfortable with processing this with exceptional clearance? Will Jack agree?"

"Yes, sir. We believe we would have sufficient circumstantial evidence to have arrested Angela Rodriguez if she were alive."

"Done. I'll call Carl Harris with that information."

Vanessa started to object, but Nick interrupted. "Nessa, I don't want you in the middle of this bit. I grew up with guys like Carl in that part of New York. I'll grant you that he's better than what I hear of his predecessors, but he's about as toothless as a rattlesnake. We know that he's been tracking your progress. He'll recognize my last name. No one messes with the Lebanese in Utica, and that's just a stone's throw away. This is a preventative measure. He'll get the message that I'm watching out for you. Trust me."

Vanessa knew Jack would be disappointed, but she was also relieved to leave the specter of Charon Springs behind. She picked up her new cases and made plans to wrap things up.

The next morning, Vanessa left her parents' house at seven thirty a.m. and parked outside Marly's place.

Tony was a surgeon. Vanessa guessed he would have left the house long ago. Just before eight, Alison left for school, driven by Charlene. A few minutes later, Pammy took off in a cute MINI Cooper. Mark would be back at Berkeley. Vanessa got out of her car.

Marly opened the door, a tiny infant nestled into her neck. Her eyes were a bit dim but firm. The baby bump was gone now, and her lanky figure was starting to reappear.

"I don't like it when people stalk me, Detective Alba."

"I wasn't stalking. I didn't want to disrupt your routine with the family. I wasn't sure on the timing."

Marly stood aside to let Vanessa pass, and they settled into the front sitting area in the bright sun. The baby squirmed and yawned on Marly's lap.

"There's a coffee machine over there that makes individual cups. If you want coffee, I'd appreciate it if you'd make me some too. But it has to be decaf."

"Tired?"

"Ooof. And I have help, so I shouldn't be complaining. Our nanny will be here soon and I'll get a little sleep. I swear he wants to eat every couple minutes, particularly at night."

Vanessa went to make coffee. By the time she returned, Marly had fallen asleep. Vanessa waited. She had time.

The baby wiggled and gave a short, piercing squawk. Marly jerked awake.

"Sorry about that. Now it's time to eat again." Despite her complaint, Marly's tone was warm. She smiled and stroked her baby, lifted her T-shirt, and offered a breast as she reached for the coffee with the other hand.

"Nice to have a nanny," Vanessa said. "I assume you're taking time off."

"A little bit, not counting a few critical meetings. I'll be back soon but on a bit more relaxed schedule. A nanny is wonderful. It's my guilty pleasure. I'd make do, but it's great to be able to off-load. Charlene and the girls take care of the house, and Mark when he's here. Even Tony chips in. We do have a house cleaner but that's every couple of weeks and this place turns upside down every day."

"I'd have thought your mother would have come out."

Marly stroked the baby's head. "My mother will come in a month or two, or three, I suppose. We aren't close. I love her, but she was so passive and never really looked out for us. I find it hard to count on her. I guess that's not very generous of me."

"I suppose she'd say that she had to figure out how to keep you fed."

"Yeah. Too bad that the only way she knew how to solve problems was to use charm and sex to get some guy to move in."

"Harris guys."

"I can't believe she still lives there. You'd think she was tethered to the Springs by a chain." Marly checked the baby's diaper and moved him to her shoulder where he burped.

"He is adorable. Look at that fuzz of red hair. What's his name?"

"James Bernard Rochford. James for Tony's father, Bernard for mine. I call him Beanie in private. That's probably not a good nickname for a kid. He's not fussy. He just wants to be fed and kept dry. Dark, violet eyes. Tony says that means they'll be brown like his. Like my dad's."

Marly put the baby in her lap with his head on her knees, and bicycled his legs.

"Why are you here, Detective?"

"We're wrapping up the case."

"So I heard. Your boss called Carl. I gather they had a good talk. Carl was impressed that your boss came from Utica. He said that you had focused on someone named Angela who served time with Louise. She's dead, right?"

"We've taken this as far as we can. There's no statute of limitations for homicide, but we have marked the case for exceptional clearance."

"Exceptional?"

"It means that we have identified a suspect but can't make an arrest. Of course, given what we know, it could well have been self-defense. Since our suspect is dead, it's unlikely we'll ever know."

Marly waggled her eyebrows. "Does that mean you'll be able to date Detective Wong?"

Vanessa sat back, startled.

Marly grinned. "I have some contacts of my own, you know. I also had a report from my mother. She said you'd had some trouble in the Springs."

Seeing that Vanessa was speechless, Marly continued her half of the conversation. "Is that it? You came to tell me that the case is going on the shelf?"

"I did come to tell you that," Vanessa said. "But the real reason I came, is to tell you that I've got your back."

It was Marly's turn to be confused. "Excuse me?"

Vanessa kept her face neutral and her voice flat.

"Don't speak. Just listen. Del and Zeke set out to kill you. It couldn't have been a random, spontaneous thing.

Del had slept with your mother, screwed your sister, and finally was going to fuck you. Permanently."

Marly stared, her face guarded.

Vanessa continued. "But you outwitted them. It was luck, of course—the kind of luck that comes from always being ready and on edge. You couldn't go to anyone. No one would stand up for you. The police avoided the Springs, you couldn't go to your mother, and Rosic was on your case. All those years later, when Louise and Troy came for revenge, it must have seemed like the same thing. Somehow you bested them, too. You're not a killer. You're a victim, but you have no trust in us. I can see that. I can see why that happened."

Marly raised her eyebrows and opened her mouth.

"Don't talk. I know what I need to know and I don't want you to say anything. I don't blame you and I'm not looking for confessions. However, I think about Carl and I worry about you. I worry about your kids. You've struck a deal, I'll bet, but Carl's not an honorable man. You know that. He'll do what's expedient. And who knows what other renegade Harris peons are out there with a grudge?"

Vanessa slapped a business card down on the table.

"My official contacts are on the front and my personal email and cell phone number are on the back. The next time you or yours get jumped or you even suspect that something's going on, you think of me. I'm in your corner. I do have your back. You can count on me."

A brief grimace crossed Marly's face. "Thank you, Detective. However misguided, I do deeply appreciate your offer and I will keep your number handy."

The two women locked eyes. Marly blinked first, picking up Vanessa's card.

"Did you kill Rosie?" Vanessa asked at last.

Marly's face was now impassive, her eyes hooded. "No, I didn't kill Rosie. Rosie was very sick."

She closed her eyes. "It's odd how fast people forget. Even I forget. Del was baby Jesus to Rosie and Zeke. He could be so charming when he wanted to be. He was also a nasty piece of work, but not all the time. He could be sweet and generous. There were people who admired him and looked up to him. He gave them jobs and money and bailed them out of jail and kept nasty husbands in line. Zeke was the same way when he was younger, or so I'm told. He was a bit more crotchety when I knew him. Of course, I also saw a different side of Del. When he got home, his façade would drop after a couple of drinks. For years I listened in on how he talked about people and what made him angry. Del was clever, but not very educated. That was the whole problem with the Harris bunch. Charon Springs had become a prison of their own making."

"And Del was very good-looking," Vanessa said.

Marly let a small laugh escape. "Yes. I knew that, but I never thought of him that way. Sometimes I'll think back on a scene or see a photograph and that will strike me. Big, blond, broad shoulders, not fat like most of the Harris types. My mother once told me she felt so privileged that he wanted her. Privileged! And don't gag, but my sister once confessed that he didn't force her to have sex with him. He seduced her. She was twelve. God, it makes my skin crawl."

Marly frowned. "When he disappeared, nothing got easier. Rosie and the rest were thrashing around in a panic and that was dangerous. I got scooped up for a beating and I don't know what would have happened if

Carl hadn't caught wind of it. He yanked me out of there, set them straight, and told me to get the hell out of Dodge. Which I did."

Marly wiped Beanie's chin. "When Del died, the center gave way. In some ways, Louise and Troy dying was just the final nail in the coffin."

"The Harris clan doesn't seem dead to me," Vanessa said. "Carl seems to be well ensconced. Larry was killed in prison a few weeks ago. Did you know that?"

"Probably because you went to see him," Marly said. "Did you think of that? Not that you got much from him, I'll bet."

Vanessa jerked as Marly's statement registered.

"I'm not particularly worried about myself, but Carl might still have you in his sights, Detective Alba," Marly said. "You and Detective Wong. I have your backs, too."

Vanessa felt a prickle on the back of her neck.

She looked out the window and noticed a young woman get out of a car. "Here's your nanny. I'll go. You won't be seeing me again unless it's in the Farmer's Market or on Castro. Or if you need me."

Marly met Vanessa's gaze. "I had a terrible childhood, but I know it was not as bad as a lot of others. I was lucky because I was just smart enough and timing was everything. Carl once asked me, what if I'd been the oldest, not Charlene? What if I hadn't been a senior and ready to leave when Del died? What if the high-tech industry wasn't so open and thriving? I can live with everything I've had to do to pull myself and the people I love into the light. I can assure you, I am no murderer. I hope that all my children—Charlene's, mine—feel that unlike me, they have the wind at their backs and that includes the law."

Vanessa drained her coffee and put both their mugs into the sink. She left by the front door and made her way to the curb. Before she opened her car door, she turned to study Marly, watching from the sitting room window. Marly raised her right hand. Vanessa returned the salute.

Perhaps Nick wasn't overprotective after all. She hoped she'd seen the last of the Harris clan.

29

Marly: Aftermath

March 12, 2013

Marly contemplated her tiny, sleeping son. Should she do anything about Carl? Could she? Sometimes less was more. That was what Carl didn't understand. *Why the hell had he arranged for Larry to get killed now?* Like Detective Alba, she saw Carl's hand in that. The man had no sense of timing.

What if Carl is thinking the same things about me? That gave her pause. It seemed unlikely, but not impossible.

She would need to soothe him. He had to stay on her side. *Take the long view.* That's what she was good at.

She closed her eyes, but jerked awake as her head nodded forward. She could have sworn she heard Del's voice calling her name. No, it was just a blue jay squabbling with a crow in the front yard.

Helen stepped out of the guest bedroom closest to the kitchen.

"Well. That was an interesting conversation." Helen moved to clean up the cups. "Do you want more?"

"Only if it's not decaf." Marly's attempt at a jocular

tone failed to materialize. She tilted her head back and allowed an audible sigh to escape.

"Time to let sleeping dogs lie, don't you think?" Helen asked, splashing in the sink. "I can't see any benefit in pursuing things in the Springs." Her voice rose at the end. It was a question.

Marly sat up straight and stared at Helen. *The woman is a mind reader.*

Helen turned, drying her hands. "Neutralize Carl. Keep him boxed in out there. That's the best way forward. Creating a power vacuum would be problematic."

Marly gazed down at Beanie, her sight glazed by sudden tears. "I have to protect him," she said. "He's so tiny and I don't have the energy to fight anymore. If Carl ends up exposing everything . . ."

"Marly, that's the sleep deprivation talking. It is time to look to the future, not the past. Don't worry. I'll talk to Betty, and she'll talk to Carl. You know she has your back just as much as that detective. And so do I."

Marly offered Helen a quavering smile. "Good. I'd hate to have to own up to anything. I've spent so long burying certain events."

Their eyes met. Helen blinked first and she turned to watch Marly's nanny stroll up the walk to the front door. "The relief shift has arrived. You go take a shower and get some sleep. You have a brand-new life ahead of you." She bent down, plucked Beanie from Marly's lap, and tucked him into the crook of her right arm.

Marly blinked and floated to her feet. As she headed for her backyard apartment, she felt as calm and at peace as she could remember. *Time for a new dream.*

ACKNOWLEDGMENTS

I owe an enormous debt to the Sisters in Crime, their Northern California chapter, and especially the Guppy (Great UnPublished) chapter. Their unflagging enthusiasm and support were instrumental in providing advice, writing courses, feedback, and encouragement—all critical for a first-time writer. My local writers group—Susannah Carlson, Andrew MacRae, Karla Rogers, Scot Friesen, Jennifer Ripley, Danielle Berggren, Vishhal Moondhra, and Michele Gibson—provided unflinching feedback, as did my Guppy Manuscript Exchange partners: Andrew MacRae, Connie Berry, Vinnie Hansen, Karen Hutchinson, and Cheryl Hollon. Special mention goes to Ramona DeFelice Long, who showed me how to write, thanks to her excellent Guppy courses.

I drew inspiration from many old friends, including Cassandra Harris Lockwood and her wonderful Harris family, my very first best friend, Elaine Fardig, and her family, the Melvilles, Chip Davis, the Shaws, Carl Schwarzer, Penny and Tony Rochford, Nancy Haas, Lieutenant Saul Jaeger of the Mountain View Police Department, Robert Hurst, and many more.

My parents, George and Betty, gave me the backing that I wanted Marly to have. Thank you, Pal, Doug, Rob, Buffy, and Erin. I am very grateful that my father always remembered I had a book coming, even after he had forgotten so many other life events.

There is a special place in heaven for my beta readers who encouraged me to continue after my first draft when I didn't even realize how much more work was required: Rob Bickford, Syddie Sowles, Pauline Ores,

Michael Reade, Cassandra Harris Lockwood, Ellen Jorgensen, and Nikki Sabin.

My deepest appreciation goes to my agent, Anne Hawkins, and to my editor, Michaela Hamilton, and the entire team at Kensington Publishing. There is no thrill quite like finding people who really get your book.

And to Central New York—the place that made me.

For those who would like to know more about the murder of my classmates Kathy Bernhardt and George Ann Formicola, I recommend *The Devil at Genesee Junction,* by Michael Benson, published by Rowman & Littlefield.

Don't miss Susan Bickford's newest novel
of chilling suspense

DREAD OF WINTER

Coming soon from Kensington Publishing Corp.

Keep reading to enjoy an intriguing excerpt . . .

1

Welcome Home

As the car rounded the last bend, Sydney tried to lean forward to catch a glimpse of her mother's house. She moved too fast. The seatbelt froze, retracted, and moved up to cut off the circulation in her neck. Resistance was futile. She would have to stay firmly pinned to her seat for a couple hundred more yards.

Midway through the turn, the back end of the car fishtailed on an icy patch hidden under the gray slush covering the road. Sydney pressed her right foot on the phantom brake on the passenger side.

Francine Buckley deftly straightened the vehicle. "Damn town. That curve isn't banked properly and they know it. Bad enough in the summer, but ice builds up there all winter, no matter how much sand and salt they throw on it. Every time I drive through town . . ." Her voice trailed off in a string of grumbled obscenities.

Sydney lifted her foot. She didn't exactly disagree, but driving a bit slower might have solved Francine's problem without any investment required by the town road crew.

"Too bad about your mom, kiddo. Man, that was fast. Glad you were able to get back in time from Colorado." Francine thumped her hands twice on the steering wheel.

"California," Sydney said. After driving in silence for over an hour, her companion now seemed to be in a mood to talk. She vaguely remembered Francine as one of the lunch ladies at the high school and wondered how well she had known Sydney's mother. Perhaps that was a silly question. Everyone knew everybody in a tiny town like Oriska, New York.

"Oh yeah. Well, a long way. I guess it goes to show. You never know when your time's going to come up. I bet you never thought you'd be coming home like this."

"I never thought I'd be coming home, period," Sydney said. She slipped the fingers of her left hand between the seatbelt and her neck.

"They don't got weather like this in California, do they?" Francine pointed her chin toward the steep drifts left by the snowplow on either side of the road.

"There's snow up high in the mountains, but it never snows where I live."

"No kidding. Sounds boring."

"I'm not complaining."

"I hear Randy didn't come to the hospital."

Sydney felt a bubble of pain move down her chest. "I kept calling his cell number and left messages. Maybe he's out of town."

"Out of something, that's for sure. Up to no good, as usual." Francine continued with a barely audible string of epithets and made a jerking-off gesture in her lap with her right hand.

Sydney had to clear her throat before she could speak. "Are you saying he's been cheating on my mother?"

"I'm saying he is a sweet-talking, good-looking guy, way younger than your mother, who has always done exactly what he wants. Just like the rest of his family. Those Jaquiths have no impulse control. What could possibly go wrong? What? Don't look at me like that. Am I right?"

"I'm not arguing with you, Francine. At least he can't cheat on her anymore. That's the upside of being dead."

Francine snorted and sped up for the last fifty feet. "Okay, here we are, then." She stomped on the brake and jammed the gearshift into park. "Looks like you got some visitors."

Sydney freed herself from the seatbelt as she studied the large black SUV with a Quebec license plate in her mother's driveway. "*Je me souviens,*" she said, reading the bottom of the rear plate. *I remember.* "I would definitely like to remember that license plate number. Just in case." Her phone was buried in a bag. She grabbed a pen from Francine's pile of possessions scattered along the dashboard, and scribbled the number on the palm of her hand.

"Whatever. Let me know about your mother's service. And put the pen back."

Sydney climbed out and gasped at the cold. She had forgotten how subzero wind could suck the breath from her lungs. *Welcome back to Central New York. Let me give you a hug.*

She wrestled her luggage from the back of Francine's car: a backpack, a wheeled suitcase, her travel purse, and a brown paper bag with her mother's effects from the hospital. She reopened the passenger door and held out two twenty-dollar bills. "Thanks, Francine. I really appreciate the ride. It would have cost a fortune to take a car service all the way from Syracuse. It was nice of you to stop by to see how she was doing."

Francine snatched the bills and stuffed them down

the front of her shirt. "Sure thing. I had to take Gladys up for her chemo today. I like it when I can get a round-trip. I thought I might be taking your mom home." She paused to cough up something disgusting into a dirty hankie. "I don't suppose you could pay me for taking your mother to the hospital, too?"

Sydney straightened up to give this some thought before she leaned into the car again. "I thought she called an ambulance."

"Ha! She'd still be lying in there today if she'd done that. She said to put it on her tab. Want to settle up? I'm never going to collect from *her*, that's for sure. Eighty-five bucks."

Sydney fished into her handbag for more bills. It appeared that settling her mother's estate would be full of surprises. Expensive ones.

She handed the bills to Francine, who put them in the same warm spot.

"Now shut the door," Francine said, checking her side-view mirror. "It's fucking freezing out there. And slam it hard. It don't like to catch in cold weather."

Sydney slammed the door as directed. She turned to study the Canadian vehicle. All she wanted to do was get inside out of the snow and cold, and find some solitude so she could cry her eyes out.

She didn't feel like entertaining visitors, and she didn't *souvenir* anyone from Quebec. Something wasn't right.

"I don't suppose you'd be willing to come in with me," she said, looking over her shoulder. But Francine had already slammed the car into drive. The backend fishtailed as her car leaped forward, showering Sydney in a spray of semi-frozen salt and sand.

"Never mind." Sydney waved at the receding rust bucket.

The house didn't appear changed from the outside. It had always been a lovely façade—a charming village farmhouse with a large, two-story living section and a single-story kitchen wing—facing the road as if it had nothing to hide.

Inside would be different this time. No screaming, no slamming doors, no tears except for her own.

She slipped on the backpack and tucked the paper bag under her left arm along with her travel purse. About eight inches of snow covered the driveway, and Sydney quickly realized the snow was too deep for the wheelies on the suitcase. Dragging the case like a dead body, she made a mental note to figure out who did the plowing around here. Maybe her mother kept a snow-blower in the barn.

The barn was a town barn—a modest structure created for the nonfarming family who built the house. It was directly attached to the house, connected via a large mudroom and laundry area. Back in the day, it must have held a couple of cows and horses and a carriage, but in recent memory it functioned as a garage and storage facility for tools and out-of-season items.

Sydney paused to glance inside the SUV. Fast-food containers littered the floor and backseat. There were no fast-food joints within twenty miles if memory served. These guys weren't local.

Two sets of footprints—boot prints, size large and extra large—led from either side of the car to the barn. The sliding door into the barn was open about two feet.

If this were California, she would have turned around. She would have called the police on her cell phone. She would have walked—no, run—to a neighbor's house.

But this was Oriska. Central New York. Somewhere between Syracuse, Binghamton, and Nowheresburg. It was January. There was no cell phone coverage. The closest neighbors had undoubtedly gone to Florida or Arizona for the winter. The police were still not her friends.

What the hell. She pushed through the last few feet into the unlit barn.

The change stopped her in her tracks. Her mother's car—a Subaru—sat waiting as expected. The rest of the interior was packed top to bottom with furniture, books, crockery, newspapers, file cabinets, old shutters, old food containers. Dirty food containers.

When had her mother turned from a collector to a hoarder? In their phone conversations, her mother raved about her thriving antique business. One more lie Sydney would never be able to put to rest.

The door to the mudroom hung wide open, spilling heated air out of the house. The boots of the two men had left clumps of ice and snow in lacy patterns. Sydney closed the mudroom door and dropped her bags before she followed the prints through a second door and into the house.

Her first impression was that black bears had come out of hibernation and invaded the kitchen and family room. Two large bodies in heavy coats and boots lounged across the couch, their feet resting on the marble coffee table—one of her mother's genuine antiques. Cigarette smoke filled the air overhead.

"Well, hey, Leslie. We've been waiting for you." The man closest to the mudroom slammed his feet to the floor and stood up.

"I'm not . . ." Sydney started to explain she wasn't Leslie and stopped. Maybe she should keep her mouth shut.

"Yeah," said the other man. He waved a tumbler filled to the brim with a golden liquid—apparently poured from the bottle of expensive scotch on the coffee table. "We were about to leave and tell Randy to take care of his own business."

"Have we met before?" Sydney asked. She decided not to ask their names but mentally labeled them René and Pierre. Their lightly accented English was excellent and colloquial, delivered in a slightly stilted, clipped manner.

"Nah," said René, the first man. "Randy said to give this package to his girlfriend at this address. He didn't want to carry it over the border." He picked up a bag with a Wegmans logo on the side and set it on the coffee table with a thump.

"Perfect. We'll take off now," Pierre said. "Thanks for the scotch."

"You're very welcome," Sydney said, eyeballing the Wegmans bag. *This could not be good. No one needs to smuggle vegetables or maple syrup from Canada.*

The two men gathered their gloves and clumped in their heavy boots toward the mudroom. Up close, Sydney could see that their eyes were bloodshot and she could smell that they hadn't bathed recently.

"Tell Randy we'll be stopping by his cabin tomorrow for the money." Pierre leaned in close, giving Sydney the opportunity to count the blackheads on his cheeks. She also noted that Pierre had never received the grooming memo that it was okay to clip nose hairs. On the bright side, his pupils were normal. He wasn't a user, even if he was too drunk to drive.

René pushed his partner aside and tapped Sydney's chest with his right forefinger. "And no sampling the merchandise. Randy says you got a taste for this stuff, so hands off. This is pure, uncut china girl. It'll kill you." He raised the finger to her face and grinned. "And that would be such a waste."

Sydney blinked and took a step back. She wasn't entirely current with drug slang, but she recalled that *china girl* meant "fentanyl."

The two Canadians disappeared into the mudroom. Sydney moved to the sitting room windows facing the driveway and watched them slog through the snow to their car. Pierre turned and waved as he climbed in.

Sydney waved back. "Yeah, yeah. *Va t'en faire foutre,* asshole." *Go fuck yourself.*

She kept watching until she was satisfied the car was out of sight before she made the rounds of locking every single door to the outside world, including the one into the barn.

Each room except the kitchen area was filled with stacks of collectibles and useless crap. Sorrow descended like a dense fog, tugging at her feet, pushing down her shoulders. By the time she returned to the kitchen sitting room area, she could feel her knees threaten to buckle.

"Did you know your mother was abusing narcotics, Ms. Graham?" the young doctor in the ICU had asked.

"Lucerno. My last name is Lucerno," Sydney answered. She forced herself to look away from her mother and the beeping machines. The doctor's nameplate read: DR. K. SINGHAL. He had introduced himself as Kamal. His brown eyes seemed warm and not judgmental. "We aren't very close. It definitely didn't come up in our phone calls. I don't see her very often."

Three times. Three times in the last thirteen years.

"I thought you said she had the flu."

"She does," Kamal replied. "The problem is that opioids suppress breathing and that led to complications."

"Pneumonia."

"Correct. She was taking a lot of codeine for the cough, in addition to her normal habit, and didn't realize she was in trouble until it was almost too late. Now she is also going through withdrawal. It's a tricky balance for us to manage."

"She's not going to make it, is she?"

Kamal put his hand on her shoulder. The nurse standing on her other side patted her back.

"We're doing all we can for her. It's good that you were able to make it here today. Why don't you go talk to her? She can't speak because of the ventilator, but she can hear you."

Sydney grasped her mother's hands and rolled them around in her own. Why were Leslie's hands so warm if the woman was dying? Sydney memorized the freckles along her mother's knuckles and the little hairs sprouting at the base of each finger. She held up her mother's right palm and measured her own against it. Identical.

All the while, Sydney spoke of cherished childhood memories, reminded her mother of the fun they had during Leslie's infrequent visits to California, and made promises for the future Sydney knew would never come to pass.

From time to time, her mother would open her eyes and gaze at Sydney with no sign of recognition. Several times, with her eyes closed, her mother squeezed Sydney's hand.

The squeezes grew fainter. Lulled by the rhythmic beeps and clicks of the machines, Sydney fell asleep with her head resting on the blankets next to her mother's chest until the beeping gave way to a final, sustained wail when her mother's heart stopped.

Now her mother's body was on its way to Martinson Funeral Home in Hartwell, and everything she took to the hospital was jammed into a brown paper bag in the mudroom.

Sydney sank to the kitchen floor. She howled like an orphaned animal and kicked her heels. She pressed her hands to her eyes and tears finally began to flow. Between moans, she screamed and thumped her head against the tiled floor.

She should have never run away. She should have stayed to protect her mother. Or at least come home to drive away Leslie's demons.

Now Sydney and her mother would never be able to take the slow route from New York to California or drive from Vancouver to Tijuana following Route 1. Leslie would never meet Sydney's someday children.

Sydney would have to live forever with a hole in her heart where family belonged.

Connect with

U S

Visit us online at
KensingtonBooks.com
to read more from your favorite authors, see books
by series, view reading group guides, and more.

Join us on social media

for sneak peeks, chances to win books and prize packs,
and to share your thoughts with other readers.

facebook.com/kensingtonpublishing
twitter.com/kensingtonbooks

Tell us what you think!

To share your thoughts, submit a review,
or sign up for our eNewsletters, please visit:
KensingtonBooks.com/TellUs.